THE OLD ARCADIA

PHILIP SIDNEY was born on 30 November 1554. He was educated at Shrewsbury School and Christ Church, Oxford; he may have spent some time also at Cambridge. In 1572 he set out for three years of foreign travel. He was in Paris at the time of the St Bartholomew's Day Massacre of Protestants; he also stayed in Frankfurt, Vienna, Padua and Venice (where Veronese painted his portrait, now lost), and made a brief excursion into Hungary. In 1577 he went to the Continent again, as an ambassador to the Imperial Court at Vienna. Soon after his return he may have begun to write the *Old Arcadia*, which he finished in 1580. *The Defence of Poetry* probably belongs to 1581, and the sonnet sequence *Astrophel and Stella* to 1581–2. Soon after this he began to recast his *Arcadia* on epic lines, a revision which he never completed. In 1583 he married Frances Walsingham, whose father was Secretary of State to the Queen. Though he was appointed royal cup-bearer in 1576, and in 1582 was knighted, he held no major office until in 1585 he was appointed Governor of the Dutch port of Flushing. In September 1586 he was shot in the thigh during a battle against the Spanish near Zutphen and died of infection just over three weeks later.

KATHERINE DUNCAN-JONES was educated at King Edward VI High School for Girls, Birmingham, and St Hilda's College, Oxford, where she obtained the Charles Oldham Shakespeare Prize and the Matthew Arnold Memorial Prize. After a year of teaching in Cambridge she was elected to a fellowship at Somerville College, Oxford. In 1972 she edited (with J. van Dorsten) *Miscellaneous Prose of Sir Philip Sidney* for the Clarendon Press; her paperback *Selected Poems of Sir Philip Sidney* (also Clarendon Press) was published in 1973. She delivered the 1980 Chatterton Lecture to the British Academy on Sidney's poetry.

THE WORLD'S CLASSICS

SIR PHILIP SIDNEY

The Countess of Pembroke's Arcadia
(The Old Arcadia)

Edited with an Introduction by
KATHERINE DUNCAN-JONES

Oxford   New York
OXFORD UNIVERSITY PRESS

Oxford University Press, Walton Street, Oxford OX2 6DP

London New York Toronto
Delhi Bombay Calcutta Madras Karachi
Kuala Lumpur Singapore Hong Kong Tokyo
Nairobi Dar es Salaam Cape Town
Melbourne Auckland
and associated companies in
Berlin Ibadan

Oxford is a trade mark of Oxford University Press

First published as a World's Classics paperback 1985
Reprinted 1990

British Library Cataloguing in Publication Data
Sidney, Sir Philip
The Countess of Pembroke's Arcadia (the old
Arcadia).—(The World's classics)
I. Title   II. Duncan-Jones, Katherine
823'.3 [F] PR2342.A6
ISBN 0–19–281690–X

Library of Congress Cataloging in Publication Data
Sidney, Philip, Sir, 1554–1586.
The Countess of Pembroke's Arcadia (the old Arcadia)
(The World's classics)
Bibliography: p.
Includes index.
I. Duncan-Jones, Katherine.   II. Title.
PR2342.A5 1985 823'.3 84–91150
ISBN 0–19–281690–X

Printed in Great Britain by
BPCC Hazell Books Ltd
Aylesbury, Bucks

CONTENTS

INTRODUCTION

'OLD' is a somewhat misleading epithet for Sidney's five-book romance, for he was very young when he wrote it. If he began it soon after returning home from his diplomatic mission to Vienna in June 1577, as Edmund Molyneux tells us,[1] he was then not yet twenty-two. Three years later, in October 1580, he promised his brother Robert a copy of his 'toyfull book' by the following February[2]—apparently the only reference to the *Arcadia* in his letters. This would make him only twenty-five when he finished it. The Phillipps MS of the *Old Arcadia* refers to it as 'made in the year 1580', and it probably was indeed completed then. We do not distinguish Keats's two versions of *Hyperion* as 'Old' and 'New', for we recognize that both are the work of a very young poet, and both are unfinished. *Mutatis mutandis*, we should approach the two *Arcadia*s in a similar way. Sidney wrote both versions while he was in his twenties, and both are unfinished, the second one radically so.

The term 'old', as applied to the *Arcadia*, derives from Fulke Greville's letter to Sidney's father-in-law and executor, Sir Francis Walsingham, written only a few weeks after Sidney's death:

Sir: This day one Ponsonby, a bookbinder in Paul's Churchyard, came to me, and told me that there was one in hand to print Sir Philip Sidney's old *Arcadia*, asking me if it were done with your honour's consent . . . Sir, I am loath to renew his memory unto you, but yet in this I might presume, for I have sent my lady your daughter at her request, a correction of that old one done 4 or 5 years since which he left in trust with me, whereof there is no more copies, and fitter to be printed than that first which is so common.[3]

'Old' here means only 'former' or 'previous'—synonymous with 'first' at the end of the sentence. From Greville's limited perspective in November 1586, we can understand his momentous decision to ensure that it was Sidney's revised but incomplete romance that reached print in 1590. We may, however, in many ways regret its consequence, which was that the 'old' version in its complete form

[1] Holinshed, *Chronicles* (1587), iii. 1554.
[2] Sidney, *Works*, ed. Feuillerat, iii. 132.
[3] PRO, SP 12/195/33. Modernized version of quotation in Robertson, p. xl.

was lost until its rediscovery by Bertram Dobell in 1907.[4] As far as Greville in 1586 was concerned, the 'old' version was already published, for there was an abundance of manuscript copies in the hands of the Sidney circle and their friends—it was 'so common'. The nine surviving manuscripts of the *Old Arcadia* probably represent dozens which were in circulation in the 1580s. It was natural that Greville should believe the 'corrected' version, with which he had been entrusted, to be superior. This version, the 'New' *Arcadia*, had the profound disadvantage of being only half written, breaking off in mid-sentence with a huge amount of unfinished business pending in its multiple plots. But its more ambitious, intricate and increasingly intellectual qualities no doubt appealed to Greville, quite apart from the value it had as the version personally entrusted to him.

From 1593 onwards the 'New' *Arcadia* was given a false completeness by being printed with Books 3–5 of the 'old' version, though it was admitted that this could provide only 'the conclusion, not the perfection of *Arcadia*'. Sidney's revised version contains many major characters and episodes which had not figured at all in the earlier work, and the pastoral intrigues of the 'old' version's Books 3–5 add inapposite complexities to the intricate and semi-tragic situations of the 'New'. In revising—or as Greville would have it, 'correcting'— his *Arcadia*, Sidney had moved perhaps irreversibly far from the limited pastoral arena, dealing in Book 3 with areas of thought and experience at which the earlier work had scarcely hinted. Arcadia, praised in the old version for its peacefulness, is here at war—a civil war with many notable casualties, such as the virtuous Argalus and Parthenia. Of the four young principals, three are in prison; the two princesses have been tortured; Musidorus, outside Cecropia's castle, is badly wounded, while inside, in the last chapter Sidney wrote, Pyrocles looks poised to recover his valour but not his dignity, since he is still disguised as a woman and taking rather unfair advantage from his disguise. By the revised Book 3 the amusing follies of mistaken or over-eager love have given place to a much darker picture of evil and moral blindness, in which the heroic energies of the two young princes are largely paralyzed. More seriously still, they have ceased to be a strong centre of narrative interest compared with the fascinatingly complex figure of Amphialus, who did not exist in the earlier version. The disjunction between the two versions, at the point where they

---

[4] *The Athenaeum*, 7 September 1907.

were cobbled together, is enormous: it is as if the head and shoulders of a man were grafted on to the hind quarters of a horse.

Yet it was this literary centaur which was read for over three hundred years. We should remember this when we contemplate the *Arcadia*'s progress from enormous popularity (throughout the seventeenth century) to neglect and even contempt from the later eighteenth century onwards. The critical history of the *Arcadia* is, until the middle of the twentieth century, the history of a long disjointed pair of fragments which Sidney himself can never have envisaged amalgamating, still less publishing. His *Old Arcadia*, as he makes clear in his dedicatory letter to his sister—'his chief safety shall be the not walking abroad'—was not intended for publication; his *New Arcadia* was unfinished, possibly unfinishable; least of all, one suspects, would he have liked to be judged by the 'composite *Arcadia*' which was fashioned from the two. No doubt from excellent motives, Greville did his beloved friend's long term fame considerable damage by preventing the publication of the 'old' *Arcadia*. C. S. Lewis made a characteristically firm case for the composite text as the one which must concern the literary historian: 'It alone is the book which lived; Shakespeare's book, Charles I's book, Milton's book, Lamb's book, our own book long before we heard of textual criticism.'[5]

But what kind of life did it really have? The honest literary historian must chronicle a steady decline in the *Arcadia*'s popularity during the eighteenth and nineteenth centuries, a major cause of which must have been the composite text's length and discontinuity. Horace Walpole in 1768 called it 'a tedious, lamentable, pedantic, pastoral romance, which the patience of a young virgin in love cannot now wade through'.[6] Hazlitt in 1820 called it 'one of the greatest monuments of the abuse of intellectual power upon record', and concluded an imaginative tirade against it by saying:

It no longer adorns the toilette or lies upon the pillow of Maids of Honour and Peeresses in their own right (the Pamelas and Philocleas of a later age), but remains upon the shelves of the libraries of the curious in long works and great names, a monument to shew that the author was one of the ablest men and worst writers of the age of Elizabeth.[7]

[5] C. S. Lewis, *English Literature in the Sixteenth Century* (1954), 333.
[6] Horace Walpole, *A Catalogue of Royal and Noble Authors of England* (1768), i. 164.
[7] William Hazlitt, *Lectures on the Age of Elizabeth*, in *Works*, ed. P. P. Howe, vi. 318–25.

Virginia Woolf echoed Hazlitt, calling the *Arcadia* 'one of those half-forgotten and deserted places' which we pause over before returning 'to its place on the bottom shelf';[8] and T. S. Eliot echoed him more concisely and damningly in calling it 'a monument of dulness'.[9] Historically and bibliographically, C. S. Lewis was right in saying that the composite *Arcadia* is the version that 'lived', for it went through fifteen editions during the seventeenth and early eighteenth centuries, until no gentleman's residence in England can have lacked a copy.[10] But as the quotations will have shown, it did not 'live' in any very positive sense, having by this century acquired a very bad name for tedium and prolixity.

A return to Sidney's original version, which has been possible only since the appearance of Feuillerat's edition in 1926, enables us to discover and enjoy a work which is bursting with young life—whose delight is that, though in a sense 'old', it is fresh, innovatory, overflowing with colour and sensation, the vigorous product of 'a young head'. The *TLS* reviewer of Feuillerat's edition called it 'a young man's work', 'almost as light-hearted an affair as "Pickwick" '. Far from being 'old' in the sense that Virginia Woolf suggested—'one of those half-forgotten and deserted places where the grasses grow over fallen statues and the rain drips and the marble steps are green with moss'—the earlier *Arcadia* offers a bright, energetic, often jokey world, as brilliant in detail as a Hilliard miniature and as assured in structure as a Ben Jonson comedy.

Structure is one of the *Old Arcadia*'s most notable features. Writing within weeks of Sidney's death, Edmund Molyneux praised its 'orderlie disposition'.[11] It is composed of five 'Books or Acts', whose organization is far from random. Overall, these terms probably reflect Sidney's admiration for two previous works of English literature. 'Books' recalls the five books of Chaucer's *Troilus and Criseyde*, the only English poem given unqualified praise by Sidney in his *Defence of Poetry*: 'Chaucer, undoubtedly, did excellently in his *Troilus and Criseyde*; of whom, truly, I know not whether to marvel more, either that he in that misty time could see so clearly, or that we in this clear age go so stumblingly after him.'[12]

[8] Virginia Woolf, 'The Countess of Pembroke's *Arcadia*', in *The Common Reader* ii (1932).

[9] T. S. Eliot, 'Apology for the Countess of Pembroke' (1932).

[10] For a full bibliography of these editions, see Bent Juel-Jensen, 'Some Uncollected Authors xxxiv: Sir Philip Sidney', *Book-Collector* xi (1962).

[11] Holinshed, *Chronicles* (1587), iii. 1554.   [12] Sidney, *Misc. Prose*, 112.

In its context, I believe this is a tribute to Chaucer's sense of form, for it comes immediately after a passage complaining of the shapeless, disordered character of recent English poetry. Contemporary poets, says Sidney, put their matter hectically into verse, 'never marshalling it into any assured rank, that almost the readers cannot tell where to find themselves'. Though Sidney's romance is comic and Chaucer's poem tragic, there are enough parallels to suggest that Sidney, like Spenser, took Chaucer as his English master. The most obvious one is the pivotal Book 3, which in both works culminates in a consummation of the love pursued with great difficulty in the previous two, and severely jeopardized in the two books following.

The other term, 'Acts', clearly refers to drama, and to Terentian five-act structure.[13] Here the English model is more dubious. Among English dramas, the only one Sidney confessed to admiring was *Gorboduc*, the five-act Senecan tragedy by Sackville and Norton dealing with abdication and civil strife in Ancient Britain. It was acted before the Queen in 1561.[14] Sidney praised it as 'full of stately speeches and well-sounding phrases, climbing to the height of Seneca his style'. The elaborate musical dumb shows dividing the acts are perhaps structurally equivalent to the Eclogues in the *Old Arcadia*, though of course very different in matter; thematically the pastorals may owe more to the intermezzi in Italian *commedia erudita*.[15]

Troilus, and to a lesser extent *Gorboduc*, may have provided the structural loom on which Sidney wove his narrative, but for his yarn he largely bypassed England in favour of Greece, Italy, France and Spain. Appropriately for a romance set in Ancient Greece, he turned to the late Greek romances for much of his setting and plot material. He drew fairly heavily on Heliodorus's *An Aethiopian History*, whose 'sugared invention of that picture of love' he classified as poetic in the *Defence*.[16] He seems also to have made some use of Achilles Tatius's *Clitophon and Leucippe*, and Apuleius's Latin *Golden Ass*, which had been translated by Adlington in 1566.

Italian literature was his richest quarry. The enormously popular *Arcadia* of Jacopo Sannazaro (Naples, 1504, and many editions

---

[13] Cf. T. W. Baldwin, *Shakespeare's Five-Act Structure* (Urbana, 1947); Robert W. Parker, 'Terentian Structure and Sidney's Original *Arcadia*', *ELR* ii (1972), 60–78.

[14] Printed as *The Tragidie of Ferrex and Porrex* (1570/1).

[15] Cf. Robertson, xxi.

[16] *Misc. Prose*, 81. The *Aethiopica* was translated as *An Aethiopian History* by Thomas Underdowne, *c.*1577.

thereafter),[17] which alternates twelve short prose descriptions with twelve verse eclogues, provided Sidney with his title, his setting, models for many of his verse forms, and even some specific lines— see for instance the note on pp. 65–6. Sannazaro gave more to Sidney's Eclogues than to his Books, and the sometimes wearisome eloquence of the melancholy gentleman shepherds is a contribution for which the modern reader may not always be grateful. A more varied Italian source was Ariosto's *Orlando Furioso*, which offered models for descriptive details and narrative techniques, especially the interrupted narrative.[18] A good example is the abrupt breaking off of Musidorus's encounter with a dozen violent peasants (p. 177), not resumed for over a hundred pages. The long romance *Amadis de Gaule*, originally Spanish but read by Sidney in the much more sophisticated French version, gave him many crucial plot details, such as the idea of falling in love with a lady's portrait and the Amazon disguise of one of the male lovers.[19] Sidney commended the reading of *Amadis*, 'which God knoweth wanteth much of a perfect poesy', as a stimulus to 'courtesy, liberality, and especially courage';[20] but it must be confessed that the elements he drew from it for his own romance were not, by and large, such wholesome ones. Another source which he drew on in considerable detail was the prose romance *Diana* by the Spanish writer Jorge de Montemayor, and its continuation by Gil Polo.[21] This pastoral romance with poems and songs offered Sidney many descriptive passages and points of detail, though it wholly lacks the vigour and forward thrust of his own narrative. *Diana* answers better than the *Old Arcadia* to Virginia Woolf's account of 'half-forgotten and deserted places', being somewhat static and limited in register. Its connection with the Sidney circle continued into the next decade, however, Bartholomew Yong's translation of it being dedicated to Lady Rich, Sidney's 'Stella'.

Classical sources, in a work of this period, may to some extent be taken as read. Sidney, however, was exceptionally well versed in

[17] There is a translation of Sannazaro's *Arcadia* by Ralph Nash (Detroit, 1966).
[18] Sir John Harington praised Sidney for this Ariostan technique in the 'Preface' to his translation of *Orlando Furioso*.
[19] See John J. O'Connor, *Amadis de Gaule and its Influence on Elizabethan Literature* (New Brunswick, 1970).
[20] Sidney, *Misc. Prose*, 92.
[21] These links are well discussed by Judith M. Kennedy in her edition of Yong's translation of *Diana* (Oxford, 1968).

classical authors, having, to adapt Ben Jonson's comment on Shakespeare, much Latin and quite a lot of Greek. He was at Shrewsbury School under the Calvinist headmaster Thomas Ashton. At Oxford he was part of a distinguished generation of undergraduates which included William Camden and Richard Hakluyt, and perhaps learned more from them than from his tutors. During his three years of Continental travel he moved in extremely varied humanist circles, acquiring as friend and mentor the Protestant statesman Hubert Languet, among many other learned friends and acquaintances. Letters of advice to his younger brother Robert and to his friend Edward Denny (both in 1580, the year he was completing the *Old Arcadia*) tell us a good deal about his energetic and wide-ranging approach to study. The classical authors whose presence can most frequently be detected in the *Old Arcadia* are Plato, Aristotle, Plutarch, Virgil, Cicero and Ovid.

In the end, however, what is most remarkable about the *Old Arcadia* is not its distillation of sources, but its originality. Though sources and influences can be identified, as I have just very superficially done, Sidney's achievement as a whole cannot be paralleled. Certainly the few English works of fiction close to it in time come nowhere near it in brilliance. We might consider, for instance, Gascoigne's *Adventures of Master F.J.* (1573 and 1575), John Grange's *The Golden Aphroditis* (1577) and Lyly's *Euphues* (1578). All of these, even Gascoigne's amusing story of adultery in a country house, are works for which allowances and excuses must be made if they are offered to a modern reader: that is, they must be viewed as primitive works of prose fiction which the contemporary reader will need to approach in a somewhat antiquarian spirit. The *Old Arcadia*, I believe (though perhaps not its Eclogues), can be as vivid and immediate a source of pleasure to modern readers as Shakespeare's comedies still are to modern audiences.

'Audience' is a helpful term for readers of the *Old Arcadia*, for Sidney's narrative voice is quasi-dramatic. Though some sheets of the *Old Arcadia* were sent by Sidney to his sister 'as fast as they were done', the majority, he reminds her, were written in her presence, and may well have been read aloud by him then and there. Many of the remarks addressed to the coterie of 'fair ladies' suggest this, and we can almost picture the young Sidney sitting as entertainer among a cluster of lively young ladies. The narrator's relationship with his audience is comfortable and intimate: 'do not think, fair ladies, his thoughts had such leisure as to run over so long a ditty' (p. 211). Still more intimate is his rapport with his central characters, especially Philoclea. One or two interjections suggest that he is to be seen as being half in love with her, rather as Chaucer's narrator is with Criseyde:

But alas, sweet Philoclea, how hath my pen forgotten thee, since to thy memory principally all this long matter is intended. Pardon the slackness to come to those woes which thou didst cause in others and feel in thyself. (p. 95)

At moments Arcadia is presented as a place far away and long ago, like Spenser's Faerie Land, a world where archetypes of all that is good and bad in contemporary England are to be found in primitive form; but more often, as here, the story is vividly immediate. The sun climbs over 'our horizon' (p. 243), and at least in the first three books, the narrator seems to be part of the story he tells. He has especially direct access to the thoughts and desires of his two princes, refining brilliantly on the Chaucerian technique of apparent sympathy. When Pyrocles disguises himself as an Amazon, the narrator seems to embark with gusto on the transformation, which entails a change of pronoun which even modern readers may find a little disquieting:

Thus did Pyrocles become Cleophila—which name for a time hereafter I will use, for I myself feel such compassion of his passion that I find even part of his fear lest his name should be uttered before fit time were for it; which you, fair ladies that vouchsafe to read this, I doubt not will account excusable. (p. 25)

This is the pantomime strategy of stimulating audience involvement through shared secrets, and its immediate effect is to create complicity with the two young princes and their amorous exploits. Yet it is undeniably deflating to Pyrocles, who is in any case only seventeen and apparently beardless, that he is referred to as 'she' until the fifth book. As the narrative proceeds there are proliferating suggestions that the princes, though lovable, are not quite so admirable as they at first appear. They may have been altruistic young giant-killers before they came to Arcadia, but their pretensions to heroism within the pastoral arena are often exceedingly suspect. When they kill a lion and a bear at the end of Book 1 the convenient provision of one beast per prince makes the encounter comic rather than threatening, little more than an amusing opportunity for them to show off to the girls. In Book 2 Pyrocles-Cleophila gives a splendid display of rhetoric after putting down the Arcadian uprising, but one which takes no account of the reality of the situation: the princes themselves are fostering 'the duke's absented manner of living', which is a prime cause of civil discontent. They are also neglecting the claims made on them by the princess Erona, who will be burned at the stake if they do not come and rescue her within a year. Though they persuade themselves that they have plenty of time in hand before they need worry about her, the long unhappy complaint of Plangus in the Second Eclogues ensures that the reader, at least, does not forget about Erona's sufferings.

As lovers, the princes are by no means so chivalrous or considerate as their language may suggest. Only the timely arrival of 'a dozen clownish villains' prevents Musidorus from raping Pamela (p. 177), enabling him later to bask in her extremely idealized image of him while well knowing it to be false (pp. 269–70). His elopement with Pamela is possible only after he has carried out a succession of highly elaborate and rather cruel tricks on the peasant family Dametas, Miso and Mopsa. The courtship stratagems of Pyrocles are still more dubious, for they require him to injure the girl he loves, who is made ill with confusion, love-melancholy and neglect, and cause lifelong misery to her mother, the passionate and imaginative Gynecia. The scene in which he encourages Gynecia to believe that he returns her passion does not show him in a very favourable light:

With that (under a feigned rage tearing her clothes) [Gynecia] discovered some parts of her fair body, which, if Cleophila's heart had not been so fully possessed as there was no place left for any new guest, no doubt it would have yielded to that gallant assault. (p. 180)

C. S. Lewis expressed horror at passages such as these revealed by the discovery of the *Old Arcadia*, preferring to see the princes as ideal types of chivalry: 'We cannot suspend our disbelief in a Musidorus who commits indecent assaults; it is as if, in some re-discovered first draft of *Emma*, we were asked to accept a Mr Woodhouse who fought a duel with Frank Churchill.'[22] Yet without these 'lapses', as Lewis calls them, the sombre fourth and fifth books lose much of their power. Sidney's complex presentation of the two princes, in which he plots the ever-widening discrepancies between their idealized pretensions and their actual self-interest, yet keeps them always the heroes, is one of the special strengths of the 'old' version. The more dignified and idealized treatment of them in the revised version is one of the changes that make the story uncompletable on the old lines. Such a passage as the debate between Pyrocles and Philoclea on

[22] C. S. Lewis, *English Literature in the Sixteenth Century* (1954), 332.

suicide in Book 4 is as fine on a semi-tragic level as anything in the later version, and its power is reinforced by the double narrative perspective which has given us so much sympathetic insight into Pyrocles's consciousness, while occasionally nudging us into a more detached consideration of his profound moral confusion. The progress of Pyrocles towards despair can be seen in the *Old Arcadia*, but not in the *New*, as being as inevitable as that of Spenser's Redcrosse. Young, blinded and foolish, Pyrocles has much to be ashamed of, and only the *Old* version makes this clear, preparing us for the sombre and frightening drama of the trial in Book 5.

Fulke Greville wrote of Sidney as being wise and grave beyond his years, 'his very play tending to enrich his mind'.[23] Though Greville prevented the publication of Sidney's youthful 'Old' *Arcadia*, it can now be seen to reflect this quality well. The *TLS* reviewer of Feuillerat's volume in 1926 found the *Old Arcadia* to be 'the work of an old young man, who, if he lose himself for a day in the fantastic invention, cannot fail to remember for an hour or two at least that he knows more than most men of his age and standing of the vicissitudes of life and the infirmities of majesty'. Like *The Importance of Being Earnest*, the original *Arcadia* is 'A Trivial Comedy for Serious People'.

[23] Fulke Greville, *Life of the Renowned Sir Philip Sidney*, ed. Nowell Smith (1907), 6.

ACKNOWLEDGEMENTS

HELP and stimulus of various kinds have been given me by Mr R. E. Alton, Mr M. Brennan, Mr E. Christiansen, Professor John Gouws, Mr V. Houliston, Mr D. C. Kay, Mr J. F. Maule, Professor G. Warkentin, Mr A. N. Wilson and Mr H. R. Woudhuysen. My greatest debt is, of course, to Sidney's previous editors, Professor W. A. Ringler and Miss Jean Robertson, on whose mighty labours my small ones depend: *sic vos non vobis*.

NOTE ON THE TEXT

THE text of the *Old Arcadia* offered here is that of the Oxford edition by Jean Robertson (1973), with a few minor corrections and emendations. This edition, based on a careful collation of the ten surviving manuscript texts of the *Old Arcadia*, is modernized, differing in that respect from W. A. Ringler's edition of Sidney's *Poems* (1962). Miss Robertson's Glossary has been included, which will be found inclusive and exact, and the explanatory notes also draw heavily on the commentaries of Ringler and Robertson.

A discussion of quantitative and accentual verse, which occurs at the end of Book 1 in two of the *Old Arcadia* MSS, is included, from Robertson's text, as Appendix A. Appendix B, a *canzone* sung by Philisides for his absent Mira, probably written in 1577–80, was first printed in the 1593 edition of the *Arcadia*; the text here is that in *Selected Poems of Sir Philip Sidney* (Oxford, 1973).

SELECT BIBLIOGRAPHY

EDITIONS: The *Old Arcadia* was first edited by Albert Feuillerat in 1926. This text, based on the very poor 'Clifford Manuscript', formed the fourth and last volume of his edition of Sidney's *Works* (reprinted, 1962). W. A. Ringler included the poems from the *Old Arcadia* in his edition of *The Poems of Sir Philip Sidney* (Oxford, 1962), and about half of these were included, in modernized spelling, in K. Duncan-Jones's *Selected Poems of Sir Philip Sidney* (Oxford, 1973). Jean Robertson's edition of *The Countess of Pembroke's Arcadia (The Old Arcadia)* (Oxford, 1973) is based on a collation of all the manuscripts, taking the St John's College, Cambridge, MS as copy-text. The present text is based on this excellent edition.

BIOGRAPHY: Fulke Greville's *Life of Sir Philip Sidney* (1652, new Oxford edition by John Gouws forthcoming) is an important document, but not a biography in the modern sense. Another interesting early 'biography' is *Nobilis*, an edifying life of Sidney written in Latin by Thomas Moffett *c.*1592 (edited and translated by V. B. Heltzel and H. H. Hudson, California, 1940). The standard modern biography is still that of M. W. Wallace (Cambridge, 1915). Roger Howell's *Sir Philip Sidney: The Shepherd Knight* (1968) is sound, but based on a less thorough sifting of primary sources than Wallace's book. Important sources that have come to light subsequently are included in James M. Osborn's *Young Philip Sidney: 1572–1577* (Yale, 1972), which weaves together in narrative form a collection of sixty-five letters to Sidney from Continental humanists (now at Yale), together with much of Sidney's correspondence with Hubert Languet. This offers a detailed guide to Sidney's European contacts in the years immediately preceding the composition of the *Old Arcadia*. Far more inclusive, however, is John Buxton's *Sir Philip Sidney and the English Renaissance* (corrected edition, 1964), which is a beautifully written study of Sidney, his circle, his patronage and the aftermath of his death. It is essential reading for anyone who wishes to understand Sidney's world. Two lively attempts to explode the 'Sidney myth' are Richard A. Lanham's 'Sidney: The Ornament of his Age' (*Southern Review*, Adelaide, 1967), and Alan Hager's 'The

Exemplary Mirage: Fabrication of Sir Philip Sidney's Biographical Image and the Sidney Reader' (*Journal of English Literary History* xlviii, 1981). The volume of essays under the editorship of J. van Dorsten and D. Baker-Smith to be published in 1986 to mark the quatercentenary of Sidney's death promises to make some further contributions to an understanding of Sidney's life and legend.

CRITICISM: Critical studies of the *Old Arcadia* which treat it separately from the revised version are not very numerous. It was enthusiastically reviewed in the *TLS* (28 October 1926; see Introduction). A short essay by Mario Praz, 'Sidney's Original *Arcadia*', gave preference to Sidney's style in the *Old* version, but slighted both (*London Mercury* xv, 1927). R. W. Zandvoort made a useful *Comparison between the two versions* (Amsterdam, 1929; reissued, New York 1969). K. O. Myrick's *Sir Philip Sidney as a Literary Craftsman* (Harvard, 1935) favoured the revised version, as being closer to epic. The second edition of his book (1965) includes a useful bibliography of Sidney studies by W. L. Godshalk. In his magisterial *English Literature in the Sixteenth Century* (1954) C. S. Lewis expressed a strong preference for the revised version (see Introduction). Richard A. Lanham in 'The *Old Arcadia*' (bound up with W. R. Davies, 'A Map of *Arcadia*', Yale Studies in English clviii, 1965) analysed the work's rhetoric skilfully, while treating it as almost wholly comic; conversely Franco Marenco, in *Arcadia Puritana* (Bari, 1968), saw it as a serious Calvinist allegory. An even narrower treatment of the *Old Arcadia* from a religious standpoint was Andrew D. Weiner's *Sir Philip Sidney and the Poetics of Protestantism* (Minnesota, 1978). The American journal *English Literary Renaissance* devoted a whole issue to Sidney in Winter 1972. This included articles dealing with the *Old Arcadia* by A. C. Hamilton, Robert W. Parker and Nancy Lindheim; it also has a useful bibliography of Sidney studies by W. L. Godshalk, updated by Godshalk in collaboration with A. J. Colainne in *ELR* (1978). A lucid and pleasing attempt to integrate both *Arcadia*s into the context of Sidney's life and personality is Dorothy Connell's *Sir Philip Sidney: The Maker's Mind* (Oxford, 1977). Richard C. McCoy's *Rebellion in Arcadia* (1979) offers a detailed analysis of political ideas in Book 3 of the *Old Arcadia*.

Sidney's poetry has been the subject of many books and articles, but the majority have taken *Astrophel and Stella* as their main focus. Theodore Spencer's 'The Poetry of Sir Philip Sidney' (*Journal of*

English Literary History xii, 1945) remains a classic treatment. Other useful studies are R. L. Montgomery, *Symmetry and Sense* (1961), David Kalstone, *Sidney's Poetry: Contexts and Interpretations* (1965), and J. G. Nichols, *The Poetry of Sir Philip Sidney* (1974). Three distinguished books which offer informed approaches to Sidney's poetic techniques, in the Eclogues and elsewhere, are John Thompson, *The Founding of English Metre* (1961), Derek Attridge, *Well-weighed syllables: Elizabethan Verse in Classical Metres* (1974), and Alastair Fowler, *Conceitful Thought* (1975). K. Duncan-Jones's 'Philip Sidney's Toys' (*Proceedings of the British Academy*, 1980) is an attempt to distinguish the juvenile character of his poems from the after-image of Sidney as a hero.

A CHRONOLOGY OF
SIR PHILIP SIDNEY

1554 Philip Sidney born at Penshurst in Kent, 30 November, and named after Philip of Spain

1564 Philip Sidney and Fulke Greville enter Shrewsbury School

1568 At Christ Church, Oxford

1572 Sets out, in the train of the Earl of Lincoln, for continental travel; witnesses the Massacre of St Bartholomew's Day in Paris, 24 August

1573 Travels to Heidelburg and Frankfurt, where he meets Hubert Languet, and to Vienna, Hungary, and Italy. Studies in Padua and Venice

1575 Returns to England by way of Vienna, Poland, and the Netherlands. Sir Henry Sidney begins his third term of office as Lord Deputy Governor of Ireland

1577 Defends his father's policy in Ireland. Is sent as ambassador to the Imperial Court; discusses Protestant League; meets William of Orange

1578 Perhaps writes *The Lady of May*. Begins to write the *Arcadia* at Wilton, the house of his sister, the Countess of Pembroke

1580 Writes to the Queen to dissuade her from marrying the Duke of Anjou. Completes the *Old Arcadia*

1581 Begins to write *Astrophel and Stella*; perhaps writes *The Defence of Poetry*. Penelope Devereux marries Lord Rich

1583 Knighted for reasons of protocol. Escorts the Duke of Alençon back to the Netherlands. Finishes *Astrophel and Stella*

1583 Marries Frances, daughter of Sir Francis Walsingham

1584 Begins to revise the *Arcadia*. Writes the *Defence of the Earl of Leicester*

1585 Begins to translate Duplessis-Mornay's *De la verité de la religion chrestienne*; perhaps translates Du Bartas's *La Semaine* and begins translation of the *Psalms*, later completed by the

Countess of Pembroke. Attempts to sail to the West Indies with Drake. Appointed Governor of Flushing

1586   Travels in the northern Netherlands. Is actively involved in politics. Wounded in a skirmish near Zutphen, 22 September; dies at Arnhem, 17 October

1587   Buried in St Paul's at the expense of Sir Francis Walsingham, his father-in-law, 16 February. Golding's completed version of *The Trueness of the Christian Religion* published

1590   The *New Arcadia* published

1591   *Astrophel and Stella* published

1593   The *New Arcadia* with Books 3–5 of the *Old Arcadia* published

1595   The *Defence of Poetry* published

1598   The composite *Arcadia* published with *Astrophel and Stella* and *Certain Sonnets*

THE COUNTESS OF PEMBROKE'S
ARCADIA

TO MY DEAR LADY AND SISTER
THE COUNTESS OF PEMBROKE*

HERE now have you (most dear, and most worthy to be most dear, lady) this idle work of mine, which I fear (like the spider's web) will be thought fitter to be swept away than worn to any other purpose. For my part, in very truth (as the cruel fathers among the Greeks were wont to do to the babes they would not foster) I could well find in my heart to cast out in some desert of forgetfulness this child which I am loath to father. But you desired me to do it, and your desire to my heart is an absolute commandment. Now it is done only for you, only to you; if you keep it to yourself, or to such friends who will weigh errors in the balance of goodwill, I hope, for the father's sake, it will be pardoned, perchance made much of, though in itself it have deformities. For indeed, for severer eyes it is not, being but a trifle, and that triflingly handled. Your dear self can best witness the manner, being done in loose sheets of paper, most of it in your presence, the rest by sheets sent unto you as fast as they were done. In sum, a young head not so well stayed as I would it were (and shall be when God will) having many many fancies begotten in it, if it had not been in some way delivered, would have grown a monster, and more sorry might I be that they came in than that they gat out. But his chief safety shall be the not walking abroad; and his chief protection the bearing the livery of your name which (if much much goodwill do not deceive me) is worthy to be a sanctuary for a greater offender. This say I because I know the virtue so; and this say I because it may be ever so; or, to say better, because it will be ever so. Read it then at your idle times, and the follies your good judgement will find in it, blame not, but laugh at. And so, looking for no better stuff than, as in a haberdasher's shop, glasses or feathers, you will continue to love the writer who doth exceedingly love you, and most most heartily prays you may long live to be a principal ornament to the family of the Sidneys.

Your loving brother,
Philip Sidney

THE FIRST BOOK OR ACT OF
THE COUNTESS OF PEMBROKE'S ARCADIA

ARCADIA*among all the provinces of Greece was ever had in singular reputation, partly for the sweetness of the air and other natural benefits, but principally for the moderate and well tempered minds of the people who (finding how true a contentation is gotten by following the course of nature, and how the shining title of glory, so much affected by other nations, doth indeed help little to the happiness of life) were the only people which, as by their justice and providence gave neither cause nor hope to their neighbours to annoy them, so were they not stirred with false praise to trouble others' quiet, thinking it a small reward for the wasting of their own lives in ravening that their posterity should long after say they had done so. Even the muses seemed to approve their good determination by choosing that country as their chiefest repairing place, and by bestowing their perfections so largely there that the very shepherds themselves had their fancies opened to so high conceits as the most learned of other nations have been long time since content both to borrow their names and imitate their cunning. In this place some time there dwelled a mighty duke named Basilius, a prince of sufficient skill to govern so quiet a country where the good minds of the former princes had set down good laws, and the well bringing up of the people did serve as a most sure bond to keep them. He married Gynecia, the daughter of the king of Cyprus; a lady worthy enough to have had her name in continual remembrance if her latter time had not blotted her well governed youth, although the wound fell more to her own conscience than to the knowledge of the world, fortune something supplying her want of virtue. Of her the duke had two fair daughters, the elder Pamela, the younger Philoclea, both so excellent in all those gifts which are allotted to reasonable creatures as they seemed to be born for a sufficient proof that nature is no stepmother to that sex, how much soever the rugged disposition of some men, sharp-witted only in evil speaking, hath sought to disgrace them. And thus grew they on in each good increase till Pamela, a year older than Philoclea, came to the point of seventeen years of age. At which time the duke Basilius—not so much stirred with the care for his country and children as with the vanity which possesseth many who, making a perpetual mansion of this poor baiting place of man's life, are desirous to know the certainty of things to come, wherein there is nothing so certain as our continual uncertainty—Basilius, I say, would needs undertake a journey to Delphos,* there by the oracle to inform himself whether the rest of his life should be continued in like tenor of happiness as thitherunto it had been, accompanied with the wellbeing of his wife and children, whereupon he had placed greatest part of his own felicity. Neither did he long stay; but the woman appointed to that impiety, furiously inspired, gave him in verse this answer:

> Thy elder care shall from thy careful face
> By princely mean be stolen and yet not lost;
> Thy younger shall with nature's bliss embrace
> An uncouth love, which nature hateth most.
> Thou with thy wife adult'ry shalt commit,
> And in thy throne a foreign state shall sit.
> All this on thee this fatal year shall hit.

Which, as in part it was more obscure than he could understand, so did the whole bear such manifest threatenings, that his amazement was greater than his fore curiosity—both passions proceeding out of one weakness: in vain to desire to know that of which in vain thou shalt be sorry after thou hast known it. But thus the duke answered though not satisfied, he returned into his country with a countenance well witnessing the dismayedness of his heart; which notwithstanding upon good considerations he thought not good to disclose, but only to one chosen friend of his named Philanax, whom he had ever found a friend not only in affection but judgement, and no less of the duke than dukedom—a rare temper, whilst most men either servilely yield to all appetites, or with an obstinate austerity, looking to that they fancy good, wholly neglect the prince's person. But such was this man; and in such a man had Basilius been happy if his mind, corrupted with a prince's fortune, had not resolved to use a friend's secrecy rather for confirmation of fancies than correcting of errors, which in this weighty matter he well showed. For having with many words discovered unto him both the cause and success of his Delphos journey, in the end he told him that, to prevent all these inconveniences of the loss of his crown and children (for as for the point of his wife, he could no way understand it), he was resolved for this fatal year to retire himself with his wife and daughters into a solitary place where, being two lodges built of purpose, he would in the one of them recommend his daughter Pamela to his principal herdman—a place in that world, not so far gone into painted vanities, of some credit—by name Dametas, in whose blunt truth he had great confidence, thinking it a contrary salve against the destiny threatening her mishap by a prince to place her with a shepherd. In the other lodge he and his wife would keep their younger jewel, Philoclea; and because the oracle touched some strange love of hers, have the more care of her, in especial keeping away her nearest kinsmen, whom he deemed chiefly understood, and therewithal all other likely to move any such humour. And so for himself, being so cruelly menaced by fortune, he would draw himself out of her way by this loneliness, which he thought was the surest mean to avoid her blows; where for his pleasure he would be recreated with all those sports and eclogues wherein the shepherds of that country did much excel. As for the government of the country, and in especial manning of his frontiers (for that only way he thought a foreign prince might endanger his crown), he would leave the charge to certain selected persons; the superintendence of all which he would commit to Philanax. And so ended he his speech, for fashion's sake asking him his counsel. But Philanax, having forthwith taken into the depth of his consideration both what the duke said and with what mind he spake it, with a true heart and humble countenance in this sort answered:

'Most redoubted and beloved prince, if as well it had pleased you at your going to Delphos, as now, to have used my humble service, both I should in better season and to better purpose have spoken, and you perhaps at this time should have been, as no way more in danger, so undoubtedly much more in quietness. I would then have said unto you that wisdom and virtue be the only destinies appointed to man to follow, wherein one ought to place all his knowledge, since they be such guides as cannot fail which, besides their inward comfort, do make a man see so direct a way of proceeding as prosperity must necessarily ensue. And, although the wickedness of the world should oppress it, yet could it not be said that evil happened to him who should fall accompanied with virtue; so that, either standing or falling with virtue, a man is never in evil case. I would then have said the heavenly powers to be reverenced and not searched into, and their mercy rather by prayers to be sought than their hidden counsels by curiosity; these kinds of soothsaying sorceries (since the heavens have left us in ourselves sufficient guides) to be nothing but fancies wherein there must either be vanity or infallibleness, and so either not to be respected or not to be prevented. But since it is weakness too much to remember what should have been done, and that your commandment stretcheth to know what shall be done, I do, most dear lord, with humble boldness say that the manner of your determination doth in no sort better please me than the cause of your going. These thirty years past have you so governed this realm that neither your subjects have wanted justice in you, nor you obedience in them; and your neighbours have found you so hurtlessly strong that they thought it better to rest in your friendship than make new trial of your enmity. If this, then, have proceeded out of the good constitution of your state, and out of a wise providence generally to prevent all those things which might encumber your happiness, why should you now seek new courses, since your own example comforts you to continue on, and that it is most certain no destiny nor influence whatsoever can bring man's wit to a higher point than wisdom and goodness? Why should you deprive yourself of governing your dukedom for fear of losing your dukedom, like one that should kill himself for fear of death? Nay rather, if this oracle be to be accounted of, arm up your courage the more against it; for who will stick to him that abandons himself? Let your subjects have you in their eyes, let them see the benefits of your justice daily more and more; and so must they needs rather like of present sureties than uncertain changes.* Lastly, whether your time call you to live or die, do both like a prince. And even the same mind hold I as touching my ladies, your daughters, in whom nature promiseth nothing but goodness, and their education by your fatherly care hath been hitherto such as hath been most fit to restrain all evil, giving their minds virtuous delights, and not grieving them for want of well ruled liberty: now to fall to a sudden straitening them, what can it do but argue suspicion, the most venomous gall to virtue? Leave women's minds, the most untamed that way of any; see whether any cage can please a bird, or whether a dog grow not fiercer with tying. What doth jealousy else but stir up the mind to think what it is from which they are restrained? For they are treasures or things of great delight which men use to hide for the aptness they have to catch men's fancies; and the thoughts once awaked to that, harder sure it is to keep those thoughts from accomplishment than it had been before to have kept the mind (which, being the chief part, by this means is defiled) from thinking. Now, for the recommending so principal a charge of her, whose mind goes beyond the governing of many hundreds of such, to such a person as Dametas is, besides that the thing in itself is strange, it comes of a very ill ground that ignorance should be the mother of faithfulness. O no, he cannot be good that knows not why he is good, but stands so far good as his fortune may keep him unassayed. But coming to that, his rude simplicity is either easily changed or easily deceived; and so grows that to be the last excuse of his fault which seemed to have been the first foundation of his faith. Thus far hath your commandment and my zeal drawn me to speak; which I, like a man in a valley may discern hills, or like a poor passenger may spy a rock, so humbly submit to your gracious consideration, beseeching you to stand wholly upon your own virtue as the surest way to maintain you in that you are, and to avoid any evil which may be imagined.'

Whilst Philanax used these words, a man might see in the duke's face that, as he was wholly wedded to his own opinion, so was he grieved to have any man say that which he had not seen. Yet did the goodwill he bare to Philanax so far prevail with him that he passed into no further choler, but with short manner asked him: 'And would you, then', said he, 'that in change of fortune I shall not change my determination, as we do our apparel according to the air, and as the ship doth her course with the wind?'

'Truly sir,' answered he, 'neither do I as yet see any change; and though I did, yet would I think a constant virtue, well settled, little subject unto it. And, as in great necessity I would allow a well proportioned change, so in the sight of an enemy to arm himself the lighter, or at every puff of wind to strike sail, is such a change as either will breed ill success or no success.'

'To give place to blows', said the duke, 'is thought no small wisdom.'

'That is true,' said Philanax, 'but to give place before they come takes away the occasion, when they come, to give place.'

'Yet the reeds stand with yielding', said the duke.

'And so are they but reeds, most worthy prince,' said Philanax, 'but the rocks stand still and are rocks.'

But the duke, having used thus much dukely sophistry to deceive himself, and making his will wisdom, told him resolutely he stood upon his own determination; and therefore willed him, with certain other he named, to take the government of the state, and especially to keep narrow watch of the frontiers. Philanax, acknowledging himself much honoured by so great trust, went with as much care to perform his commandment as before he had with faith yielded his counsel, which in the latter short disputations he had rather proportioned to Basilius's words than to any towardness of argument. And Basilius, according to his determination, retired himself into the solitary place of the two lodges, where he was daily delighted with the eclogues and pastimes of shepherds. In the one of which lodges he himself remained with his wife and the beauty of the world, Philoclea;* in the other, near unto him, he placed his daughter Pamela with Dametas, whose wife was Miso and daughter Mopsa, unfit company for so excellent a creature, but to exercise her patience and to serve for a foil to her perfections.

Now, newly after that the duke had begun this solitary life, there came (following the train their virtues led them) into this country two young princes: the younger, but chiefer,* named Pyrocles, only son to Euarchus, king of Macedon; the other his cousin german, Musidorus, duke of Thessalia; both like in virtues, near in years, near in blood, but nearest of all in friendship. And because this matter runs principally of them, a few more words how they came hither will not be superfluous. Euarchus, king of Macedon, a prince of such justice that he never thought himself privileged by being a prince, nor did measure greatness by anything but by goodness; as he did thereby root an awful love in his subjects towards him, so yet could he not avoid the assaults of envy—the enemy and yet the honour of virtue. For the kings of Thrace, Pannonia, and Epirus, not being able to attain his perfections, thought in their base wickedness best to take away so odious a comparison, lest his virtues, joined now to the fame and force of the Macedonians, might in time both conquer the bodies and win the minds of their subjects. And thus conspiring together, they did three sundry ways enter into his kingdom at one time. Which sudden and dangerous invasions, although they did nothing astonish Euarchus, who carried a heart prepared for all extremities (as a man that knew both what ill might happen to a man never so prosperous, and withal what the uttermost of that ill was), yet were they cause that Euarchus did send away his young son Pyrocles, at that time but six years old, to his sister, the dowager and regent of Thessalia, there to be brought up with her son Musidorus. Which, though it proceeded of necessity, yet was not the counsel in itself unwise, the sweet emulation that grew being an excellent nurse of the good parts in these two princes, two princes indeed born to the exercise of virtue. For they, accompanying the increase of their years with the increase of all good inward and outward qualities, and taking very timely into their minds that the divine part of man was not enclosed in this body for nothing, gave themselves wholly over to those knowledges which might in the course of their life be ministers to well doing. And so grew they on till Pyrocles came to be seventeen and Musidorus eighteen years of age; at which time Euarchus, having after ten years' war conquered the kingdom of Thrace and brought the other two to be his tributaries, lived in the principal city of Thrace called at that time Byzantium, whither he sent for his son and nephew to delight his aged eyes in them and to make them enjoy the fruits of his victories. But so pleased it God, who reserved them to greater traverses,* both of good and evil fortune, that the sea, to which they committed themselves, stirred with terrible tempest, forced them to fall far from their course upon the coast of Lydia where, what befell unto them, what valiant acts they did, passing in one year's space through the lesser Asia, Syria, and Egypt, how many ladies they defended from wrongs, and disinherited persons restored to their rights, it is a work for a higher style than mine. This only shall suffice: that their fame returned so fast before them into Greece that the king of Macedon received that as the comfort of their absence, although accompanied with so much more longing as he found the manifestation of their worthiness greater. But they, desirous more and more to exercise their virtues and increase their experience, took their journey from Egypt towards Greece. Which they did, they two alone, because, that being their native country they might have the most perfect knowledge of it; wherein they that hold the countenances of princes have their eyes most dazzled.

And so, taking Arcadia in their way, for the fame of the country, they came thither newly after that this strange solitariness had possessed Basilius. Now so fell it unto them that they, lodging in the house of Kerxenus, a principal gentleman in Mantinea, so was the city called, near to the solitary dwelling of the duke, it was Pyrocles' either evil or good fortune walking with his host in a fair gallery that he perceived a picture, newly made by an excellent artificer, which contained the duke and duchess with their younger daughter Philoclea, with such countenance and fashion as the manner of their life held them in, both the parents' eyes cast with a loving care upon their beautiful child, she drawn as well as it was possible art should counterfeit so perfect a workmanship of nature. For therein, besides the show of her beauties, a man might judge even the nature of her countenance, full of bashfulness, love, and reverence—and all by the cast of her eye—, mixed with a sweet grief to find her virtue suspected. This moved Pyrocles to fall into questions of her; wherein being answered by the gentleman as much as he understood, which was of her strange kind of captivity; neither was it known how long it should last; and there was a general opinion grown the duke would grant his daughters in marriage to nobody. As the most noble heart is most subject unto it, from questions grew to pity; and when with pity once his heart was made tender, according to the aptness of the humour, it received straight a cruel impression of that wonderful passion which to be defined is impossible, by reason no words reach near to the strange nature of it. They only know it which inwardly feel it. It is called love. Yet did not the poor youth at first know his disease, thinking it only such a kind of desire as he was wont to have to see unwonted sights, and his pity to be no other but the fruits of his gentle nature. But even this arguing with himself came of a further thought; and the more he argued, the more his thought increased. Desirous he was to see the place where she remained, as though the architecture of the lodges would have been much for his learning; but more desirous to see herself, to be judge, forsooth, of the painter's cunning—for thus at the first did he flatter himself, as though his wound had been no deeper. But when within short time he came to the degree of uncertain wishes, and that those wishes grew to unquiet longings; when he could fix his thoughts upon nothing but that, within a little varying, they should end with Philoclea; when each thing he saw seemed to figure out some part of his passions, and that he heard no word spoken but that he imagined it carried the sound of Philoclea's name; then did poor Pyrocles yield to the burden, finding himself prisoner before he had leisure to arm himself, and that he might well, like the spaniel, gnaw upon the chain that ties him, but he should sooner mar his teeth than procure liberty. Then was his chief delight secretly to draw his dear friend a-walking to the desert*of the two lodges where he saw no grass upon which he thought Philoclea might hap to tread but that he envied the happiness of it; and yet, with a contrary folly, would sometimes recommend his whole estate unto it. Till at length love, the refiner of invention, put in his head a way how to come to the sight of his Philoclea; for which he with great speed and secrecy prepared everything that was necessary for his purpose, but yet would not put it in execution till he had disclosed it to Musidorus, both to perform the true laws of friendship and withal to have his counsel and allowance. And yet, out of the sweetness of his disposition, was bashfully afraid to break it with him to whom (besides other bonds), because he was his elder, he bare a kind of reverence, until some fit opportunity might, as it were, draw it from him. Which occasion time shortly presented unto him.

For Musidorus, having informed himself fully of the strength and riches of the country; of the nature of the people, and of the manner of their laws; and seeing the duke's court could not be visited, and that they came not without danger to that place, prohibited to all men but to certain shepherds, grew no less weary of his abode there than marvelled of the great delight Pyrocles took in that place. Whereupon one day, at Pyrocles' earnest request being walked thither again, began in this manner to say unto him:

'A mind well trained and long exercised in virtue, my sweet and worthy cousin, doth not easily change any course it once undertakes but upon well grounded and well weighed causes; for being witness to itself of his own inward good, it finds nothing without it of so high a price for which it should be altered. Even the very countenance and behaviour of such a man doth show forth images of the same constancy by maintaining a right harmony betwixt it and the inward good in yielding itself suitable to the virtuous resolutions of the mind. This speech I direct to you, noble friend Pyrocles, the excellency of whose mind and well chosen course in virtue, if I do not sufficiently know, having seen such rare demonstrations of it, it is my weakness and not your unworthiness. But as indeed I do know it, and knowing it, most dearly love both it and him that hath it, so must I needs say that since our late coming into this country I have marked in you, I will not say an alteration, but a relenting, truly, and slacking of the main career you had so notably begun and almost performed; and that, in such sort as I cannot find sufficient reasons in my great love towards you how to allow it. For, to leave off other secreter arguments which my acquaintance with you makes me easily find, this in effect to any man may be manifest: that, whereas you were wont, in all the places you came, to give yourself vehemently to knowledge of those things which might better your mind; to seek the familiarity of excellent men in learning and

soldiery; and lastly, to put all these things in practice both by con-
tinual wise proceeding and worthy enterprises, as occasions fell for
them; you now leave all these things undone; you let your mind fall
asleep, besides your countenance troubled (which surely comes not
out of virtue; for virtue, like the clear heaven, is without clouds);
and lastly, which seemeth strangest unto me, you haunt greatly this
place, wherein, besides the disgrace that might fall of it (which, that
it hath not already fallen upon you, is rather luck than providence,
this duke having sharply forbidden it), you subject yourself to
solitariness, the sly enemy that doth most separate a man from well
doing.'

These words, spoken vehemently and proceeding from so dearly
an esteemed friend as Musidorus, did so pierce poor Pyrocles that
his blushing cheeks did witness with him he rather could not help,
than did not know, his fault. Yet, desirous by degrees to bring his
friend to a gentler consideration of him, and beginning with two or
three broken sighs, answered him to this purpose:

'Excellent Musidorus, in the praises you gave me in the beginning
of your speech, I easily acknowledge the force of your goodwill unto
me; for neither could you have thought so well of me if extremity of
love had not something dazzled your eyes, nor you could have loved
me so entirely if you had not been apt to make so great, though
undeserved, judgement of me. And even so must I say of those
imperfections, to which though I have ever through weakness been
subject, yet you by the daily mending of your mind have of late
been able to look into them, which before you could not discern; so
that the change you spake of falls not out by my impairing but by
your bettering. And yet, under the leave of your better judgement,
I must needs say thus much, my dear cousin, that I find not myself
wholly to be condemned because I do not with a continual
vehemency follow those knowledges which you call the bettering of
my mind; for both the mind itself must, like other things, sometimes
be unbent,*or else it will be either weakened or broken, and these
knowledges, as they are of good use, so are they not all the mind may
stretch itself unto. Who knows whether I feed not my mind with
higher thoughts? Truly, as I know not all the particularities, so yet
see I the bounds of all those knowledges; but the workings of the
mind, I find, much more infinite than can be led unto by the eye or
imagined by any that distract their thoughts without themselves.
And in such contemplations, or, as I think, more excellent, I enjoy

my solitariness; and my solitariness, perchance, is the nurse of these contemplations. Eagles, we see, fly alone; and they are but sheep which always herd together. Condemn not, therefore, my mind sometimes to enjoy itself, nor blame not the taking of such times as serve most fit for it!'

And here Pyrocles suddenly stopped, like a man unsatisfied in himself, though his wit might well have served to have satisfied another. And so, looking with a countenance as though he desired he should know his mind without hearing him speak, and yet desirous to speak to breathe out some part of his inward evil, sending again new blood to his face, he continued his speech in this manner:

'And lord! dear cousin,' said he, 'doth not the pleasantness of this place carry in itself sufficient reward for any time lost in it, or for any such danger that might ensue? Do you not see how everything conspires together to make this place a heavenly dwelling? Do you not see the grass, how in colour they excel the emeralds, everyone striving to pass his fellow—and yet they are all kept in an equal height? And see you not the rest of all these beautiful flowers, each of which would require a man's wit to know, and his life to express? Do not these stately trees seem to maintain their flourishing old age with the only happiness of their seat, being clothed with a continual spring because no beauty here should ever fade? Doth not the air breathe health, which the birds, delightful both to the ear and eye, do daily solemnize with the sweet concent of their voices? Is not every echo here a perfect music? And these fresh and delightful brooks, how slowly they slide away, as loath to leave the company of so many things united in perfection! And with how sweet a murmur they lament their forced departure! Certainly, certainly, cousin, it must needs be that some goddess this desert belongs unto, who is the soul of this soil; for neither is any less than a goddess worthy to be shrined in such a heap of pleasures, nor any less than a goddess could have made it so perfect a model of the heavenly dwellings.'

And so he ended, with a deep sigh, ruefully casting his eye upon Musidorus, as more desirous of pity than pleading. But Musidorus had all this while held his look fixed upon Pyrocles' countenance, and with no less loving attention marked how his words proceeded from him. But in both these he perceived such strange diversities that they rather increased new doubts than gave him ground to settle any judgement; for, besides his eyes sometimes even great with tears, the oft changing of his colour, with a kind of shaking unstaidness over all his body, he might see in his countenance some great determination mixed with fear, and might perceive in him store of thoughts rather stirred than digested, his words interrupted continually with sighs which served as a burden to each sentence, and the tenor of his speech (though of his wonted phrase) not knit together to one constant end but rather dissolved in itself, as the vehemency of the inward passion prevailed: which made Musidorus frame his answer nearest to that humour which should soonest put out the secret. For, having in the beginning of Pyrocles' speech which defended his solitariness framed in his mind a reply against it in the praise of honourable action (in showing that such kind of contemplation is but a glorious title to idleness; that in action a man did not only better himself but benefit others; that the gods would not have delivered a soul into the body which hath arms and legs (only instruments of doing) but that it were intended the mind should employ them; and that the mind should best know his own good or evil by practice; which knowledge was the only way to increase the one and correct the other; besides many other better arguments which the plentifulness of the matter yielded to the sharpness of his wit), when he found Pyrocles leave that, and fall to such an affected praising of the place, he left it likewise, and joined therein with him because he found him in that humour utter most store of passion. And even thus, kindly embracing him, he said:

'Your words are such, noble cousin, so sweetly and strongly handled in the praise of solitariness, as they would make me likewise yield myself up unto it, but that the same words make me know it is more pleasant to enjoy the company of him that can speak such words than by such words to be persuaded to follow solitariness. And even so do I give you leave, sweet Pyrocles, ever to defend solitariness so long as, to defend it, you ever keep company. But I marvel at the excessive praises you give to this desert. In truth, it is not unpleasant; but yet, if you would return into Macedon, you should see either many heavens or find this no more than earthly. And even Tempe, in my Thessalia, where you and I (to my great happiness) were brought up together, is nothing inferior unto it. But I think you will make me see that the vigour of your wit can show itself in any subject; or else you feed sometimes your solitariness with the conceits of the poets whose liberal pens can as easily travel over mountains as molehills,* and so (like well disposed men) set up everything to the highest note—especially when they put such words in the mouth of one of these fantastical mind-infected people that children and musicians call lovers.'

This word of 'lover' did no less pierce poor Pyrocles than the right tune of music toucheth him that is sick of the tarantula. There was not one part of his body that did not feel a sudden motion, the heart drawing unto itself the life of every part to help it, distressed with the sound of that word. Yet, after some pause, lifting up his eyes a little from the ground, and yet not daring to place them in the face of Musidorus, armed with the very countenance of the poor prisoner at the bar whose answer is nothing but 'guilty', with much ado he brought forth this question:

'And alas,' said he, 'dear cousin, what if I be not so much the poet, the freedom of whose pen can exercise itself in anything, as even that very miserable subject of his cunning whereof you speak?'

'Now the eternal gods forbid', mainly cried out Musidorus. But Pyrocles, having broken the ice, pursued on in this manner:

'And yet such a one am I,' said he, 'and in such extremity as no man can feel but myself, nor no man believe; since no man ever could taste the hundredth part of that which lies in the inwardmost part of my soul. For since it was the fatal overthrow of all my liberty to see in the gallery of Mantinea the only Philoclea's picture, that beauty did pierce so through mine eyes to my heart that the impression of it doth not lie but live there, in such sort as the question is not now whether I shall love or no, but whether loving, I shall live or die.'

Musidorus was no less astonished with these words of his friend than if, thinking him in health, he had suddenly told him that he felt the pangs of death oppress him. So that, amazedly looking upon him (even as Apollo is painted*when he saw Daphne suddenly turned to a laurel), he was not able to say one word; but gave Pyrocles occasion, having already made the breach, to pass on in this sort:

'And because I have laid open my wound, noble cousin,' said he, 'I will show you what my melancholy hath brought forth for the preparation at least of a salve, if it be not in itself a medicine. I am resolved, because all direct ways are barred me of opening my suit to the duke, to take upon me the estate of an Amazon lady going about the world to practise feats of chivalry and to seek myself a worthy husband. I have already provided all furniture necessary for it; and my face, you see, will not easily discover me. And hereabout will I haunt till, by the help of this disguising, I may come to the presence of her whose imprisonment darkens the world, that my own eyes may be witnesses to my heart it is great reason why he should be thus captived. And then, as I shall have attained to the first degree of my happiness, so will fortune, occasion, and mine own industry put forward the rest. For the principal point is to set in a good way the thing we desire; for then will time itself daily discover new secret helps. As for my name, it shall be Cleophila, turning Philoclea to myself, as my mind is wholly turned and transformed into her. Now therefore do I submit myself to your counsel, dear cousin, and crave your help.'

And thus he ended, as who should say, 'I have told you all, have pity on me.' But Musidorus had by this time gathered his spirits together, dismayed to see him he loved more than himself plunged in such a course of misery. And so, when Pyrocles had ended, casting a ghastful countenance upon him, as if he would conjure some strange spirit he saw possess him, with great vehemency uttered these words:

'And is it possible that this is Pyrocles, the only young prince in the world, formed by nature and framed by education to the true exercise of virtue? Or is it, indeed, some Amazon Cleophila that hath counterfeited the face of my friend in this sort to vex me? For likelier, sure, I would have thought it that any outward face might have been disguised than that the face of so excellent a mind could have been thus blemished. O sweet Pyrocles, separate yourself a little, if it be possible, from yourself, and let your own mind look upon your own proceedings; so shall my words be needless, and you best instructed. See with yourself how fit it will be for you in this your tender youth (born so great a prince, of so rare, not only expectation, but proof, desired of your old father, and wanted of your native country, now so near your home) to divert your thoughts from the way of goodness to lose, nay to abuse, your time; lastly, to overthrow all the excellent things you have done, which have filled the world with your fame (as if you should drown your ship in the long-desired haven, or like an ill player should mar the last act of his tragedy). Remember (for I know you know it) that, if we will be men, the reasonable part of our soul is to have absolute commandment,* against which if any sensual weakness arise, we are to yield all our sound forces to the overthrowing of so unnatural a rebellion; wherein, how can we want courage, since we are to deal against so weak an adversary that in itself is nothing but weakness? Nay, we are to resolve that if reason direct it, we must do it; and if we must do it, we will do it; for to say I cannot is childish, and I will not womanish. And see how extremely every way you endanger your mind; for to take this woman's habit, without you frame your behaviour accordingly, is wholly vain; your behaviour can never come kindly from you but as the mind is proportioned unto it. So that you must resolve, if you will play your part to any purpose, whatsoever peevish imperfections are in that sex, to soften your heart to receive them—the very first down step to all wickedness. For do not deceive yourself, my dear cousin; there is no man suddenly either excellently good or extremely evil, but grows either as he holds himself up in virtue or lets himself slide to viciousness. And let us see what power is the author of all these troubles: forsooth, love; love, a passion, and the basest and fruitlessest of all passions. Fear breedeth wit; anger is the cradle of courage; joy openeth and enableth the heart; sorrow, as it closeth it, so yet draweth it inward to look to the correcting of itself. And so all of them generally have power towards some good, by the direction of reason. But this bastard love (for, indeed, the name of love is unworthily applied to so hateful a humour as it is, engendered betwixt lust and idleness), as the matter it works upon is nothing but a certain base weakness, which some gentle fools call a gentle heart; as his adjoined companions be unquietness, longings, fond comforts, faint discomforts, hopes, jealousies, ungrounded rages, causeless yieldings; so is the highest end it aspires unto a little pleasure, with much pain before, and great repentance after. But that end, how endlessly it runs to infinite evils, were fit enough for the matter we speak of; but not for your ears, in whom, indeed, there is so much true disposition to virtue. Yet thus much of his worthy effects in yourself is to be seen: that it utterly subverts the course of nature in making reason give place to sense, and man to woman. And truly, I think, hereupon it first gat the name of love. For, indeed, the true love hath that excellent nature in it, that it doth transform the very essence of the lover into the thing loved, uniting and, as it were, incorporating it with a secret and inward working. And herein do these kinds of love imitate the excellent; for, as the love of heaven makes one heavenly, the love of virtue, virtuous, so doth the love of the world make one become worldly. And this effeminate love of a woman doth so womanize a man that, if you yield to it, it will not only make you a famous Amazon, but a launder, a distaff-spinner,* or whatsoever other vile occupation their idle heads can imagine and their weak hands perform. Therefore, to trouble you no longer with my tedious but loving words, if either you remember what you are, what you have been, or what you must be; if you consider what it is that moves you, or for what kind of creature you are moved, you shall find the cause so small, the effects so dangerous, yourself so unworthy to run into the one or to be driven by the other, that I doubt not I shall quickly have occasion rather to praise you for having conquered it than to give you any further counsel how to do it.'

Pyrocles' mind was all this while so fixed upon another devotion that he no more attentively marked his friend's discourse than the child that hath leave to play marks the last part of his lesson, or the diligent pilot in a dangerous tempest doth attend to the unskilful words of the passenger. Yet, the very sound having left the general points of his speech in his mind, the respect he bare to his friend brought forth this answer, having first paid up his late-accustomed tribute of sighs:

'Dear and worthy friend, whatsoever good disposition nature hath bestowed on me, or howsoever that disposition hath been by bringing up confirmed, this must I confess: that I am not yet come to that degree of wisdom to think lightly of·the sex of whom I have my life; since, if I be anything (which your friendship rather finds than I acknowledge), I was to come to it born of a woman and nursed of a woman. And certainly (for this point of your speech doth nearest touch me) it is strange to see the unmanlike cruelty of mankind who, not content with their tyrannous ambition to have brought the others' virtuous patience under them, like childish masters, think their masterhood nothing without doing injury to them who (if we will argue by reason) are framed of nature with the same parts of the mind for the exercise of virtue as we are. And, for example, even this estate of Amazons, which I now for my greatest honour do seek to counterfeit, doth well witness that, if generally the sweetness of their disposition did not make them see the vainness of these things which we account glorious, they neither want valour of mind, nor yet doth their fairness take away their force. And truly, we men and praisers of men should remember that, if we have such excellencies, it is reason to think them excellent creatures of whom we are, since a kite never brought forth a good flying hawk. But to tell you true, I do both disdain to use any more words of such a subject which is so praised in itself as it needs no praises; and withal fear lest my conceit (not able to reach unto them) bring forth words which for their un-worthiness may be a disgrace to them I so inwardly honour. Let this suffice: that they are capable of virtue. And virtue, you yourself say, is to be loved; and I, too, truly. But this I willingly confess: that it likes me much better when I find virtue in a fair lodging than when I am bound to seek it in an ill-favoured creature, like a pearl in a dunghill.'

And here Pyrocles stayed as to breathe himself, having been transported with a little vehemency because it seemed him Musidorus had over bitterly glanced against the reputation of woman-kind. But then quieting his countenance, as well as out of an unquiet mind it might be, he thus proceeded on:

'And poor love,' said he, 'dear cousin, is little beholding unto you, since you are not contented to spoil it of the honour of the highest power of the mind (which notable men have attributed unto it), but you deject it below all other passions—in truth, something strangely since, if love receive any disgrace, it is by the company of those passions you prefer unto it. For those kinds of bitter objections (as that lust, idleness, and a weak heart should be, as it were, the matter and form of love), rather touch me, dear Musidorus, than love. But I am good witness of mine own imperfections, and therefore will not defend myself. But herein, I must say, you deal contrary to yourself; for, if I be so weak, then can you not with reason stir me up, as you did, by the remembrance of mine own virtue. Or if indeed I be virtuous, then must you confess that love hath his working in a virtuous heart. And so no doubt hath it, whatsoever I be. For, if we love virtue, in whom shall we love it but in virtuous creatures?— Without your meaning be I should love this word of virtue when I see it written in a book. Those troublesome effects you say it breeds be not the fault of love, but of him that loves, as an unable vessel to bear such a power—like ill eyes, not able to look on the sun, or like a weak brain, soonest overthrown with the best wine. Even that heavenly love you speak of is accompanied in some hearts with hopes, griefs, longings, and despairs. And in that heavenly love, since there are two parts (the one, the love itself; the other, the excellency of the thing loved), I (not able at the first leap to frame both in myself) do now, like a diligent workman, make ready the chief instrument and first part of that great work, which is love itself. Which, when I have a while practised in this sort, then you shall see me turn it to greater matters. And thus gently you may, if it please you, think of me. Neither doubt you, because I wear a woman's apparel, I will be the more womanish; since, I assure you, for all my apparel, there is nothing I desire more than fully to prove myself a man in this enterprise. Much might be said in my defence, much more for love, and most of all for that divine creature which hath joined me and love together. But these disputations are fitter for quiet schools*than my troubled brains, which are bent rather in deeds to perform, than in words to defend, the noble desire that possesseth me.'

'O lord,' said Musidorus, 'how sharp-witted you are to hurt yourself!'

'No,' answered he, 'but it is the hurt you speak of which makes me so sharp-witted.'

'Even so', said Musidorus, 'as every base occupation makes one sharp in that practice and foolish in all the rest.'

'Nay rather', answered Pyrocles, 'as each excellent thing, once well learned, serves for a measure of all other knowledges.'

'And is that become', said Musidorus, 'a measure for other things, which never received measure in itself?'

'It is counted without measure', answered Pyrocles, 'because the workings of it are without measure; but otherwise in nature it hath measure, since it hath an end allotted unto it.'

'The beginning being so excellent, I would gladly know the end.'

'Enjoying', answered Pyrocles, with a deep sigh.

'O', said Musidorus, 'now set you forth the baseness of it since, if it end in enjoying, it shows all the rest was nothing.'

'You mistake me,' answered Pyrocles, 'I spake of the end to which it is directed; which end ends not no sooner than the life.'

'Alas! Let your own brain disenchant you', said Musidorus.

'My heart is too far possessed', said Pyrocles.

'But the head gives you direction.'

'And the heart gives me life', answered Pyrocles.

But Musidorus was so grieved to see his beloved friend obstinate, as he thought to his own destruction, that it forced him, with more than accustomed vehemency, to speak these words:

'Well, well,' said he, 'you list to abuse yourself. It was a very white and red virtue which you could pick out by the sight of a picture. Confess the truth, and you shall find the uttermost was but beauty; a thing which, though it be in as great excellency in yourself as may be in any, yet am I sure you make no further reckoning of it than of an outward fading benefit nature bestowed upon you. And yet, such is your want of a true-grounded virtue (which must be like itself in all points) that what you wisely count a trifle in yourself, you fondly become a slave unto in another. For my part, I now protest I have left nothing unsaid which my wit could make me know, or my most entire friendship to you requires of me. I do now beseech you, even for the love betwixt us (if this other love have left any in you towards me), and for the remembrance of your old careful father (if you can remember him, that forgets yourself), lastly, for Pyrocles' own sake (who is now upon the point of falling or rising), to purge your head of this vile infection. Otherwise, give me leave rather in absence to bewail your mishap than to bide the continual pang of seeing your danger with mine eyes.'

The length of these speeches before had not so much cloyed Pyrocles (though he were very impatient of long deliberations) as this last farewell of him he loved as his own life did wound his soul— as, indeed, they that think themselves afflicted are apt to conceive unkindness deeply—; insomuch that, shaking his head, and delivering some show of tears, he thus uttered his griefs:

'Alas,' said he, 'Prince Musidorus, how cruelly you deal with me! If you seek the victory, take it; and if you list, triumph. Have you all the reason of the world, and with me remain all the imperfections; yet such as I can no more lay from me than the crow can be persuaded by the swan to cast off his blackness. But truly, you deal with me like a physician that, seeing his patient in a pestilent fever, should chide him instead of ministering help, and bid him be sick no more; or rather, like such a friend that, visiting his friend condemned to perpetual prison and loaden with grievous fetters, should will him to shake off his fetters, or he would leave him. I am sick, and sick to the death. I am prisoner; neither is there any redress but by her to whom I am slave. Now, if you list, leave him that loves you in the highest degree; but remember ever to carry this with you: that you abandon your friend in his greatest need.'

And herewith, the deep wound of his love being rubbed afresh with this new unkindness, began, as it were, to bleed again, in such sort that he was unable to bear it any longer; but, gushing out abundance of tears and crossing his arms*over his woeful heart, he sank down to the ground. Which sudden trance went so to the heart of Musidorus that, falling down by him, and kissing the weeping eyes of his friend, he besought him not to make account of his speech which, if it had been over vehement, yet was it to be borne withal, because it came out of a love much more vehement; that he had never thought fancy could have received so deep a wound, but now finding in him the force of it, he would no further contrary it, but employ all his service to medicine it in such sort as the nature of it required. But even this kindness made Pyrocles the more melt in the former unkindness, which his manlike tears well showed, with a silent look upon Musidorus, as who should say, 'and is it possible that Musidorus should threaten to leave me?' And this strook Musidorus's mind and senses so dumb, too, that for grief not being able to say anything, they rested with their eyes placed one upon another, in such sort as might well paint out the true passion of unkindness, which is never aright but betwixt them that most dearly love.

And thus remained they a time, till at length Musidorus, embracing him, said, 'And will you thus shake off your friend?'

'It is you that shake off me,' said Pyrocles, 'being, for my unperfectness, unworthy of your friendship.'

'But this,' said Musidorus, 'shows you much more unperfect, to be cruel to him that submits himself unto you. But since you are unperfect,' said he, smiling, 'it is reason you be governed by us wise and perfect men. And that authority will I begin to take upon me with three absolute commandments: the first, that you increase not your evil with further griefs; the second, that you love Philoclea with all the powers of your mind; and the last commandment shall be that you command me to do you what service I can towards the attaining of your desires.'

Pyrocles' heart was not so oppressed with the two mighty passions of love and unkindness but that it yielded to some mirth at this commandment of Musidorus that he should love Philoclea. So that, something clearing his face from his former shows of grief, 'Well', said he, 'dear cousin, I see by the well choosing of your commandments that you are far fitter to be a prince than a councillor. And therefore I am resolved to employ all my endeavour to obey you, with this condition: that the commandments you command me to lay upon you shall only be that you continue to love me, and look upon my imperfections with more affection than judgement.'

'Love you,' said he, 'alas, how can my heart be separated from the true embracing of it without it burst by being too full of it? But,' said he, 'let us leave off these flowers of new-begun friendship; and since you have found out that way as your readiest remedy, let us go put on your transforming apparel. For my part, I will ever remain hereabouts, either to help you in any necessity or, at least, to be partaker of any evil may fall unto you.'

Pyrocles, accepting this as a most notable testimony of his long-approved friendship, and returning to Mantinea where, having taken leave of their host (who, though he knew them not, was in love with their virtue), and leaving with him some apparel and jewels, with opinion they would return after some time unto him, they departed thence to the place where he had left his womanish apparel which, with the help of his friend, he had quickly put on in such sort as it might seem love had not only sharpened his wits but nimbled his hands in anything which might serve to his service. And to begin with his head, thus was he dressed: his hair (which the young men of Greece ware very long, accounting them most beautiful that had that in fairest quantity) lay upon the upper part of his forehead in locks, some curled and some, as it were, forgotten, with such a careless care, and with an art so hiding art, that he seemed he would lay them for a paragon whether nature simply, or nature helped by cunning, be the more excellent. The rest whereof was drawn into a coronet of gold, richly set with pearls, and so joined all over with gold wires, and covered with feathers of divers colours, that it was not unlike to a helmet, such a glittering show it bare, and so bravely it was held up from the head. Upon his body he ware a kind of doublet of sky-colour satin, so plated over with plates of massy gold that he seemed armed in it; his sleeves of the same, instead of plates, was covered with purled lace. And such was the nether part of his garment; but that made so full of stuff, and cut after such a fashion that, though the length fell under his ankles, yet in his going one might well perceive the small of the leg which, with the foot, was covered with a little short pair of crimson velvet buskins, in some places open (as the ancient manner was) to show the fairness of the skin. Over all this he ware a certain mantle of like stuff, made in such manner that, coming under his right arm, and covering most part of that side, it touched not the left side but upon the top of the shoulder where the two ends met, and were fastened together with a very rich jewel, the device whereof was this: an eagle covered with the feathers of a dove, and yet lying under another dove, in such sort as it seemed the dove preyed upon the eagle, the eagle casting up such a look as though the state he was in liked him, though the pain grieved him.* Upon the same side, upon his thigh he ware a sword (such as we now call scimitars), the pommel whereof was so richly set with precious stones as they were sufficient testimony it could be no mean personage that bare it. Such was this Amazon's attire: and thus did Pyrocles become Cleophila—which name for a time hereafter I will use, for I myself feel such compassion of his passion that I find even part of his fear lest his name should be uttered before fit time were for it; which you, fair ladies that vouchsafe to read this, I doubt not will account excusable. But Musidorus, that had helped to dress his friend, could not satisfy himself with looking upon him, so did he find his excellent beauty set out with this new change, like a diamond set in a more advantageous sort. Insomuch that he could not choose, but smiling said unto him:

'Well,' said he, 'sweet cousin, since you are framed of such a loving mettle, I pray you, take heed of looking yourself in a glass lest Narcissus's fortune fall unto you. For my part, I promise you, if I were not fully resolved never to submit my heart to these fancies, I were like enough while I dressed you to become a young Pygmalion.'*

'Alas,' answered Cleophila, 'if my beauty be anything, then will it help me to some part of my desires; otherwise I am no more to set by it than the orator by his eloquence that persuades nobody.'

'She is a very invincible creature, then,' said he, 'for I doubt me much, under your patience, whether my mistress, your mistress, have a greater portion of beauty.'

'Speak not that blasphemy, dear friend,' said Cleophila, 'for if I have any beauty, it is the beauty which the imagination of her strikes into my fancies, which in part shines through my face into your eyes.'

'Truly,' said Musidorus, 'you are grown a notable philosopher of fancies.'

'Astronomer,' answered Cleophila, 'for they are heavenly fancies.'

In such friendly speeches they returned again to the desert of the two lodges, where Cleophila desired Musidorus he would hide himself in a little grove where he might see how she could play her part; for there, she said, she was resolved to remain till, by some good favour of fortune, she might obtain the sight of her whom she bare continually in the eyes of her mind. Musidorus obeyed her request, full of extreme grief to see so worthy a mind thus infected; besides he could see no hope of success, but great appearance of danger. Yet, finding it so deeply grounded that striving against it did rather anger than heal the wound, and rather call his friendship in question than give place to any friendly counsel, he was content to yield to the force of the present stream, with hope afterwards, as occasion fell out, to prevail better with him; or at least to adventure his life in preserving him from any injury might be offered him. And with the beating of those thoughts, remained he in the grove till, with a new fullness, he was emptied of them—as you shall after hear.

In the mean time, Cleophila walking up and down in that solitary place, with many intricate determinations, at last wearied both in mind and body, sat her down, and beginning to tune her voice, with many sobs and tears, sang this song which she had made since her first determination thus to change her estate:

> Transformed in show, but more transformed in mind,
> I cease to strive, with double conquest foiled;
> For (woe is me) my powers all I find
> With outward force and inward treason spoiled.
>
> For from without came to mine eyes the blow,
> Whereto mine inward thoughts did faintly yield;
> Both these conspired poor reason's overthrow;
> False in myself, thus have I lost the field.
>
> And thus mine eyes are placed still in one sight,
> And thus my thoughts can think but one thing still;
> Thus reason to his servants gives his right;
> Thus is my power transformed to your will.
> What marvel, then, I take a woman's hue,
> Since what I see, think, know, is all but you?

I might entertain you, fair ladies, a great while, if I should make as many interruptions in the repeating as she did in the singing. For no verse did pass out of her mouth but that it was waited on with such abundance of sighs, and, as it were, witnessed with her flowing tears, that, though the words were few, yet the time was long she employed in uttering them; although her pauses chose so fit times that they rather strengthened a sweeter passion than hindered the harmony. Musidorus himself (that lay so as he might see and hear these things) was yet more moved to pity by the manner of Cleophila's singing than with anything he had ever seen—so lively an action doth the mind, truly touched, bring forth. But so fell it out that, as with her sweet voice she recorded once or twice the last verse of her song, it awakened the shepherd Dametas, who at that time had laid his sleepy back upon a sunny bank not far thence, gaping as far as his jaws would suffer him. But being troubled out of his sleep (the best thing his life could bring forth) his dull senses could not convey the pleasure of the excellent music to his rude mind, but that he fell into a notable rage. Insomuch that, taking a hedging bill lay by him, he guided himself by the voice till he came to the place where he saw Cleophila sitting, wringing her hands, and with some few words to herself, breathing out part of the vehemency of that passion which she had not fully declared in her song. But no more were his eyes taken with her beauty than his ears with her music. But beginning to swear by the pantable of Pallas, Venus's waistcoat, and such other oaths as his rustical bravery could imagine, leaning his hands upon his bill, and his chin upon his hands, he fell to mutter such railings and cursings against her as a man might well see he had passed through the discipline of an alehouse. And because you may take the better into your fancies his mannerliness, the manner of the man shall in few words be described. He was a short lean fellow, of black hair, and notably backed for a burden, one of his eyes out, his nose turned up to take more air, a seven or eight long black hairs upon his chin, which he called his beard; his breast he ware always unbuttoned for heat, and yet a stomacher before it for cold; ever untrussed, yet points hanging down, because he might be trussed if he list; ill gartered for a courtlike carelessness; only well shod for his father's sake, who had upon his death bed charged him to take heed of going wet. He had for love chosen his wife Miso, yet so handsome a beldam that she was counted a witch only for her face and her splay foot. Neither inwardly nor outwardly was there anything good in her but that she observed decorum, having in a wretched body a froward mind. Neither was there any humour in which her husband and she could ever agree, but in disagreeing. Betwixt these two issued forth mistress Mopsa, a fit woman to participate of both their perfections. But because Alethes, an honest man of that time, did her praises in verse, I will only repeat them and spare mine own pen, because she bare the sex of a woman; and these they were:

What length of verse can serve brave Mopsa's good to show,
  Whose virtues strange, and beauties such, as no man them may
                                                        know?
Thus shrewdly burdened then, how can my muse escape?
  The gods must help and precious things must serve to show her
                                                        shape.

Like great god Saturn fair, and like fair Venus chaste;
As smooth as Pan, as Juno mild, like goddess Iris fast.
With Cupid she foresees, and goes god Vulcan's pace;
And for a taste of all these gifts, she borrows Momus' grace.*
    Her forehead jacinth like, her cheeks of opal hue,
Her twinkling eyes bedecked with pearl, her lips of sapphire blue;
Her hair pure crapal stone; her mouth O heav'nly wide;
Her skin like burnished gold, her hands like silver ore untried.
    As for those parts unknown, which hidden sure are best,
    Happy be they which will believe, and never seek the rest.

    The beginning of this Dametas's credit with Basilius was by the
duke's straying out of his way one time a-hunting where, meeting
this fellow, and asking him the way, and so falling into other ques-
tions, he found some of his answers touching husbandry matters (as
a dog sure, if he could speak, had wit enough to describe his kennel)
not unsensible; and all uttered with such a rudeness, which the duke
interpreted plainness*(although there be great difference betwixt
them), that the duke, conceiving a sudden delight in his entertain-
ment, took him to his court, with apparent show of his good opinion;
where the flattering courtier had no sooner taken the prince's mind
but that there were straight reasons to confirm the duke's doing, and
shadows of virtues found for Dametas. His silence grew wit, his
bluntness integrity, his beastly ignorance virtuous simplicity; and
the duke (according to the nature of great persons, in love with that
he had done himself) fancied that the weakness was in him, with his
presence, would grow wisdom. And so, like a creature of his own
making, he liked him more and more. And thus gave he him first the
office of principal herdman. And thus lastly did he put his life into
his hands—although he grounded upon a great error; for his quality
was not to make men, but to use men according as men were, no
more than an ass will be taught to manage, a horse to hunt, or a
hound to bear a saddle, but each to be used according to the force
of his own nature.
    But Dametas, as I said, suddenly awaked, remembering the duke's
commandment, and glad he might use his authority in chiding, came
swearing to the place where Cleophila was, with a voice like him that
plays Hercules in a play and, God knows, never had Hercules' fancy
in his head. The first word he spake, after his railing oaths, was 'Am
not I Dametas? Why, am not I Dametas?'

These words made Cleophila lift up her eyes upon him, and seeing what manner of man he was, the height of her thoughts would not suffer her to yield any answer to so base a creature; but casting again down her eyes, leaning upon the ground, and putting her cheek in the palm of her hand, fetched a great sigh, as if she had answered him, 'my head is troubled with greater matters'. Which Dametas (as all persons witnesses of their own unworthiness are apt to think they are contemned) took in so heinous a chafe that, standing upon his tiptoes, and staring as if he would have had a mote pulled out of his eye, 'Why,' said he, 'thou woman or boy, or both, or whatsoever thou be, I tell thee, here is no place for thee; get thee gone, I tell thee, it is the duke's pleasure. I tell thee, it is master Dametas's pleasure.'

Cleophila could not choose but smile at him, and yet, taking herself with the manner, spake these words to herself:

'O spirit', said she, 'of mine, how canst thou receive any mirth in the midst of thine agonies? And thou, mirth, how darest thou enter into a mind so grown of late thy professed enemy?'

'Thy spirit,' said Dametas, 'dost thou think me a spirit? I tell thee I am the duke's officer, and have the charge of him and his daughters.'

'O pearl,' said sobbing Cleophila, 'that so vile an oyster should keep thee!'

'By the combcase of Diana!' sware Dametas, 'this woman is mad; oysters and pearls; dost thou think I will buy oysters? I tell thee, get thee packing, or else I must needs be offended.'

'O sun,' said Cleophila, 'how long shall this cloud live to darken thee, and the poor creatures that live only by thee be deprived of thee?'

These speeches to herself put Dametas out of all patience; so that, hitting her upon the breast with the blunt end of his bill, 'Maid Marian,'*said he, 'am not I a personage to be answered?'

But Cleophila no sooner felt the blow but that, the fire sparkling out of her eyes, and rising up with a right Pyrocles countenance in a Cleophila face, 'Vile creature,' said she, laying her hand upon her sword, 'force me not to defile this sword in thy base blood!'

Dametas, that from his childhood had ever feared the blade of a sword, ran back backwards, with his hands above his head, at least twenty paces, gaping and staring with the very countenance of those clownish churls that by Latona's*prayer were turned into frogs. At length staying, he came a little nearer her again, but still without the compass of blows, holding one leg, as it were, ready to run away;

and then fell to scolding and railing, swearing it was but a little
bashfulness in him that had made him go back; and that if she
stayed any longer he would make her see his blood came out of the
eldest shepherd's house in that country. But seeing her walk up and
down without marking what he said, he went for more help to his
own lodge where, knocking a good while, at length he cried to his
wife Miso that in a whore's name she should come out to him. But
instead of that, he might hear a hollow rotten voice that bid him
let her alone, like a knave as he was, for she was busy about my
lady Pamela. This dashed poor Dametas more than anything, for
old acquaintance had taught him to fear that place; and therefore,
calling with a more pitiful voice to his daughter, he might see a face
look out of a window, enough to have made any blind man in love.
It was mistress Mopsa that, instead of answer, asked him whether
he were mad to forget his duty to her mother. Dametas shrunk
down his shoulders, like the poor ass that lays down his ears when
he must needs yield to the burden; and yet his tongue, the valiantest
part of him, could not forbear to say these words: 'Here is foreign wars
abroad, and uncivil wars at home—and all with women. Now', said he,
'the black jaundice and the red flix take all the warbled kind of you!'

And with this prayer, he went to the other lodge where the duke
lay at that time sleeping, as it was in the heat of the day. And there
he whistled, and stamped, and knocked, crying 'Ho! my liege!' with
such faces as might well show what a deformity a passion can bring
a man unto when it is not governed with reason; till at length the
fair Philoclea came down in such loose apparel as was enough to
have bound any man's fancies, and with a sweet look asking him
what he would have. Dametas, without any reverence, commanded
her in the duke's name she should tell the duke he was to speak with
the duke, for he forsooth had things to tell the duke that pertained
to the duke's service. She answered him he should be obeyed, since
such was the fortune of her and her sister. And so went she to tell
her father of Dametas's being there, leaving him chafing at the door
and whetting his bill, swearing if he met her again neither she nor
the tallest woman in the parish should make him run away any more.

But the duke, understanding by his jewel Philoclea that some-
thing there was which greatly troubled Dametas's conscience, came
presently down unto him to know the matter; where he found
Dametas, talking to himself, and making faces like an ape that had

newly taken a purgation, pale, shaking, and foaming at the mouth. And a great while it was before the duke could get any word of him. At length, putting his leg before him (which was the manner of his curtsy), he told the duke that, saving the reverence of his duty, he should keep himself from thenceforward, he would take no more charge of him. The duke, accustomed to take all well at his hands, did but laugh to see his rage, and, stroking his head, desired him of fellowship to let him know the matter.

'I tell you', saith Dametas, 'it is not for me to be an officer without I may be obeyed.'

'But what troubles thee, my good Dametas?' said the duke.

'I tell you', said Dametas, 'I have been a man in my days, whatsoever I be now.'

'And reason,' answered the duke, 'but let me know that I may redress thy wrongs.'

'Nay,' says Dametas, 'no wrongs neither. But thus falls out the case, my liege; I met with such a mankind creature yonder, with her sword by her hip, and with such a visage as, if it had not been for me and this bill, God save it, she had come hither and killed you and all your house.'

'What, strike a woman!' said the duke.

'Indeed,' said Dametas, 'I made her but a little weep, and after I had pity of her.'

'It was well and wisely done,' said the duke, 'but I pray thee show me her.'

'I pray you,' said Dametas, 'first call for more company to hold me from hurting her; for my stomach riseth against her.'

'Let me but see the place', said the duke, 'and then you shall know whether my words or your bill be the better weapon.'

Dametas went stalking on before the duke as if he had been afraid to wake his child; and then, pointing with his bill towards her, was not hasty to make any nearer approaches. But the duke no sooner saw Cleophila but that he remained amazed at the goodliness of her stature and the stateliness of her march (for at that time she was walking with a countenance well setting forth an extreme distraction of her mind), and, as he came nearer her, at the excellent perfection of her beauty; insomuch that, forgetting any anger he conceived in Dametas's behalf, and doing reverence to her, as to a lady in whom he saw much worthy of great respect, 'Fair lady,' said he 'it is nothing strange that such a solitary place as this should receive solitary persons; but much do I marvel how such a beauty as yours is could be suffered to be thus alone.'

She, looking with a grave majesty upon him, as if she found in herself cause why she should be reverenced, 'They are never alone', said she, 'that are accompanied with noble thoughts.'

'But those thoughts', said the duke (replying for the delight he had to speak further with her), 'cannot in this your loneliness neither warrant you from suspicion in others nor defend you from melancholy in yourself.'

Cleophila, looking upon him as though he pressed her further than needed, 'I seek no better warrant', said she, 'than mine own conscience, nor no greater pleasure than mine own contentation.'

'Yet virtue seeks to satisfy others', said Basilius.

'Those that be good,' answered Cleophila, 'and they will be satisfied as long as they see no evil.'

'Yet will the best in this country', said the duke, 'suspect so excellent a beauty, being so weakly guarded.'

'Then are the best but stark naught,' answered Cleophila, 'for open suspecting others comes of secret condemning themselves. But in my country,' said she, continuing her speech with a brave vehemency, 'whose manners I am in all places to maintain and reverence, the general goodness which is nourished in our hearts makes everyone think that strength of virtue in another whereof they find the assured foundation in themselves.'

But Basilius, who began to feel the sparkles of those flames which shortly after burned all other thoughts out of his heart, felt such a music, as he thought, in her voice, and such an eye-pleasing in her face, that he thought his retiring into this solitary place was well employed if it had been only to have met with such a guest. And therefore, desirous to enter into nearer points with her, 'Excellent lady,' said he, 'you praise so greatly, and yet so wisely, your country that I must needs desire to know what the nest is out of which such birds do fly.'

'You must first deserve that knowledge', said she, 'before you obtain it.'

'And by what means', said Basilius, 'shall I deserve to know your estate?'

'By letting me first know yours', answered she.

'To obey you,' said he, 'I will do it; although it were so much more reason yours should be known first, as you do deserve in all points to be preferred. Know you, fair lady,' said he, 'that my name is Basilius, unworthy duke of this country; the rest, either fame hath already brought to your ears, or, if it please you to make this place happy by your presence, at more leisure you shall understand of me.'

Cleophila (who had from the beginning suspected it should be he, but would not seem she did so, to keep her majesty the better), making some reverence unto him, 'Mighty prince,' said she, 'let my not knowing of you serve for the excuse of my boldness, and the little reverence I do you, impute it to the manner of my country, which is the invincible land of the Amazons, myself niece to Senicia, queen thereof, lineally descended of the famous Penthesilea,* slain before Troy by the bloody hand of Pyrrhus. I, having in this my youth determined to make the world see the Amazons' excellencies, as well in private as in public virtues, have passed many dangerous adventures in divers countries, till the unmerciful sea deprived me of all my company; so that shipwrack brought me to this realm, and uncertain wandering guided me to this place.'

Whoever saw a man to whom a beloved child long lost did, un-looked for, return might easily figure unto his fancy the very fashion of Basilius's countenance—so far had love become his master. And so had this young siren charmed his old ears, insomuch that, with more vehement importunacy than any greedy host would use to well acquainted passengers, he fell to entreat her abode there for some time. She, although nothing could come fitter to the very point of her desire, yet had she already learned that womanish quality to counterfeit backwardness in that she most wished; so that he, desirous to prove whether intercession coming out of fitter mouths might better prevail, called to Dametas, and commanded him to bring forth his wife and two daughters—three ladies, although of diverse, yet all of excellent beauty: the duchess Gynecia, in grave matronlike attire, with a countenance and behaviour far unlike to fall into those inconveniences she afterwards tasted of. The fair Pamela, whose noble heart had long disdained to find the trust of her virtue reposed in the hands of a shepherd, had yet, to show an obedience, taken on a shepherdish apparel, which was of russet velvet, cut after their fashion, with a straight body, open breasted, the nether part full of pleats, with wide open sleeves, hanging down very low; her hair at the full length, only wound about with gold lace—by the comparison to show how far her hair did excel in colour; betwixt her breasts, which sweetly rase up like two fair mountainets in the pleasant vale of Tempe, there hanged down a jewel which she had devised as a picture of her own estate. It was a perfect white lamb*tied at a stake with a great number of chains, as it had been feared lest the silly creature should do some great harm; neither had she added any word unto it, but even took silence as the word of the poor lamb, showing such humbleness as not to use her own voice for complaint of her misery.

But when the ornament of the earth, young Philoclea, appeared in her nymphlike apparel, so near nakedness as one might well discern part of her perfections, and yet so apparelled as did show she kept the best store of her beauties to herself; her excellent fair hair drawn up into a net made only of itself (a net indeed to have caught the wildest disposition); her body covered with a light taffeta garment, so cut as the wrought smock came through it in many places (enough to have made a very restrained imagination have thought what was under it); with the sweet cast of her black eye which seemed to make a contention whether that in perfect blackness, or her skin in perfect whiteness,* were the most excellent; then, I say, the very clouds seemed to give place to make the heaven more fair. At least, the clouds of Cleophila's thoughts quite vanished, and so was her brain fixed withal that her sight seemed more forcible and clear than ever before or since she found it, with such strange delight unto her (for still, fair ladies, you remember that I use the she-title to Pyrocles, since so he would have it) that she stood like a well wrought image, with show of life, but without all exercise of life, so forcibly had love transferred all her spirits into the present contemplation of the lovely Philoclea. And so had it been like enough she would have stayed long time but that by chance Gynecia stepped betwixt her sight and the lady Philoclea, and the change of the object made her recover her senses; so that she could with good manner receive the salutation of the duchess and the princess Pamela, doing them yet no further reverence than one princess useth to another. But when she came to the lady Philoclea, she fell down on her knees, taking by force her fair hands and kissing them with great show of extreme affection, and with a bowed-down countenance began this speech unto her: 'Divine lady,' said she, 'let not the world nor these great princes marvel to see me contrary to my manner do this especial honour unto you, since all, both men and women, owe this homage to the perfection of your beauty.'

Philoclea's blushing cheeks quickly witnessed how much she was abashed to see this singularity used to herself; and therefore, causing Cleophila to rise, 'Noble lady,' said she, 'it is no marvel to see your judgement much mistaken in my beauty, since you begin with so great an error as to do more honour unto me than to them to whom I myself owe all service.'

'Rather', answered Cleophila, 'that shows the power of your beauty which hath forced me to fall into such an error, if it were an error.'

'You are so acquainted', said Philoclea, sweetly smiling, 'with your own beauty that it makes you easily fall into the discourse of beauty.'

'Beauty in me!' said Cleophila, deeply sighing, 'Alas! if there be any, it is in mine eyes, which your happy presence hath imparted unto them.'

Basilius was even transported with delight to hear these speeches betwixt his well beloved daughter and his better loved lady; and so made a sign to Philoclea that she should entreat her to remain with them; which she willingly obeyed, for already she conceived delight in Cleophila's presence, and therefore said unto her: 'It is a great happiness, I must confess, to be praised of them that are themselves most praiseworthy. And well I find you are an invincible Amazon, since you will overcome in a wrong matter. But if my beauty be anything', said she, 'then let it obtain thus much of you: that you will remain in this company some time, to ease your own travail, and our solitariness.'

'First let me die', said Cleophila, 'before any word spoken by such a mouth should come in vain. I yield wholly to your commandment, fearing nothing but that you command that which may be troublesome to yourself.'

Thus, with some other words of entertaining, her staying was concluded, to the unspeakable joy of the duke—although, perchance, with some little envy in the other ladies, to see young Philoclea's beauty so greatly advanced. You ladies know best whether sometimes you feel impression of that passion; for my part, I would hardly think that the affection of a mother and the noble mind of Pamela could be overthrown with so base a thing as envy is—especially Pamela, to whom fortune had already framed another, who no less was dedicated to her excellencies than Cleophila was to Philoclea's perfections, as you shall shortly hear. For the duke going into the lodge with his wife and daughters, Cleophila desired them to excuse her for a while, for that she had thoughts to pass over with herself; and that shortly after she would come in to them—indeed meaning to find her friend Musidorus, and to glory with him of the happiness of her choice. But when she looked in the grove and could nowhere find him, marvelling something at it, she gave herself to feed those sweet thoughts which now had the full possession of her heart, sometimes thinking how far Philoclea herself passed her picture, sometimes fore-imagining with herself how happy she should be if she could obtain her desires; till, having spent thus an hour or two, she might perceive afar off one coming towards her, in the apparel of a shepherd, with his arms hanging down, going a kind of languishing pace, with his eyes sometimes cast up to heaven as though his fancies strave to mount up higher, sometimes thrown down to the ground as if the earth could not bear the burden of his pains. At length she heard him, with a lamentable tune, sing these few verses:

> Come shepherd's weeds, become your master's mind:
> Yield outward show, what inward change he tries:
> Nor be abashed, since such a guest you find,
> Whose strongest hope in your weak comfort lies.

> Come shepherd's weeds, attend my woeful cries:
> Disuse yourselves from sweet Menalcas' voice:
> For other be those tunes which sorrow ties
> From those clear notes which freely may rejoice.
>   Then pour out plaint, and in one word say this:
>   Helpless his plaint who spoils himself of bliss.

And having ended, she might see him strike himself upon the breast, uttering these words: 'O miserable wretch, whither do thy destinies guide thee?'

It seemed to Cleophila that she knew the voice; and therefore drawing nearer, that her sight might receive a perfect discerning, she saw plainly, to her great amazement, it was her dear friend Musidorus. And now having named him, methinks it reason I should tell you what chance brought him to this change. I left him lately, if you remember, fair ladies, in the grove by the two lodges, there to see what should befall to his dear new-transformed friend. There heard he all the complaints (not without great compassion) that his friend made to himself; and there (not without some laughter) did he see what passed betwixt him and Dametas, and how stately he played the part of Cleophila at the duke's first coming. And falling into many kind fancies towards him, sometimes pitying his case, sometimes praising his behaviour, he would often say to himself: 'O sweet Pyrocles, how art thou bewitched! Where is thy virtue? Where is the use of thy reason? Much am I inferior to thee in all the powers of the mind; and yet know I that all the heavens cannot bring me to such a thraldom.'

Scarcely, think I, he had spoken those words but that the duchess, being sent for to entertain Cleophila, came out with her two daughters; where the beams of the princess Pamela's beauty had no sooner stricken into his eyes but that he was wounded with more sudden violence of love than ever Pyrocles was. Whether indeed it were that this strange power would be bravely revenged of him for the bitter words he had used, or that his very resisting made the wound the crueller (as we see the harquebus doth most endamage the stiffest metal), or rather that the continual healthfulness of his mind made this sudden ill the more incurable (as the soundest bodies, once infected, are most mortally endangered); but howsoever the cause was, such was the effect that, not being able to bear the vehement pain, he ran away through the grove, like a madman, hoping perchance (as the fever-sick folks do) that the change of places might ease his grief. But therein was his luck indeed better than his providence; for he had not gone a little but that he met with a shepherd (according to his estate, handsomely apparelled) who was as then going to meet with other shepherds (as upon certain days they had accustomed) to do exercises of activity and to play new-invented eclogues before the duke. Which, when Musidorus had learned of him (for love is full of desire, and desire is always inquisitive), it came straight into his head that there were no better way for him to come by the often enjoying of the princess Pamela's sight than to take the apparel of this shepherd upon him. Which he quickly did, giving him his own much richer; and withal, lest the matter by him might be discovered, hired him to go without stay into Thessalia, writing two or three words by him, in a pair of tables well closed up, to a servant of his that he should, upon the receipt, arrest and keep him in good order till he heard his further pleasure. Yet before Menalcas departed (for so was his name), he learned of him both his own estate and the manner of their pastimes and eclogues. And thus furnished, he returned again to the place where his heart was pledged, so oppressed in mind that it seemed to him his legs were uneath able to bear him. Which grief he uttered in the doleful song I told you of before, and was cause that his dear he-she friend, Cleophila, came unto him; who, when she was assured it was he (with wonted entireness embracing him), demanded of him what sudden thing had thus suddenly changed him; whether the goddess of those woods had such a power to transform everybody; or whether, indeed, as he had always in all enterprises most faithfully accompanied her, so he would continue to match her in this new metamorphosis. But Musidorus, looking dolefully upon her, wringing his hands, and pouring out abundance of tears, began to recount unto her all this I have already told you, but with such passionate dilating of it that, for my part, I have not a feeling insight enough into the matter to be able lively to express it. Sufficeth it that whatsoever a possessed heart with a good tongue, to a dear friend, could utter was at that time largely set forth. The perfect friendship Cleophila bare him, and the great pity she (by good experience) had of his case could not keep her from smiling at him, remembering how vehemently he had cried out against the folly of lovers; so that she thought good a little to punish him, playing with him in this manner: 'Why, how now, dear cousin,' said she, 'you that were even now so high in the pulpit against love, are you now become so mean an auditor? Remember that love is a passion, and that a worthy man's reason must ever have the masterhood.'

'I recant, I recant!' cried Musidorus, and withal falling down prostrate, 'O thou celestial, or infernal, spirit of love', said he, 'or what other heavenly or hellish title thou list to have, for both those effects I find in myself, have compassion of me, and let thy glory be as great in pardoning them that be submitted to thee as in conquering those that were rebellious!'

'No, no!' said Cleophila, yet further to urge him, 'I see you well enough; you make but an interlude of my mishaps, and do but counterfeit thus to make me see the deformity of my passions. But take heed,' said she, 'cousin, that this jest do not one day turn into earnest.'

'Now I beseech thee,' said Musidorus, taking her fast by the hand, 'even by the truth of our friendship (of which, if I be not altogether an unhappy man, thou hast some remembrance), and by those sacred flames (which I know have likewise nearly touched thee), make no

jest of that which hath so earnestly pierced me through; nor let that
be light to thee which is to me so burdenous that I am not able
to bear it.'

Musidorus did so lively deliver out his inward griefs that
Cleophila's friendly heart felt a great impression of pity withal—as
certainly all persons that find themselves afflicted easily fall to com-
passion of them who taste of like misery, partly led by the common
course of humanity, but principally because, under the image of
them, they lament their own mishaps; and so the complaints the
others make seem to touch the right tune of their own woes. Which
did mutually work so in these two young princes that, looking rue-
fully one upon the other, they made their speech a great while
nothing but doleful sighs. Yet sometimes they would yield out such-
like lamentations: 'Alas! What further evil hath fortune reserved for
us, or what shall be the end of this our tragical pilgrimage? Ship-
wracks, daily dangers, absence from our country, have at length
brought forth this captiving of us within ourselves which hath trans-
formed the one in sex, and the other in state, as much as the utter-
most work of changeable fortune can be extended unto.'

And then would they kiss one another, vowing to continue par-
takers of all either good or evil fortune. And thus perchance would
they have forgotten themselves some longer time, but that Basilius,
whose heart was now set on fire with his new mistress, finding her
absence long, sent out Dametas to her to know if she would com-
mand anything, and to invite her to go with his wife and daughters
to a fair meadow thereby to see the sports and hear the eclogues of
his country shepherds. Dametas came out with two or three swords
about him, his hedging bill on his neck, and a chopping knife under
his girdle, armed only behind, as fearing most the blows that might
fall upon the reins of his back; for, indeed, Cleophila had put such a
sudden fear into his head that from thenceforth he was resolved never
to come out any more ill provided. Yet had his blunt brains per-
ceived some favour the duke bare to this new-come lady; and so
framing himself thereunto (as without doubt the most servile flattery
is most easy to be lodged in the most gross capacity; for their
ordinary conceit draws a yielding to their greatness, and then have
they not wit to discern right degrees of goodness), he no sooner saw
her but, with head and arms, he laid his reverence before her,
enough to have made a man forswear all courtesy. And then, in the
duke's name, did he require her she would take pains to see their

pastorals (for so their sports were termed); but when he spied Musidorus standing by her (for his eye had been placed all this while upon her), not knowing him, he would fain have persuaded himself to have been angry but that he durst not. Yet, muttering and champing as though his cud troubled him, he gave occasion to Musidorus to come nearer him, and to feign a tale of his own life: that he was a younger brother of the shepherd Menalcas, by name Dorus, sent by his father in his tender age to Athens, there to learn some cunning more than ordinary for to excel his fellow shepherds in their eclogues; and that his brother Menalcas, lately gone thither to fetch him home, was deceased; where, upon his deathbed, he had charged him to seek the service of Dametas, and to be wholly and only guided by his counsel, as one in whose judgement and integrity the duke had singular confidence; for token whereof he gave him a sum of gold in ready coin which Menalcas had bequeathed him upon condition he should receive this poor Dorus into his service, that his mind and manners might grow the better by his daily example. Dametas no sooner saw the gold but that his heart was presently infected with the self-conceit he took of it; which, being helped with the tickling of Musidorus's praises, so turned the brain of good Dametas that he became slave to that which he that would be his servant bestowed on him, and gave in himself an example for ever that the fool can never be honest since, not being able to balance what points virtue stands upon, every present occasion catches his senses, and his senses are masters of his silly mind. Yet, for countenance's sake, he seemed very squeamish, in respect he had the charge of the princess Pamela, to accept any new servant into his house. But such was the secret operation of the gold, helped with the persuasions of the Amazon Cleophila, who said it was pity so proper a young man should be anywhere else than with so good a master, that in the end he agreed to receive him for his servant, so as that day in their pastorals he proved himself active in mind and body.

And thus went they to the lodge, with greater joy to Musidorus (now only poor shepherd Dorus) than all his life before had ever brought forth unto him—so manifest it is that the greatest point outward things can bring a man unto is the contentment of the mind,* which once obtained, no state is miserable; and without that, no prince's seat restful. There found they Gynecia, with her two daughters, ready to go to the meadow; whither also they went. For, as for Basilius, he desired to stay behind them to debate a little with himself of this new guest that had entered and possessed his brains. There, it is said, the poor old Basilius, now alone (for, as I said, the rest were gone to see the pastorals), had a sufficient eclogue* in his own head betwixt honour, with the long experience he had had of the world, on the one side, and this new assault of Cleophila's beauty on the other side. There hard by the lodge walked he, carrying this unquiet contention about him. But passion ere long had gotten the absolute masterhood, bringing with it the show of present pleasure, fortified with the authority of a prince whose power might easily satisfy his will against the far-fet (though true) reasons of the spirit— which, in a man not trained in the way of virtue, have but slender working. So that ere long he utterly gave himself over to the longing desire to enjoy Cleophila, which finding an old broken vessel of him, had the more power in him than, perchance, it would have had in a younger man. And so, as all vice is foolish, it wrought in him the more absurd follies. But thus, as I say, in a number of intermixed imaginations, he stayed solitary by the lodge, waiting for the return of his company from the pastorals, some good space of time, till he was suddenly stirred out of his deep muses by the hasty and fearful running unto him of most part of the shepherds who came flying from the pastoral sports, crying to one another to stay and save the duchess and young ladies. But even whilst they cried so they ran away as fast as they could; so that the one tumbled over the other, each one show-ing he would be glad his fellow should do valiantly, but his own heart served him not. The duke, amazed to see such extreme shows of fear, asked the matter of them. But fear had so possessed their inward parts that their breath would not serve to tell it him, but after such a broken manner that I think it best not to trouble you, fair ladies, with their panting speeches; but to make a full declara-tion of it myself. And thus it was: Gynecia, with her two daughters, Cleophila, the shepherds Dorus and Dametas, being parted from the duke whom they left solitary at the lodge, came into the fair meadow appointed for their shepherdish pastimes. It was, indeed, a place of great delight, for through the midst of it there ran a sweet brook which did both hold the eye open with her beautiful streams and close the eye with the sweet purling noise it made upon the pebble-stones it ran over; the meadow itself yielding so liberally all sorts of flowers that it seemed to nourish a contention betwixt the colour and the smell whether in his kind were the more delightful. Round about the meadow, as if it had been to enclose a theatre, grew all such sorts of trees as either excellency of fruit, stateliness of growth, continual greenness, or poetical fancies have made at any time famous. In most part of which trees there had been framed by art such pleasant arbours that it became a gallery aloft, from one tree to the other, almost round about, which below yielded a perfect shadow, in those hot countries counted a great pleasure.

In this place, under one of the trees, the ladies sat down, inquiring many questions of young Dorus (now newly perceived of them), whilst the other shepherds made them ready to the pastimes. Dorus, keeping his eye still upon the princess Pamela, answered with such a trembling voice and abashed countenance, and oftentimes so far from the matter, that it was some sport to the ladies, thinking it had been want of education which made him so discountenanced with unwonted presence. But Cleophila (that saw in him the glass of her own misery), taking the fair hand of Philoclea, and with more than womanish ardency kissing it, began to say these words: 'O love, since thou art so changeable in men's estates, how art thou so constant in their torments?'—when suddenly there came out of the wood a monstrous lion, with a she-bear of little less fierceness, which, having been hunted in forests far off, had by chance come to this place where such beasts had never before been seen. Which, when the shepherds saw, like silly wretches that think all evil is ever next themselves, ran away in such sort as I told you till they came to the duke's presence. There might one have seen at one instant all sorts of passions lively painted out in the young lovers' faces—an extremity of love shining in their eyes; fear for their mistresses; assured hope in their own virtue; anger against the beasts; joy that occasion employed their service; sorrow to see their ladies in agony. For, indeed, the sweet Philoclea no sooner espied the ravenous lion but that, opening her arms, she fell so right upon the breast of Cleophila, sitting by her, that their faces at unawares closed together, which so transported all whatsoever Cleophila was that she gave leisure to the lion to come very near them before she rid herself from the dear arms of Philoclea. But necessity, the only overruler of affections, did force her then gently to unfold herself from those sweet embracements; and so drawing her sword, waited the present assault of the lion who, seeing Philoclea fly away, suddenly turned after her. For, as soon as she had risen up with Cleophila, she ran as fast as her delicate legs would carry her towards the lodge after the fugitive shepherds. But Cleophila, seeing how greedily the lion went after the prey she herself so much desired, it seemed all her spirits were kindled with an unwonted fire; so that, equalling the lion in swiftness, she overtook him as he was ready to have seized himself of his beautiful chase, and disdainfully saying 'are you become my competitor?'—strake him so great a blow upon the shoulder that she almost cleaved him asunder. Yet the valiant beast turned withal so far upon the weapon, that with his paw he did hurt a little the left shoulder of Cleophila; and mortal it would have been had not the death wound Cleophila, with a new thrust, gave unto him taken away the effect of his force. But therewithal he fell down, and gave Cleophila leisure to take off his head to carry it for a present to her lady Philoclea, who all this while, not knowing what was done behind her, kept on her course, as Arethusa when she ran from Alpheus,* her light nymphlike apparel being carried up with the wind, that much of those beauties she would at another time have willingly hidden were presented to the eye of the twice-wounded Cleophila; which made Cleophila not follow her over hastily lest she should too soon deprive herself of that pleasure. But, carrying the lion's head in her hand, did not fully overtake her till they came both into the presence of Basilius, at that time examining the shepherds of what was passed, and preparing himself to come to their succour. Neither were they long there but that Gynecia came to them; whose look had all this while been upon the combat, eyeing so fixedly Cleophila's manner of fighting that no fear did prevail over her but, as soon as Cleophila had cut off his head, and ran after Philoclea, she could not find in her heart but to run likewise after Cleophila. So that it was a new sight fortune had prepared to those woods, to see these three great personages thus run one after the other, each carried away with the violence of an inward evil: the sweet Philoclea, with such fear that she thought she was still in the lion's mouth; Cleophila, with a painful delight she had to see without hope of enjoying; Gynecia, not so much with the love she bare to her best beloved daughter as with a new wonderful passionate love had possessed her heart of the goodly Cleophila. For so the truth is that, at the first sight she had of Cleophila, her heart gave her she was a man* thus for some strange cause disguised, which now this combat did in effect assure her of, because she measured the possibility of all women's hearts out of her own. And this doubt framed in her a desire to know, and desire to know brought forth shortly such longing to enjoy that it reduced her whole mind to an extreme and unfortunate slavery—pitifully, truly, considering her beauty and estate; but for a perfect mark of the triumph of love who could in one moment overthrow the heart of a wise lady, so that neither honour long maintained, nor love of husband and children, could withstand it. But of that you shall after hear; for now, they being come before the duke, and the fair Philoclea scarcely then stayed from her fear, Cleophila, kneeling down, presented the head of the lion unto her with these words: 'Only lady,' said she, 'here see you the punishment of that unnatural beast which, contrary to his own kind, would have wronged prince's blood; neither were his eyes vanquished with the duty all eyes bear to your beauty.'

'Happy am I and my beauty both', answered the fair Philoclea (the blood coming again to her cheeks, pale before for fear), 'that you, excellent Amazon, were there to teach him good manners.'

'And even thank that beauty,' said Cleophila, 'which forceth all noble swords to be ready to serve it.'

Having finished these words, the lady Philoclea perceived the blood that ran abundantly down upon Cleophila's shoulder; so that starting aside, with a countenance full of sweet pity, 'Alas,' said she, 'now perceive I my good hap is waited on with great misfortune, since my safety is wrought with the danger of a much more worthy person.'

'Noble lady,' answered she, 'if your inward eyes could discern the wounds of my soul, you should have a plentifuller cause to exercise your compassion.'

But it was sport to see how in one instant both Basilius and Gynecia (like a father and mother to a beloved child) came running to see the wound of Cleophila; into what rages Basilius grew, and what tears Gynecia spent—for so it seemed that love had purposed to make in those solitary woods a perfect demonstration of his unresistible force, to show that no desert place can avoid his dart. He must fly from himself that will shun his evil. But so wonderful and in effect incredible was the passion which reigned as well in Gynecia as Basilius (and all for the poor Cleophila, dedicated another way) that it seems to myself I use not words enough to make you see how they could in one moment be so overtaken. But you, worthy ladies, that have at any time feelingly known what it means, will easily believe the possibility of it. Let the ignorant sort of people give credit to them that have passed the doleful passage, and daily find that quickly is the infection gotten which in long time is hardly cured.

Basilius sometimes would kiss her forehead, blessing the destinies that had joined such beauty and valour together. Gynecia would kiss her more boldly, by the liberty of her womanish show, although her heart were set of nothing less; for already was she fallen into a jealous envy against her daughter Philoclea, because she found Cleophila showed such extraordinary dutiful favour unto her; and even that settled her opinion the more of her manhood. And this doubtful jealousy served as a bellows to kindle the violent coals of her passion. But as the over kind nurse may sometimes with kissing forget to give the child suck so had they, with too much kindness, unkindly forgotten the wound of Cleophila, had not Philoclea, whose heart had not yet gone beyond the limits of a right goodwill, advised herself, and desired her mother to help her to dress the wound of Cleophila. For both those great ladies were excellently seen in that part of surgery—an art in that age greatly esteemed because it served as a minister to virtuous courage, which in those worthy days was even by ladies more beloved than any outward beauty. So to the great comfort of Cleophila, more to feel the delicate hands of Philoclea than for the care she had of her wound, these two ladies had quickly dressed it, applying so precious a balm as all the heat and pain was presently assuaged, with apparent hope of soon amendment. In which doing, I know not whether Gynecia took some greater conjectures of Cleophila's sex. But even then, and not before, did Cleophila remember herself of her dear friend Musidorus; for having only had care of the excellent Philoclea, she never missed neither her friend nor the princess Pamela—not so much to be marvelled at in her, since both the duke and duchess had forgotten their daughter, so were all their thoughts plunged in one place. Besides Cleophila had not seen any danger was like to fall unto him, for her eye had been still fixed upon Philoclea, and that made her the more careless. But now, with a kind of rising in her heart, lest some evil should be fallen to her chosen friend, she hastily asked what was become of the princess Pamela, with the two shepherds, Dametas and Dorus. And then the duke and Gynecia remembered their forgetfulness, and with great astonishment made like inquiry for her. But of all the company of the shepherds (so had the lion's sight put them from themselves), there was but one could say anything of her; and all he said was this: that as he ran away he might perceive a great bear run directly towards her. Cleophila (whose courage was always ready without deliberation) took up the sword lying by her, with mind to bestow her life for the succour or revenge of her Musidorus and the gracious Pamela. But as she had run two or three steps, they might all see Pamela coming betwixt Dametas and Dorus, Pamela having in her hand the paw of the bear which the shepherd Dorus had newly presented unto her, desiring her to keep it, as of such a beast which, though she was to be punished for her over great cruelty, yet was her wit to be esteemed, since she could make so sweet a choice. Dametas for his part came piping and dancing, the merriest man of a parish; but when he came so near as he might be heard of the duke, he sang this song for joy of their success:

> Now thanked be the great god Pan
> That thus preserves my loved life:
> Thanked be I that keep a man
> Who ended hath this fearful strife:
> So if my man must praises have,
> What then must I that keep the knave?
>
> For as the moon the eye doth please
> With gentle beams not hurting sight,
> Yet hath sir sun the greatest praise,
> Because from him doth come her light:
> So if my man must praises have,
> What then must I that keep the knave?

It were a very superfluous thing to tell you how glad each party was of the happy returning from these dangers, and doubt you not, fair ladies, there wanted no questioning how things had passed; but because I will have the thanks myself, it shall be I you shall hear it of. And thus the ancient records of Arcadia say it fell out: the lion's presence had no sooner driven away the heartless shepherds, and followed, as I told you, the excellent Philoclea, but that there came out of the same woods a monstrous she-bear which, fearing to deal with the lion's prey, came furiously towards the princess Pamela who, whether it were she had heard that such was the best refuge against that beast, or that fear (as it fell out most likely) brought forth the effects of wisdom, she no sooner saw the bear coming towards her but she fell down flat upon her face. Which when the prince Musidorus saw (whom, because such was his pleasure, I am bold to call the shepherd Dorus), with a true resolved magnanimity, although he had no other weapon but a great shepherd's knife, he leaped before the head of his dear lady, and saying these words unto her, 'Receive here the sacrifice of that heart which is only vowed to

your service', attended with a quiet courage the coming of the bear
which, according to the manner of that beast's fight, especially
against a man that resists them, rase up upon her hinder feet, so
to take him in her ugly paws. But, as she was ready to give him a
mortal embracement, the shepherd Dorus, with a lusty strength and
good fortune, thrust his knife so right into the heart of the beast that
she fell down dead without ever being able to touch him. Which
being done, he turned to his lady Pamela (at that time in a swoon
with extremity of fear), and softly taking her in his arms, he took
the advantage to kiss and re-kiss her a hundred times, with such
exceeding delight that he would often after say he thought the joy
would have carried his life from him, had not the grief he conceived
to see her in such case something diminished it. But long in that
delightful agony he was not; for the lady Pamela, being come out of
her swoon, opened her fair eyes, and seeing herself in the hands of
this new-come shepherd, with great disdain put him from her. But
when she saw the ugly bear lying hard by her, starting aside (for
fear gave not reason leave to determine whether it were dead or no),
she forgot her anger, and cried to Dorus to help her. Wherefore he,
cutting off the forepaw of the bear, and showing unto her the bloody
knife, told her she might well by this perceive that there was no
heart so base, nor weapon so feeble, but that the force of her beauty
was well able to enable them for the performance of great matters.
She, inquiring the manner, and whether himself were hurt, gave him
great thanks for his pains, with promise of reward. But being
ashamed to find herself so alone with this young shepherd, looked
round about if she could see anybody; and at length they both per-
ceived the gentle Dametas, lying with his head and breast as far as
he could thrust himself into a bush, drawing up his legs as close unto
him as he could. For, indeed, as soon as he saw the bear coming
towards him (like a man that was very apt to take pity of himself), he
ran headlong into this bush, with full resolution that, at the worst
hand, he would not see his own death. And when Dorus pushed him,
bidding him be of good courage, it was a great while before they
could persuade him that Dorus was not the bear; so that he was fain
to pull him out by the heels, and show him her as dead as he could
wish her—which, you may believe me, was a very joyful sight unto
him. And yet, like a man of a revengeful spirit, he gave the dead body
many a wound, swearing by much it was pity such beasts should be
suffered in a commonwealth. And then, with as immoderate joy as
before with fear (for his heart was framed never to be without a

passion), he went by his fair charge, dancing, piping, and singing; till they all came to the presence of the careful company, as before I told you. Thus now this little, but noble, company united again together, the first thing was done was the yielding of great thanks and praises of all sides to the virtuous Cleophila. The duke told with what a gallant grace she ran after Philoclea with the lion's head in her hand, like another Pallas with the spoils of Gorgon.* Gynecia sware she saw the very face of young Hercules killing the Nemean lion;* and all, with a grateful assent, confirmed the same praises. Only poor Dorus, though of equal desert, yet not proceeding from equal estate, should have been left forgotten, had not Cleophila (partly to put by the occasion of her own excessive praises, but principally for the true remembrance she had of her professed friend), with great admiration, spoken of his hazardous act, asking afresh (as if she had never before known him) what he was, and whether he had haunted that place before, protesting that, upon her conscience, she could not think but that he came of some very noble blood—so noble a countenance he bare, and so worthy an act he had performed. This Basilius took (as the lover's heart is apt to receive all sudden sorts of impression) as though his mistress had given him a secret reprehension that he had not showed more gratefulness to the valiant Dorus. And therefore, as nimbly as he could, began forthwith to inquire of his estate, adding promise of great rewards—among the rest offering to him that, if he would exercise his valour in soldiery, he would commit some charge unto him under Philanax, governor of his frontiers. But Dorus, whose ambition stretched a quite other way, having first answered (touching his estate) that he was brother to the shepherd Menalcas whom the duke had well known, and excused his going to soldiery by the unaptness he found in himself that way, told the duke that his brother, in his last testament, had commanded him to dedicate his service to Dametas; and therefore, as well for due obedience thereto as for the satisfaction of his own mind (which was wholly set upon pastoral affairs), he would think his service greatly rewarded if he might obtain by that means to live in the sight of the duke more than the rest of his fellows, and yet practise that his chosen vocation. The duke, liking well of his modest manner, charged Dametas to receive him like a son in his house, telling him, because of his tried valour, he would have him be as a guard to his daughter Pamela, to whom likewise he recommended him, sticking not to say such men were to be cherished since she was in danger of some secret misadventure.

All this while Pamela said little of him, and even as little did Philoclea of Cleophila; although everybody else filled their mouths with their praises. Whereof seeking the cause that they which were most bound said least, I note this to myself, fair ladies, that even at this time they did begin to find they themselves could not tell what kind of inclination towards them; whereof feeling a secret accusation in themselves, and in their simplicity not able to warrant it, closed up all such motion in secret, without daring scarcely to breathe out the names of them who already began to breed unwonted war in their spirits. For, indeed, fortune had framed a very stage-play of love among these few folks, making the old age of Basilius, the virtue of Gynecia, and the simplicity of Philoclea, all affected to one; but by a three-headed kind of passion: Basilius assuring himself she was, as she pretended, a young lady, but greatly despairing for his own unworthiness's sake; Gynecia hoping her judgement to be right of his disguising, but therein fearing a greater sore if already his heart were pledged to her daughter. But sweet Philoclea grew shortly after of all other into worst terms; for taking her to be such as she professed, desire she did, but she knew not what; and she longed to obtain that whereof she herself could not imagine the mean, but full of unquiet imaginations rested only unhappy because she knew not her good hap. Cleophila hath (I think) said enough for herself to make you know, fair ladies, that she was not a little enchanted; and as for Dorus, a shepherd's apparel upon a duke of Thessalia will answer for him. Pamela was the only lady that would needs make open war upon herself, and obtain the victory; for, indeed, even now find she did a certain working of a new-come inclination to Dorus. But when she found perfectly in herself whither it must draw her, she did overmaster it with the consideration of his meanness. But how therein Dorus sought to satisfy her you shall after hear; for now the day being closed up in darkness the duke would fain have had Cleophila gone to rest, because of her late-received wound. But she (that found no better salve than Philoclea's presence) desired first that by torchlight they might see some of the pastorals the lion's coming had disordered. Which accordingly was done; whereof I will repeat you a few to ease you, fair ladies, of the tediousness of this long discourse.

Here ends the first book or act.

HERE BEGINS THE FIRST ECLOGUES

THE manner of the Arcadian shepherds was, when they met together, to pass their time, either in such music as their rural education could afford them, or in exercise of their body and trying of masteries. But, of all other things, they did especially delight in eclogues; wherein sometimes they would contend for a prize of well singing, sometimes lament the unhappy pursuit of their affections, sometimes, again, under hidden forms utter such matters as otherwise were not fit for their delivery. Neither is it to be marvelled that they did so much excel other nations in that quality since, from their childhood, they were brought up unto it, and were not such base shepherds as we commonly make account of, but the very owners of the sheep themselves, which in that thrifty world the substantiallest men would employ their whole care upon. And when they had practised the goodness of their wit in such sports, then was it their manner ever to have one who should write up the substance of that they said; whose pen, having more leisure than their tongues, might perchance polish a little the rudeness of an unthought-on song.*But the peace wherein they did so notably flourish, and especially the sweet enjoying of their peace to so pleasant uses, drew divers strangers, as well of great as of mean houses, especially such whom inward melancholies made weary of the world's eyes, to come and live among them, applying themselves to their trade: which likewise was many times occasion to beautify more than otherwise it would have been this pastoral exercise. But nothing lifted it up to so high a key as the presence of their own duke who, not only by looking on but by great courtesy and liberality, animated the shepherds the more exquisitely to seek a worthy accomplishment of his good liking, as this time after the valiant killing of the beasts by the two disguised princes performed. The duke (because Cleophila so would have it) used the artificial day of torches to lighten the sports their inventions could minister. And yet, because many more shepherds were newly come than at the first were, he did, with a gentle manner, chastise the cowardice of the fugitive shepherds with making them for that night the torch bearers; and the others later come, he willed, with all freedom of speech and behaviour, to keep their accustomed method; which they prepared themselves to do, while he sat himself down, having on the one side the duchess, but of his heart side the fair Cleophila. To whom speaking in looks (for as yet his tongue was not come to a thorough boldness), he sought to send the first ambassade of his passions—little marked of Cleophila whose eyes seemed to have changed sight with Philoclea's eyes (whom Gynecia had of purpose placed by herself), so attentive looks were mutually fixed between them, to the greatest corrosive to Gynecia that can be imagined, whose love-open sight did more and more pierce into the knowledge of Cleophila's counterfeiting, which likewise more and more fortified her unlawful desires; yet with so great and violent a combat with herself as the suppression of a long-used virtue comes to. But another place shall serve to manifest her agonies; this, being dedicated only to pastorals, shall bend itself that way, and leave all those princely motions to their considerations that, untold, can guess what love means—whereof the princess Pamela, that sat next to Cleophila, was most free, having in her mind used Dorus's baseness as a shield against his worthiness. But they being set in order, Dametas, who much disdained (since his late authority) all his old companions, brought his servant Dorus in good acquaintance and allowance of them; and himself stood like a director over them, with nodding, gaping, winking or stamping, showing how he did like or mislike those things he did not understand. The first sports the shepherds showed were full of such leaps and gambols as (being accorded to the pipe which they bare in their mouths even as they danced) made a right picture of their chief god Pan and his companions, the satyrs. Then would they cast away their pipes and, holding hand in hand, dance as it were in a brawl by the only cadence of their voices, which they would use in singing some short couplets; whereto the one half beginning, the other half answered; as, the one half saying:

We love, and have our loves rewarded.

The others would answer:

We love, and are no whit regarded.

The first again:

We find most sweet affection's snare.

With like tune, it should be (as in a choir) sent back again:

That sweet, but sour despairful care.

A third time likewise thus:

Who can despair whom hope doth bear?

The answer:

> And who can hope who feels despair?

Then, all joining their voices, and dancing a faster measure, they would conclude with some such words:

> As without breath no pipe doth move,
> No music kindly without love.

Having thus varied both their songs and dances into diverse sorts of inventions, their last sport was one of them to provoke another to a more large expressing of his passions: which Lalus, a shepherd accounted one of the best singers among them, having marked in Dorus's dancing no less good grace and handsome behaviour than extreme tokens of a troubled mind, he began first with his pipe, and then with his voice, thus to challenge Dorus; and was by him answered in the underwritten sort:

Lalus. Come, Dorus, come, let songs thy sorrows signify;
> And if, for want of use, thy mind ashamed is,
> That very shame with love's high title dignify.
> No style is held for base where love well named is:
> Each ear sucks up the words a true love scattereth,
> And plain speech oft than quaint phrase better framed is.

Dorus. Nightingales seldom sing, the pie still chattereth;
> The wood cries most before it throughly kindled be;
> Deadly wounds inward bleed, each slight sore mattereth;
> Hardly they herd which by good hunters singled be;
> Shallow brooks murmur most, deep silent slide away,
> Nor true love loves his loves with others mingled be.

Lalus. If thou wilt not be seen, thy face go hide away,
> Be none of us, or else maintain our fashion:
> Who frowns at others' feasts doth better bide away.
> But if thou hast a love, in that love's passion,
> I challenge thee, by show of her perfection,
> Which of us two deserveth most compassion.

Dorus. Thy challenge great, but greater my protection:
> Sing, then, and see (for now thou hast inflamed me)
> Thy health too mean a match for my infection.
> No, though the heav'ns for high attempt have blamed me,
> Yet high is my attempt. O muse, historify
> Her praise, whose praise to learn your skill hath framed me.

Lalus. Muse, hold your peace! But thou, my god Pan, glorify
My Kala's gifts, who with all good gifts filled is.
Thy pipe, O Pan, shall help, though I sing sorrily.
A heap of sweets she is, where nothing spilled is,
Who, though she be no bee, yet full of honey is:
A lily field, with plough of rose, which tilled is.
Mild as a lamb, more dainty than a cony is:
Her eyes my eyesight is, her conversation
More glad to me than to a miser money is.
What coy account she makes of estimation!
How nice to touch, how all her speeches peised be!
A nymph thus turned, but mended in translation.

Dorus. Such Kala is; but ah, my fancies raised be
In one whose name to name were high presumption,
Since virtues all, to make her title, pleased be.
O happy gods, which by inward assumption
Enjoy her soul, in body's fair possession,
And keep it joined, fearing your seat's consumption.
How oft with rain of tears skies make confession
Their dwellers rapt with sight of her perfection,
From heav'nly throne to her heav'n use digression.
Of best things then what world can yield confection
To liken her? Deck yours with your comparison:
She is herself of best things the collection.

Lalus. How oft my doleful sire cried to me, 'tarry son',
When first he spied my love? How oft he said to me,
'Thou art no soldier fit for Cupid's garrison.
My son, keep this that my long toil hath laid to me:
Love well thine own; methinks, wool's whiteness passeth all:
I never found long love such wealth hath paid to me.'
This wind he spent; but when my Kala glasseth all
My sight in her fair limbs, I then assure myself,
Not rotten sheep, but high crowns she surpasseth all.
Can I be poor, that her gold hair procure myself?
Want I white wool, whose eyes her white skin garnished?
Till I get her, shall I to keep inure myself?

Dorus. How oft, when reason saw love of her harnished
With armour of my heart, he cried, 'O vanity,

To set a pearl in steel so meanly varnished!
Look to thyself; reach not beyond humanity;
    Her mind, beams, state, far from thy weak wings banished;
    And love which lover hurts is inhumanity.'
Thus reason said: but she came, reason vanished;
    Her eyes so mast'ring me that such objection
    Seemed but to spoil the food of thoughts long famished.
Her peerless height my mind to high erection
    Draws up; and if, hope failing, end life's pleasure,
    Of fairer death how can I make election?

Lalus. Once my well-waiting eyes espied my treasure,
    With sleeves turned up, loose hair, and breasts enlarged,
    Her father's corn (moving her fair limbs) measure.
'O', cried I, 'of so mean work be discharged:
    Measure my case, how by thy beauty's filling
    With seed of woes my heart brim-full is charged.
Thy father bids thee save, and chides for spilling.
    Save then my soul, spill not my thoughts well heaped,
    No lovely praise was ever got with killing.'
These bold words she did hear, this fruit I reaped,
    That she, whose look alone might make me blessed,
    Did smile on me, and then away she leaped.

Dorus. Once, O sweet once,* I saw, with dread oppressed,
    Her whom I dread; so that with prostrate lying
    Her length the earth in love's chief clothing dressed.
I saw that richess fall, and fell a-crying:
    'Let not dead earth enjoy so dear a cover,
    But deck therewith my soul for your sake dying.
Lay all your fear upon your fearful lover:
    Shine eyes on me, that both our lives be guarded;
    So I your sight, you shall yourselves recover.'
I cried, and was with open rays rewarded;
    But straight they fled, summoned by cruel honour,
    Honour, the cause desert is not regarded.

Lalus. This maid, thus made for joys, O Pan, bemoan her,
    That without love she spends her years of love:
    So fair a field would well become an owner.
And if enchantment can a hard heart move,

Teach me what circle may acquaint her sprite,
Affection's charms in my behalf to prove.
The circle is my round-about-her sight:
   The power I will invoke dwells in her eyes:
   My charm should be she haunt me day and night.

Dorus. Far other care, O muse, my sorrow tries,
   Bent to such one, in whom, myself must say,
   Nothing can mend one point that in her lies.
What circle, then, in so rare force bears sway?
   Whose sprite all sprites can spoil, raise, damn, or save:
   No charm holds her, but well possess she may;
Possess she doth, and makes my soul her slave:
   My eyes the bands, my thoughts the fatal knot.
   No thralls like them that inward bondage have.

Lalus. Kala, at length, conclude my ling'ring lot:
   Disdain me not, although I be not fair.
   Who is an heir of many hundred sheep
Doth beauties keep, which never sun can burn,
   Nor storms do turn: fairness serves oft to wealth.
   Yet all my health I place in your goodwill:
Which if you will (O do) bestow on me,
   Such as you see, such still you shall me find:
   Constant and kind. My sheep your food shall breed,
Their wool your weed: I will you music yield
   In flow'ry field; and as the day begins
   With twenty gins we will the small birds take,
And pastimes make, as nature things hath made.
   But when in shade we meet of myrtle boughs,
   Then love allows, our pleasures to enrich,
The thought of which doth pass all worldly pelf.

Dorus. Lady yourself, whom neither name I dare,
   And titles are but spots to such a worth,
   Hear plaints come forth from dungeon of my mind:
The noblest kind rejects not others' woes.
   I have no shows of wealth: my wealth is you,
   My beauty's hue your beams, my health your deeds;
My mind for weeds your virtue's liv'ry wears.
   My food is tears; my tunes waymenting yield;

Despair my field; the flowers spirit's wars;
My day new cares; my gins my daily sight,
In which do light small birds of thoughts o'erthrown.
My pastimes none; time passeth on my fall.
Nature made all, but me of dolours made.
I find no shade, but where my sun doth burn;
No place to turn; without, within, it fries;
Nor help by life or death who living dies.

Lalus. But if my Kala this my suit denies,
    Which so much reason bears,
    Let crows pick out mine eyes which too much saw.
    If she still hate love's law,
    My earthy mould doth melt in wat'ry tears.

Dorus. My earthy mould doth melt in wat'ry tears,
    And they again resolve
    To air of sighs, sighs to the heart's fire turn,
    Which doth to ashes burn;
    Thus doth my life within itself dissolve.

Lalus. Thus doth my life within itself dissolve,
    That I grow like the beast
    Which bears the bit a weaker force doth guide,
    Yet patient must abide;
    Such weight it hath which once is full possessed.

Dorus. Such weight it hath which once is full possessed
    That I become a vision,
    Which hath in other's head his only being
    And lives in fancy's seeing.
    O wretched state of man in self-division!

Lalus. O wretched state of man in self-division!
        O well thou say'st! A feeling declaration
        Thy tongue hath made of Cupid's deep incision.
    But now hoarse voice doth fail this occupation,
        And others long to tell their loves' condition:
        Of singing thou hast got the reputation.

Dorus. Of singing thou hast got the reputation
        Good Lalus mine; I yield to thy ability:

My heart doth seek another estimation.
But ah, my muse, I would thou hadst facility
　To work my goddess so by thy invention
　On me to cast those eyes, where shine nobility:
Seen and unknown; heard, but without attention.

The eclogue betwixt Lalus and Dorus of every one of the be-
holders received great commendations, saving only of the two grave
shepherds, Geron and Dicus, who both plainly protested it was pity
wit should be employed about so very a toy as that they called love
was—Geron thereto the more inclined, as that age, having taken
from him both the thoughts and fruits of that passion, wished all
the world proportioned to himself. But Dicus, whether for certain
mischances of his own, or out of a better judgement, which saw the
bottom of things, did more detest and hate love than the most
envious man doth in himself cherish and love hate. Which, as he
did at all times publicly profess, so now he came, as a man should
say, armed to show his malice; for in the one hand he bare a whip,
in the other a naked Cupid, such as we commonly set him forth.
But on his breast he ware a painted table, wherein he had given
Cupid a quite new form, making him sit upon a pair of gallows,
like a hangman, about which there was a rope very handsomely
provided; he himself painted all ragged and torn, so that his skin
was bare in most places, where a man might perceive all his body full
of eyes, his head horned with the horns of a bull, with long ears
accordingly, his face old and wrinkled, and his feet cloven. In his
right hand, he was painted holding a crown of laurel, in his left a
purse of money; and out of his mouth hung a lace which held the
pictures of a goodly man and an excellent fair woman. And with
such a countenance he was drawn as if he had persuaded every man
by those enticements to come and be hanged there. The duke
laughed when he saw Dicus come out in such manner, and asked him
what he meant by such transforming the gentle Cupid. But Dicus,
as if it had been no jesting matter, told him plainly that long they
had done the heavens wrong to make Cupid a god, and much more
to the fair Venus to call him her son—indeed, the bastard of false
Argus,*who, having the charge of the deflowered Io (what time she
was a cow), had traitorously in that shape begot him of her; and that
the naughtiness of men's lust had given him so high a title. Everyone

of the company (except old Geron) began to stamp with their feet, and hiss at him, as thinking he had spoken an unpardonable blasphemy. But Geron, well backing him in it, Dicus boldly stepped forth and, after having railed at the name of Cupid as spitefully as he could devise, calling to Pan to help his song in revenge of his losing the fair Syrinx,* he thus, tuning his voice to a rebeck, sang against him:

> Poor painters oft with silly poets join
> To fill the world with strange but vain conceits:
> One brings the stuff, the other stamps the coin,
> Which breeds naught else but glosses of deceits.
>   Thus painters Cupid paint, thus poets do,
>   A naked god, blind, young, with arrows two.
>
> Is he a god, that ever flies the light?
> Or naked he, disguised in all untruth?
> If he be blind, how hitteth he so right?
> Or is he young, that tamed old Phoebus' youth?
>   But arrows two, and tipped with gold or lead:
>   Some hurt, accuse a third with horny head.
>
> No, nothing so; an old false knave he is,
> By Argus got on Io, then a cow,
> What time for her Juno her Jove did miss,
> And charge of her to Argus did allow.
>   Mercury killed his false sire for this act,
>   His dam, a beast, was pardoned beastly fact.
>
> With father's death, and mother's guilty shame,
> With Jove's disdain at such a rival's seed,
> The wretch compelled, a runagate became,
> And learned what ill a miser state doth breed;
>   To lie, to steal, to pry, and to accuse,
>   Naught in himself, each other to abuse.
>
> Yet bears he still his parents' stately gifts,
> A horned head, cloven foot, and thousand eyes,
> Some gazing still, some winking wily shifts,
> With long large ears where never rumour dies.
>   His horned head doth seem the heav'n to spite:
>   His cloven foot doth never tread aright.

Thus half a man, with man he easily haunts,
Clothed in the shape which soonest may deceive:
Thus half a beast, each beastly vice he plants
In those weak hearts that his advice receive.
    He prowls each place still in new colours decked,
    Sucking one's ill, another to infect.

To narrow breasts he comes all wrapped in gain:
To swelling hearts he shines in honour's fire:
To open eyes all beauties he doth rain;
Creeping to each with flatt'ring of desire.
    But for that love is worst which rules the eyes,
    Thereon his name, there his chief triumph lies.

Millions of years this old drivel Cupid lives;
While still more wretch, more wicked he doth prove:
Till now at length that Jove him office gives
(At Juno's suit who much did Argus love),
    In this our world a hangman for to be
    Of all those fools that will have all they see.

He had not fully ended his last words of his invective song when a young shepherd named Histor who, while Dicus was singing, sometimes with his eyes up to heaven, sometimes seeming to stop his ears, did show a fearful mislike of so unreverent reproaches, with great vehemency desired all the hearers to take heed how they seemed to allow any part of his speech against so revengeful a god as Cupid was, who had even in his first magistracy showed against Apollo the heat of his anger. 'But', said he, 'if you had heard or seen such violence of his wrath as I even yesterday, and the other day, have, you would tremble at the recital of his name.'

The duke and all the rest straight desired him to tell what it was; and he (seeming loath, lest his words might disgrace the matter) told them that, as he was two days before sitting in the shade of a bush, he did hear the most wailful lamentation of an Iberian nobleman called Plangus (uttered to the wise shepherd Boulon) that he thought any words could express; and all touching a pitiful adventure, the ground and maintenance whereof was only Cupid. 'And that song', said he, 'for in a song I gathered it, would I let you hear but that, for the better understanding, I must first repeat the subject thereof. This Plangus, when no persuasion of the wise Boulon could keep him from the pitiful complaining of his sorrows, yet yielded so much to my request as to harbour with me these last days in my simple cabin where, with much entreaty, he told me this pitiful story:*

That of late there reigned a king of Lydia who had for the blessing of his marriage his only daughter Erona, a princess worthy for her beauty as much praise as beauty may be praised. This Erona being fourteen years old, seeing the country of Lydia so much devoted to Cupid as that in each place his naked pictures and images were superstitiously adored, procured so much of her father (either moved thereunto by the hate of that god, or the shamefast consideration of such nakedness) utterly to deface and pull down all those pictures of him; which how terribly he punished quickly after appeared. For she had not lived a year longer when she was stricken with most obstinate love to a young man, but of mean parentage, in her father's court, named Antiphilus; so mean as that he was but the son of her nurse, and by that means came known of her. And so ill could she conceal this fire, and so wilfully persevered she in it, that her father offering her the marriage of the great Otanes, king of Persia (who desired her more than the joys of heaven), she, for Antiphilus's sake, refused him. Many ways her father did seek to withdraw her from it; sometimes persuasions, sometimes threatenings, sometimes hiding Antiphilus and giving her to understand he was fled the country; lastly making a solemn execution to be done of another under the name of Antiphilus, whom he kept in prison. But neither she liked persuasions, nor feared threatenings, nor changed for absence; and when she thought him dead, it was manifestly seen she sought all means, as well by poison as knife, to follow him. This so brake the father's heart with grief that, leaving things as he found them, he shortly after died. Then forthwith Erona, being seized of the crown, sought to satisfy her mind with Antiphilus's marriage.

But before she could accomplish it, she was overtaken with a cruel war the king Otanes made upon her, only for her person, towards whom, for her ruin, love had kindled his cruel heart: indeed cruel and tyrannous; for being far too strong in the field, he spared not man, woman, nor child, but with miserable tortures slew them, although his fair sister Artaxia (who accompanied him in the army) sought all means to mollify his rage; till lastly he besieged Erona in her best city, vowing he would have her either by force or otherwise. And to the extremity he had brought her when there landed in Lydia, driven thither by tempest, two excellent young princes, as Plangus named them, Pyrocles, prince of Macedon, and Musidorus, duke of Thessalia (at these words, a man might easily have perceived a starting and blushing, both in Cleophila and Dorus; but being utterly unsuspected to be such, they were unmarked). Those two princes, as well to help the weaker as for the natural hate the Grecians bare the Persians, did so much with their incomparable valour as that they gat into the city, and by their presence much repelled Otanes' assaults. Which he understanding to be occasioned by them, made a challenge of three princes in his retinue against those two princes and Antiphilus; and that thereupon the matter should be decided, with compact that neither should help his fellows, but of whose side the more overcame, with him the victory should remain. Of his side was Barzanes, lord of Hyrcania, against Pyrocles; Nardes, satrapas of Mesopotamia, to fight with Musidorus; and against Antiphilus he placed this same Plangus, second son to the king of Iberia, who served him with dear estimation. And so it fell out that Pyrocles and Musidorus overcame both their adversaries, but of the other side Plangus took Antiphilus prisoner. Under which colour, as though the matter had been equal (though indeed it was not), Otanes continued his war; and to bring Erona to a compelled yielding, sent her one day word that the next morrow he would, before the walls of her town, strike off Antiphilus's head, if she yielded not to his desire.

Then, lo, was Cupid's work well seen; for he had brought this miserable princess to such a case as she had love against love. For if she loved him (as unmeasurably she did), then could she condescend to no other; again, if she loved him, then must she save his life; which two things were impossible to be joined together. But the matchless courage of those two princes prevented him, and preserved her; for the same night, with a desperate camisado, they pierced into the midst of his army where Otanes, valiantly defending himself, was by Pyrocles slain, and Antiphilus by Musidorus rescued. Plangus, seeing no other remedy, conveyed in safety to her country the fair Artaxia, now queen of Persia, who, with the extremest lamentations could issue out of a woman's mouth, testified to the world her new greatness did no way comfort her in respect of her brother's loss; whom she studied all means possible to revenge upon every one of the occasioners.

But thus was Antiphilus redeemed, and (though against the consent of all the Lydian nobility) married to Erona. In which case the two Greek princes left them, being called away by one of the notablest adventures in the world. But the vindicative Cupid, who had given Erona only so much time of sweetness as to make the miseries more cruel that should fall upon her, had turned Antiphilus's heart while he was Otanes' prisoner quite from her to queen Artaxia; insomuch that, longing to have the great crown of Persia on his head and, like a base man suddenly advanced, having no scope of his insolence, made Artaxia secretly understand (who, he knew, mortally hated Erona) that, if she would reward his vehement loving of her with marriage, he would either by poison or otherwise make away the beautiful Erona, and so, with the might of Persia, easily join those two kingdoms together. The wise Artaxia, that had now a good entrance to her desires, finely handled the vile Antiphilus and brought his heart to such a wicked paradise that one day, under colour of hunting, he enticed abroad the excellent Erona to a place where he had laid some of Artaxia's men in ambushment, and there delivered both himself and her into their hands; who conveying them to their mistress, Antiphilus was justly rewarded of his expected marriage. For she presently gave him into the hands of four valiant gentlemen, who dearly had loved their master Otanes, to be slain with as many deaths as their wit and hate could find out. Which accordingly was done, and he held a whole month together in continual wretchedness, till at last his life left him, rather with continuance of the miserable pain than any violent stroke added unto him. As for Erona, she put her in prison, swearing that, if by that time two year she did not bring Pyrocles and Musidorus to fight with those four (who would prove upon them they had traitorously killed her brother Otanes), she should be publicly burned at a stake; which likewise she should be, if Pyrocles and his fellow were overcome. But if they would take the matter upon them, then should they have a free camp granted them to try the matter in the court of the king of Parthia, because they might hold hers for suspected. This did she hoping that the courage of the two young princes would lead them to so unequal a match, wherein she rested assured their death, and so consequently her revenge, should be fully performed. But Erona, because she might exceed even misery with misery, did not, for all the treachery of Antiphilus (able to make any love a mortal hatred), nor yet for his death (the breaker of all worldly fancies), leave to love Antiphilus and to hate herself since she had lost him. And in respect of his revenge upon those four his murderers (not for her own life, which she was weary of), she desired that Pyrocles and Musidorus might against the day be brought thither, having such confidence in the notable proofs she had seen of their virtue that those four should not be able to withstand them, but suffer death for killing her (in spite of hate) beloved Antiphilus. But whom to send for their search she knew not, when Cupid (I think for some greater mischief) offered this Plangus unto her, who from the day of her first imprisonment was so extremely enamoured of her that he had sought all means how to deliver her. But that being impossible, for the narrow watch was of her, he had (as well he might, being greatly trusted of Artaxia) conference with Erona; and, although she would promise no affection in reward (which was finished absolutely in Antiphilus), yet he took upon him the quest of those two heroical princes who, in this mean time, had done such famous acts that all Asia was full of their histories. But he, having travelled a whole year after them, and still hearing their doings notably recounted, yet could never (being stayed by many misadventures) fully overtake them; but was newly come into Egypt after they had shipped themselves thence for Greece; and into Greece likewise followed, taking this country in his way because mariners had told him such a ship had touched upon the south part of Peloponnesus, where it was my hap to hear him make the pitifullest lamentation that ever before came into mine ears. Neither could the wise Boulon (who had found him making the like doleful complaints, as his mind otherwise occupied led him contrary to these woods) anything mitigate his agonies; but, as he told us (having likewise at our request recounted the full story of those two rare princes), his purpose was to go into Thessalia and Macedon where, if he cannot hear of them, he will return into Persia, and either find some way to preserve Erona or burn at the stake with her.'

Great was the compassion Cleophila and Dorus conceived of the queen Erona's danger—which was the first enterprise they had ever entered into; and therefore (besides their noble humanity) they were loath their own worthy work should be spoiled. Therefore, considering they had almost a year of time to succour her, they resolved as soon as this their present action (which had taken full possession of all their desires) were brought to any good point they would forthwith take in hand that journey; neither should they need in the meantime anything reveal themselves to Plangus (who, though unwittingly, had now done his errand). To which they thought themselves in honour bound, since Artaxia laid treason to their charge. But how that fancy was stopped shall be after told.

Now Dorus desired Histor to repeat the lamentable song he first spake of; and Histor was ready to do it when out starts old Geron and said it was very undecent a young man's tongue should possess so much time, and that age should become an auditor. And therefore, bending himself to another young shepherd named Philisides*who neither had danced nor sung with them, and had all this time lain upon the ground at the foot of a cypress tree, leaning upon his elbow, with so deep a melancholy that his senses carried to his mind no delight from any of their objects, he strake him upon the shoulder with a right old man's grace that will seem livelier than his age will afford him; and thus began his eclogue unto him:

Geron   Philisides   Histor

Geron. Up, up, Philisides, let sorrows go,
   Who yields to woe doth but increase his smart.
   Do not thy heart to plaintful custom bring,
   But let us sing, sweet tunes do passions ease,
   An old man hear, who would thy fancies raise.

Philisides. Who minds to please the mind drowned in annoys
   With outward joys, which inly cannot sink,
   As well may think with oil to cool the fire;
   Or with desire to make such foe a friend,
   Who doth his soul to endless malice bend.

Geron. Yet sure an end to each thing time doth give,
   Though woes now live, at length thy woes must die.
   Then virtue try, if she can work in thee
   That which we see in many time hath wrought,
   And weakest hearts to constant temper brought.

Philisides. Who ever taught a skill-less man to teach,
   Or stop a breach, that never cannon saw?
   Sweet virtue's law bars not a causeful moan.
   Time shall in one my life and sorrows end,
   And me perchance your constant temper lend.

Geron. What can amend where physic is refused?

The wits abused with will no counsel take.
Yet for my sake discover us thy grief.
Oft comes relief when most we seem in trap.
The stars thy state, fortune may change thy hap.

Philisides. If fortune's lap became my dwelling place,
And all the stars conspired to my good,
Still were I one, this still should be my case,
Ruin's relic,* care's web, and sorrow's food;
Since she, fair fierce, to such a state me calls,
Whose wit the stars, whose fortune fortune thralls.

Geron. Alas, what falls are fall'n unto thy mind
That there where thou confessed thy mischief lies
Thy wit dost use still still more harms to find?
Whom wit makes vain, or blinded with his eyes,
What counsel can prevail, or light give light,
Since all his force against himself he tries?
Then each conceit that enters in by sight
Is made forsooth a jurat of his woes:
Earth, sea, air, fire, heav'n, hell, and ghastly sprite.
Then cries to senseless things which neither knows
What aileth thee, and if they knew thy mind
Would scorn in man (their king) such feeble shows.
Rebel, rebel, in golden fetters bind
This tyrant love; or rather do suppress
Those rebel thoughts which are thy slaves by kind.
Let not a glitt'ring name thy fancy dress
In painted clothes, because they call it love.
There is no hate that can thee more oppress.
Begin (and half the work is done) to prove
By raising up, upon thyself to stand;
And think she is a she that doth thee move.
He water ploughs, and soweth in the sand,*
And hopes the flick'ring wind with net to hold,
Who hath his hopes laid up in woman's hand.
What man is he that hath his freedom sold?
Is he a manlike man that doth not know man
Hath power that sex with bridle to withhold?
A fickle sex, and true in trust to no man;
A servant sex, soon proud if they be coyed;

And to conclude, thy mistress is a woman.*

Histor. Those words did once the loveliest shepherd*use
    That erst I knew, and with most plainful muse;
    Yet not of women judging, as he said,
    But forced with rage, his rage on them upbraid.

Philisides. O gods, how long this old fool hath annoyed
    My wearied ears! O gods, yet grant me this,
    That soon the world of his false tongue be void.
    O noble age who place their only bliss
    In being heard until the hearer die,
    Utt'ring a serpent's mind with serpent's hiss!
    Then who will hear a well authorized lie
    (And patience hath), let him go learn of him
    What swarms of virtues did in his youth fly
    Such hearts of brass, wise heads, and garments trim
    Were in his days: which heard, one nothing hears,
    If from his words the falsehood he do skim.
    And herein most their folly vain appears,
    That since they still allege, *When they were young*,
    It shows they fetch their wit from youthful years.
    Like beast for sacrifice where, save the tongue
    And belly, naught is left; such sure is he,
    This 'live-dead man in this old dungeon flung.
    Old houses are thrown down for new we see;
    The oldest rams are culled from the flock;
    No man doth wish his horse should aged be;
    The ancient oak well makes a fired block;
    Old men themselves do love young wives to choose;
    Only fond youth admires a rotten stock.
    Who once a white long beard well handle does
    (As his beard him, not he his beard, did bear),
    Though cradle-witted, must not honour lose.
    O when will men leave off to judge by hair,
    And think them old that have the oldest mind,
    With virtue fraught and full of holy fear?

Geron. If that thy face were hid, or I were blind,
    I yet should know a young man speaketh now,
    Such wand'ring reasons in thy speech I find.

He is a beast that beast's use will allow
For proof of man who, sprung of heav'nly fire,
Hath strongest soul when most his reins do bow.
But fondlings fond know not your own desire,
Loath to die young, and then you must be old,
Fondly blame that to which yourselves aspire.
But this light choler that doth make you bold,
Rather to wrong than unto just defence,
Is passed with me, my blood is waxen cold.
Thy words, though full of malapert offence,
I weigh them not, but still will thee advise
How thou from foolish love mayst purge thy sense.
First, think they err that think them gaily wise
Who well can set a passion out to show;
Such sight have they that see with goggling eyes.
Passion bears high when puffing wit doth blow,
But is indeed a toy; if not a toy,
True cause of ills, and cause of causeless woe.
If once thou mayst that fancy gloss destroy
Within thyself, thou soon wilt be ashamed
To be a player of thine own annoy.
Then let thy mind with better books be tamed,
Seek to espy her faults as well as praise,
And let thine eyes to other sports be framed.
In hunting fearful beasts do spend some days,
Or catch the birds with pitfalls, or with lime,
Or train the fox that trains so crafty lays.
Lie but to sleep, and in the early prime
Seek skill of herbs in hills, haunt brooks near night,
And try with bait how fish will bite sometime.
Go graft again, and seek to graft them right,
Those pleasant plants, those sweet and fruitful trees,
Which both the palate and the eyes delight.
Cherish the hives of wisely painful bees;
Let special care upon thy flock be stayed;
Such active mind but seldom passion sees.

Philisides. Hath any man heard what this old man said?
  Truly, not I who did my thoughts engage
  Where all my pains one look of hers hath paid.

Histor. Thus may you see how youth esteemeth age,
  And never hath thereof arightly deemed,
  While hot desires do reign in fancy's rage,
  Till age itself do make itself esteemed.

Geron was even out of countenance, finding the words he thought
were so wise win so little reputation at this young man's hands; and
therefore, sometimes looking upon an old acquaintance of his called
Mastix, one of the repiningest fellows in the world, and that beheld
nobody but with a mind of mislike (saying still the world was amiss,
but how it should be amended he knew not), sometimes casting his
eyes to the ground, even ashamed to see his grey hairs despised, at
last he spied his two dogs, whereof the elder was called Melampus,
and the younger Lælaps (indeed the jewels he ever had with him),
one brawling with the other. Which occasion he took to restore
himself to his countenance, and rating Melampus, he began to
speak to his dogs as if in them a man should find more obedience
than in unbridled young men:

Geron   Mastix

Geron. Down, down, Melampus; what? your fellow bite?
  I set you o'er the flock I dearly love
  Them to defend, not with yourselves to fight.
  Do you not think this will the wolves remove
  From former fear they had of your good minds,
  When they shall such divided weakness prove?
  What if Lælaps a better morsel finds
  Than thou erst knew? Rather take part with him
  Than jarl: lo, lo, even these how envy blinds!
  And thou, Lælaps, let not pride make thee brim
  Because thou hast thy fellow overgone,
  But thank the cause, thou seest, when he is dim.
  Here, Lælaps, here; indeed, against the foen
  Of my good sheep thou never truce-time took:
  Be as thou art, but be with mine at one.
  For though Melampus like a wolf do look
  (For age doth make him of a wolvish hue),
  Yet have I seen when well a wolf he shook.
  Fool that I am that with my dogs speak Grew.
  Come nar, good Mastix, 'tis now full tway score

Of years (alas) since I good Mastix knew.
Thou heardst e'en now a young man sneb me sore
Because I red him as I would my son.
Youth will have will, age must to age therefore.

Mastix. What marvel if in youth such faults be done,
Since that we see our saddest shepherds out
Who have their lesson so long time begun?
Quickly secure, and easily in doubt,
Either asleep be all if naught assail,
Or all abroad if but a cub start out.
We shepherds are like them that under sail
Do speak high words when all the coast is clear,
Yet to a passenger will bonnet vail.
'I con thee thank' to whom thy dogs be dear,
But commonly like curs we them entreat,
Save when great need of them perforce appear,
Then him we kiss whom late before we beat
With such intemperance, that each way grows
Hate of the first, contempt of later feat.
And such discord 'twixt greatest shepherds flows,
That sport it is to see with how great art
By justice' work they their own faults disclose;
Like busy boys to win their tutor's heart,
One saith he mocks; the other saith he plays;
The third his lesson missed; till all do smart.
As for the rest, how shepherds spend their days
At blow point, hot cockles, or else at keels,*
While, 'Let us pass our time', each shepherd says.
So small account of time the shepherd feels,
And doth not feel that life is naught but time,*
And when that time is past, death holds his heels.
To age thus do they draw their youthful prime,
Knowing no more than what poor trial shows,
As fish sure trial hath of muddy slime.
This pattern good unto our children goes,
For what they see their parents love or hate
Their first caught sense prefers to teacher's blows.
These cocklings cockered we bewail too late
When that we see our offspring gaily bent,

Women manwood, and men effeminate.

Geron. Fie, man; fie, man; what words hath thy tongue lent?
Yet thou art mickle warse than ere was I,
Thy too much zeal I fear thy brain hath spent.
We oft are angrier with the feeble fly
For business where it pertains him not
Than with the pois'nous toads that quiet lie.
I pray thee what hath e'er the parrot got,
And yet they say he talks in great men's bow'rs?
A cage (gilded perchance) is all his lot.
Who off his tongue the liquor gladly pours
A good fool called with pain perhaps may be,
But e'en for that shall suffer mighty lours.
Let swan's example*sicker serve for thee,
Who once all birds in sweetly singing passed,
But now to silence turned his minstrelsy.
For he would sing, but others were defaced:
The peacock's pride, the pie's pilled flattery,
Cormorant's glut, kite's spoil, kingfisher's waste,
The falcon's fierceness, sparrow's lechery,
The cuckoo's shame, the goose's good intent,
E'en turtle touched he with hypocrisy.
And worse of other more; till by assent
Of all the birds, but namely those were grieved,
Of fowls there called was a parliament.
There was the swan of dignity deprived,
And statute made he never should have voice,
Since when, I think, he hath in silence lived.
I warn thee therefore (since thou mayst have choice)
Let not thy tongue become a fiery match,
No sword so bites as that ill tool annoys.
Let our unpartial eyes a little watch
Our own demean, and soon we wonder shall
That, hunting faults, ourselves we did not catch.
Into our minds let us a little fall,
And we shall find more spots than leopard's skin.
Then who makes us such judges over all?
But farewell now, thy fault is no great sin,
Come, come, my curs, 'tis late, I will go in.

And away with his dogs straight he went, as if he would be sure to have the last word, all the assembly laughing at the lustiness of the old fellow, who departed muttering to himself he had seen more in his days than twenty of them. But as he went out, Dorus seeing a lute lying under the princess Pamela's feet, glad to have such an errand to approach her, he came, but came with a dismayed grace, all his blood stirred betwixt fear and desire; and playing upon it with such sweetness as everybody wondered to see such skill in a shepherd, he sang unto it with a sorrowing voice these elegiac verses:

- - - - - ∪ ∪ - ∪ ∪ - ∪ ∪ - -

- - - ∪ ∪ - - ∪ ∪ - ∪ ∪ -

Dorus. Fortune, Nature, Love, long have contended about me,
    Which should most miseries cast on a worm that I am.
Fortune thus gan say: 'Misery and misfortune is all one,
    And of misfortune, Fortune hath only the gift.
With strong foes on land, on seas with contrary tempests,
    Still do I cross this wretch, what so he taketh in hand.'
'Tush, tush', said Nature, 'this is all but a trifle, a man's self
    Gives haps or mishaps, e'en as he ord'reth his heart.
But so his humour I frame, in a mould of choler adusted,*
    That the delights of life shall be to him dolorous.'
Love smiled, and thus said: 'Want joined to desire is unhappy.
    But if he naught do desire, what can Heraclitus ail?
None but I works by desire; by desire have I kindled in his soul
    Infernal agonies unto a beauty divine,
Where thou, poor Nature, left'st all thy due glory to Fortune.
    Her virtue is sovereign, Fortune a vassal of hers.'
Nature abashed went back; Fortune blushed, yet she replied thus:
    'And e'en in that love shall I reserve him a spite.'
Thus, thus, alas! woeful in nature, unhappy by fortune,
    But most wretched I am now love awakes my desire.

Nota*

The rules observed in these English measured verses be these:

Consonant before consonant always long, except a mute and a liquid (*as rĕfrain*), such indifferent.

Single consonants commonly short, but such as have a double sound (as *lăck*, *wĭll*, *tĭll*) or such as the vowel before doth produce long (as *hāte*, *debāte*).

Vowel before vowel or diphthong before vowel always short, except such an exclamation as *ōh*; else the diphthongs always long and the single vowels short.

Because our tongue being full of consonants and monosyllables, the vowel slides away quicklier than in Greek or Latin, which be full of vowels and long words. Yet are such vowels long as the pronunciation makes long (as *glōry*, *lādy*), and such like as seem to have a diphthong sound (as *shōw*, *blōw*, *dīe*, *hīgh*).

Elisions, when one vowel meets with another, used indifferently as the advantage of the verse best serves; for so in our ordinary speech we do (for as well we say *thou art* as *th'art*), and like scope doth Petrarch take to himself sometimes to use apostrophe, sometimes not.

For the words derived out of Latin and other languages, they are measured as they are denizened in English and not as before they came over sea (for we say not *fortūnate* though the Latin say *fortūna*, nor *usūry* but *ūsury* in the first); so our language hath a special gift in altering them and making them our own.

Some words especially short.

Particles used now long, now short (as *bŭt*, *ŏr*, *nŏr*, *ŏn*, *tŏ*).

Some words, as they have diverse pronunciations, to be written diversely, (as some say *thōugh*, some pronounce it *thŏ*).

As for *wĕe*, *thĕe*, *shĕe*, though they may seem to be a double vowel by the wrong orthography, be here short, being indeed no other than the Greek iota; and the like of our *o*, which some write double in this word *dŏo*.

Dorus, when he had sung this, having had all the while a free beholding of the fair Pamela (who could well have spared such honour, and defended the assault he gave unto her face with bringing a fair stain of shamefastness unto it), let fall his arms and remained so fastened in his thoughts as if Pamela had grafted him there to grow in continual imagination. But Cleophila espying it, and fearing he should too much forget himself, she came to him and took out of his hand the lute; and laying fast hold of Philoclea's face with her eyes, she sang these sapphics,*speaking as it were to her own hope:

    ‿ − − − − ‿ ‿ − ‿ − ‿

    ‿ − − − − ‿ ‿ − ‿ − −

    − ‿ ‿ − − ‿ ‿ − ‿ − ‿

        − ‿ ‿ − −

Cleophila.   If mine eyes can speak to do hearty errand,
            Or mine eyes' language she do hap to judge of,
            So that eyes' message be of her received,
                Hope, we do live yet.

But if eyes fail then, when I most do need them,
Or if eyes' language be not unto her known,
So that eyes' message do return rejected,
            Hope, we do both die.

Yet dying, and dead, do we sing her honour;
So become our tombs monuments of her praise;
So becomes our loss the triumph of her gain;
            Hers be the glory.

If the senseless spheres do yet hold a music,
If the swan's sweet voice be not heard, but at death,
If the mute timber when it hath the life lost,
            Yieldeth a lute's tune,

Are then human minds privileged so meanly
As that hateful death can abridge them of power
With the voice of truth to record to all worlds
            That we be her spoils?

Thus not ending, ends the due praise of her praise;
Fleshly veil consumes, but a soul hath his life,
Which is held in love; love it is that hath joined
            Life to this our soul.

But if eyes can speak to do hearty errand,
Or mine eyes' language she do hap to judge of,
So that eyes' message be of her received,
            Hope we do live yet.

Great was the pleasure of Basilius, and greater would have been
Gynecia's but that she found too well it was intended to her
daughter. As for Philoclea, she was sweetly ravished withal; when
Dorus, desiring in a secret manner to speak so of their cases as per-
chance the parties intended might take some light of it, making low
reverence to Cleophila, he began this provoking song in hexameter
verse unto her. Whereunto she, soon finding whither his words were
directed (in like tune and like verse), answered as followeth:

Dorus   Cleophila

Dorus. Lady, reserved by the heav'ns to do pastors' company honour,
      Joining your sweet voice to the rural muse of a desert,
      Here you fully do find this strange operation of love,
      How to the woods love runs as well as rides to the palace,

Neither he bears reverence to a prince nor pity to beggar,
But (like a point in midst of a circle) is still of a nearness,
All to a lesson he draws, nor hills nor caves can avoid him.

Cleophila.   Worthy shepherd, by my song to myself all favour is
  happened,
That to the sacred muse my annoys somewhat be revealed,
Sacred muse, who in one contains what nine do in all them.
But O, happy be you which safe from fiery reflection
Of Phoebus' violence in shade of stately cypress tree,
Or pleasant myrtle, may teach th'unfortunate Echo
In these woods to resound the renowned name of a goddess.
Happy be you that may to the saint, your only Idea
(Although simply attired), your manly affection utter.
Happy be those mishaps which, justly proportion holding,
Give right sound to the ears, and enter aright to the judgement;
But wretched be the souls which, veiled in a contrary subject,
How much more we do love, so the less our loves be believed.
What skill serveth a sore of a wrong infirmity judged?
What can justice avail to a man that tells not his own case?
You, though fears do abash, in you still possible hopes be:
Nature against we do seem to rebel, seem fools in a vain suit.
But so unheard, condemned, kept thence we do seek to abide in,
Self-lost and wand'ring, banished that place we do come from,
What mean is there, alas, we can hope our loss to recover?
What place is there left we may hope our woes to recomfort?
Unto the heav'ns? our wings be too short, th'earth thinks us a
  burden;
Air, we do still with sighs increase; to the fire? we do want none.
And yet his outward heat our tears would quench, but an inward
Fire no liquor can cool: Neptune's seat would be dried up there.
Happy shepherd, with thanks to the gods, still think to be thankful,
That to thy advancement their wisdoms have thee abased.

Dorus. Unto the gods with a thankful heart all thanks I do render,
That to my advancement their wisdoms have me abased.
But yet, alas! O but yet, alas! our haps be but hard haps,
Which must frame contempt to the fittest purchase of honour.
Well may a pastor plain, but alas his plaints be not esteemed.
Silly shepherd's poor pipe, when his harsh sound testifies our
  woes,

Into the fair looker-on, pastime, not passion, enters.
And to the woods or brooks, who do make such dreary recital
What be the pangs they bear, and whence those pangs be derived,
Pleased to receive that name by rebounding answer of Echo,
And hope thereby to ease their inward horrible anguish,
Then shall those things ease their inward horrible anguish
When trees dance to the pipe, and swift streams stay by the music,
Or when an echo begins unmoved to sing them a love song.
Say then what vantage do we get by the trade of a pastor?
(Since no estates be so base, but love vouchsafeth his arrow,
Since no refuge doth serve from wounds we do carry about us,
Since outward pleasures be but halting helps to decayed souls)
Save that daily we may discern what fire we do burn in.
Far more happy be you, whose greatness gets a free access,
Whose fair bodily gifts are framed most lovely to each eye.
Virtue you have, of virtue you have left proofs to the whole world,
And virtue is grateful with beauty and richess adorned,
Neither doubt you a whit, time will your passion utter.
Hardly remains fire hid where skill is bent to the hiding,
But in a mind that would his flames should not be repressed,
Nature worketh enough with a small help for the revealing.
Give therefore to the muse great praise in whose very likeness
You do approach to the fruit your only desires be to gather.

Cleophila. First shall fertile grounds not yield increase of a good seed;
   First the rivers shall cease to repay their floods to the ocean;
   First may a trusty greyhound transform himself to a tiger;
   First shall virtue be vice, and beauty be counted a blemish,
   Ere that I leave with song of praise her praise to solemnize,
   Her praise, whence to the world all praise had his only beginning:
   But yet well I do find each man most wise in his own case.
   None can speak of a wound with skill, if he have not a wound felt.*
   Great to thee my estate seems, thy estate is blest by my judgement:
   And yet neither of us great or blest deemeth his own self.
   For yet (weigh this, alas!) great is not great to a greater.
   What judge you doth a hillock show by the lofty Olympus?
   Such this small greatness doth seem compared to the greatest.
   When cedars to the ground be oppressed by the weight of an emmet,

Or when a rich ruby's just price be the worth of a walnut,
Or to the sun for wonders seem small sparks of a candle:
Then by my high cedar, rich ruby, and only shining sun,
Virtue, richess, beauties of mine shall great be reputed.
O no, no, hardy shepherd, worth can never enter a title,
Where proofs justly do teach, thus matched, such worth to be
    naught worth.
Let not a puppet abuse thy sprite, kings' crowns do not help them
From the cruel headache, nor shoes of gold do the gout heal,
And precious couches full oft are shaked with a fever.
If then a bodily evil in a bodily gloss be not hidden,
Shall such morning dews be an ease to the heat of a love's fire?

Dorus. O glitt'ring miseries of man, if this be the fortune
Of those fortune lulls, so small rest rests in a kingdom.
What marvel though a prince transform himself to a pastor?
Come from marble bowers, many times the gay harbour of anguish,
Unto a silly cabin, though weak, yet stronger against woes.
Now by thy words I begin, most famous lady, to gather
Comfort into my soul. I do find, I do find, what a blessing
Is chanced to my life, that from such muddy abundance
Of carking agonies (to estates which still be adherent)
Destiny keeps me aloof. For if all thy estate to thy virtue
Joined, by thy beauty adorned, be no means these griefs to
    abolish;
If neither by that help, thou canst climb up to thy fancy,
Nor yet, fancy so dressed, do receive more plausible hearing;
Then do I think, indeed, that better it is to be private
In sorrow's torments than, tied to the pomps of a palace,
Nurse inward maladies, which have not scope to be breathed out,
But perforce digest all bitter juices of horror
In silence, from a man's own self with company robbed.
Better yet do I live, that though by my thoughts I be plunged
Into my life's bondage, yet may disburden a passion
(Oppressed with ruinous conceits) by the help of an outcry:
Not limited to a whisp'ring note, the lament of a courtier,
But sometimes to the woods, sometimes to the heavens, do decipher,
With bold clamour unheard, unmarked, what I seek, what I suffer:
And when I meet these trees,*in the earth's fair livery clothed,
Ease I do feel (such ease as falls to one wholly diseased)

For that I find in them part of my estate represented.

A   B   A Victory
Laurel shows what I seek, by the myrrh is showed how I seek it,   B Lamenta-
                                                                                            tion
C   C Quietness
Olive paints me the peace that I must aspire to by conquest: D Love
D   E   E Refusal
Myrtle makes my request, my request is crowned with a willow.
F   F Death
Cypress promiseth help, but a help where comes no recomfort.

Sweet juniper saith this, though I burn, yet I burn in a sweet fire.

Yew doth make me bethink what kind of bow the boy holdeth

Which shoots strongly without any noise and deadly without
    smart.

Fir trees great and green, fixed on a high hill but a barren,

Like to my noble thoughts, still new, well placed, to me fruitless.

Fig that yields most pleasant fruit, his shadow is hurtful,

Thus be her gifts most sweet, thus more danger to be near her,

But in a palm when I mark how he doth rise under a burden,

And may I not (say I then) get up though griefs be so weighty?

Pine is a mast to a ship, to my ship shall hope for a mast serve?

Pine is high, hope is as high; sharp-leaved, sharp yet be my hope's
    buds.

Elm embraced by a vine, embracing fancy reviveth.

Poplar changeth his hue from a rising sun to a setting:

Thus to my sun do I yield, such looks her beams do afford me.

Old aged oak cut down, of new works serves to the building:

So my desires, by my fear cut down, be the frames of her honour.

Ash makes spears which shields do resist, her force no repulse takes:

Palms do rejoice to be joined by the match of a male to a female,

And shall sensive things be so senseless as to resist sense?

Thus be my thoughts dispersed, thus thinking nurseth a thinking,

Thus both trees and each thing else be the books of a fancy.

But to the cedar, queen of woods, when I lift my beteared eyes,

Then do I shape to myself that form which reigns so within me,

And think there she do dwell and hear what plaints I do utter:

When that noble top doth nod, I believe she salutes me;

When by the wind it maketh a noise, I do think she doth answer.

Then kneeling to the ground, oft thus do I speak to that image:

'Only jewel, O only jewel, which only deservest

That men's hearts be thy seat and endless fame be thy servant,

O descend for a while from this great height to behold me,

But naught else do behold (else is naught worth the beholding)
Save what a work by thyself is wrought: and since I am altered
Thus by thy work, disdain not that which is by thyself done.
In mean caves oft treasure abides, to an hostry a king comes.
And so behind foul clouds full oft fair stars do lie hidden.'

Cleophila. Hardy shepherd, such as thy merits, such may be her insight
Justly to grant thy reward, such envy I bear to thy fortune.
But to myself what wish can I make for a salve to my sorrows,
Whom both nature seems to debar from means to be helped,
And if a mean were found, fortune th'whole course of it hinders.
Thus plagued how can I frame to my sore any hope of amendment?
Whence may I show to my mind any light of a possible escape?
Bound, and bound by so noble bands as loath to be unbound,
Gaoler I am to myself, prison and prisoner to mine own self.
Yet be my hopes thus placed, here fixed lives my recomfort,
That that dear diamond, where wisdom holdeth a sure seat,
Whose force had such force so to transform, nay to reform me,
Will at length perceive these flames by her beams to be kindled,
And will pity the wound festered so strangely within me.
O be it so, grant such an event, O gods, that event give.
And for a sure sacrifice I do daily oblation offer
Of my own heart, where thoughts be the temple, sight is an altar.
But cease, worthy shepherd, now cease we to weary the hearers
With moanful melodies, for enough our griefs be revealed,
If by the parties meant our meanings rightly be marked,
And sorrows do require some respite unto the senses.

What exclaiming praises Basilius gave first to Cleophila's song, and now to this eclogue, any man may guess that knows love is better than a pair of spectacles to make everything seem greater which is seen through it; and then is it never tongue-tied where fit commendation (whereof womankind is so lickerous) is offered unto it. But the wasting of the torches served as a watch unto them to make them see the time's waste. And therefore the duke, though unwilling, rase from his seat (which he thought excellently settled of the one side), and considering Cleophila's late hurt, persuaded her to take that far spent night's rest. And so of all sides they went to recommend themselves to the elder brother of Death.

Here end the first eclogues of the
Countess of Pembroke's Arcadia.

THE SECOND BOOK OR ACT

In these pastoral pastimes a great number of days were sent to follow their flying predecessors, while the cup of poison, which was deeply tasted of all this noble company, had left no sinew of theirs without mortally searching into it; yet never manifesting his venomous work till once that, having drawn out the evening to his longest line, no sooner had the night given place to the breaking out of the morning's light and the sun bestowed his beams upon the tops of the mountains but that the woeful Gynecia (to whom rest was no ease) had left her loathed lodging and gotten herself into the solitary places those deserts were full of, going up and down with such unquiet motions as the grieved and hopeless mind is wont to bring forth. There appeared unto the eyes of her judgement the evils she was like to run into, with ugly infamy waiting upon them; she saw the terrors of her own conscience; she was witness of her long-exercised virtue, which made this vice the fuller of deformity. The uttermost of the good she could aspire unto was but a fountain of danger; and the least of her dangers was a mortal wound to her vexed spirits; and lastly, no small part of her evils was that she was wise to see her evils. Insomuch that, having a great while cast her countenance ghastly about her, as if she had called all the powers of the whole world to be witness of her wretched estate, at length casting up her watery eyes to heaven: 'O sun,' said she, 'whose unspotted light directs the steps of mortal mankind, art thou not ashamed to impart the clearness of thy presence to such an over-thrown worm as I am? O you heavens, which continually keep the course allotted unto you, can none of your influences prevail so much upon the miserable Gynecia as to make her preserve a course so long embraced by her? O deserts, deserts, how fit a guest am I for you, since my heart is fuller of wild ravenous beasts than ever you were! O virtue, how well I see thou wert never but a vain name and no essential thing, which hast thus left thy professed servant when she had most need of thy lovely presence! O imperfect proportion of reason, which can too much foresee, and so little prevent! Alas, alas,' said she, 'if there were but one hope for all my pains, or but one excuse for all my faultiness! But, wretch that I am, my torment is beyond all succour, and my ill-deserving doth exceed my ill fortune. For nothing else did my husband take this strange resolution to live so solitary, for nothing else have the winds delivered this strange guest to my country, for nothing else have the destinies reserved my life to this time, but that only I, most wretched I, should become a plague to myself, and a shame to womankind. Yet if my desire, how unjust so ever it be, might take effect, though a thousand deaths followed it, and every death were followed with a thousand shames, yet should not my sepulchre receive me without some contentment. But alas, sure I am not that Cleophila is such as can answer my love. And if she be, how can I think she will, since this disguising must needs come for some foretaken conceit? And either way, wretched Gynecia, where canst thou find any small ground-plot for hope to dwell upon? No, no, it is Philoclea his heart is set upon (if he be a he); it is my daughter which I have borne to supplant me. But if it be so, the life I have given thee, ungrateful Philoclea, I will sooner with these hands bereave thee of than my birth shall glory she hath bereaved me of my desires. In shame there is no comfort but to be beyond all bounds of shame.'

Having spoken this, she began to make a piteous war with her fair hair when she might hear not far from her an extremely doleful voice, but so suppressed with a kind of whispering note that she could not conceive the words distinctly. But as a lamentable tune is the sweetest music to a woeful mind, she drew thither near away in hope to find some companion of her misery. And as she paced on, she was stopped with a number of trees so thickly placed together that she was afraid she should with rushing through stop the speech of the lamentable party, which she was so desirous to understand. And therefore, sitting her down as softly as she could (for she was now in distance to hear), she might first perceive a lute, excellently well played upon, and then the same doleful voice accompanying it with these few verses:

In vain, mine eyes, you labour to amend
    With flowing tears your fault of hasty sight;
Since to my heart her shape you so did send
    That her I see, though you did lose your light.

In vain, my heart, now you with sight are burned,
    With sighs you seek to cool your hot desire;
Since sighs (into mine inward furnace turned)
    For bellows serve to kindle more the fire.

> Reason in vain (now you have lost my heart)
>   My head you seek, as to your strongest fort;
> Since there mine eyes have played so false a part
>   That to your strength your foes have sure resort.
>   And since in vain I find were all my strife,
>   To this strange death I vainly yield my life.

The ending of the song served but for a beginning of new plaints; as if the mind, oppressed with too heavy a burden of cares, was fain to discharge itself in all manners, and as it were paint out the hideousness of the pain in all sorts of colours. For the woeful person, as if the lute had ill joined to the voice, threw it down to the ground with suchlike words: 'Alas, poor lute, how much thou art deceived to think that in my miseries thou couldst ease my woes, as in my careless times thou wert wont to please my fancies! The time is changed, my lute, the time is changed; and no more did my joyful mind then receive everything to a joyful consideration than my careful mind now makes each thing taste like the bitter juice of care. The evil is inward, my lute, the evil is inward; which all thou dost doth serve but to make me think more freely of; and the more I think, the more cause I find of thinking, but less of hoping. The discord of my thoughts, my lute, doth ill agree to the concord of thy sweet strings; therefore, be not ashamed to leave thy master, since he is not afraid to forsake himself.'

And thus much spoken, instead of a conclusion, was closed up with so hearty a groaning that Gynecia could not refrain to show herself, thinking such griefs could serve fitly for nothing but her own fortune. But as she came into the little arbour of this sorrowful music, her eyes met with the eyes of Cleophila (which was the party that thus had witnessed her sorrow), so that either of them remained confused with a sudden astonishment, Cleophila fearing lest she had heard some part of those sorrows which she had risen up that morning early of purpose to breathe out in secret to herself. But Gynecia a great while stood still, with a kind of dull amazement, looking steadfastly upon her. At length returning to some use of herself, she began to say to Cleophila that she was sorry she would venture herself to leave her rest, being not altogether healed of her hurt. But as if the opening of her mouth to Cleophila had opened some great flood-gap of sorrow, whereof her heart could not bear the violent issue, she sank to the ground with her hands over her face, crying vehemently: 'Cleophila, help me! O Cleophila, have pity of me!'

Cleophila ran to her, marvelling what sudden sickness had thus possessed her; and beginning to ask her the cause of her sorrow, and offering her service to be employed by her, Gynecia opening her eyes wildly upon her, pricked with the flames of love and the torments of her own conscience: 'O Cleophila, Cleophila,' said she, 'dost thou offer me physic which art my only poison, or wilt thou do me service which hast already brought me into eternal slavery?'

Cleophila yet more marvelling, and thinking some extreme pain did make her rave, 'Most excellent lady,' said she, 'you were best to retire yourself into your lodging that you the better may pass over this sudden fit.'

'Retire myself,' said Gynecia, 'if I had retired myself into myself when thou (to me unfortunate guest) camest to draw me from myself, blessed had I been, and no need had I had of thy counsel. But now, alas, I am forced to fly to thee for succour whom I accuse of all my hurt; and make thee judge of my cause who art the only author of my mischief.'

Cleophila, yet more astonished, 'Madam,' said she, 'whereof do you accuse me that I will not clear myself; or wherein may I stead you that you may not command me?'

'Alas,' answered Gynecia, 'what shall I say more? Take pity of me, O Cleophila, but not as Cleophila, and disguise not with me in words, as I know thou dost in apparel.'

Cleophila was stricken even dead with that word, finding herself discovered. But as she was amazedly thinking what to answer her, they might see old Basilius pass hard by them, without ever seeing them, complaining likewise of love very freshly, and ending his complaint with this song, love having renewed both his invention and voice:

Let not old age disgrace my high desire,
    O heav'nly soul in human shape contained.
Old wood inflamed doth yield the bravest fire,
    When younger doth in smoke his virtue spend.

Ne let white hairs (which on my face do grow)
    Seem to your eyes of a disgraceful hue;
Since whiteness doth present the sweetest show,
    Which makes all eyes do honour unto you.

Old age is wise and full of constant truth;
  Old age well stayed from ranging humour lives;
Old age hath known whatever was in youth;
  Old age o'ercome, the greater honour gives.
    And to old age since you yourself aspire,
    Let not old age disgrace my high desire.

Which being done, he looked very curiously upon himself, sometimes fetching a little skip, as if he had said his strength had not yet forsaken him. But Cleophila having in this time gotten some leisure to think for an answer, looking upon Gynecia as if she thought she did her some wrong, 'Madam,' said she, 'I am not acquainted with these words of disguising; neither is it the profession of an Amazon; neither are you a party with whom it is to be used. If my service may please you, employ it, so long as you do me no wrong in misjudging of me.'

'Alas, Cleophila,' said Gynecia, 'I perceive you know full little how piercing the eyes are of a true lover. There is no one beam of those thoughts you have planted in me but is able to discern a greater cloud than you do go in. Seek not to conceal yourself further from me, nor force not the passion of love into violent extremities!'

Now was Cleophila brought to an exigent, when the duke, turning his eye that way through the trees, perceived his wife and mistress together; so that, framing the most lovely countenance he could, he came straightway towards them, and at the first word, thanking his wife for having entertained Cleophila, desired her she would now return into the lodge because he had certain matters of state to impart to the lady Cleophila. The duchess, being nothing troubled with jealousy in that point, obeyed the duke's commandment, full of raging agonies, and determinately bent that, as she would seek all loving means to win Cleophila, so she would stir up terrible tragedies rather than fail of her intent.

But as soon as Basilius was rid of his wife's presence, falling down on his knees, 'O lady,' said he, 'which have only had the power to stir up again those flames which had so long lain dead in me, see in me the power of your beauty which can make old age come to ask counsel of youth, and a prince unconquered to become a slave to a stranger. And when you see that power of yours, love that at least in me, since it is yours, although of me you see nothing to be loved.'

'Worthy prince,' answered Cleophila, taking him up from his

kneeling, 'both your manner and your speech are so strange unto me as I know not how to answer it better than with silence.'

'If silence please you', said the duke, 'it shall never displease me, since my heart is wholly pledged to obey you. Otherwise, if you would vouchsafe mine ears such happiness as to hear you, they shall but convey your words to such a mind which is with the humblest degree of reverence to receive them.'

'I disdain not to speak to you, mighty prince,' said Cleophila, 'but I disdain to speak to any matter which may bring mine honour into question.'

And therewith, with a brave counterfeited scorn, she departed from the duke, leaving him not so sorry for this short answer as proud in himself that he had broken the matter. And thus did the duke, feeding his mind with these thoughts, pass great time in writing of verses, and making more of himself than he was wont to do; that with a little help he would have grown into a pretty kind of dotage.

But Cleophila, being rid of this loving, but little loved, company, 'Alas,' said she, 'poor Pyrocles, was ever one but I that had received wrong, and could blame nobody; that, having more than I desire, am still in want of that I would? Truly, Love, I must needs say thus much on thy behalf, thou hast employed my love there where all love is deserved; and for recompense hast sent me more love than ever I desired. Yet a child indeed thou showest thyself that thinkest to glut me with quantity, as though therein thou didst satisfy the heart another way dedicated. But what wilt thou do, Pyrocles? Which way canst thou find to rid thee of these intricate troubles? To her whom I would be known to, I live in darkness; and to her am revealed from whom I would be most secret. What shield shall I find against the doting love of Basilius and the violent passion of Gynecia? And if that be done, yet how am I the nearer to quench the fire that consumes me? Well, well, sweet Philoclea, my whole confidence must be builded in thy divine spirit, which cannot be ignorant of the cruel wound I have received by you.'

Thus did Cleophila wade betwixt small hopes and huge despairs, whilst in the mean time the sweet Philoclea found strange unwonted motions in herself. And yet the poor soul could neither discern what it was, nor whither the vehemency of it tended. She found a burning affection towards Cleophila; an unquiet desire to be with her; and yet she found that the very presence kindled the desire. And examining in herself the same desire, yet could she not know to what the desire inclined. Sometimes she would compare the love she bare to Cleophila with the natural goodwill she bare to her sister; but she perceived it had another kind of working. Sometimes she would wish Cleophila had been a man, and her brother; and yet, in truth, it was no brotherly love she desired of her. But thus, like a sweet mind not much traversed in the cumbers of these griefs, she would even yield to the burden, rather suffering sorrow to take a full possession than exercising any way her mind how to redress it.

Thus in this one lodge was lodged each sort of grievous passions, while in the other the worthy Dorus was no less tormented, even with the extremest anguish that love at any time can plague the mind withal. He omitted no occasion whereby he might make Pamela see how much extraordinary devotion he bare to her service, and daily withal strave to make himself seem more worthy in her sight; that desert being joined to affection might prevail something in the wise princess. But too well he found that a shepherd's either service or affection was but considered of as from a shepherd, and the liking limited to that proportion. For indeed Pamela, having had no small stirring of her mind towards him, as well for the goodliness of his shape as for the excellent trial of his courage, had notwithstanding, with a true-tempered virtue, sought all this while to overcome it; and a great mastery, although not without pain, she had wrought with herself. When Dorus saw of the one side that the highest point this service could bring him to should be but to be accounted a good servant, and of the other that, for the suspiciousness of Dametas and Miso, with his young mistress Mopsa, he could never get any piece of time to give Pamela to understand the estate either of himself or affection—for Dametas, according to the right constitution of a dull head, thought no better way to show himself wise than by suspecting everything in his way. Which suspicion Miso, for the shrewdness of her brain, and Mopsa, for a certain unlikely envy she had caught against Pamela's beauty, were very glad to execute. Insomuch that Dorus was ever kept off, and the fair Pamela restrained to a very unworthy servitude. Dorus, finding his service by this means lightly regarded, his affection despised, and himself unknown, was a great while like them that in the midst of their leap know not where to light. Which in doleful manner, he would oftentimes utter, and make those desert places of counsel in his miseries. But in the end (seeing that nothing is achieved before it be attempted, and that lying still doth never go forward), he resolved to take this mean for the manifesting of his mind—although it should have seemed to have been a way the more to have darkened it: he began to counterfeit the extremest love towards Mopsa that might be; and as for the love, so lively indeed it was in him (although to another subject) that little he needed to counterfeit any notable demonstration of it. He would busily employ himself about her, giving her daily some country tokens, and making store of love songs unto her. Whereby, as he wan Dametas's heart, who had before borne him a certain rude envy for the favour the duke had lately showed unto him, so likewise did the same make Pamela begin to have the more consideration of him —for indeed so falls it often in the excellent women that even that which they disdain to themselves yet like they not that others should win it from them. But the more she marked the expressing of Dorus's affection towards Mopsa, the more she thought she found such phrases applied to Mopsa as must needs argue either great ignorance or a second meaning in Dorus; and so to this scanning of him was she now content to fall, whom before she was resolved to banish from her thoughts. As one time among the rest, Mopsa being alone with Pamela, Dorus with a face full of cloudy fancies came suddenly unto them, and taking a harp sang this passioned song:

> Since so mine eyes are subject to your sight,
> That in your sight they fixed have my brain;
> Since so my heart is filled with that light,
> That only light doth all my life maintain.
>
> Since in sweet you all goods so richly reign,
> That where you are no wished good can want;
> Since so your living image lives in me,
> That in myself yourself true love doth plant;
> How can you him unworthy then decree,
> In whose chief part your worths implanted be?

The song being ended, which he had oftentimes broken off in the midst with grievous sighs which overtook every verse he sang, he let fall his harp from him, and casting his eye sometimes upon Mopsa, but settling his sight principally upon Pamela: 'And is it only the fortune, most beautiful Mopsa,' said he, 'of wretched Dorus that fortune must be the measure of his mind? Am I only he that, because

I am in misery, more misery must be laid upon me? Must that which should be cause of compassion become an argument of cruelty against me? Alas, excellent Mopsa, consider that a virtuous prince requires the life of his meanest subject, and the heavenly sun disdains not to give light to the smallest worm. O Mopsa, Mopsa, if my heart could be as manifest to you as it is uncomfortable to me, I doubt not the height of my thoughts should well countervail the lowness of my quality. Who hath not heard of the greatness of your estate? Who sees not that your estate is much excelled with that sweet uniting of all beauties which remaineth and dwelleth with you? Who knows not that all these are but ornaments of that divine spark within you which, being descended from heaven, could not elsewhere pick out so sweet a mansion? But if you will know what is the bond that ought to knit all these excellencies together, it is a kind mercifulness to such a one as is in soul devoted to those perfections.'

Mopsa (who already had had a certain smackering towards Dorus) stood all this while with her hand sometimes before her face, but most commonly with a certain special grace of her own, wagging her lips and grinning instead of smiling. But all the words he could get of her was (wrying her waist): 'In faith, you jest with me; you are a merry man indeed!'

But Pamela did not so much attend Mopsa's entertainment as she marked both the matter Dorus spake and the manner he used in uttering it. And she saw in them both a very unlikely proportion to mistress Mopsa, so that she was contented to urge a little further of him: 'Master Dorus,' said the fair Pamela, 'methinks you blame your fortune very wrongfully, since the fault is not in fortune but in you that cannot frame yourself to your fortune; and as wrongfully you do require Mopsa to so great a disparagement as to her father's servant, since she is not worthy to be loved that hath not some feeling of her own worthiness.'

Dorus stayed a good while after her words in hope she would have continued her speech, so great a delight he received in hearing her. But seeing her say no further, with a quaking all over his body, he thus answered her: 'Lady most worthy of all duty, how falls it out that you in whom all virtue shines will take the patronage of fortune, the only rebellious handmaid against virtue—especially since before your eyes you have a pitiful spectacle of her wickedness, a forlorn creature which must remain not such as I am but such as she makes me, since she must be the balance of worthiness or disparagement? Yet alas, if the condemned man may even at his death have leave to speak, let my mortal wound purchase thus much consideration, since the perfections are such in the party I love as the feeling of them cannot come into any unnoble heart. Shall that heart, which doth not only feel them but hath all the workings of his life placed in them, shall that heart, I say, lifted up to such a height, be counted base? O let not an excellent spirit do itself such wrong as to think where it is placed, embraced, and loved, there can be any unworthiness; since the weakest mist is not easilier driven away by the sun than that is chased away with so high thoughts.'

'I will not deny,' answered the gracious Pamela, 'but that the love you bear to Mopsa hath brought you to the consideration of her virtues, and the consideration may have made you the more virtuous, and so the more worthy. But even that, then, you must confess you have received of her, and so are rather gratefully to thank her than to press any further till you bring something of your own by which to claim it. And truly, Dorus, I must in Mopsa's behalf say thus much to you: that if her beauties have so overtaken you, it becometh a true love to have your heart more set upon her good than your own, and to bear a tenderer respect to her honour than your satisfaction.'

'Now, by my halidom, madam,' said Mopsa, throwing a great number of sheep's eyes*upon Dorus, 'you have even touched mine own mind to the quick, forsooth.'

Dorus, finding that the policy he had used had at leastwise procured thus much happiness unto him as that he might even in his lady's presence discover the sore which had deeply festered within him, and that she could better conceive his reasons applied to Mopsa than she would have vouchsafed them whilst herself was a party, thought good to pursue on his good beginning using this fit occasion of Pamela's wit and Mopsa's ignorance. Therefore with an humble but piercing eye, looking upon Pamela as if he had rather be condemned by her mouth than highly exalted by the other, turning himself to Mopsa, but keeping his eye where it was, 'Fair Mopsa', said he, 'well do I find by the wise knitting together of your answer that any disputation I can use is as much too weak as I unworthy. I find my love shall be proved no love, without I leave to love, being too unfit a vessel in whom so high thoughts should be engraved. Yet, since the love I bear you hath so joined itself to the best part of my life, as the one cannot depart but that the other will follow, before I seek to obey you in making my last passage, let me know which is my unworthiness, either of mind, estate, or both.'

Mopsa was about to say 'in neither', for her heart did even quab with overmuch kindness, when Pamela, with a more favourable countenance than before, finding how apt he was to fall into despair, told him he might therein have answered himself, for besides that it was granted him that the inward feeling of Mopsa's perfections had greatly beautified his mind, there was none could deny but that his mind and body of themselves deserved great allowance. 'But Dorus', said she, 'you must so far be master of your love as to consider that since the judgement of the world stands upon matter of fortune, and that the sex of womankind of all other is most bound to have regardful eye to men's judgements, it is not for us to play the philosophers in seeking out your hidden virtues, since that which in a wise prince would be counted wisdom, in us will be taken for a light-grounded affection; so is not one thing one, done by divers persons.'

There is no man in a burning fever feels so great contentment in cold water greedily received (which, as soon as the drink ceaseth, the heat reneweth) as poor Dorus found his soul refreshed with her sweetly pronounced words, and newly and more violently again inflamed as soon as she had closed up her delightful speech with no less well graced silence. But remembering in himself that as well the soldier dies which stands still as he that gives the bravest onset, and seeing that to the making up of his fortune there wanted nothing so much as the making known of his estate, with a face well witnessing how deeply his soul was possessed, and with the most submissive behaviour that a thralled heart could express, even as if his words had been too thick for his mouth, at length spake to this purpose: 'Alas, most worthy princess,' said he, 'and do not then your own sweet words sufficiently testify that there was never man could have a juster action against filthy fortune than I, since all other things being granted me, her blindness is my only let? O heavenly gods, I would either she had such eyes as were able to discern my deserts, or I were blind not to see the daily cause of my misfortune! But yet,' said he, 'most honoured lady, if my miserable speeches have not already cloyed you, and that the very presence of such a wretch become not hateful in your eyes, let me reply thus much further against my mortal sentence by telling you a story which happened in this same country long since (for woes make the shortest time seem long), whereby you shall see that my estate is not so contemptible but that a prince hath been content to take the like upon him, and by that only hath aspired to enjoy a mighty princess.'

Pamela graciously hearkened, and he told his tale in this sort: 'In the country of Thessalia (alas, why name I that accursed country which brings forth nothing but matters for tragedies? But name it I must); in Thessalia, I say, there was—well may I say there was—a prince. No! no prince, whom bondage wholly possessed, but yet accounted a prince, and named Musidorus. O Musidorus! Musidorus! But to what serve exclamations where there are no ears to receive the sound? This Musidorus, being yet in the tenderest age, his aged father paid up to nature her last duties, leaving his child to the faith of friends and the proof of time. Death gave him not such pangs as the foresightful care he had of his silly successor. And yet, if in his foresight he could have seen so much, happy was that good prince in his timely departure which barred him from the knowledge of his son's miseries, which his knowledge could neither have prevented nor relieved. The young Musidorus being thus (as for the first pledge of the destinies' goodwill) deprived of his principal stay, was yet for some years after (as if the stars would breathe themselves for a greater mischief) lulled up in as much good luck as the heedful love of his doleful mother and the flourishing estate of his country could breed unto him. But when the time now came that misery seemed to be ripe for him, because he had age to know misery, I think there was a conspiracy in all heavenly and earthly things to frame fit occasions to lead him unto it. His people (to whom all foreign matters in foretime were odious) began now to wish in their beloved prince experience by travel. His dear mother (whose eyes were held open only with the joy of looking upon him) did now dispense with the comfort of her widowed life, desiring the same her subjects did, for the increase of her son's worthiness. And hereto did Musidorus's own virtue (see how virtue can be a minister to mischief) sufficiently provoke him. For, indeed, thus much I must say for him (although the likeness of our mishaps makes me presume to pattern myself unto him) that well doing was at that time his scope, from which no faint pleasures could withhold him. But the present occasion (which did knit all these together) was his uncle, the king of Macedon, who (having lately before gotten such victories as were beyond expectation) did at this time send both for the prince, his son (brought up together, to avoid the wars, with Musidorus) and for Musidorus himself, that his joy might be the more full having such partakers of it. But, alas, to what a sea of miseries my plaintful tongue doth lead me!'

And thus out of breath, rather with that he thought than with that he said, Dorus stayed his speech till Pamela showing by countenance that such was her pleasure, he thus continued it: 'These two young princes, to satisfy the king, took their way by sea towards Byzantium, where at that time his court was. But when the conspired heavens had gotten this subject of their wrath upon so fit a place as the sea was, they straight began to breathe out in boisterous winds some part of their malice against him. So that, with the loss of all his navies, he only with the prince, his cousin, were cast aland, far off from the place whither their desires would have guided them. O cruel winds in your unconsiderate rages, why either began you this fury, or why did you not end it in his end? But your cruelty was such as you would spare his life for many deathful torments. To tell you what pitiful mishaps fell to the young prince of Macedon, his cousin, I should too much fill your ears with strange horrors; neither will I stay upon those laboursome adventures, nor loathsome misadventures, to which and through which his fortune and courage conducted him. My speech hasteth itself to come to the full point of all Musidorus's infortunes. For as we find the most pestilent diseases do gather into themselves all the infirmities with which the body before was annoyed, so did his last misery embrace in the extremity of itself all his former mischiefs. Arcadia, Arcadia was the place prepared to be the stage of his endless overthrow; Arcadia was (alas, well might I say it is) the charmed circle where all his spirits should for ever be enchanted. For here and nowhere else did his infected eyes make his mind know what power heavenly beauty hath to throw it down to hellish agonies. Here, here did he see the Arcadian duke's eldest daughter; in whom he forthwith placed so all his hopes of joy and joyful parts of his heart, that he left in himself nothing but a maze of longing and a dungeon of sorrow. But alas, what can saying make them believe whom seeing cannot persuade? Those pains must be felt before they be understood; no outward utterance can command a conceit. Such was as then the state of the duke as it was no time by direct means to seek her; and such was the state of his captived will as he could delay no time of seeking her. In this entangled case, he clothed himself in a shepherd's weed, that under the baseness of that form he might at least have free access to feed his eyes with that which should at length eat up his heart. In which doing, thus much without doubt he hath manifested: that this estate is not always to be rejected, since under that veil there may be hidden things to be esteemed. And that if he might, with taking on a shepherd's look, cast up his eyes to the fairest princess nature in that time created, the like, nay the same, desire of mine need no more to be disdained or held for disgraceful. But now, alas, mine eyes wax dim, my tongue begins to falter, and my heart to want force to help either, with the feeling remembrance I have in what heap of miseries the caitiff prince lay at this time buried. Pardon therefore, most excellent princess, if I cut off the course of my dolorous tale, since (if I be understood) I have said enough for the defence of my baseness. And for that which after might befall to that pattern of ill fortune, the matters are too monstrous for my capacity. His hateful destinies must best declare their own workmanship.'

He ended thus his speech. But withal began to renew his accustomed plaints and humble intercessions to Mopsa, who (having no great battle in her spirit) was almost brought asleep with the sweet delivery of his lamentations. But Pamela (whom liking had made willing to conceive, and natural wisdom able to judge) let no word slip without his due pondering; even love began to revive his flames, which the opinion she had of his meanness had before covered in her. She well found he meant the tale by himself, and that he did under that covert manner make her know the great nobleness of his birth. But no music could with righter accords possess her senses than every passion he expressed had his mutual working in her. Full well she found the lively image of a vehement desire in herself, which ever is apt to receive belief, but hard to ground belief. For as desire is glad to embrace the first show of hope, so by the same nature is desire desirous of a perfect assurance. She did immediately catch hold of his signifying himself to be a prince, and did glad her heart with having a reasonable ground to build her love upon. But straight the longing for assurance made suspicions arise and say unto herself, 'Pamela, take heed! The sinews of wisdom is to be hard of belief. Who dare place his heart in so great places dare frame his head to as great feignings?' Dorus, that found his speeches had given alarum to her imaginations, to hold her the longer in them and bring her to a dull yielding-over her forces (as the nature of music is to do), he took up his harp and sang these few verses:

> My sheep are thoughts, which I both guide and serve:
> Their pasture is fair hills of fruitless love:
> On barren sweets they feed, and feeding starve:
> I wail their lot, but will not other prove.
> My sheephook is wanhope which all upholds:
> My weeds, desire, cut out in endless folds.
>> What wool my sheep shall bear, while thus they live,
>> In you it is, you must the judgement give.

The music added to the tale, and both fitted to such motions in her as now began again to be awaked, did steal out of the fair eyes of Pamela some drops of tears; although with great constancy she would fain have overmastered at least the show of any such weakness. At length, with a sigh come up even to her mouth and there stopped: 'But lord,' said she, 'if such were the prince's burning affection, what could he hope by living here, if it were not to grow purer in the fire like a salamander?'

'And even so too,' answered Dorus, 'but withal perchance (for what cannot love hope?) he hoped to carry away the fire with him.'

'With him,' said she, 'now what could induce a princess to go away with a shepherd?'

'Principally,' said he, 'the virtuous gratefulness for his affection; then, knowing him to be a prince; and lastly, seeing herself in unworthy bondage.'

Pamela found in her conscience such an accusing of secret consent thereto that she thought it safest way to divert the speech, lest in parley the castle might be given up. And therefore, with a gracious closing up of her countenance towards Dorus, she willed Mopsa to take good heed to herself, for her shepherd could speak well. 'But truly Mopsa,' said she, 'if he can prove himself such as he saith (I mean the honest shepherd Menalcas's brother and heir), I know no reason why a better than you need think scorn of his affectionate suit.'

Mopsa did not love comparisons, but yet, being far spent towards Dorus, she answered Pamela that, for all his quaint speeches, she would keep her honesty close enough. And that, as for the high way of matrimony, she would go never a furlong further till my master, her father, did speak the whole word himself. But ever and anon turning her muzzle towards Dorus, she threw such a prospect upon him as might well have given a surfeit to any light lover's stomach. But Dorus, full of inward joy that he had wrought his matters to such a towardness, took out of his bag a very rich jewel, kept among other of his precious things, which because of the device he thought fittest to give. It was an altar of gold, very full of the most esteemed stones, dedicated to Pollux who, because he was made a god for his brother Castor's virtue, all the honour men did to him seemed to have their final intent to the greater god Castor; about it was written in Roman words, *Sic vos non vobis*.* And kneeling down to the fair princess Pamela, he desired her she would in his behalf bestow it upon the cruel-hearted Mopsa who was as then benumbed with joy, seeing so fair a present. Pamela gave it to her, having received into her own mind a great testimony of the giver's worthiness.

But alas, sweet Philoclea, how hath my pen forgotten thee, since to thy memory principally*all this long matter is intended. Pardon the slackness to come to those woes which thou didst cause in others and feel in thyself. The sweet-minded Philoclea was in their degree of well doing to whom the not knowing of evil serveth for a ground of virtue, and hold their inward powers in better temper with an unspotted simplicity than many who rather cunningly seek to know what goodness is than willingly take into themselves the following of it. True it is that that sweet and simple breath of heavenly goodness is the easier to fall because it hath not passed through the worldly wickedness, nor feelingly found the evil that evil carrieth with it. As now the amiable Philoclea, whose eyes and senses had received nothing but according as the natural course of each thing required, whose tender youth had obediently lived under her parents' behests without the framing (out of her own will) the forechoosing of anything, was suddenly (poor soul) surprised before she was aware that any matter laid hold of her. Neither did she consider that the least gap a sea wins is enough without gainstriving industry to overflow a whole country; but finding a mountain of burning desire to have overwhelmed her heart, and that the fruits thereof, having new won the place, began to manifest themselves with horrible terrors of danger, dishonour and despair, she did suffer her sweet spirits to languish under the heavy weight, thinking it impossible to resist, as she found it deadly to yield. Thus ignorant of her own disease, although (full well) she found herself diseased, her greatest pleasure was to put herself into some lonely place where she might freely feed the humour that did tyrannize within her: as one night that, the moon being full did show herself in her most perfect beauty, the unmatched Philoclea secretly stale from her parents (whose eyes were now so bent upon another subject that the easier she might get her desired advantage); and going with uncertain paces to a little wood, where many times before she had delighted to walk, her rolling eye lighted upon a tuft of trees, so closely set together as with the shade the moon gave through it, it bred a fearful devotion to look upon it. But well did she remember the place, for there had she often defended her face from the sun's rage, there had she enjoyed herself often while she was mistress of herself and had no other thoughts but such as might arise out of quiet senses. But the principal cause that made her remember it was a fair white marble stone that should seem had been dedicated in ancient time to the sylvan gods; which she finding there a few days before Cleophila's coming, had written these words upon it as a testimony of her mind against the suspicion she thought she lived in. The writing was this:

> Ye living powers enclosed in stately shrine
> Of growing trees, ye rural gods that wield
> Your sceptres here, if to your ears divine
> A voice may come which troubled soul doth yield,
>   This vow receive, this vow O gods maintain:
>   My virgin life no spotted thought shall stain.
>
> Thou purest stone, whose pureness doth present
> My purest mind; whose temper hard doth show
> My tempered heart; by thee my promise sent
> Unto myself let after-livers know.
>   No fancy mine, nor others' wrong suspect
>   Make me, O virtuous Shame, thy laws neglect.
>
> O Chastity, the chief of heav'nly lights,
> Which makes us most immortal shape to wear,
> Hold thou my heart, establish thou my sprites;
> To only thee my constant course I bear.
>   Till spotless soul unto thy bosom fly,
>   Such life to lead, such death I vow to die.

But now that her memory served as an accuser of her change, and that her own hand-writing was there to bear testimony of her fall, she went in among the few trees, so closed in the top together as they seemed a little chapel; and there might she by the moonlight perceive the goodly stone which served as an altar in that woody devotion. But neither the light was enough to read the words, and the ink was already foreworn and in many places blotted; which as she perceived, 'Alas,' said she, 'fair marble, which never receivedst spot but by my writing, well do these blots become a blotted writer; but pardon her which did not dissemble then, although she have changed since. Enjoy, and spare not, the glory of thy nature which can so constantly bear the marks of my inconstancy!' And herewith hiding her eyes awhile with her soft hands, there came into her head certain verses which, if the light had suffered, she would fain presently have adjoined as a retractation to the other. The verses were to this effect:

> My words, in hope to blaze my steadfast mind,
> This marble chose, as of like temper known:
> But lo, my words defaced, my fancies blind,
> Blots to the stone, shame to myself I find;
>   And witness am, how ill agree in one,
>   A woman's hand with constant marble stone.
>
> My words full weak, the marble full of might;
> My words in store, the marble all alone;
> My words black ink, the marble kindly white;
> My words unseen, the marble still in sight,
>   May witness bear, how ill agree in one,
>   A woman's hand with constant marble stone.

But seeing she could not see so perfectly as to join this recantation to the former vow, laying all her fair length under one of the trees, for a while the poor soul did nothing but turn up and down and hide her face, as if she had hoped to turn away the fancy that mastered her, or could have hidden herself from her own thoughts. At length with a whispering voice to herself, 'O me, unfortunate wretch,' said she, 'what poisonous heats be these that thus possess me? How hath the sight of this strange guest invaded my soul? Alas, what entrance found this desire; or what strength had it thus to conquer me?' Then looking to the stars, which had perfectly as then beautified the clear sky, 'My parents', said she, 'have told me that in these fair heavenly bodies there are great hidden deities which have their working in the ebbing and flowing of our estates. If it be so, then, O ye stars, judge rightly of me; and if I have willingly made myself a prey to fancy, or if by any idle lusts I framed my heart fit for such an impression, then let this plague daily increase in me till my name be made odious to womankind. But if extreme and unresistible violence have oppressed me, who will ever do any of you sacrifice, O ye stars, if you do not succour me—no, no, you cannot help me; my desire must needs be waited on with shame, and my attempt with danger. And yet are these but childish objections. It is the impossibility that doth torment me; for unlawful desires are punished after the effect of enjoying, but impossible desires are plagued in the desire itself.' Then would she wish to herself (for even to herself she was ashamed to speak it out in words) that Cleophila might become a young transformed Caeneus.*'For', said she, 'if she were a man I might either obtain my desire, or have cause to hate for refusal'—besides the many duties Cleophila did to her assured her Cleophila might well want power, but not will, to please her. In this depth of her muses there passed a cloud betwixt her sight and the moon which took away the present beholding of it. 'O Diana,' said Philoclea, 'I would either the cloud that now hides the light of my virtue would as easily pass away as you will quickly overcome this let; or else that you were for ever thus darkened to serve for a better excuse of my outrageous folly.' In this diverse sort of strange discourses would she ravingly have remained, but that she perceived by the high climbing of the moon the night was far spent. And therefore, with stealing steps she returned to the lodge where, for all the lateness, she found her father and mother giving a tedious entertainment to Cleophila, oppressed with being loved almost as much as with loving. Basilius, not so wise in covering his passion, would fall to those immoderate praises which the foolish lover ever thinks short of his mistress, although they reach far beyond the heavens; but Gynecia, whom womanly modesty did more outwardly bridle, yet did many times use the advantage of her sex in kissing Cleophila (which did indeed but increase the rage of her inward fury)—both immoderately feeding their eyes with one intention, though by contrary means. But once Cleophila could not stir but that, as if they had been puppets whose motions stood only upon her pleasure, they would with forced steps and gazing looks follow her. Basilius's mind Gynecia well perceived, and could well have found in her heart to laugh at—if her fortune might have endured mirth. But all Gynecia's actions were by Basilius interpreted as proceeding from jealousy; Cleophila betwixt both (like the poor child whose father while he beats him will make him believe it is for love, or as the sick man to whom the physician swears the medicine he proffers is of a good taste), their love was hateful, their courtesy troublesome, their presence cause of her absence thence where her heart lived.

Philoclea coming among them made them all perceive it was time to rest their bodies, how little part soever their minds took of it. And therefore, bringing Cleophila to her chamber, Basilius and Gynecia retired them to theirs, where Basilius being now asleep and all the lights (which naturally keep a cheerfulness in the mind) put out, Gynecia (kneeling up in her bed) began with a soft voice and swollen heart to renew the curses of her birth; and then in a manner embracing her bed, 'Ah chastest bed of mine,' said she, 'which never heretofore couldst accuse me of one defiled thought, how canst thou now receive this disastered*changeling? Happy, happy be only they which be not, and thy blessedness only in this respect: thou mayst feel that thou hast no feeling!' With that she furiously tare off great part of her fair hair: 'Take here, O forgotten virtue,' said she, 'this miserable sacrifice'—more she would have said, but that Basilius, awaked with the noise, took her in his arms and began to comfort her, the goodman thinking it was all for love of him—which humour, if she would a little have maintained, perchance it might have weakened his new-conceived heats. But he, finding her answers wandering from the purpose, left her to herself, glad the next day to take the advantage of her dead sleep (which her overwatched sorrow had laid upon her) to have the more conference with the afflicted Cleophila who, baited on this fashion by these two lovers, and ever kept from any means to declare herself to Philoclea, was in far harder estate than the pastor Dorus; for he had but to do, in his pursuit, with shepherdish folks who troubled him with a little envious care and affected diligence. But Cleophila was waited on by princes, and watched by the two wakeful eyes of love and jealousy.

But this morning of Gynecia's sleep, Basilius gave her occasion to go beyond him in this sort. Cleophila thus at one instant both besieged and banished, found in herself a daily increase of her violent desires which, as a river, his current being stopped, doth the more swell, so did her heart, the more impediments she met, the more vehemently strive to overpass them. The only recreation she could find in all her anguish was to visit sometimes that place where first she was so happy as to see the cause of her unhap. There would she kiss the ground, and thank the trees; bless the air, and do dutiful reverence to everything that she thought did accompany her at the first meeting. But as love, though it be a passion, hath in itself a very active manner of working, so had she in her brain all sorts of invention by which she might come to some satisfaction of it. But still the cumbersome company of her two ill-matched lovers was a cruel bar unto it; till this morning that Basilius, having combed and tricked himself more curiously than any time forty winters before, did find her given over to her muses, which she did express in this song, to the great pleasure of the good old Basilius who retired himself behind a tree, while she with a most sweet voice did utter these passionate verses:

> Loved I am, and yet complain of love;
> As loving not, accused, in love I die.
> When pity most I crave, I cruel prove;
> Still seeking love, love found as much I fly.
>
> Burnt in myself I muse at others' fire;
> What I call wrong, I do the same, and more;
> Barred of my will, I have beyond desire;
> I wail for want, and yet am choked with store.
>
> This is thy work, thou god for ever blind;
> Though thousands old, a boy entitled still.
> Thus children do the silly birds they find
> With stroking hurt, and too much cramming kill.
> > Yet thus much love, O love, I crave of thee:
> > Let me be loved, or else not loved be.

Basilius made no great haste from behind the tree till he perceived she had fully ended her music; but then, loath to lose the precious fruit of time, he presented himself unto her, falling down upon both his knees, and holding up his hands, as the old governess of Danae is painted,*when she suddenly saw the golden shower: 'O heavenly woman or earthly goddess,' said he, 'let not my presence be odious unto you, nor my humble suit seem of small weight in your ears. Vouchsafe your eyes to descend upon this miserable old man whose life hath hitherto been maintained but to serve as an increase of your beautiful triumphs. You only have overthrown me, and in my bondage consists my glory. Suffer not your own work to be despised of you, but look upon him with pity whose life serves for your praise.'

Cleophila, keeping a countenance askances she understood him not, told him it became her ill to suffer such excessive reverence of him, but that it worse became her to correct him to whom she owed duty; that the opinion she had of his wisdom was such as made her esteem greatly of his words, but that the words themselves sounded so as she could not imagine what they might intend.

'Intend!', said Basilius (almost proud with being asked the question). 'Alas,' said he, 'what may they intend but a refreshing of my soul, an assuaging of my heat, and enjoying those your excellencies wherein my life is upheld and my death threatened?'

Cleophila, lifting up her face as if she had received a mortal injury of him; 'And is this the devotion your ceremonies', said she, 'have been bent unto? Is it the disdain of my estate or the opinion of my lightness that have emboldened such base fancies towards me? Enjoying, quoth you! Now little joy come to them that yield to such enjoying!'

Poor Basilius was so appalled that his legs bowed under him, his eyes waxed staring dead, and (his old blood going to his heart) a general shaking all over his body possessed him. At length, with a wan mouth, he was about to give a stammering answer when Cleophila, seeing it was now time to make her profit of his folly, with something a relented countenance said unto him: 'Your words, mighty prince, were unfit either for you to speak or me to hear; but yet the large testimony I see of your affection makes me willing to suppress a great number of errors. Only thus much I think good to say: that these same words in my lady Philoclea's mouth, as from one woman to another, might have had a better grace, and perchance have found a gentler receipt. Desire holds the senses open, and a lover's conceit is very quick.'

Basilius no sooner received this answer but that, as if speedy flight might save his life, he turned without any ceremony away from Cleophila and ran with all speed his body would suffer him towards his fair daughter Philoclea, whom he found at that time watching her mother Gynecia taking such rests as unquiet sleeps and fearful dreams would yield her. Basilius delayed no time, but with all those conjuring prayers which a father's authority may lay upon an humble child besought her she would preserve his life in whom her life was begun; she would save his grey hairs from rebuke, and his aged mind from despair; that if she were not cloyed with his company, and that she thought not the earth overburdened with him, she would cool his fiery plague, which was to be done but with her breath; that in fine whatsoever he was, he was nothing but what it pleased Cleophila—he lived in her, and all the powers of his spirits depended of her; that if she continued cruel he could no more sustain himself than the earth remain fruitful in the sun's continual absence. He concluded she should in one payment requite all his deserts; and that she needed not disdain any service, though never so base, which was warranted by the sacred name of a father.

Philoclea more glad than ever she had known herself that she might by this occasion enjoy the private conference of Cleophila, yet had so sweet a feeling of virtue within her mind that she would not suffer a vile colour to be cast over her high thoughts, but with an humble look and obedient heart answered her father that there needed neither promise nor persuasion unto her to make her do her uttermost for her father's service; that, for Cleophila's favour in all virtuous sort, she would seek it towards him; and that, as she would not pierce further into his meaning than himself should declare, so would she interpret all his doings to be accomplished in goodness. And therefore desired, if otherwise it should be, he would not impart it to her, who then should be forced to begin by true obedience a show of disobedience, rather performing his general commandment (which had ever been to embrace virtue) than any new particular sprung out of passion and contrary to the former.

Basilius, that did but desire by her means to have the beginning of a more free access unto Cleophila, allowed her reasons and accepted her service, desiring but a speedy return of comfort. Away departed the most excellent Philoclea with a new field of fancies in her travailed mind; for well she saw her father was now grown her adverse party, and yet her own fortune such as she must needs favour her rival who might have show of hope where herself was out of possibility of help. But as she walked a little on she saw at a river's side a fair lady whose face was so bent over the river that her flowing tears continually fell into the water, much like as we see in some pleasant gardens costly images are set for fountains, which yield abundance of waters to the delightful streams that run under them.

Newly was Philoclea departed out of the chamber when Gynecia, troubled with a fearful dream, frightfully awaked. The dream was this: it seemed unto her to be in a place full of thorns which so molested her as she could neither abide standing still nor tread safely going forward. In this case she thought Cleophila, being upon a fair hill, delightful to the eye and easy in appearance, called her thither; but thither with much anguish being come, Cleophila was vanished, and she found nothing but a dead body which seeming at the first with a strange smell so to infect her as she was ready to die likewise, within a while the dead body (she thought) took her in his arms and said: 'Gynecia, here is thy only rest.' With that she awaked, crying very loud: 'Cleophila! Cleophila!' But remembering herself, and seeing her husband by (as a guilty conscience doth more suspect than is suspected), she turned her call and called for Philoclea. Basilius (that God knows knew no reason why he might spare to tell it) told her Philoclea was gone to entertain the lady Cleophila who had long remained in solitary muses. Gynecia, as if she had heard her last doom pronounced against her, with a side look and changing face: 'O my lord,' said she, 'what mean you to suffer these young folks together?'

Basilius smiling, took her in his arms: 'Sweet wife,' said he, 'I thank you for your care of your child, but they must be youths of other mettle than Cleophila that can endanger her.'

'O but'—cried out Gynecia; and therewith she stopped. For then indeed did her spirit suffer a right conflict betwixt the force of love and the rage of jealousy. Many times was she about to satisfy the spite of her mind and tell Basilius what, and upon what reasons, she thought Cleophila to be far other than the outward appearance. But those many times were all put back by the manifold forces of her vehement love. Fain she would have barred her daughter's hap; but loath she was to cut off her own hope. Often she offered to have risen to have broken that which her jealousy made her imagine, much more than so stolen a leisure could suffer. But Basilius, who had no less desire to taste of his daughter's labour, would never suffer it, swearing he saw sickness in his wife's face, and therefore would not the air should have his power over her. Thus did Gynecia eat of her jealousy, pine in her love, and receive kindness nowhere but from the fountain of unkindness.

In the mean time Philoclea saw the doleful lady, and heard her plaint which was uttered in this sort: 'Fair streams', said she, 'that do vouchsafe in your clearness to represent unto me my blubbered face, stay a little your course, and receive knowledge of my unfortunate fortune; or if the violence of your spring command you to haste away to pay your duties to your great mother the sea, yet carry with you these few words, and let the uttermost ends of the world know them. A love as clear as yourselves, employed to a love (I fear) as cold as yourselves, makes me increase your flood with my tears and continue my tears in your presence.' With that she took a willow stick and wrote in a sandy bank*these verses:

> Over these brooks, trusting to ease mine eyes
> (Mine eyes e'en great in labour with their tears),
> I laid my face (my face wherein there lies
> Clusters of clouds which no sun ever clears).
>   In wat'ry glass my watered eyes I see:
>   Sorrows ill eased, where sorrows painted be.
>
> My thoughts, imprisoned in my secret woes,
> With flamy breath do issue oft in sound:
> The sound to this strange air no sooner goes
> But that it doth with echo's force rebound
>   And make me hear the plaints I would refrain:
>   Thus outward helps my inward griefs maintain.
>
> Now in this sand I would discharge my mind,
> And cast from me part of my burd'nous cares:
> But in the sands my pains foretold I find,
> And see therein how well the writer fares.
>   Since stream, air, sand, mine eyes and ears conspire:
>   What hope to quench where each thing blows the fire?

Philoclea at the first sight well knew this was Cleophila (for so indeed it was); but as there is nothing more agreeable than a beloved voice, she was well content to hear her words which she thought might with more cause have been spoken by her own mouth. But when Cleophila did both cease to speak and had ended her writing, Philoclea gave herself to be seen unto her, with such a meeting of both their eyes together, with such a mutual astonishment to them both as it well showed each party had enough to do to maintain their vital powers in their due working. At length Philoclea, having a while mused how to wade betwixt her own hopeless affection and her father's unbridled hope, with blushing cheeks and eyes cast down to the ground, began to say: 'My father, to whom I owe myself, and therefore must perform all duties unto—', when Cleophila straitly embracing her, and (warranted by a womanly habit) often kissing her, desired her to stay her sweet speech, for well she knew her father's errand, and should soon receive a sufficient answer. But now she demanded leave, not to lose this long-sought-for commodity of time, to ease her heart thus far: that if in her agonies her destiny was to be condemned by Philoclea's mouth, at least Philoclea might know whom she had condemned. Philoclea easily yielded to this request; and therefore, sitting down together upon the green bank hard by the river, Cleophila long in a deep doubt how to begin (though she had often before thought of it), with panting heart brought it forth in this manner: 'Most beloved lady, the incomparable worthiness of yourself, joined to the greatness of your estate, and the importance of the thing whereon my life consisteth, doth require both length of time in the beginning and many ceremonies in the uttering my enforced speech. But the small opportunity of envious occasion, with the malicious eye hateful love doth cast upon me, and the extreme bent of my affection, which will either break out in words or break my heart, compel me, not only to embrace the smallest time I may obtain, but to lay aside all respects due to yourself in respect of my own life, which is now or never to be preserved. I do therefore vow to you hereafter never more to omit all dutiful forms; do you now only vouchsafe to hear the matters of a most perplexed mind. If ever the sound of love have come to your ears, or if ever you have understood what force it hath had to conquer the strongest hearts and change the most settled estates, receive here, not only an example of those strange tragedies, but one that in himself hath contained all the particularities of their misfortunes; and from henceforth believe it may be, since you shall see it is. You shall see, I say, a living image and a present story of the best pattern love hath ever showed of his workmanship. But alas, whither goest thou, my tongue; or how doth my heart consent to adventure the revealing my nearest touching secrets? But spare not my speech; here is the author of thy harms, the witness of thy words, and the judge of thy life! Therefore again I say, I say, O only princess attend here a miserable miracle of affection! Behold here before your eyes Pyrocles, prince of Macedon, whom you only have brought to this fall of fortune and unused metamorphosis; whom you only have made neglect his country, forget his father, and lastly forsake himself! My suit is to serve you, and my end to do you honour. Your fair face hath many marks in it of amazement at my words; think then what his amazement is from whence they come, since no words can carry with them the life of the inward feeling. If the highest love in no base person may bear place in your judgement, then may I hope your beauty will not be without pity. If otherwise you be (alas, but let it never be so) resolved, yet shall not my death be without comfort, receiving it by your sentence.'

The joy which wrought into Pygmalion's mind*while he found his beloved image wax little and little both softer and warmer in his folded arms, till at length it accomplished his gladness with a perfect woman's shape, still beautified with the former perfections, was even such as, by each degree of Cleophila's words, stealingly entered into Philoclea's soul, till her pleasure was fully made up with the manifesting of his being, which was such as in hope did overcome hope. Yet did a certain spark of honour arise in her well disposed mind, which bred a starting fear to be now in secret with him in whose presence, notwithstanding, consisted her comfort—such contradictions there must needs grow in those minds which neither absolutely embrace goodness nor freely yield to evil. But that spark soon gave place, or at least gave no more light in her mind than a candle doth in the sun's presence; but even astonished with a surfeit of joy, and fearful of she knew not what (as he that newly finds much treasure is most subject to doubts), with a shrugging kind of tremor through all her principal parts, she gave these affectionate words for answer: 'Alas, how painful a thing it is to a divided mind to make a well joined answer; how hard it is to bring inward shame to outward confession; and how foolish, trow you, must that answer be which is made one knows not to whom! Shall I say, "O Cleophila"? Alas, your words be against it! Shall I say, "prince Pyrocles"? Wretch that I am, your show is manifest against it. But this, this, I well may say: if I had continued as I ought Philoclea, you had either never been or ever been Cleophila; you had either never attempted this change, fed with hope, or never discovered it, stopped with despair. But I fear me my behaviour ill governed gave you the first comfort. I fear me my affection ill hid hath given you this last assurance. If my castle had not seemed weak, you would never have brought these disguised forces. No, no; I have betrayed myself. It was well seen I was glad to yield before I was assaulted. Alas, what then shall I do? Shall I seek far-fetched inventions? Shall I seek to lay colours over my decayed thoughts? Or rather, though the pureness of my virgin mind be stained, let me keep the true simplicity of my word. True it is (alas, too true it is), O Cleophila (for so I love to call thee, since in that name my love first began, and in the shade of that name my love shall best lie hidden), that even while so thou wert (what eye bewitched me I know not) my passions were far fitter to desire than to be desired. Shall I say then I am sorry, or that my love must be turned to hate, since thou art turned to Pyrocles? How may that well be; since, when thou wert Cleophila, the despair thou mightst not be thus did then most torment me? Thou hast then the victory; use it now with virtue, since from the steps of virtue my soul is witness to itself it never hath, and pledge to itself it never shall decline no way to make me leave to love thee, but by making me think thy love unworthy of me.'

Pyrocles, so carried up with joy that he did not envy the gods' felicity, presented her with some jewels of inestimable price as tokens both of his love and quality, and for a conclusion of proof showed her letters from his father, king Euarchus, unto him; which hand she happily knew, as having kept divers which passed betwixt her father and him. There, with many such embracings as it seemed their souls desired to meet and their hearts to kiss as their mouths did, they passed the promise of marriage.

But Gynecia's restless affection and furious jealousy had by this time prevailed so much with her husband as to come to separate them. O jealousy, the frenzy of wise folks, the well wishing spite and unkind carefulness, the self-punishment for other's fault and self-misery in other's happiness, the sister of envy, daughter of love, and mother of hate, how couldst thou so quickly get thee a seat in the unquiet heart of Gynecia, a lady very fair in her strongest age, known wise and esteemed virtuous? It was thy breeder's power that planted thee there; it was the inflaming agonies of affection that drew on the fever of thy sickness in such sort that nature gave place. The growing of her daughter seemed the decay of herself. The blessings of a mother turned to the curses of a competitor, and the fair face of Philoclea appeared more horrible in her sight than the image of death. Possessed with these devils of love and jealousy, the great and wretched lady Gynecia had rid herself from her tedious husband (who thought now he might freely give her leave to go, hoping his daughter by that time had performed his message) and, as soon as she was alone, with looks strangely cast about her, she began to denounce war to all the works of earth and powers of heaven. But the envenomed heat which lay within her gave her not scope for many words, but (with as much rageful haste as the Trojan women went to burn Aeneas's ships)*she ran headlongly towards the place where she guessed her daughter and Cleophila might be together. Yet by the way there came into her mind an old song which she thought did well figure her fortune. The song was this, though her leisure served her not as then to sing it:

With two strange fires of equal heat possessed,
The one of love, the other jealousy,
Both still do work, in neither find I rest;
For both, alas, their strengths together tie;
The one aloft doth hold the other high.
    Love wakes the jealous eye lest thence it moves;
    The jealous eye, the more it looks, it loves.

These fires increase, in these I daily burn:
They feed on me, and with my wings do fly:
My lively joys to doleful ashes turn:
Their flames mount up, my powers prostrate lie:
They live in force, I quite consumed die.
    One wonder yet far passeth my conceit:
    The fuel small, how be the fires so great?

Being come where they were, to the great astonishment of the sweet Philoclea (whose conscience now began to know cause of blushing), for first salutation she gave an eye to her daughter full of the same disdainful scorn which Pallas showed to the poor Arachne*that durst contend with her for the prize of well weaving. Yet see, the force of love did so much rule her that, though for Cleophila's sake she did detest her, yet for Cleophila's sake she used no harder words to her than to bid her go home and accompany her solitary father.

Then began she to display to Cleophila the storehouse of her deadly desires, when suddenly the confused rumour of a mutinous multitude gave just occasion to Cleophila to break off any such conference (for well they found they were no friendly voices they heard), and to retire with as much diligence as conveniently they could towards the lodge. Yet before they could win the lodge by twenty paces, they were overtaken by an unruly sort of clowns which, like a violent flood, were carried they themselves knew not whither. But as soon as they came within the compass of blows, like enraged beasts, without respect of their estates or pity of their sex, they ran upon these fair ladies, to show the right nature of a villain, never thinking his estate happy but when he is able to do hurt. Yet so many as they were, so many almost were the minds all knit together only in madness. Some cried 'take!', some 'kill!', some 'save!'; but even they that cried 'save!' ran for company with them that meant to kill. Everyone commanded, none obeyed. He only seemed to have most pre-eminence that was most rageful. Cleophila, whose virtuous courage was ever awake in her, drawing out her sword, kept a while the villains at a bay while the ladies gat themselves into the lodge, out of which the good old Basilius, having put on an armour long before untried, came to prove his authority among his subjects, or at least to adventure his life with his dear mistress. The ladies in the mean time tremblingly attended the issue of this dangerous adventure. But Cleophila did quickly make them perceive that one eagle is worth a great number of kites. No blow she strake that did not suffice for a full reward of him that received it. Yet at length the many hands would have prevailed against these two, had not the noble shepherd Dorus heard this noise and come to their succour.

Dorus had been upon a fine little hill not far off, in the company of some other shepherds, defending him from the sun's heat with the shade of a few pleasant myrtle trees, feeding his master's sheep, practising his new-learned shepherd's pipe, and singing with great joy for the long-pursued victory he had lately gotten of the gracious Pamela's favour—victory so far as the promising affection came unto, he having lately (keeping still his disguised manner) opened more plainly both his mind and estate. His song, as the shepherds after recounted it, was this:

> Feed on my sheep; my charge, my comfort, feed;
> With sun's approach your pasture fertile grows,
> O only sun that such a fruit can breed.
>
> Feed on my sheep, your fair sweet feeding flows,
> Each flow'r, each herb, doth to your service yield,
> O blessed sun whence all this blessing goes.
>
> Feed on my sheep, possess your fruitful field,
> No wolves dare howl, no murrain can prevail,
> And from the storms our sweetest sun will shield.
>
> Feed on my sheep, sorrow hath stricken sail,
> Enjoy my joys, as you did taste my pain,
> While our sun shines no cloudy griefs assail.

> Feed on my sheep, your native joys maintain,
>   Your wool is rich; no tongue can tell my gain.

His song being ended, the young shepherd Philisides at that time in his company, as if Dorus's joy had been a remembrance to his sorrow, tuning his voice in doleful manner, thus made answer unto him, using the burden of his own words:

> Leave off my sheep: it is no time to feed,
>   My sun is gone, your pasture barren grows,
>   O cruel sun, thy hate this harm doth breed.

> Leave off my sheep, my show'r of tears o'erflows,
>   Your sweetest flow'rs, your herbs, no service yield,
>   My sun, alas, from me for ever goes.

> Leave off my sheep, my sighs burn up your field,
>   My plaints call wolves, my plagues in you prevail,
>   My sun is gone, from storms what shall us shield?

> Leave off my sheep, sorrow hath hoised sail,
>   Wail in my woes, taste of your master's pain,
>   My sun is gone, now cloudy griefs assail.
>   Leave leaving not my mourning to maintain,
>   You bear no wool, and loss is all my gain.

Before Philisides had finished the last accent of his song, the horrible cries of the mad multitude gave an untimely conclusion to his passionate music. But Dorus had straight represented before the eyes of his careful love the peril wherein his other soul might be. Therefore, taking no other weapon than his sheephook (which he thought sufficient because it had sufficed to bring him in a towardness of his most redoubted conquest), he gave example to Philisides and some other of the best-minded shepherds to follow him. First he went to Pamela's lodge, where finding her already close in a strong cave a little way from the lodge, not possible to be entered into by force, with Miso, Mopsa, and Dametas (who would not that time of day have opened the entry to his father), he led his little troop to the other lodge, where he saw Cleophila, having three of that rustic rout dead at her feet, and bathed in the blood of a great number other; but both she and the duke so sore wearied with the excessive number of them that they were but resolved to sell their lives at a dear price, when Dorus coming in, and crying, 'courage, here is Dorus!' to his dear friend Cleophila, felled one of them with his sheephook, and taking his bill from him, valiantly seconded by Philisides and the other honest shepherds, made so fair way among them that he wan time for them all to recover the lodge, and to give the rebels a face of wood of the outside.* The joy Gynecia and Philoclea felt in seeing them safely come in, whom both they loved, and in whom their lives consisted, would have been unspeakable had it not been much kept down with the savage howlings the rascals made without; who now began to seek fire to burn the gates, seeing otherwise they were unlikely to prevail.

But before I tell you what came thereof, methinks it reason you know what raging motion was the beginning of this tumult. Bacchus, they say, was begotten with thunder. I think that made him ever since so full of stir and debate. Bacchus, indeed, it was which sounded the first trumpet of this rude alarum, a manner the Arcadians had to solemnize their prince's birthdays with banqueting together as largely as the quality of the company could suffer—a barbarous opinion, to think with vice to do honour, or with activity in beastliness to show abundance of love. This custom, being general, was particularly this time of Basilius's nativity observed by a town near the desert of the two lodges called Phagona.* There, being chafed with wine and emboldened with the duke's absented manner of living, there was no matter their ears had ever heard of that grew not to be a subject of their winy conference. Public affairs were mingled with private grudge; neither was any man thought of wit that did not pretend some cause of mislike. Railing was counted the fruit of freedom, and saying nothing had his uttermost praise in ignorance. At the length the prince's person fell to be their table-talk; and to speak licentiously of that was a tickling point of courage to them. A proud word did swell in their stomachs, and disdainful reproaches to great persons had put on a shadow of greatness in their base minds. Till at length, the very unbridled use of words having increased fire to their minds (which thought their knowledge notable because they had at all no knowledge to condemn their own want of knowledge), they descended to a direct mislike of the duke's living from among them. Whereupon it were tedious to write their far-fetched constructions; but the sum was he disdained them, and what were the shows of his estate if their arms maintained him not? Who would call him duke if he had not a people? When certain of them of wretched estates (and worse minds), whose fortunes change could not impair, began to say a strange woman had now possessed their prince and government; Arcadians were too plain-headed to give the prince counsel. What need from henceforward to fear foreign enemies, since they were conquered without stroke striking, their secrets opened, their treasures abused, themselves triumphed over, and never overthrown? If Arcadia grew loathsome in the duke's sight, why did he not rid himself of the trouble? There would not want those should take so fair a cumber in good part. Since the country was theirs and that the government was an adherent to the country, why should they that needed not be partakers of the danger, be partakers with the cause of the danger? 'Nay rather', said they, 'let us begin that which all Arcadia will follow. Let us deliver our prince from foreign hands, and ourselves from the want of a prince. Let us be the first to do that which all the rest think. Let it be said the Phagonians are they which are not astonished with vain titles that have their forces but in our forces. Lastly, to have said and heard so much was as punishable as to have attempted; and to attempt they had the glorious show of commonwealth with them.'

These words being spoken, like a furious storm presently took hold of their well inclined brains. There needed no drum where each man cried; each spake to other, that spake as fast to him; and the disagreeing sound of so many voices was the only token of their unmeet agreement. Thus was their banquet turned to a battle, their winy mirths to bloody rages, and the happy prayers for the duke to monstrous threatening his estate; the solemnizing his birthday tended to the cause of his funerals. But as rage hath (besides his wickedness) that folly that, the more it seeks to hurt, the less it considers how to be able to hurt, they never weighed how to arm themselves, but took up everything for a weapon that fury offered to their hands: some swords and bills; there were other took pitchforks and rakes, converting husbandry to soldiery. Some caught hold of spits, things serviceable for the lives of men, to be the instruments of their deaths; and there wanted not such which held the same pots wherein they had drunk to the duke's health to use them (as they could) to his mischief. Thus armed, thus governed, adding fury to fury and increasing rage with running, they went headlong towards the duke's lodge, no man in his own heart resolved what was the uttermost he would do when he came thither. But as mischief is of such nature that it cannot stand but with strengthening one evil by another, and so multiply in itself till it come to the highest, and then fall with his own weight, so to their minds once past the bounds of obedience more and more wickedness opened itself, and they which first pretended to succour him, then to reform him, now thought no safety to themselves without killing him.

In this mad mood Cleophila's excellent valour, joined to Basilius, and succoured by the worthy Dorus and his fellow shepherds, made them feel the smart of their folly; till, for last extremity, they sought for unmerciful fire to be their foregoer. Then did the ladies with pitiful shrieks show the deadly fear they had of a present massacre, especially the sweet Philoclea who ever caught hold of Cleophila, so by the folly of love hindering the succour; which succour she desired. But Cleophila, seeing no way of defence, nor time to deliberate, thought the only mean with extraordinary boldness to overcome boldness, and with danger to avoid danger. And therefore, when they were even ready to put fire, she caused the gate to be opened by Dorus, who stood there ready to do his uttermost for her defence; for all the rest cried to her she should not so adventure her life. And so, with her sword by her side, ready but not drawn, she issued among them. The blows she had dealt before (though all in general were hasty) made each of them take breath before they brought themselves suddenly over near her; so that she had time to get up to the judgement seat of the duke which, according to the guise of that country, was hard before the court gate. There she paused a while, making sign with her hand unto them that she had something to say would please them. Truly, outward graces are not without their efficacies; the goodliness of her shape, with that quiet magnanimity represented in her face in this uttermost peril, did even fix the eyes of the barbarous people with admiration upon her. And the nature of man is such that, as they leave no rageful violence unattempted while their choler is nourished with resistance, so, when the very subject of their wrath is unlooked-for offered to their hands, it makes them at least take a pause before they determine cruelty. Cleophila (whose wits were not dismayed) quickly spied her coming had bred an alteration; and therefore, meaning to use the advantage of time, and to speak determinately while she might be heard, with a brave unbashed countenance, thus said: 'An unused thing it is, and I think not heretofore seen, O Arcadians, that a woman should give public counsel to men; a stranger to the country people; and that lastly in such a presence a private person, as I am, should possess the regal throne. But the strangeness of your action makes that used for virtue which your violent necessity imposeth. For certainly a woman may well speak to such men who have forgotten all manly government; a stranger may with reason instruct such subjects that neglect due points of subjection. And is it marvel this place is entered into by another, since your own duke after thirty years' government dare not show his face to his faithful people? Hear therefore, O Arcadians, and be ashamed! Against whom hath this zealous rage been stirred? Whither have you bent these manful weapons of yours? In this quiet harmless lodge there are harboured no Trojans, your ancient enemies; nor Persians, whom you have in present fear.* Here lodge none but such as either you have great cause to love, or no cause to hate. But none other most sure it can be: is it I, O Arcadians, against whom your anger is armed? Am I the mark of your vehement quarrel? If it be so, that innocency shall not be a stop for fury; if it be so, that the law of hospitality may not defend a stranger fled to your arms for succour; if lastly it be so, that so many valiant men's courages can be inflamed to the mischief of one hurtless woman, I refuse not to make my life a sacrifice to your wrath. Exercise in me your indignation, so it go no further. I am content to pay the great favours I have received among you with the usury of my well deserving life. I present it here unto you, O Arcadians, if that may satisfy you, rather than you (called over the world the wise and quiet Arcadians) should be so vain as to attempt that alone which all your country will abhor; than you should show yourselves so ungrateful as to forget the fruit of so many years peaceable government, or so unnatural as not to have any fury over-mastered with the holy name of your natural duke. For such a hellish madness, I know, will never enter into your hearts as to attempt anything against his person; which no successor, though never so hateful to him, will, for his own sake, ever leave unpunished. Neither can your wonted valour be turned to such a baseness as, instead of a duke delivered unto you by so many royal ancestors, to take the tyrannous yoke of your fellow subject, in whom the innate meanness will bring forth ravenous covetousness, and the newness of his estate suspectful cruelty. Imagine what would your enemies more wish unto you than to see you with your own hands overthrow your estate? O what would the first Arcadians, your worthy predecessors, say if they lived at this time and saw their offspring defacing such an excellent monarchy, which they with much labour and blood so wisely established? No, no, your honest hearts will neither so gratify your hateful neighbours, nor so degenerate from your famous ancestors. I see in your countenances, now virtuously settled, nothing but love and duty to him who for your only sakes doth embrace the government. The uncertainty of his estate made you take arms; now you see him well, with the same love lay them down. If now you end, as I know you will, he will take no other account of you but as of a vehement, I must confess over vehement, affection; the only continuance should prove a wickedness. But it is not so; I see very well you began with zeal and will end with reverence.'

The action Cleophila used, with a sweet magnanimity and stately mildness, did so pierce into their hearts (whom the taking of breath had cooled, and leisure had taught doubts) that, instead of roaring cries, there was now heard nothing but a confused muttering whether her saying was to be followed, betwixt doubt to pursue and fear to leave. Glad everyone would have been it had never been begun; but how to end it (each afraid of his companion) they knew not—so much easier it is to inflame than to quench, to tie than to loose knots. But Cleophila, to take an assured possession of their minds which she found began to waver, 'Loyal Arcadians,' said she, 'now do I offer unto you the manifesting of your duties. All those that have taken arms for the duke's safety, let them turn their backs to the gate with their weapons bent against such as would hurt the sacred person of the duke.'

O weak trust of the many-headed multitude, whom inconstancy only doth guide at any time to well doing! Let no man lay confidence there where company takes away shame, and each may lay the fault in his fellow. The word no sooner came from Cleophila but that there were shouts of joy, with 'God save the duke!'; and they with much jollity grown to be the duke's guard that but then before meant to be his murderers. And, indeed, no ill way it is in such mutinies to give them some occasion of such service as they may think in their own judgements may countervail their trespass. Yet was not this done with such an unity of hearts but that their faces well showed it was but a sheep's draught,* and no thirst of goodwill: namely some of them who, as they were forwardest in the mischief, could least persuade a pardon to themselves, would fain have made a resistance to the rest. But their fellows, that were most glad to have such a mean to show their loyalty, dispatched most of them with a good rule: that to be leaders in disobedience teacheth ever disobedience to the same leaders. So was this ungracious motion converted into their own bowels, and they by a true judgement grown their own punishers; till the duke promising a general pardon, most part with marks of their folly returned home, saving a few to the number of a dozen, in whom their own naughtiness could suffer no assurance, fled to certain woods not far off, where they kept themselves to see how the pardon should be observed; where feeding wildly upon grass and such other food, drinking only water, they were well disciplined from their drunken riots.

To describe unto you the miserable fear Cleophila's lovers lived in while she stood at the discretion of those undiscreet rebels, how at every angry countenance any of them made they thought a knife was laid upon their own throat, would require as many words as to make you know how full they were now of unspeakable joy that they saw, besides the safety of their own estates, the same wrought (and safely wrought) by her mean in whom they had placed all their delights. There wanted no embracements, no praises of her virtue, no outward signs of their inward affection. But as they were in the midst of those unfeigned ceremonies, a gittern ill played on, accompanied with a hoarse voice (who seemed to sing maugre the muses, and to be merry in spite of fortune), made them look the way of the ill-noised song. But the song was this:

A hateful cure with hate to heal:
A bloody help with blood to save:
A foolish thing with fools to deal:
Let him be bobbed that bobs will have.
    But who by means of wisdom high
    Hath saved his charge? It is e'en I.

Let others deck their pride with scars,
And of their wounds make brave lame shows:
First let them die, then pass the stars,
When rotten Fame will tell their blows.
    But eye from blade, and ear from cry:
    Who hath saved all? It is e'en I.

They had soon perceived it was master Dametas, who came with no less lifted up countenance than if he had passed over the bellies of all his enemies; so wise a point he thought he had performed in using the natural strength of his cave. But never was it his doing to come so soon thence till the coast were more assuredly clear; for it was a rule with him that after great storms there ever fell a few drops before they be fully finished. But Pamela (who had now experienced how much care doth solicit a lover's heart) used this occasion of going to her parents—indeed, unquiet till her eye might assure her how her shepherd had gone through the danger. Basilius, with the sight of Pamela, of whom almost his head (otherwise occupied) had lost the wonted remembrance, was suddenly stricken into a devout kind of admiration. And therefore presently commanded his wife and daughters to assist him in a sacrifice he would make to Apollo. 'For even now', said he, 'do I find the force of his oracle.' He would not, for all that, reveal the secret thereof; for that no man ever knew of him but his best trusted friend Philanax. But in his mind thus he construed it:

That where the oracle said his elder care should by princely mean be stolen away from him, and yet not lost, it was now performed, since Cleophila had as it were robbed from him the care of his first begotten child; yet was it not lost, since in his heart the ground of it remained. His younger should with nature's bliss embrace the love of Cleophila, because he had so commanded her for his service to do; yet should it be with as much hate of nature, for being so hateful an opposite to the jealousy he thought her mother had of him. The third was it which most rejoiced him; for now he interpreted the meaning thereof that he should accomplish his unlawful desires with Cleophila, and that after (by the death of Gynecia) she should become his wife. And no less comfort received he of the last point; for that he thought the threatening influence to his estate was in this passed, in respect Cleophila had, as you have heard, possessed his regal throne. Thus the fawning humour of false hope made him take everything to his own best; and such is the selfness of affection that, because his mind ran wholly upon Cleophila, he thought the gods in their oracles did mind nothing but her. These many good successes, as well essential as imaginative, made him grateful to Apollo; and therefore, excluding all the rest saving his wife and daughters (as their manner was when they privately made oblations to their household gods), after sacrifice done, they sang together this their yearly-used hymn:

Apollo great, whose beams the greater world do light,
And in our little world dost clear our inward sight,
Which ever shines, though hid from earth by earthly shade,

Whose lights do ever live, but in our darkness fade;
Thou God, whose youth was decked with spoil of Python's skin
(So humble knowledge can throw down the snakish sin),
Latona's son, whose birth in pain and travail long
Doth teach to learn the good what travails do belong;
In travail of our life (a short but tedious space
While brickle hour-glass runs) guide thou our panting race:
Give us foresightful minds; give us minds to obey
What foresight tells; our thoughts upon thy knowledge stay.
Let so our fruits grow up that nature be maintained;
But so our hearts keep down, with vice they be not stained.
Let this assured hold our judgements ever take,
That nothing wins the heav'n but what doth earth forsake.

As soon as he had ended his devotion, the coming thither together of
a great number of shepherds (which had followed Dorus to succour
him) remembered Basilius to call again for the pastorals; which in
this sort was handled.

Here ends the second book or act.

HERE BEGIN THE SECOND ECLOGUES

THE rude tumult of the Phagonians gave occasion to the honest shepherds to begin their pastorals this day with a dance which they called the skirmish betwixt Reason and Passion. For seven shepherds, which were named the reasonable shepherds, joined themselves, four of them making a square and the other two going a little wide of either side, like wings for the main battle, and the seventh man foremost, like the forlorn hope, to begin the skirmish. In like order came out the seven appassionate shepherds, all keeping the pace of their foot by their voice and sundry consorted instruments they held in their arms. And first the foremost of the reasonable side began to sing:

> Thou rebel vile, come, to thy master yield.

And the other that met with him answered:

> No tyrant, no; mine, mine shall be the field.

Reason. Can Reason then a tyrant counted be?
Passion. If Reason will that Passions be not free.
R.   But Reason will that Reason govern most.
P.   And Passion will that Passion rule the roast.
R.   Your will is will; but Reason reason is.
P.   Will hath his will when Reason's will doth miss.
R.   Whom Passion leads unto his death is bent.
P.   And let him die, so that he die content.
R.   By nature you to Reason faith have sworn.
P.   Not so, but fellowlike together born.
R.   Who Passion doth ensue lives in annoy.
P.   Who Passion doth forsake lives void of joy.
R.   Passion is blind, and treads an unknown trace.
P.   Reason hath eyes to see his own ill case.

Then, as they approached nearer, the two of Reason's side, as if they shot at the other, thus sang:

R.   Dare Passions then abide in Reason's light?
P.   And is not Reason dimmed with Passion's might?

R.   O foolish thing which glory dost destroy!
P.   O glorious title of a foolish toy!
R.   Weakness you are, dare you with our strength fight?
P.   Because our weakness weak'neth all your might.
R.   O sacred Reason, help our virtuous toils!
P.   O Passion, pass on feeble Reason's spoils!
R.   We with ourselves abide a daily strife.
P.   We gladly use the sweetness of our life.
R.   But yet our strife sure peace in end doth breed.
P.   We now have peace, your peace we do not need.

Then did the two square battles meet and, instead of fighting, embrace one another, singing thus:

R.   We are too strong; but Reason seeks not blood.
P.   Who be too weak do feign they be too good.
R.   Though we cannot o'ercome, our cause is just.
P.   Let us o'ercome, and let us be unjust.
R.   Yet Passion, yield at length to Reason's stroke.
P.   What shall we win by taking Reason's yoke?
R.   The joys you have shall be made permanent.
P.   But so we shall with grief learn to repent.
R.   Repent indeed, but that shall be your bliss.
P.   How know we that, since present joys we miss?
R.   You know it not; of Reason therefore know it.
P.   No Reason yet had ever skill to show it.
R.P. Then let us both to heav'nly rules give place,
        Which Passions kill, and Reason do deface.

Then embraced they one another, and came to the duke who framed his praises of them according to Cleophila's liking, that sat at that time betwixt the duke and duchess, as if she had had her choice of drowning or burning. But her two unrestrained parts, the mind and eye, had their free convoy to the delicate Philoclea, whose look was not short in well requiting it; although she knew it was a hateful sight to the marking eye of her jealous mother. But Dicus, that had in this time taken a great liking of Dorus for the good parts he found above his age in him, had a delight to taste the fruits of his wit—though in a subject which he himself most of all other despised; and so entered into speech with him in the manner of this following eclogue:

Dicus   Dorus

Dicus. Dorus, tell me,*where is thy wonted motion
To make these woods resound thy lamentation?
Thy saint is dead, or dead is thy devotion.
For who doth hold his love in estimation,
To witness that he thinks his thoughts delicious,
Seeks to make each thing badge of his sweet passion.

Dorus. But what doth make thee, Dicus, so suspicious
Of my due faith, which needs must be immutable?
Who others' virtue doubt, themselves are vicious.
Not so; although my metal were most mutable,
Her beams have wrought therein most sure impression:
To such a force soon change were nothing suitable.

Dicus. The heart well set doth never shun confession:
If noble be thy bands, make them notorious:
Silence doth seem the mask of base oppression.
Who glories in his love doth make love glorious:
But who doth fear, or bideth muett wilfully,
Shows guilty heart doth deem his state opprobrious.
Thou, then, that fram'st both words and voice most skilfully,
Yield to our ears a sweet and sound relation,
If love took thee by force, or caught thee guilefully.

Dorus. If sunny beams shame heav'nly habitation;
If three-leaved grass seem to the sheep unsavoury,
Then base and sour is love's most high vocation.
Or if sheep's cries can help the sun's own bravery,
Then may I hope my pipe may have ability
To help her praise, who decks me in her slavery.
No, no; no words ennoble self-nobility.
As for your doubts, her voice was it deceived me,
Her eyes the force beyond my possibility.

Dicus. Thy words well voiced, well graced, had almost heaved me
Quite from myself to love love's contemplation;
Till of these thoughts thy sudden end bereaved me.
Go on, therefore, and tell us by what fashion
In thy own proof he gets so strange possession;
And how possessed, he strengthens his invasion?

Dorus. Sight is his root, in thought is his progression,
      His childhood wonder, prenticeship attention,
      His youth delight, his age the soul's oppression;
   Doubt is his sleep, he waketh in invention;
      Fancy his food, his clothing is of carefulness;
      Beauty his book, his play lovers' dissension;
   His eyes are curious search, but veiled with warefulness;
      His wings desire oft clipped with desperation;
      Largess his hands could never skill of sparefulness.
   But how he doth by might or by persuasion
      To conquer, and his conquest how to ratify,
      Experience doubts, and schools hold disputation.

Dicus. But so thy sheep may thy good wishes satisfy
      With large increase, and wool of fine perfection,
      So she thy love, her eyes thy eyes may gratify,
   As thou wilt give our souls a dear refection,
      By telling how she was, how now she framed is
      To help or hurt in thee her own infection.

Dorus. Blest be the name wherewith my mistress named is;
      Whose wounds are salves, whose yokes please more than
                                    pleasure doth:
      Her stains are beams, virtue the fault she blamed is.
   The heart, eye, ear here only find his treasure doth:
      All numb'ring arts her endless graces number not:
      Time, place, life, wit scarcely her rare gifts measure doth.
   Is she in rage? So is the sun in summer hot,
      Yet harvest brings. Doth she, alas, absent herself?
      The sun is hid; his kindly shadows cumber not.
   But when to give some grace she doth content herself,
      O then it shines; then are the heav'ns distributed,
      And Venus seems, to make up her, she spent herself.
   Thus then (I say) my mischiefs have contributed
      A greater good by her divine reflection;
      My harms to me, my bliss to her attributed.
   Thus she is framed: her eyes are my direction;
      Her love my life; her anger my instruction;
      Lastly, what so she be, that's my protection.

Dicus. Thy safety sure is wrapped in destruction;
      For that construction*thy own words do bear.
      A man to fear a woman's moody eye,
Or reason lie a slave to servile sense,
      There seek defence where weakness is the force,
      Is late remorse in folly dearly bought.

Dorus. If I had thought to hear blasphemous words,
      My breast to swords, my soul to hell have sold
      I sooner would than thus my ears defile
With words so vile, which viler breath doth breed.
      O herds, take heed! for I a wolf have found
      Who, hunting round the strongest for to kill,
      His breast doth fill with earth of others' woe,
      And loaden so, pulls down; pulled down, destroys.
      O shepherd boys, eschew these tongues of venom
      Which do envenom both the soul and senses!
      Our best defences are to fly these adders.
      O tongues, right ladders made to climb dishonour,
      Who judge that honour which hath scope to slander!

Dicus. Dorus, you wander far in great reproaches,
      So love encroaches on your charmed reason;
      But it is season for to end our singing,
      Such anger bringing; as for me, my fancy
In sick man's franzy rather takes compassion
      Than rage for rage: rather my wish I send to thee,
      Thou soon may have some help or change of passion.
      She oft her looks, the stars her favour, bend to thee:
      Fortune store, Nature health, Love grant persuasion.
A quiet mind none but thyself can lend to thee,
      Thus I commend to thee all our former love.

Dorus. Well do I prove error lies oft in zeal;
      Yet is it seal (though error) of true heart.
      Naught could impart such heats to friendly mind.
But for to find thy words did her disgrace,
      Whose only face the little heaven is,
Which who doth miss his eyes are but delusions,
      Barred from their chiefest object of delightfulness,
      Thrown on this earth the chaos of confusions.

As for thy wish to my enraged spitefulness,
  The lovely blow with rare reward, my prayer is
  Thou mayst love her that I may see thy sightfulness.
The quiet mind (whereof myself impairer is,
  As thou dost think) should most of all disquiet me
  Without her love than any mind who fairer is.
Her only cure from surfeit woes can diet me:
  She holds the balance of my contentation:
  Her cleared looks (naught else) in storms can quiet me.
Nay, rather than my ease discontentation
  Should breed to her, let me for ay dejected be
  From any joy which might her grief occasion.
With so sweet plagues my happy harms infected be:
  Pain wills me die, yet will of death I mortify;
  For though life irks, in life my loves protected be.
Thus for each change my changeless heart I fortify.

When they had ended to the good pleasing of the assistants,
especially of Cleophila who never forgat to give due commendation
to her friend Dorus, the more to advance him in his pursuit (although
therein he had brought his matters to a more wished conclusion
than yet she knew of), out starts a jolly younker (his name was Nico)
whose tongue had borne a very itching silence all this while; and
having spied one Pas (a mate of his as mad as himself—both indeed
lads to climb any tree in the world), he bestowed this manner of
salutation upon him, and was with like reverence requited:

Nico Pas Dicus*

Nico. And are you there, old Pas? In truth I ever thought
  Among us all we should find out some thing of naught.

Pas. And I am here the same, so mote I thrive and thee,
  Despaired in all this flock to find a knave but thee.

Nico. Ah, now I see why thou art in thyself so blind;
  Thy grey hood hides the thing that thou despair'st to find.

Pas. My grey hood is mine own, all be it be but grey,
  Not as the scrip thou stal'st while Dorcas sleeping lay.

Nico. Mine was the scrip; but thou, that seeming rayed with love,
  Didst snatch from Cosma's hand her green ywroughten glove.

Pas. Ah fool, so courtiers do. But who did lively skip
  When for a treen-dish stol'n thy father did thee whip?

Nico. Indeed the witch thy dam her crouch from shoulder spread,
  For pilf'ring Lalus' lamb, with crouch to bless thy head.

Pas. My voice the lamb did win, Menalcas was our judge
  Of singing match we made, whence he with shame did trudge.

Nico. Couldst thou make Lalus fly? so nightingales avoid
  When with the cawing crows their music is annoyed.

Pas. Nay, like to nightingales the other birds give ear,
  My pipe and song made him both song and pipe forswear.

Nico. I think it well; such voice would make one music hate:
  But if I had been there, th'hadst met another mate.

Pas. Another sure, as is a gander from a goose;
  But still when thou dost sing methinks a colt is loose.

Nico. Well aimed, by my hat; for as thou sangst last day
  The neighbours all did cry, 'Alas, what ass doth bray?'

Pas. But here is Dicus old; let him then speak the word
  To whether with best cause the nymphs fair flow'rs afford.

Nico. Content; but I will lay a wager hereunto,
  That profit may ensue to him that best can do.
  I have (and long shall have) a white great nimble cat,
  A king upon a mouse, a strong foe to a rat;
  Fine ears, long tail he hath, with lion's curbed claw
  Which oft he lifteth up, and stays his lifted paw,
  Deep musing to himself, which after-mewing shows,
  Till with licked beard his eye of fire espy his foes.
  If thou (alas, poor if!) do win, then win thou this;
  And if I better sing, let me thy Cosma kiss.

Pas. Kiss her? Now mayst thou kiss. I have a fitter match:
  A pretty cur it is; his name iwis is Catch,
  No ear nor tail he hath, lest they should him disgrace,
  A ruddy hair his coat, with fine long speckled face:
  He never musing stands, but with himself will play,
  Leaping at every fly, and angry with a flea:
  He eft would kill a mouse, but he disdains the fight,
  And makes our home good sport with dancing bolt upright.
  This is my pawn; the prize let Dicus' judgement show:
  Such odds I willing lay; for him and you I know.

Dicus. Sing then my lads, but sing with better vein than yet,

Or else who singeth worse, my skill will hardly hit.

Nico. Who doubts but Pas' fine pipe again will bring
　　The ancient praise to Arcad shepherds' skill?
　　Pan is not dead since Pas begins to sing.

Pas. Who evermore will love Apollo's quill,
　　Since Nico doth to sing so widely gape?
　　Nico his place far better furnish will.

Nico. Was this not he who, for Syringa's scape
　　Raging in woes, first pastors taught to plain?
　　Do you not hear his voice, and see his shape?

Pas. This is not he that failed her to gain,
　　Which made a bay, made bay a holy tree;
　　But this is one that doth his music stain.

Nico. O fauns, O fairies all, and do you see
　　And suffer such a wrong? A wrong, I trow,
　　That Nico must with Pas compared be.

Pas. O nymphs, I tell you news, for Pas you know;
　　While I was warbling out your wonted praise,
　　Nico would needs with Pas his bagpipe blow.

Nico. If never I did fail your holydays,
　　With dances, carols, or with barleybreak,*
　　Let Pas now know how Nico maketh lays.

Pas. If each day hath been holy for your sake
　　Unto my pipe, O nymphs, now help my pipe,
　　For Pas well knows what lays can Nico make.

Nico. Alas, how oft I look on cherries ripe
　　Methinks I see the lips my Leuca hath,
　　And wanting her, my weeping eyes I wipe.

Pas. Alas, when I in spring meet roses rathe,
　　And think from Cosma's sweet red lips I live,
　　I leave mine eyes unwiped, my cheeks to bathe.

Nico. As I of late near bushes used my sieve,
　　I spied a thrush where she did make her nest;
　　That will I take, and to my Leuca give.

Pas. But long have I a sparrow gaily dressed,
　　As white as milk, and coming to the call,

To put it with my hand in Cosma's breast.

Nico. I oft do sue, and Leuca saith I shall;
But when I did come near with heat and hope,
She ran away and threw at me a ball.

Pas. Cosma once said she left the wicket ope
For me to come; and so she did. I came,
But in the place found nothing but a rope.

Nico. When Leuca doth appear the sun for shame
Doth hide himself; for to himself he says,
If Leuca live, she darken will my fame.

Pas. When Cosma doth come forth the sun displays
His utmost light; for well his wit doth know
Cosma's fair beams emblemish much his rays.

Nico. Leuca to me did yestermorning show
In perfect light, which could not me deceive,
Her naked leg, more white than whitest snow.

Pas. But yesternight by light I did receive
From Cosma's eyes, which full in darkness shine,
I saw her arm where purest lillies cleave.

Nico. She once stark nak'd did bathe a little tine;
But still (methought), with beauties from her fell,
She did the water wash, and make more fine.

Pas. She once, to cool herself, stood in a well;
But ever since that well is well besought,
And for rose-water sold of rarest smell.

Nico. To river's bank, being a-walking brought,
She bid me spy her baby in the brook.
Alas (said I) this babe doth nurse my thought.

Pas. As in a glass I held she once did look,
I said my hands well paid her for mine eyes,
Since in my hands self goodly sight she took.

Nico. O if I had a ladder for the skies,
I would climb up, and bring a pretty star
To wear upon her neck that open lies.

Pas. O if I had Apollo's golden car,
I would come down and yield to her my place,

That (shining now) she then might shine more far.

Nico. Nothing, O Leuca, shall thy fame deface,
   While shepherds' tunes be heard, or rhymes be read,
   Or while that shepherds love a lovely face.

Pas. Thy name, O Cosma, shall with praise be spread
   As far as any shepherds piping be,
   As far as love possesseth any head.

Nico. Thy monument is laid in many a tree,
   With name engraved; so though thy body die,
   The after-folks shall wonder still at thee.

Pas. So oft these woods have heard me 'Cosma' cry,
   That after death to heav'n in woods' resound,
   With echo's help, shall 'Cosma, Cosma' fly.

Nico. Peace, peace, good Pas, thou weariest e'en the ground
   With sluttish song; I pray thee learn to blea,
   For good thou mayst yet prove in sheepish sound.

Pas. My father hath at home a pretty jay,
   Go win of him (for chatt'ring) praise or shame;
   For so yet of a conquest speak thou may.

Nico. Tell me (and be my Pan) the monster's name
   That hath four legs, and with two only goes;
   That hath four eyes, and only two can frame.

Pas. Tell this (and Phoebus be): what monster grows
   With so strong lives that body cannot rest
   In ease until that body life forgoes?*

Dicus. Enough, enough; so ill hath done the best
   That, since the having them to neither's due,
   Let cat and dog fight which shall have both you.

Some speech there straight grew among the hearers what they should mean by the riddles of the two monsters. But Cleophila, whose heart better delighted in wailful ditties as more according to her fortune, she desired Histor he would repeat the lamentation some days before he told them that he had heard of a stranger made to the wise Boulon—indeed Cleophila desirous to hear of Plangus's love, whose valour she had well seen (though against herself) in the combat of the six princes. Basilius, as soon as he understood Cleophila's pleasure, commanded Histor upon pain of his life (as though everything were a matter of life and death that pertained to his mistress's service) immediately to sing it; who, with great cunning varying his voice according to the diversity of the persons, thus performed his pleasure:

Histor

As I behind a bush did sit
I silent heard more words of wit
Than erst I knew; but first did plain
The one, which tother would refrain.

Plangus   Boulon

Plangus. Alas, how long this pilgrimage doth last?
    What greater ills have now the heav'ns in store
    To couple coming harms with sorrows past?
Long since my voice is hoarse, and throat is sore,
    With cries to skies, and curses to the ground;
    But more I plain, I feel my woes the more.
Ah where was first that cruel cunning found
    To frame of earth a vessel of the mind,
    Where it should be to self-destruction bound?
What needed so high sprites such mansions blind?
    Or wrapped in flesh what do they here obtain,
    But glorious name of wretched human-kind?
Balls to the stars, and thralls to Fortune's reign;
    Turned from themselves, infected with their cage,
    Where death is feared, and life is held with pain.
Like players placed to fill a filthy stage,
    Where change of thoughts one fool to other shows,
    And all but jests, save only sorrow's rage.
The child feels that; the man that feeling knows,
    With cries first born,* the presage of his life,
    Where wit but serves to have true taste of woes.
A shop of shame, a book where blots be rife
    This body is; this body so composed
    As in itself to nourish mortal strife.
So diverse be the elements disposed
    In this weak work that it can never be
    Made uniform to any state reposed.
Grief only makes his wretched state to see
    (E'en like a top which naught but whipping moves)

This man, this talking beast, this walking tree.
Grief is the stone which finest judgement proves;
    For who grieves not hath but a blockish brain,
    Since cause of grief no cause from life removes.

Boulon. How long wilt thou with moanful music stain
    The cheerful notes these pleasant places yield,
    Where all good haps a perfect state maintain?

Plangus. Cursed be good haps, and cursed be they that build
    Their hopes on haps, and do not make despair
    For all these certain blows the surest shield.
Shall I that saw Erona's shining hair
    Torn with her hands, and those same hands of snow
    With loss of purest blood themselves to tear,
Shall I that saw those breasts where beauties flow,
    Swelling with sighs, made pale with mind's disease,
    And saw those eyes (those suns) such show'rs to show,
Shall I whose ears her mournful words did seize
    (Her words in syrup laid of sweetest breath),
    Relent those thoughts which then did so displease?
No, no; despair my daily lesson saith,
    And saith, although I seek my life to fly,
    Plangus must live to see Erona's death.
Plangus must live some help for her to try
    Though in despair, for love so forceth me;
    Plangus doth live, and shall Erona die?
Erona die? O heav'n (if heav'n there be)
    Hath all thy whirling course so small effect?
    Serve all thy starry eyes this shame to see?
Let dolts in haste some altars fair erect
    To those high pow'rs which idly sit above,
    And virtue do in greatest need neglect.

Boulon. O man, take heed how thou the gods do move
    To causeful wrath which thou canst not resist.
    Blasphemous words the speaker vain do prove.
Alas, while we are wrapped in foggy mist
    Of our self-love (so passions do deceive)
    We think they hurt when most they do assist.
To harm us worms should that high justice leave

His nature? nay, himself? for so it is.
What glory from our loss can he receive?
But still our dazzled eyes their way do miss,
    While that we do at his sweet scourge repine,
    The kindly way to beat us on to bliss.
If she must die, then hath she passed the line
    Of loathsome days, whose loss how canst thou moan,
    That dost so well their miseries define?
But such we are, with inward tempest blown
    Of winds quite contrary in waves of will:
    We moan that lost, which had we did bemoan.

Plangus. And shall she die, shall cruel fire spill
    Those beams that set so many hearts on fire?
    Hath she not force e'en death with love to kill?
Nay, e'en cold death inflamed with hot desire
    Her to enjoy (where joy itself is thrall)
    Will spoil the earth of his most rich attire.
Thus death becomes a rival to us all,
    And hopes with foul embracements her to get,
    In whose decay virtue's fair shrine must fall.
O virtue weak, shall death his triumph set
    Upon thy spoils, which never should lie waste?
    Let death first die; be thou his worthy let.
By what eclipse shall that sun be defaced?
    What mine hath erst thrown down so fair a tower?
    What sacrilege hath such a saint disgraced?
The world the garden is, she is the flower
    That sweetens all the place; she is the guest
    Of rarest price, both heav'n and earth her bower.
And shall (O me) all this in ashes rest?
    Alas, if you a phoenix new will have
    Burnt by the sun, she first must build her nest.
But well you know the gentle sun would save
    Such beams so like his own, which might have might
    In him, the thoughts of Phaethon's dam to grave.
Therefore, alas, you use vile Vulcan's spite,
    Which nothing spares, to melt that virgin wax
    Which while it is, it is all Asia's light.
O Mars, for what doth serve thy armed axe?

To let that witold beast consume in flames
Thy Venus' child, whose beauty Venus lacks?
O Venus (if her praise no envy frames
    In thy high mind) get her thy husband's grace.
    Sweet speaking oft a currish heart reclaims.
O eyes of mine where once she saw her face
    (Her face which was more lively in my heart),
    O brain where thought of her hath only place,
O hand, which touched her hand when we did part;
    O lips, that kissed that hand with my tears sprent;
    O tongue, then dumb, not daring tell my smart;
O soul, whose love in her is only spent,
    What e'er you see, think, touch, kiss, speak, or love,
    Let all for her, and unto her be bent.

Boulon. Thy wailing words do much my spirits move,
    They uttered are in such a feeling fashion
    That sorrow's work against my will I prove.
Methinks I am partaker of thy passion,
    And in thy case do glass mine own debility—
    Self-guilty folk most prone to feel compassion.
Yet reason saith, reason should have ability
    To hold these worldly things in such proportion
    As let them come or go with e'en facility.
But our desire's tyrannical extortion
    Doth force us there to set our chief delightfulness
    Where but a baiting place*is all our portion.
But still, although we fail of perfect rightfulness,
    Seek we to tame these childish superfluities?
    Let us not wink though void of purest sightfulness;
For what can breed more peevish incongruities
    Than man to yield to female lamentations?
    Let us some grammar learn of more congruities.

Plangus. If through mine ears pierce any consolations
    By wise discourse, sweet tunes, or poet's fiction;
    If aught I cease these hideous exclamations,
While that my soul, she, she lives in affliction;
    Then let my life long time*on earth maintained be,
    To wretched me the last worst malediction.
Can I, that know her sacred parts, restrained be

From any joy; know fortune's vile displacing her,
In moral rules let raging woes contained be?
Can I forget, when they in prison placing her,
    With swelling heart in spite and due disdainfulness
    She lay for dead, till I helped with unlacing her?
Can I forget from how much mourning plainfulness
    With diamond in window glass she graved,
    'Erona die, and end this ugly painfulness'?
Can I forget in how strange phrase she craved
    That quickly they would her burn, drown, or smother,
    As if by death she only might be saved?
Then let me eke forget one hand from other;
    Let me forget that Plangus I am called;
    Let me forget I am son to my mother;
But if my memory thus must be thralled
    To that strange stroke which conquered all my senses,
    Can thoughts still thinking so rest unappalled?

Boulon. Who still doth seek against himself offences,
    What pardon can avail? Or who employs him
    To hurt himself, what shields can be defences?
Woe to poor man: each outward thing annoys him
    In diverse kinds; yet as he were not filled,
    He heaps in inward grief that most destroys him.
Thus is our thought with pain for thistles tilled:
    Thus be our noblest parts dried up with sorrow:
    Thus is our mind with too much minding spilled.
One day lays up stuff of grief for the morrow;
    And whose good hap doth leave him unprovided,
    Condoling cause of friendship he will borrow.
Betwixt the good and shade of good divided,
    We pity deem that which but weakness is;
    So are we from our high creation slided.
But Plangus, lest I may your sickness miss
    Or rubbing, hurt the sore, I here do end.
    The ass did hurt*when he did think to kiss.

Histor. Thus did they say, and then away did wend;
    High time for me, for scattered were my sheep
    While I their speech in my rude rhyming penned.
Yet for that night my cabin did them keep

While Plangus did a story strange declare;
But hoarse and dry, my pipes I now must spare.

So well did Histor's voice express the passion of Plangus that all the princely beholders were stricken into a silent consideration of it; indeed everyone making that he heard of another the balance of his own troubles. Pamela was the first that commanded her thoughts to give place to some necessary words; and so, remembering herself what Histor had said the other time of the pastorals touching Musidorus (which as then she regarded not), she now desired him, if he did bear it in memory, that he would tell what strange adventure it was that had led away the two Greek princes from Erona, after they had slain Otanes and settled her in her kingdom. And when she had asked thus much, having had nothing but vehement desire to her counsel, her sweet body did even tremble for fear lest she had done amiss. But glad was her shepherd, not to have his doings spoken of, but because any question of him proceeded out of that mouth. Histor made answer that Plangus indeed had before his departure towards Thessalia and Macedon, at his importunate desire, made a brief declaration unto him thereof, but always with protestation that such things they were as many particularities of them had been full works to excellent historiographers; and that the first adventure was a man of monstrous bigness and force (and therefore commonly called a giant) who had wasted all the whole country of Paphlagonia by the help of a strong castle in the top of a high rock, where he kept a most terrible dragon which he had with such art from youth trained up that it was much more at his commandment than the best reclaimed hawk; so that it would fly abroad and do incredible damage, and ever duly return again to the castle where the giant kept no living man but himself. This, besides his own force, forced the miserable people to come to what composition he would: which was that monthly they should send him two maids not above sixteen years old, and two boys or young men under nineteen. The women he used at his beastly pleasure, and kept them imprisoned in his castle; the young men he was wont to sacrifice to an idol. This being come to the ears of those valiant young princes who (the harder a thing were the more their hearts rase unto it) went to the desolate people, and there (after many horrible complaints of parents whose children by public force were taken from them) they offered themselves to pay the next month's wages, if better they could not do. Their beauty made all the people pity them, but in the end self-respect prevailed over the pity, and the time being come, they armed themselves secretly under their long garments, and carrying short swords under their arms, were in that sort brought unto him by a man appointed to deliver them, for more the giant would not suffer to enter; who, when he saw their faces, was a proud man of so goodly a sacrifice. But they were no sooner in but that, drawing out their swords, they made him look to his own life. Which he did, running to a horse-load of a mast*he always used, and so weaponed (for armed he ever went) he let loose his trusty dragon. And so matched that ill-favoured couple with the matchless princes, who (having an excellent strength, and courage to make that strength awake) had within small space dispatched the world of those monsters, Pyrocles having killed the dragon and Musidorus the giant. What honours were done unto them by that people (which they continually observe as towards their savers) were superfluous to tell.

But thence were they led by the fame of a great war betwixt two brethren, where the younger had rebelled against the elder (being king of Syria), forced thereunto because he had taken away from him the principality of Damascus which their father in partage had bestowed upon him. There did they show as much their wisdom as their valour; for the one putting himself of the one side, and the other of the other, they so behaved themselves that either part thought they had the bravest champion in the world, insomuch as both were content to let the matter be tried by them to save the blood of so many which of both sides were but one people. But they (having the matter without exception put into their hands) instead of fighting fell to arbitrage, and making the brothers see the shamefulness of their fault so to sever themselves whom nature in their very beginning had so nearly knit, and yet remembering that whosoever hath thoroughly offended a prince can never think himself in perfect safety under him, they did determine that the king, giving in riches to his brother as much as his principality came unto, should enjoy Damascus; and they, finding the younger a prince of great worthiness, did so much by their credit with the Paphlagonians that they married him to the inheritrix of that goodly province—leaving in this sort a perpetual monument of wit, liberality, and courage.

But after this the next notable chance fell unto them (for many hundred of their valiant acts Plangus said he neither could tell, nor much time would serve for the repeating) was by the great lady of Palestina's means (called Andromana) who, hearing of their singular valour, sent to beseech their aid against a young prince of Arabia who had promised her marriage, and upon that having gotten a child of her, had now left her. They, though they knew she should have done well to have been sure of the church before he had been sure of the bed, yet pitying womanhood and desiring to know what answer the Arabian could make for himself, they went to offer themselves unto her. But they had not been there a while, and made her see their activity in jousts and their valour in particular combats, but that she had quite forgotten her old fancy that had cost her so dear, and was grown into the miserablest and strangest passion of love that can be imagined; for she loved them both with equal ardency. The only odds was that when she saw Pyrocles she thought she most desired him, and when she looked on Musidorus then was Pyrocles overweighed. At these words a man might have seen the eyes both of Pamela and Philoclea cast upon their servants to see whether they had committed any trespass or no. But Histor proceeded on in declaring her divided desire. When she looked on Musidorus then thought she a sweet brownness to be the most delightful beauty; but when she marked Pyrocles' pure white and red (for such difference Plangus said was betwixt them) then roses and lilies were the fairest flowers. Musidorus as the elder and stronger, Pyrocles as the younger and more delicate, contented her. In fine, she would wish sometimes Musidorus to be Pyrocles, another time Pyrocles to be Musidorus; but still she would have both hers. But those two princes (that seemed to love anything better than love) did so utterly discomfort her that she was forced to fly to force and put them both (by a sleight she played) in prison, where what allurements she used indifferently were long to tell. But at length they obstinately so much more refusing her (as their courages disdained to be compelled to anything), they had been like enough to have tarried there a good number of days but that the Arabian prince (hearing of their imprisonment) grew proud of his strength, and entered into Palestina with hope to conquer it. Which the people feeling (whether the lady would or no), delivered the prisoners, who having likewise by their good conduct delivered them of the Arabians, they themselves went into Egypt, as well to fly such a heart-burning woman (who shortly after, as Plangus said, had likewise forgotten them and, after divers changes, at last married herself to an apple-monger) as because they heard great fame of the king of Egypt's court, to be by reason of his magnificence full of valiant knights, as also his country well policied with good laws and customs, worthy to be learned.

But many notable accidents met with them as they passed the desert way betwixt Palestina and Egypt, worthy to have whole books written of them. But Plangus's appassionate mind could not brook long discourses, and therefore hasted himself to let me know the generality of their doings, which certainly were such as made me greatly delighted to hear them.

'But did he tell you no further', said the sweetest Philoclea, 'of those princes?'

'Yes', answered Histor, 'of a strange chance fell to them in Egypt, and that was this: riding together about six miles from the great city of Memphis they heard a pitiful cry as of one that either extreme grief or present fear had made his voice his best instrument of defence. They went the next way they thought should guide them to the party, and there found they a young man, well apparelled and handsomely proportioned, in the hands of four murdering villains who were ready to slay him, having stayed for nothing but that he told them he knew a place where a great treasure was hid. The covetousness of that made them delay the killing of him till one of the four, weary to follow him any longer, was ready to have given his mortal wound, at which he cried. But the other three stopped their fellow, when (in good time for him) came in these two princes who (seeing, how justly soever he had deserved death, that the manner was unjust by which they sought to lay it upon him) came in among them with threatenings if they did not let him loose. But the four (better knowing their own number than the others' valour) scorned their commandment, till by the death of three of them the fourth was taught with running away to leave the prisoner to their discretion; who (falling on his knees unto them as to the bestowers of a life upon him) told them the ground of his mischance, to this purpose: that he was a servant and of nearest credit to Amasis, son and heir to Sesostris, king of Egypt, and being of one age was also so like him as hardly (but by the great difference of their outward estates) the one could be known from the other; that the king Sesostris, after the death of Amasis's mother, had married a young woman who had turned the ordinary course of stepmother's hate to so unbridled a love towards her husband's son Amasis that neither the name of a father in him, of a husband in her, nor of a mother and son between themselves, could keep her back from disorderly seeking that of Amasis which is a wickedness to accept. But he (besides his duty to virtue) having his heart already pledged to Artaxia, queen of Persia, the more she loved him, the more detested her; which finding her hot spirits to work upon, shame, disdain, and lust converted all her affection to a most revengeful hatred, insomuch that all her study was for some naughty policy to over-throw him, whereof in the end this young man offered her occasion. For considering the resemblance he bare to his master, she began to make the poor youth believe she did extremely affect him in respect of that likeness; which he, privy to all his master's counsels, well knew she immoderately loved. Thermuthis (for so the young man was called) thought himself advanced to the stars when he saw so fair a queen bend her goodwill towards him, which she (so far was she become a slave to sin) sealed unto him with the fruition of her unchaste body. When she thus had angled Thermuthis then began she to accuse Amasis to his father as having sought to defile his bed; which opinion being something gotten in, though not fully imprinted in Sesostris's head, she caused Thermuthis (who was fully at her devotion) to come one night in his master's apparel he had that day worn to her chamber with his sword ready to kill the king as he slept, for so had she persuaded him to do. But as soon as he entered into the chamber she awaked the king, and making him see him he took to be his son (being deceived by candle-light and his raiment) in that order coming to kill him, the poor Thermuthis astonished and running away, she sent those four trusty servants after him, to whom she had beforehand given charge to have eye of him, and as soon as he should fly out of the chamber to follow him (under colour to help him by her commandment) till they trained him into some secret place, and there murder him. And thus much one of them appointed to kill him (who was the man the queen of Egypt most trusted) had revealed unto him, thinking his speedy death should keep it from being opened. "And", said Thermuthis, "by this time I fear the king hath done some hurt to my dear master, whom thus miserably I have ruined."

And indeed so the king meant to have done, and presently to have killed him, whom she caused to be brought by force out of his lodging, as though thither he had fled to shift himself, and so escape—the poor prince newly being come out of his sleep, and with his amazedness rather condemning himself than otherwise. But the king (neither taking pains to examine the matter to the uttermost, nor so much as to hear what Amasis could say in a matter by many circumstances easy enough to have been refelled), he presently caused him to be carried to the Red Sea, there to be put in a ship without any man but himself in it, and so to be left to the wind's discretion. But the two princes, having understood the beginning of this matter by Thermuthis, taking him with them, they entered into Memphis as the poor prince was some few miles already carried out towards his ship of death. Which they understanding, and fearing they should not have leisure to tell the king and save him, they first pursued after him and by force of arms, joined with the help of some of the country who were willing to help their prince, they rescued him out of their hands and, bringing him back to the king, made him understand the whole circumstances by Thermuthis's confession; whose pardon they got, considering what a fault the king himself had done to run so hastily in the condemning his only son in a cause might both by Thermuthis's absence and many other ways have been proved contrary. As for his wife, she was past either pardoning or punishing; for when she heard the matter was revealed, she killed herself. "Thence," Plangus said, "having left the father and son in unity, and Amasis acknowledging his life of them with great love (which notwithstanding he could not have done if he had known how Artaxia hated them), they returned, as it was thought, to Greece-ward; whom he had still followed, and by many misfortunes could never find. And now his last hope is in one of their countries, being nevertheless in great doubt that they are already perished by sea."'

Thus did Histor epitomise the worthy acts of those two worthies, making (though unknown) their own ears witnesses of their glory; which in no respect rejoiced them so much as that their beloved ladies heard it, of whose esteeming them they had tenderest regard, and chiefly desired they might know it was no dishonour they sought unto them whose honour they held in more precious reckoning than their own lives. But indeed unmeasurable was the contentment of the two ladies who, besides love had taught them to trust, might find by the circumstance of these things that these could be no other than their lovers, although either's heart was so deeply plunged in her own that she never pained herself to call in question her sister's case; so that neither Pamela ever took conceit of the

Amazon, nor Philoclea of the shepherd. As for Gynecia, such an inward lordship Cleophila held in her that she saw only her, she heard nobody but her, and thought of nothing but of her; so that Histor's narration passed through her ears without any marking, judging (as commonly they do that are full of thoughts) by the beginning that it should nothing appertain to the party upon whom she knit all her imagining power. The duke would divers times very fain have broken off Histor's speech but that, finding Cleophila yield him acceptable audience, he was in doubt to displease her. But well afraid he was lest the great praises he gave to the famous Pyrocles might kindle Cleophila's heart unto him; for comparing their worthiness he was forced to confess in himself there would prove a noble match between them, which made him fear that Cleophila's young mind might be stirred that way. Therefore, as soon, or rather before, Histor had ended, lest he might renew again some mention of those two princes, he called to Philisides who (according to his custom) sat so melancholy as though his mind were banished from the place he loved to be, imprisoned in his body; and desired him he would begin some eclogue with some other of the shepherds according to the accustomed guise. Philisides (though very unwilling) at the duke's commandment offered to sing with Lalus; but Lalus directly refused him, saying he should within few days be married to the fair Kala and since he had gotten his desire, he would sing no more. Then the duke willed Philisides to declare the discourse of his own fortunes, unknown to them as being a stranger in that country. But he prayed the duke to pardon him, the time being far too joyful to suffer the rehearsal of his miseries. But to satisfy Basilius some way, he began an eclogue betwixt himself and the echo, framing his voice so in those desert places as what words he would have the echo reply unto, those he would sing higher than the rest, and so kindly framed a disputation betwixt himself and it; which, with these hexameters in the following order, he uttered:

Philisides   *Echo*

$$- - \cup \cup - - - \cup \cup - \cup \cup - -$$

Fair rocks, goodly rivers, sweet woods, when shall I
    see peace?   Peace.
Peace? What bars me my tongue? Who is it that
    comes me so nigh?   I.
Oh! I do know what guest I have met; it is echo.   'Tis echo.

Well met, echo, approach; then tell me thy will too.   I will too.
  Echo, what do I get yielding my sprite to my griefs?   Griefs.
What medicine may I find for a pain that draws me to
  death?   Death.
O poisonous medicine! What worse to me can be than
  it?   It.
In what state was I then, when I took this deadly
  disease?   Ease.
And what manner a mind which had to that humour
  a vein?   Vain.
Hath not reason enough vehemence the desire to
  reprove?   Prove
Oft prove I; but what salve when reason seeks to be
  gone?   One.
Oh! What is it? What is it that may be a salve to my
  love?   Love.
What do lovers seek for, long seeking for to enjoy?   Joy.
What be the joys for which to enjoy they went to the
  pains?   Pains.
Then to an earnest love what doth best victory lend?   End.
End? But I can never end; love will not give me the
  leave.   Leave.
How be the minds disposed that cannot taste thy
  physic?   Sick.
Yet say again thy advice for th'ills that I told thee.   I told thee.
Doth th'infected wretch of his ill th'extremity know?   No.
But if he know not his harms what guides hath he
  whilst he be blind?   Blind.
What blind guides can he have that leans to a fancy?   A fancy.
Can fancies want eyes, or he fall that steppeth aloft?   Oft.
What causes first made these torments on me to light?   Light.
Can then a cause be so light that forceth a man to go
  die?   Aye.
Yet tell what light thing I had in me to draw me to
  die?   Eye.
Eyesight made me to yield, but what first pierced to
  mine eyes?   Eyes.
Eyes' hurters, eyes' hurt, but what from them to me
  falls?   Falls.
But when I first did fall, what brought most fall to my
  heart?   Art.

Art? What can be that art which thou dost mean by thy speech?	Speech.
What be the fruits of speaking art? What grows by the words?	Words.
O much more than words: those words served more to me bless.	Less.
O when shall I be known where most to be known I do long?	Long.
Long be thy woes for such news, but how recks she my thoughts?	Oughts.
Then, then what do I gain, since unto her will I do wind?	Wind.
Wind, tempests, and storms; yet in end what gives she desire?	Ire.
Silly reward! Yet among women hath she of virtue the most.	Most.
What great name may I give to so heav'nly a woman?	A woe-man.
Woe, but seems to me joy that agrees to my thought so.	I thought so.
Think so, for of my desired bliss it is only the course.	Curse.
Cursed be thyself for cursing that which leads me to joys.	Toys.
What be the sweet creatures where lowly demands be not heard?	Hard.
Hard to be got, but got constant, to be held like steels.	Eels.
How can they be unkind? Speak for th'hast narrowly pried.	Pride.
Whence can pride come there, since springs of beauty be thence?	Thence.
Horrible is this blasphemy unto the most holy.	O lie.
Thou li'st false echo, their minds as virtue be just.	Just.
Mock'st thou those diamonds which only be matched by the gods?	Odds.
Odds? What an odds is there since them to the heav'ns I prefer?	Err.
Tell yet again me the names of these fair formed to do ev'ls.	Dev'ls.
Dev'ls? If in hell such dev'ls do abide, to the hells I do go.	Go.

Philisides was commended for the placing of his echo, but little did he regard their praises; who had set the foundation of his honour there where he was most despised. And therefore returning again to the train of his desolate pensiveness, Cleophila seeing nobody offer to fill the stage, as if her long-restrained conceits did now burst out of prison, she thus (desiring her voice should be accorded to nothing but to Philoclea's ears) threw down the burden of her mind in Anacreon's kind of verses:*

My muse what ails this ardour
To blaze my only secrets?
Alas, it is no glory
To sing my own decayed state.
Alas, it is no comfort
To speak without an answer.
Alas, it is no wisdom
To show the wound without cure.

My muse what ails this ardour?
My eyes be dim, my limbs shake,
My voice is hoarse, my throat scorched,
My tongue to this my roof cleaves,
My fancy amazed, my thoughts dulled,
My heart doth ache, my life faints,
My soul begins to take leave.
So great a passion all feel,
To think a sore so deadly
I should so rashly rip up.

My muse what ails this ardour?
If that to sing thou art bent,
Go sing the fall of old Thebes,
The wars of ugly centaurs,
The life, the death of Hector,
So may thy song be famous;
Or if to love thou art bent,
Recount the rape of Europe,

Adonis' end, Venus' net,
The sleepy kiss the moon stale;
So may thy song be pleasant.

My muse what ails this ardour
To blaze my only secrets?
Wherein do only flourish
The sorry fruits of anguish,
The song thereof a last will,
The tunes be cries, the words plaints,
The singer is the song's theme
Wherein no ear can have joy,
Nor eye receives due object,
Ne pleasure here, ne fame got.

My muse what ails this ardour?
'Alas', she saith, 'I am thine,
So are thy pains my pains too.
Thy heated heart my seat is
Wherein I burn, thy breath is
My voice, too hot to keep in.
Besides, lo here the author
Of all thy harms; lo here she
That only can redress thee,
Of her I will demand help.'

My muse, I yield, my muse sing,
But all thy song herein knit:
The life we lead is all love,
The love we hold is all death,
Nor aught I crave to feed life,
Nor aught I seek to shun death,
But only that my goddess
My life, my death, do count hers.

Basilius, when she had fully ended her song, fell prostrate upon the
ground, and thanked the gods they had preserved his life so long as
to hear the very music they themselves used in an earthly body.
And then with like grace to Cleophila, never left entreating her till
she had (taking a lyra Basilius held for her) sung these phaleuciacs:*

— — — ∪ ∪ — ∪ — ∪ — ∪

Reason, tell me thy mind, if here be reason
In this strange violence, to make resistance.
Where sweet graces erect the stately banner
Of virtue's regiment, shining in harness

Of fortune's diadems, by beauty mustered.
Say then, Reason, I say what is thy counsel?

Her loose hair be the shot, the breasts the pikes be,
Scouts each motion is, the hands the horsemen,
Her lips are the riches the wars to maintain,
Where well couched abides a coffer of pearl,
Her legs carriage is of all the sweet camp.
Say then, Reason, I say what is thy counsel?

Her cannons be her eyes, mine eyes the walls be,
Which at first volley gave too open entry,
Nor rampire did abide; my brain was up blown,
Undermined with a speech, the piercer of thoughts.
Thus weakened by myself, no help remaineth.
Say then, Reason, I say what is thy counsel?

And now fame, the herald of her true honour,
Doth proclaim (with a sound made all by men's mouths)
That nature, sovereign of earthly dwellers,
Commands all creatures to yield obeisance
Under this, this her own, her only darling.
Say then, Reason, I say what is thy counsel?

Reason sighs, but in end he thus doth answer:
'Naught can reason avail in heav'nly matters.'
Thus nature's diamond, receive thy conquest,
Thus pure pearl, I do yield my senses and soul.
Thus sweet pain, I do yield what e'er I can yield.
Reason look to thyself, I serve a goddess.

Dorus had long, he thought, kept silence from saying somewhat
which might tend to the glory of her in whom all glory (to his
seeming) was included. But now he brake it, singing these verses,
called asclepiadics:*

— — — ∪ ∪ — — ∪ ∪ — ∪

O sweet woods, the delight of solitariness!
O how much I do like your solitariness!
Where man's mind hath a freed consideration
Of goodness to receive lovely direction;
Where senses do behold th'order of heav'nly host,
And wise thoughts do behold what the creator is.

O.A.—8

Contemplation here holdeth his only seat,
Bounded with no limits, borne with a wing of hope,
Climbs even unto the stars; nature is under it.
Naught disturbs thy quiet, all to thy service yield,
Each sight draws on a thought (thought mother of science),
Sweet birds kindly do grant harmony unto thee,
Fair trees' shade is enough fortification,
Nor danger to thyself, if be not in thyself.

O sweet woods, the delight of solitariness!
O how much I do like your solitariness!
Here no treason is hid, veiled in innocence,
Nor envy's snaky eye finds any harbour here,
Nor flatterers' venomous insinuations,
Nor cunning humorists' puddled opinions,
Nor courteous ruin of proffered usury,
Nor time prattled away, cradle of ignorance,
Nor causeless duty, nor cumber of arrogance,
Nor trifling title of vanity dazzleth us,
Nor golden manacles stand for a paradise,
Here wrong's name is unheard; slander a monster is.
Keep thy sprite from abuse, here no abuse doth haunt.
What man grafts in a tree dissimulation?

O sweet woods, the delight of solitariness!
O how well I do like your solitariness!
Yet dear soil, if a soul closed in a mansion
As sweet as violets, fair as a lily is,
Straight as cedar, a voice stains the canary birds,
Whose shade safety doth hold, danger avoideth her:
Such wisdom that in her lives speculation:
Such goodness that in her simplicity triumphs:
Where envy's snaky eye winketh or else dieth,
Slander wants a pretext, flattery gone beyond:
Oh! If such a one have bent to a lonely life,
Her steps glad we receive, glad we receive her eyes.
    And think not she doth hurt our solitariness,
    For such company decks such solitariness.

The other shepherds were offering themselves to have continued
the sports, but the night had so quietly spent most part of herself

among them that the duke, for that time, licensed them; and so bringing Cleophila to her lodging (who would much rather have done the same for Philoclea), of all sides they went to counterfeit a sleep in their beds, for a true one their agonies could not afford them. Yet there they lay (for so might they be most solitary for the food of their thoughts) till it was near noon the next day. After which Basilius was to continue his Apollo devotions, and the others to meditate upon their private desires.

Here ends the second eclogues.

THE THIRD BOOK OR ACT

THE next day, which followed a night full of passions, and yet brought in himself new matter to increase them (time upon time still adding growth to a well-rooted inclination), while the duke in the afternoon time was busy about Apollo's rites, Cleophila (to whom the not-enjoying her dear friend Dorus had been one of her burdenous griefs) took hold of this opportunity, and calling her beloved cousin with her, went to the same place where first she had revealed unto him her enclosed passion and was by him (as you may remember) with a friendly sharpness reprehended. There, sitting down among the sweet flowers (whereof that country was very plentiful) under the pleasant shade of a broad-leaved sycamore, they recounted one to another their strange pilgrimage of passions, omitting nothing which the open-hearted friendship is wont to lay forth, where there is cause to communicate both joys and sorrows— for, indeed, there is no sweeter taste of friendship than the coupling of their souls in this mutuality either of condoling or comforting, where the oppressed mind finds itself not altogether miserable, since it is sure of one which is feelingly sorry for his misery; and the joyful spends not his joy either alone or there where it may be envied, but may freely send it to such a well-grounded object, from whence he shall be sure to receive a sweet reflection of the same joy, and (as in a clear mirror of sincere goodwill) see a lively picture of his own gladness. Then would there arise betwixt them loving debates of their ladies' beauties, of their own constancies; and sometimes gloriously strive whether had been the most wretched.

'O my Dorus, my Dorus,' said Cleophila, 'who would ever have thought so good a schoolmaster as you were to me could for lack of living have been driven to shepherdry?'

'Even the same', said Dorus, 'that would have thought so true a chaste boy as you were could have become a counterfeit courtesan. But', said he, 'see whether you can show me so fair spoils of your victory'—and therewith he drew out a glove of Pamela's done with murrey silk and gold lace, and (not without tender tears kissing it) he put it again in his bosom, and sang these two stanzas:*

Sweet glove, the witness of my secret bliss
(Which hiding didst preserve that beauty's light
That, opened forth, my seal of comfort is),
Be thou my star in this my darkest night,
Now that mine eyes their cheerful sun doth miss
Which dazzling still, doth still maintain my sight;
   Be thou, sweet glove, the anchor of my mind,
   Till my frail bark his hav'n again do find.

Sweet glove, the sweet despoils of sweetest hand,
Fair hand, the fairest pledge of fairer heart,
True heart, whose truth doth yield to truest band,
Chief band, I say, which ties my chiefest part,
My chiefest part, wherein do chiefly stand
Those secret joys, which heav'n to me impart,
   Unite in one, my state thus still to save;
   You have my thanks, let me your comfort have.

'Alas,' said Cleophila, when she had awhile paused after her friend's music, 'can you not joy sufficiently in your joys, but you must use your joys as if you would vauntingly march over your friend's miseries? Be happy still, my Dorus, but wish the same hap to him whom goodwill doth make to place much of his hap in you.'

'Not the same hap,' said Dorus smiling, 'Philoclea's hap I freely grant you; but I pray you let not your Amazon eyes be busy upon the lady Pamela, for her looks have an attractive power in them, and your heart is not of the hardest metal.'

'And are you afraid of that?' said Cleophila. 'From henceforward be not, for hardly are stars seen in daylight. But I would fain know what assurance you have of the changing favour of fortune. I have heard of them that dreamed much of holding great treasures, and when they waked found nothing in their hands but a bedstaff. Glad would I be to be assured of your well-being, for methinks the gods be too unequal to mankind if they suffer not good to come from one kinsman to another by a secret infusion, as we find daily evil doth by a manifest infection. Therefore, since your joy was such as you could find in your heart to sing it, do now for my sake vouchsafe to say it.'

'My joys are such', said Dorus, 'as neither suffer in themselves uncertainty, nor are in danger by inconstancy. Let me, therefore, do no wrong to my motherly destinies, which have woven me so blessed a web, by ungrateful forgetting their favours; and since I have often tired the muses with the hideous tune of my doleful affects, I will now sauce those sorrows with some more pleasant exercises.' And so took he his shepherd's pipe, and with the sounding that, first seeming to invite the birds to mark his music, he after laid down his pipe and sang these following:

> The merchant man, whom gain doth teach the sea
> Where rocks do wait for them the winds do chase,
> Beaten with waves, no sooner kens the bay
> Where he was bound to make his marting place,
>   But fear forgot, and pains all overpast,
>   Make present ease receive the better taste.
>
> The labourer, which cursed earth up tears
> With sweaty brows, sometimes with watered eyes,
> Oft scorching sun, oft cloudy darkness fears,
> While upon chance his fruit of labour lies;
>   But harvest come, and corn in fertile store,
>   More in his own he toiled, he glads the more.
>
> Thus in my pilgrimage of mated mind,
> Seeking the saint in whom all graces dwell,
> What storms found me, what torments I did find,
> Who seeks to know acquaints himself with hell;
>   But now success hath got above annoys,
>   That sorrow's weight doth balance up these joys.

'Truly', said Cleophila, 'among so many qualities as all ages have attributed to Cupid, I did never think him so good a minstrel that in such short space could make his scholar so musical as you be. But although, for my part, the stars have not held wholly an angry aspect towards me, yet lest envious fortune should spite at the too much boasting of your blessedness, I will mingle your comical tunes with my long-used tragical notes, and will stain a little the fullness of your hopes with the hanging on of my tedious fears.' Therewith lying down with her face upward towards heaven, with her eye so settled as one might well perceive it was nothing her eye could then see which busied her common sense, with a fainting kind of voice she thus sang:

> The merchant man, whom many seas have taught
> What horrors breed where wind dominion bears,

Yet never rock, nor race, such terror brought
As near his home when storm or shelf he fears;
   For nature hath that never failing scope,
   Most loath to lose, the most approaching hope.

The labourer, whom tired body makes
Hold dear his work, with sighs each change attends,
But at no change so pinching care he takes
As happy shows of corn when harvest sends;
   For reason will, great sight of hoped bliss,
   Make great the loss, so great the fear to miss.

Thus tossed in my ship of huge desire,
Thus toiled in my work of raging love,
Now that I spy the hav'n my thoughts require,
Now that some flow'r of fruit my pains do prove,
   My dreads augment the more in passion's might,
   Since love with care, and hope with fear do fight.

As she had ended the last word, she took Dorus in her arms: 'Ah!
my Dorus,' said she, 'these be as yet my harvests; these be as yet the
gains of my traffic! But I conjure thee by the inviolate name of our
friendship, or (if your new flames have made that smoke) by the fair
hair of Pamela, that you tell me the story of your loving adventures,
that thus short of me, as I think, in affection, you have gotten so
much the fore-foot in affection's reward.'

'Alas,' said Dorus, with a changed countenance, 'the cruel
schoolmaster makes the silly child think a little play great sport, and
how much the more we need great help, small help seems the greater
unto us; for long beaten in miseries, it makes us measure our minds
by our powers and not by our wishes, and the heart stuffed up with
woefulness is glad greedily to suck the thinnest air of comfort. Far
am I (God knows) from the place where I hope to stop, but yet well
advanced am I from thence where I took my start.' Then did he
declare unto her the discourse of all that with which heretofore,
fair ladies, perchance I have troubled you: How Pamela, out of a
virtuous resolution in respect of his outward inequality, had wholly
disdained to speak with him, and misliked the shows he had made of
his love; the strait he was in to make himself known (he being
enviously looked upon, and she narrowly guarded); that in the end
he was forced to counterfeit a love to Mopsa, and tell her whatsoever

he would have Pamela understand; how in his tale he answered Pamela's wit and abused Mopsa's ignorance—the manner whereof you have before, fair ladies, understood. And further, since that time having plainly found there wanted no liking in Pamela, if she might have assurance of his worthiness, he had (still under the colour of asking her whether it were not fit for Mopsa so to do) concluded with her the stealing her away to the next seaport, under vehement oath to offer no force unto her till he had invested her in the duchy of Thessalia; that one of the greatest matters had won her to this was the strange humours she saw her father lately fallen into, and unreasonable restraint of her liberty (whereof she knew no cause but light-grounded jealousies), added to the hate of that manner of life, and confidence she had in his virtue; that now they waited for nothing but some fit time by the absence of their three loathsome companions in whom folly engendered suspicion. 'And therefore now', said Dorus, 'my dear cousin (to whom nature began my friendship, education confirmed it, and virtue hath made it eternal), here have I discovered the very foundation whereupon my life is built. Be you the judge betwixt me and my fortune. The violence of love is not unknown unto you; and I know my case shall never want pity in your consideration. How all the joys of my heart do leave me in thinking I must for a time be absent from you! The eternal truth is witness unto me, I know I should not so sensibly feel the pangs of my last departure. But this enchantment of my restless desire hath such authority in myself above myself that I am become a slave unto it. I have no more freedom in mine own determinations. My thoughts are now all bent how to carry away my burdenous bliss. Yet, most beloved cousin, rather than you should think I do herein violate that holy band of true friendship wherein I unworthy am knit unto you, command my stay. Perchance the force of your commandment may work such impression into my heart, which no reason of mine own can imprint unto it. For the gods forbid the foul word of abandoning Pyrocles might ever be objected to the faithful Musidorus! But if you can spare my presence (whose presence no way serves you, and by the division of these two lodges is not oft with you); nay, if you can think my absence may (as it shall) stand you in stead by bringing such an army hither as shall make Basilius (willing or unwilling) to know his own hap in granting you Philoclea, then I will cheerfully go about this my most desired enterprise, and shall think the better half of it already achieved, being begun in the fortunate hour of my friend's contentment.'

These words, as they were not knit together with such a constant course of flowing eloquence as Dorus was wont to use, so was his voice interrupted with sighs and his countenance with interchanging colour dismayed—so much his own heart did find him faulty to unbend any way the continual use of their dear friendship. But, O feminine love, what power thou holdest in men's hearts! Many times he had been desirous to signify his happy success and final determination with Pamela, but his heart would never serve him to come to this point, till one word at this time emboldened another kindly to discover to his friend his own unkindness. Cleophila (who had before purposed to make the like declaration upon what slippery grounds her hopes stood, and yet how far her hopes in Philoclea were advanced, how far by Gynecia they were hindered), when this last determination of Dorus strake her attentive ears, she stayed a great while oppressed with a dead amazement. There came straight before her mind, made tender with woes, the images of her own fortune; her tedious longings; her causes to despair; the cumbersome folly of Basilius; the enraged jealousy of Gynecia; herself a prince without retinue, a man annoyed with the troubles of womankind, loathsomely loved, and dangerously loving; and now, for the perfecting of all, her friend to be taken away by himself, to make the loss the greater by the unkindness. But within a while she resolutely passed over all inward objections; and therefore, preferring her friend's profit to her own desire, with a quiet but hearty*look, she thus answered him:

'If I bare thee this love, virtuous Musidorus, for mine own sake, and that our friendship grew because I for my part might rejoice to enjoy such a friend, I should now so thoroughly feel mine own loss that I should call the heavens and earth to witness how cruelly ye rob me of my greatest comfort, measuring the breach of friendship by mine own passion. But because indeed I love thee for thyself, and in my judgement judge of thy worthiness to be loved, I am content to leave all that which might please myself. I am content to build my pleasure upon thy comfort; and then will I deem my hap in friendship great when I shall see thee, whom I love, happy. Let me be only sure thou lovest me still—the only prize of true affection. Go therefore on, worthy Musidorus, with the guide of virtue and service of fortune. Let thy loves be loved, thy desires prosperous, thy escape safe, and thy journey easy. Let everything yield his help to thy desert. For my part, absence shall not take thee from mine eyes, nor afflictions shall bar me from gladding in thy good; nor a possessed heart shall keep thee from the place it hath forever allotted unto thee.'

Dorus would fain have replied again, to have made a liberal confession that Cleophila had of her side the advantage of well performing friendship; but partly his own grief of parting from one he loved so dearly, partly the kind care in what state he should leave Cleophila, bred such a conflict in his mind that many times he wished he had either never attempted, or never revealed, this secret enterprise.

But Cleophila, who had now looked to the uttermost of it, and established her mind upon an assured determination: 'My only friend,' said she, 'since to so good towardness your courteous destinies have conducted you, let not a ceremonial consideration of our mutual love be a bar unto it. I joy in your presence; but I joy more in your good. That friendship brings forth the fruits of enmity which prefers his own tenderness before his friend's damage. For my part, my greatest grief herein shall be I can be no further serviceable unto you.'

'O Cleophila,' said Dorus, with his eyes even covered with water, 'I did not think so soon to have displayed my determination unto you, but to have made my way first into your loving judgement. But, alas, as your sweet disposition drew me so far, so doth it now strengthen me in it. To you, therefore, be the due commendation given, who can conquer me in love, and love in wisdom. As for me, then shall goodness turn to evil, and ungratefulness be the token of a true heart, when Pyrocles shall not possess a principal seat in my soul, when the name of Pyrocles shall not be held of me in devout reverence.'

I think they would never have come to the cruel instant of parting, nor to the ill-faring word of farewell, had not Cleophila seen afar off the old Basilius who had been everywhere to seek her since he had ended his sacrifice; and now being come within compass of discerning her, he began to frame the loveliest countenance he could, stroking up his legs, setting his beard in due order, and standing bolt upright.

'Alas,' said Cleophila, 'behold an evil foretoken of our sorrowful departure!*Yonder see I one of my furies which doth daily vex me. Farewell, farewell, my Musidorus! The gods make fortune to wait on thy virtues, and make me wade through this lake of wretchedness!'

Dorus burst out into a flood of tears, wringing her fast by the hand: 'No, no,' said he, 'I go blindfold whither the course of my ill-hap carries me; for now, too late, my heart gives me this our separating can never be prosperous. But if I live, attend me here shortly with an army.'

Thus both appalled with the grievous renting of their long combination (having first resolved with themselves that, whatsoever evil fell unto them, they should never upon no occasion utter their names—for the conserving the honour of their royal parentage—but took other names they agreed upon), they took diverse ways: Dorus to the lodge-ward, where his heavy eyes might be something refreshed; Cleophila towards Basilius, saying to herself with a scornful smiling, 'yet hath not my friendly fortune wholly deprived me of a pleasant companion.'

Basilius had inquired of his daughter Philoclea what receipt his desires found in Cleophila, and had some comfort of her: that, by her own good entertainment, she did imagine his cause was not ungrateful unto her. And now, having with much search come to her presence, doubt and desire bred a great quarrel in his mind; for late experience had taught him to doubt, and true feeling of love made doubts dangerous. But the working of his desire had ere long won the field; and therefore, with the most submissive manner his behaviour could yield: 'O goddess', said he, 'towards whom I have the greatest feeling of religion, be not displeased at some show of devotion I have made to Apollo, since he (if he know anything) knows that my heart bears far more awful reverence to yourself than to any unseen deity.'

'You will ever be deceived in me,' answered Cleophila, 'I will make myself no competitor with Apollo; neither can blasphemies to him be duties to me.'

With that, Basilius took out of his bosom certain verses he had written, and kneeling down, presented them to her. They contained this:

Phoebus farewell, a sweeter saint I serve.
The high conceits thy heav'nly wisdoms breed
My thoughts forget: my thoughts which never swerve
From her in whom is sown their freedom's seed,
And in whose eyes my daily doom I read.

Phoebus farewell, a sweeter saint I serve.

Thou art far off, thy kingdom is above;
She heav'n on earth with beauties doth preserve.
Thy beams I like, but her clear rays I love;
Thy force I fear, her force I still do prove.

Phoebus yield up thy title in my mind.
She doth possess; thy image is defaced.
But if thy rage some brave revenge will find
On her, who hath in me thy temple razed,
Employ thy might, that she my fires may taste;
   And how much more her worth surmounteth thee,
   Make her as much more base by loving me.

'This is my hymn to you,' said he, 'not left me by my ancestors, but begun in myself. The temple wherein it is daily sung is my soul, and the sacrifice I offer to you withal is all whatsoever I am.'

Cleophila (who ever thought she found in his speeches the ill taste of a medicine, and the operation of a poison) would have suffered a disdainful look to have been the only witness of her good acceptation, but that Basilius began afresh to lay before her many pitiful prayers; and in the end to conclude that he was fully of opinion the hateful influence which had made him embrace this solitary life was now passed over him, and withal living so weakly guarded, the late tumult had taught him what dangers he might fall into. Therefore he was now inclined to return to his palace in Mantinea, and there he hoped he should be better able to show how much he desired to make all he had hers—with many other such honey words which my pen grows almost weary to set down.

This, indeed, nearly pierced Cleophila; for the good beginning she had obtained of Philoclea made her desire to continue the same trade till unto the more perfecting of her desires; and to come to any public place she did deadly fear, lest her mask by many eyes might the sooner be discovered, and so her hopes stopped, and the state of her joys endangered. Therefore awhile she rested, musing at the daily changing labyrinth of her own fortune; but in herself determined it was her only best to keep him there, and with favours to make him love the place where the favours were received, as disgraces had made him apt to change the soil. Therefore, casting a kind of corner look upon him, 'it is truly said', said she, 'that age cooleth the blood. How soon, good man, you are terrified before you

THE THIRD BOOK OR ACT 157

receive any hurt! Do you not know that daintiness is kindly unto us, and that hard obtaining is the excuse of women's granting? Yet speak I not as though you were like to obtain, or I to grant; but because I would not have you imagine I am to be won by courtly vanities, or esteem a man the more because he hath handsome men to wait on him when he is afraid to live without them.'

You might have seen Basilius humbly swell, and with a lowly look stand upon his tiptoes—such diversity her words delivered unto him. 'O Hercules,' answered he, 'Basilius afraid! Or his blood cold, that boils in such a furnace! Care I who is with me while I enjoy your presence, or is any place good or bad to me but as it please you to bless or curse it? O let me be but armed in your good grace, and I defy whatsoever there is or can be against me! No, no! your love is forcible, and my age is not without vigour.'

Cleophila thought it not good for his stomach to receive a surfeit of too much favour; and therefore thinking he had enough for the time to keep him from any sudden removing, with a certain gracious bowing down of her head towards him, she turned away, saying she would leave him at this time, to see how temperately he could use so bountiful a measure of her kindness.

Basilius (that thought every drop a flood, that bred any refreshment) durst not further press her, but, with an ancient modesty, left her to the sweet repast of her own fancies.

Cleophila, as soon as he was departed, went towards Pamela's lodge, in hope again to have seen her friend Dorus, to have pleased herself with a new painful farewell. But being come even near the lodge, she saw the mouth of a cave, made as it should seem by nature in despite of art, so fitly did the rich growing marble serve to beautify the vault of the first entry. Underfoot the ground seemed mineral, yielding such a glistering show of gold in it as, they say, the river Tagus carries in his sandy bed. The cave framed out into many goodly spacious rooms, even such as the self-liking men have with long and learned delicacy found out the most easeful. There ran through it a little sweet river which had left the face of the earth to drown herself for a small way in this dark, but pleasant, mansion. The very first show of the place enticed the melancholy mind of Cleophila to yield herself over there to the flood of her own thoughts. And therefore, sitting down in the first entry of the cave's mouth, with a song she had lately made she gave doleful way to her bitter affects. She sang to this effect:

Since that the stormy rage of passions dark
(Of passions dark, made dark by beauty's light)
With rebel force hath closed in dungeon dark
My mind ere now led forth by reason's light;

Since all the things which give mine eyes their light
Do foster still the fruit of fancies dark,
So that the windows of my inward light
Do serve to make my inward powers dark;

Since, as I say, both mind and senses dark
Are hurt, not helped, with piercing of the light;
While that the light may show the horrors dark,
But cannot make resolved darkness light;

   I like this place where, at the least, the dark
   May keep my thoughts from thought of wonted light.

Instead of an instrument, her song was accompanied with the wringing of her hands, the closing of her weary eyes, and even sometimes cut off with the swelling of her sighs, which did not suffer the voice to have his free and native passage. But as she was awhile musing upon her song, raising up her spirits, which were something fallen into the weakness of lamentation, considering solitary complaints do no good to him whose help stands without himself, she might afar off first hear a whispering sound which seemed to come from the inmost part of the cave, and being kept together with the close hollowness of the place, had (as in a trunk) the more liberal access to her ears. And by and by she might perceive the same voice deliver itself into musical tunes, and with a base lyre give forth this song:

Hark, plaintful ghosts! Infernal furies, hark
Unto my woes the hateful heav'ns do send—
The heav'ns conspired to make my vital spark
A wretched wrack, a glass of ruin's end!

Seeing, alas, so mighty powers bend
Their ireful shot against so weak a mark,
Come cave, become my grave; come death, and lend
Receipt to me within thy bosom dark!
For what is life to daily dying mind
Where, drawing breath, I suck the air of woe;
Where too much sight makes all the body blind,

> And highest thoughts downward most headlong throw?
> > Thus then my form, and thus my state I find:
> > Death wrapped in flesh, to living grave assigned.

And pausing but a little, with moanful melody it continued this octave:

> Like those sick folks, in whom strange humours flow,
> Can taste no sweets, the sour only please;
> So to my mind, while passions daily grow,
> Whose fiery chains upon his freedom seize,
> > Joys strangers seem, I cannot bide their show,
> > Nor brook aught else but well acquainted woe.
> > Bitter grief tastes me best, pain is my ease,
> > Sick to the death, still loving my disease.

'O Venus,' said Cleophila, 'who is this so well acquainted with me, that can make so lively a portraiture of my miseries? It is surely the spirit appointed to have care of me which doth now in this dark place bear part with the complaints of his unhappy charge. For if it be so, that the heavens have at all times a measure of their wrathful harms, surely so many have come to my blissless lot that the rest of the world hath too small a proportion to make with cause so wailful a lamentation. But', said she, 'whatsoever thou be, I will seek thee out; for thy music well assures me we are at least hand fellow prentices to one ungracious master.' So rase she and went, guiding herself by the still plaining voice, till she saw upon a stone a little wax light set, and under it a piece of paper with these verses very lately (as it should seem) written in it:

> How is my sun, whose beams are shining bright,
> Become the cause of my dark ugly night?
> Or how do I, captived in this dark plight,
> Bewail the case, and in the cause delight?
> My mangled mind huge horrors still do fright,
> With sense possessed, and claimed by reason's right:
> Betwixt which two in me I have this fight,
> Where whoso wins, I put myself to flight.

> Come, cloudy fears, close up my dazzled sight;
> Sorrow, suck up the marrow of my might;
> Due sighs, blow out all sparks of joyful light;
> Tire on, despair, upon my tired sprite!

> An end, an end, my dulled pen cannot write,
> Nor mazed head think, nor falt'ring tongue recite!

And hard underneath the sonnet were these words written:

> This cave is dark, but it had never light.
> This wax doth waste itself, yet painless dies.
> These words are full of woes, yet feel they none.
>
> I darkened am, who once had clearest sight.
> I waste my heart, which still new torment tries.
> I plain with cause, my woes are all mine own.
>
> No cave, no wasting wax, no words of grief,
> Can hold, show, tell, my pains without relief.

She did not long stay to read the words, for not far off from the stone she might discern in a dark corner a lady lying with her face so prostrate upon the ground as she could neither know nor be known. But (as the general nature of man is desirous of knowledge, and sorrow especially glad to find fellows) she went as softly as she could convey her foot near unto her, where she heard these words come, with vehement sobbings, from her:

'O darkness,' said she, 'which doth lightsomely, methinks, make me see the picture of my inward darkness, since I have chosen thee to be the secret witness of my sorrows, let them receive a safe receipt in thee, and esteem them not tedious! But, if it be possible, let the uttering them be some discharge to my overladen breast. Alas, sorrow, now thou hast the full sack of my conquered spirits, rest thyself awhile, and set not still new fire to thy own spoils. O accursed reason, how many eyes thou hast to see thy evils, and how dim, nay blind, thou art in preventing them! Forlorn creature that I am, I would I might be freely wicked, since wickedness doth prevail; but the footsteps of my overtrodden virtue lie still as bitter accusations unto me. I am divided in myself; how can I stand? I am overthrown in myself; who shall raise me? Vice is but a nurse of new agonies, and the virtue I am divorced from makes the hateful comparison the more manifest. No, no, virtue; either I never had but a shadow of thee, or thou thyself art but a shadow, for how is my soul abandoned! How are all my powers laid waste! My desire is pained, because it cannot hope; and if hope came, his best should be but mischief. O strange mixture of human minds: only so much good left as to make us languish in our own evils! Ye infernal furies—for it is too late for me to awake my dead virtue, or to place my comfort in the angry gods—ye infernal furies, I say, aid one that dedicates herself unto you! Let my rage be satisfied, since the effect of it is fit for your service; neither be afraid to make me too happy, since nothing can come to appease the smart of my guilty conscience! I desire but to assuage the sweltering of my hellish longing. Dejected Gynecia!'

Cleophila no sooner heard the name of Gynecia but that, with a cold sweat all over her, as if she had been ready to tread upon a deadly stinging adder, she would have withdrawn herself, but her own passion made her yield more unquiet motions than she had done in coming; so that she was perceived, and Gynecia suddenly risen up. For, indeed, it was Gynecia gotten into this cave (the same cave wherein Dametas had safely kept Pamela in the late uproar) to pass her pangs with change of places. And as her mind ran still upon Cleophila, her piercing lover's eye had soon found it was she; and seeing in her a countenance to fly away, she fell down at her feet, and catching fast hold of her:

'Alas,' said she, 'whither or from whom dost thou fly away? The savagest beasts are won with service, and there is no flint but may be mollified. How is Gynecia so unworthy in thine eyes; or whom cannot abundance of love make worthy? O think not that cruelty or ungratefulness can flow from a good mind! O weigh, alas, weigh with thyself the new effects of this mighty passion: that I, unfit for my state, uncomely for my sex, must become a suppliant at thy feet! By the happy woman that bare thee, by all the joys of thy heart and success of thy desire, I beseech thee turn thyself into some consideration of me, and rather show pity in now helping me than in too late repenting my death, which hourly threatens me.'

Cleophila, imputing it to one of her continual mishaps thus to have met with this lady, with a full weary countenance: 'Without doubt, madam,' said she, 'where the desire is such as may be obtained, and the party well deserving as yourself, it must be a great excuse that may well colour a denial; but when the first motion carries with it a direct impossibility, then must the only answer be comfort without help and sorrow to both parties: to you, not obtaining; to me, not able to grant.'

'O,' said Gynecia, 'how good leisure you have to frame these scornful answers! Is Gynecia thus to be despised? Am I so vile a worm in your sight? No, no, trust to it, hard-hearted tiger, I will not be the only actor of this tragedy! Since I must fall, I will press down some others with my ruins; since I must burn, my spiteful neighbours shall feel of my fire! Dost thou not perceive that my diligent eyes have pierced through the cloudy mask of thy disguisement? Have I not told thee, O fool (if I were not much more fool), that I know thou wouldst abuse us with thy outward show? Wilt thou still attend the rage of love in a woman's heart? The girl, thy well chosen mistress, perchance shall defend thee when Basilius shall know how thou hast sotted his mind with falsehood, and falsely sought the dishonour of his house. Believe it, believe it, unkind creature, I will end my miseries with a notable example of revenge; and that accursed cradle of mine shall feel the smart of my wound, thou of thy tyranny, and lastly, I confess, myself of my own work!'

Cleophila (that had long before doubted herself to be discovered by her, and now plainly finding it) was, as the proverb saith, like them that hold the wolf by the ears: bitten while they hold, and slain if they loose. If she held her off, in these wonted terms, she saw rage would make her love work the effects of hate; to grant unto her, her heart was so bound upon Philoclea, it had been worse than a thousand deaths. Yet found she it was necessary for her to come to a resolution; for Gynecia's sore could bide no leisure, and once discovered, besides the danger of Philoclea, her desires should be forever utterly stopped. She remembered withal the words of Basilius; how apt he was to leave this life, and return to his court (a great bar to her hopes). Lastly, she considered Dorus's enterprise might bring some strange alteration of this their well liked fellowship. So that, encompassed with these instant difficulties, she bent her spirits to think of a remedy which might at once both save her from them, and serve her to the accomplishment of her only pursuit. Lastly she determined thus: that there was no way but to yield to the violence of their desires, since striving did the more chafe them; and that following their own current, at length of itself it would bring her to the other side of her burning desires.

But methinks I hear the shepherd Dorus calling me to tell you something of his hopeful adventures. Whosoever hath found by experience how unspeakable a comfort a true friend is (where there is so sincere a participating of each other's fortune as a man is sure either to have help or comfort) may hold easily in his conjecture the present case of divided Dorus—divided betwixt love and friendship. But love carrying with it, besides all force of such arguments of which affectionated brains are never unprovided, the continual sting of insatiate desire, had (as you have heard) gotten the fort; though without prejudice of his loyal friendship, which doth never bar the mind from his free satisfaction. Yet still Dorus (a cruel judge over himself) thought he was some ways faulty, and applied his mind how to amend it with a speedy and behoveful return. But then was his first study how to get away, whereto already he had Pamela's consent, confirmed and concluded under the name of Mopsa in her own presence—Dorus taking this way, that whatsoever he would have of Pamela, he would ask her whether in such a case it were not best for Mopsa so to behave herself: thus was Mopsa's envy made an instrument of that she did envy, as already you have understood by the relation Dorus made thereof to Cleophila. Now that Dorus had passed over his first and most feared difficulty, he busied his spirits how to come to the harvest of his desires, whereof he had so fair a a show; and thereunto (having gotten leave for some days of his master Dametas, who began to account him as his son-in-law) he roamed round about the desert to find some unknown way, that might bring him to the next seaport, as much as might be out of all course of other passengers. Which all very well succeeding him, and he having hired a bark for his life's traffic, and provided horses to carry her thither, returned homeward, now come to the last point of his care: how to go beyond the loathsome watchfulness of these three uncomely companions. And therein did wisely consider how they were to be taken, with whom he had to deal, remembering that in the particularities of everybody's mind and fortune there are particular advantages by which they are to be held. The muddy mind of Dametas he found most easily stirred with covetousness; the cursed mischievous heart of Miso most apt to be tickled with jealousy, as whose rotten brain could think well of nobody; but young mistress Mopsa, who could open her eyes upon nothing that did not all to-bewonder her, he thought curiosity the fittest bait for her. And first for Dametas: Dorus, having employed a whole day's work about a ten mile off from the lodge (quite contrary way to that he meant to take with Pamela) in digging and opening the ground under an ancient oak that stood there, in such sort as might longest hold Dametas's greedy hopes in some show of comfort, he came to his master with a countenance mixed betwixt cheerfulness and haste; and taking him by the right hand as if he had a great matter of faithful secrecy to reveal unto him:

'Master', said he, 'I did never think that the gods had appointed my mind, freely brought up, to have so longing a desire to serve you, but that they minded thereby to bring some extraordinary fruit to one so beloved of them as your honesty makes me think you are. This binds me even in conscience to disclose that which I persuade myself is allotted unto you, that your fortune may be of equal balance with your deserts.'

He said no further, because he would let Dametas play upon the bit awhile; who, not understanding what his words intended, yet well finding they carried no evil news, was so much the more desirous to know the matter as he had free scope to imagine what measure of good hap himself would. Therefore, putting off his cap to him (which he had never done before), and assuring him he should have Mopsa though she had been all made of cloth of gold, he besought Dorus not to hold him long in hope for that he found it a thing his heart was not able to bear.

'Master,' answered Dorus, 'you have so satisfied me with promising me the uttermost of my desired bliss that, if my duty bound me not, I were in it sufficiently rewarded. To you, therefore, shall my good hap be converted, and the fruit of all my labour dedicated.' Therewith he told him how under an ancient oak (the place he made him easily understand by sufficient marks he gave unto him) he had found, digging but a little depth, scatteringly lying a great number of rich medals; and that, piercing further into the ground, he had met with a great stone which, by the hollow sound it yielded, seemed to be the cover of some greater vault, and upon it a box of cypress with the name of the valiant Aristomenes* graven upon it; and within the box he found certain verses which signified that some depth again under that all his treasures lay hidden, what time for the discord fell out in Arcadia* he lived banished.

Therewith he gave Dametas certain medals of gold he had long kept about him, and asked him, because it was a thing much to be kept secret, and a matter one man in twenty hours might easily perform, whether he would have him go and seek the bottom of it—which he had refrained to do till he knew his mind—promising he would faithfully bring him what he found; or else that he himself would do it, and be the first beholder of that comfortable spectacle.

No man need doubt which part Dametas would choose, whose

fancy had already devoured all this great riches, and even now began to grudge at a partner, before he saw his own share. Therefore, taking straight a strong jade, laden with spades and mattocks (which he meant to bring back otherwise laden), he went in all speed thitherward, taking leave of nobody; only desiring Dorus he would look well to the princess Pamela, promising him mountains of his own labour, which nevertheless he little meant to perform—like a fool, not considering that no man is to be moved with part that neglects the whole. Thus away went Dametas, having already made an image in his fancy what palaces he would build, how sumptuously he would fare, and among all other things imagined what money to employ in making coffers to keep his money. His ten miles seemed twice so many leagues; and yet, contrary to the nature of it, though it seemed long, it was not wearisome. Many times he cursed his horse's want of consideration that in so important a matter would make no greater speed; many times he wished himself the back of an ass to help to carry away the new-sought riches—an unfortunate wisher, for if he had as well wished the head, it had been granted him. At length, being come to the tree which he hoped should bear so golden acorns, down went all his instruments, and forthwith to the renting up of the hurtless earth; where by and by he was caught with the lime of a few promised medals, which was so perfect a pawn unto him of his further expectation that he deemed a great number of hours well employed in groping further unto it (which with logs and great stones was made as cumbersome as might be), till at length with sweaty brows he came to the great stone—a stone, God knows, full unlike to the cover of a monument, but yet there was the cypress box with Aristomenes graven upon it, and these verses written in it:

A banished man, long barred from his desire
By inward lets of them his state possessed,
Hid here his hopes, by which he might aspire
To have his harms with wisdom's help redressed.

Seek then, and see what man esteemeth best,
All is but this, this is our labour's hire,
Of this we live, in this we find our rest,
Who hold this fast no greater wealth require.

Look further then, so shalt thou find at least
A bait most fit for hungry-minded guest.

He opened the box, and to his great comfort read them, and with fresh courage went about to lift up that stone.

But in the mean time I must tell you that Dametas was not half a mile gone to the treasure-ward when Dorus came to Miso, whom he found sitting in the chimney's end, babbling to herself, and showing in all her gestures that she was loathsomely weary of the world, not for any hope of a better life, but finding no one good,* neither in mind nor body, whereout she might nourish a quiet thought, having long since hated each thing else, began now to hate herself. Before this sweet-humoured dame Dorus set himself, and framed towards her such a smiling countenance as might seem to be mixed between a tickled mirth and a forced pity. Miso (to whom cheerfulness in others was ever a sauce of envy in herself) took quickly mark of his behaviour, and with a look full of forworn spite:

'Now the devil', said she, 'take these villains that can never leave grinning because I am not so fair as mistress Mopsa! To see how the skipjack looks at me!'

Dorus, that had the occasion he desired, 'Truly mistress', answered he, 'my smiling is not at you, but at them that are from you; and indeed I must needs a little accord my countenance with others' sport.' And therewithal took her in his arms, and rocking her to and fro, 'In faith, mistress,' said he, 'it is high time for you to bid good night forever, since others can possess your place in your own time.'

Miso, that was never void of malice enough to suspect the uttermost evil, to satisfy a further shrewdness took on a present mildness, and gently desired him to tell her what he meant, 'for', said she, 'I am like enough to be knavishly dealt with by that churl my husband.'

Dorus fell off from the matter again, as if he had meant no such thing, till by much refusing her entreaty, and vehemently stirring up her desire to know, he had strengthened a credit in her to that he should say; and then with a formal countenance, as if the conscience of the case had touched himself, 'Mistress,' said he, 'I am much perplexed in mine own determination, for my thoughts do ever will me to do honestly, but my judgement fails me what is honest, betwixt the general rule that entrusted secrecies are holily to be observed, and the particular exception that the dishonest secrecies are to be revealed—especially there where by revealing they may either be prevented or at least amended. Yet in this balance your judgement weighs me down, because I have confidence in it, that

you will use what you know moderately, and rather take such faults
as an advantage to your own good desert than by your bitter using it
be content to be revenged on others with your own harms. So it is,
mistress', said he, 'that yesterday driving my sheep up to the stately
hill which lifts his head over the fair city of Mantinea I happened,
upon the side of it in a little falling of the ground which was a
rampire against the sun's rage, to perceive a young maid, truly of the
finest stamp of beauty; and that which made her beauty the more
admirable, there was at all no art added to the helping of it. For her
apparel was but such as shepherds' daughters are wont to wear; and
as for her hair, it hong down at the free liberty of his goodly length,
but that sometimes falling before the clear stars of her sight, she was
forced to put it behind her ears, and so open again the treasure of
her perfections, which that for a while had in part hidden. In her
lap there lay a shepherd, so wrapped up in that well liked place that I
could discern no piece of his face; but as mine eyes were attent in
that, her angelic voice strake mine ears with this song:

> My true love hath my heart, and I have his,
> By just exchange, one for the other given.
> I hold his dear, and mine he cannot miss:
> There never was a better bargain driven.
>
> His heart in me, keeps me and him in one,
> My heart in him, his thoughts and senses guides.
> He loves my heart, for once it was his own:
> I cherish his, because in me it bides.
>
> His heart his wound received from my sight:
> My heart was wounded, with his wounded heart,
> For as from me on him his hurt did light,
> So still methought in me his hurt did smart:
> > Both equal hurt, in this change sought our bliss:
> > My true love hath my heart, and I have his.

But, as if the shepherd that lay before her had been organs which
were only to be blown by her breath, she had no sooner ended with
the joining her sweet lips together but that he recorded to her music
this rural poesy:

> O words which fall like summer dew on me,
> O breath more sweet than is the growing bean,

O tongue in which all honeyed liquors be,
O voice that doth the thrush in shrillness stain,
  Do you say still, this is her promise due,
  That she is mine, as I to her am true.

Gay hair, more gay than straw when harvest lies,
Lips red and plum, as cherry's ruddy side,
Eyes fair and great, like fair great ox's eyes:
O breast in which two white sheep swell in pride
  Join you with me, to seal this promise due,
  That she be mine, as I to her am true.

But thou white skin, as white as cruds well pressed,
So smooth as sleekstone-like it smooths each part,
And thou dear flesh, as soft as wool new dressed,
And yet as hard as brawn made hard by art;*
  First four but say, next four their saying seal,
  But you must pay the gage of promised weal.

And with the conclusion of his song he embraced her about the knees: 'O sweet Charita,' said he, 'when shall I enjoy the rest of my toiling thoughts, and when shall your blissful promise (now due) be verified with just performance?' With that I drew nearer to them, and saw (for now he had lifted up his face to glass himself in her fair eyes) that it was my master Dametas'—but here Miso interrupted his tale with railing at Dametas with all those exquisite terms which I was never good scold enough to imagine.

But Dorus (as if he had been much offended with her impatience) would proceed no further till she had vowed more stillness: 'For', said he, 'if the first drum thus chafe you, what will you be when it comes to the blows?' Then he told her how, after many familiar entertainments betwixt them, Dametas (laying before her his great credit with the duke, and withal giving her very fair presents, with promise of much more) had in the end concluded together to meet as that night at Mantinea in the Oudemian street*at Charita's uncle's house about ten of the clock. After which bargain Dametas had spied Dorus, and calling him to him, had with great bravery told him all his good hap, willing him in any case to return to the old witch Miso ('for so indeed, mistress, of liveliness, and not of ill will, he termed you'), and to make some honest excuse of his absence; 'for', said he, kissing Charita, 'if thou didst know what a life I lead with that drivel, it would make thee even of pity receive me into thy only comfort.'

'Now mistress,' said he, 'exercise your discretion, which if I were well assured of, I would wish you to go yourself to Mantinea, and (lying secret in some one of your gossips' houses till the time appointed come) so may you find them together, and using mercy, reform my master from his evil ways.'

There had nothing more enraged Miso than the praises Dorus gave to Charita's beauty, which made her jealousy swell the more with the poison of envy; and that being increased with the presents she heard Dametas had given her (which all seemed torn out of her bowels), her hollow eyes yielded such wretched looks as one might well think Pluto at that time might have had her soul very good cheap. But when the fire of spite had fully caught hold of all her inward parts, then whosoever would have seen the picture of Alecto,* or with what manner of countenance Medea*killed her own children, needed but take Miso for the full satisfaction of that point of his knowledge. She, that could before scarce go but supported by crutches, now flew about the house, borne up with the wings of anger. There was no one sort of mortal revenge that had ever come to her ears but presented itself now to her gentle mind. At length, with few words (for her words were choked up with the rising of her revengeful heart), she ran down, and with her own hands saddled a mare of hers—a mare that seven year before had not been acquainted with a saddle—and so to Mantinea she went, casting with herself how she might couple shame with the punishment of her accursed husband—but the person is not worthy in whose passion I should too long stand.

Therefore now must I tell you that mistress Mopsa (who was the last party Dorus was to practise his cunning withal) was, at the parting of her parents, attending upon the princess Pamela, whom because she found to be placed in her father's house, she knew it was for suspicion the duke had of her. This made Mopsa, with a right base nature (which joys to see any hard hap happen to them they deem happy), grow proud over her, and use great ostentation of her own diligence in prying curiously into each thing that Pamela did. Neither is there anything sooner overthrows a weak heart than opinion of authority (like too strong a liquor for so feeble a glass); which joined itself to the humour of envying Pamela's beauty so far that oft she would say to herself: 'if she had been born a duchess as well as Pamela, her perfections then should have been as well seen as

Pamela's.' With this manner of woman, and placed in these terms, had Dorus to play his last part, which he would quickly have dispatched, in tying her up in such a manner that she should little have hindered his enterprise, but that the virtuous Pamela (when she saw him so minded) by countenance absolutely forbade it, resolutely determining she would not leave behind her any token of wrong, since the wrong done to herself was the best excuse of her escape. So that Dorus was compelled to take her in the manner he first thought of, and accordingly, Pamela sitting musing at the strange attempt she had condescended unto, and Mopsa hard by her (looking in a glass with very partial eyes), Dorus put himself between them, and casting up his face to the top of the house, shrugging all over his body, and stamping sometimes upon the ground, gave Mopsa occasion (who was as busy as a bee to know anything) to ask her lover Dorus what ailed him that made him use so strange a behaviour?

He (as if his spirits had been ravished at some supernatural contemplation) stood still mute, sometimes rubbing his forehead, sometimes starting in himself; that he set Mopsa in such an itch of inquiry that she would have offered her maidenhead rather than be long kept from it. Dorus not yet answering to the purpose, still keeping his amazement: 'O Hercules,' said he, 'resolve me in this doubt! A tree to grant one's wishes! Is this the cause of the duke's solitary life? Which part shall I take? Happy in either; unhappy because I cannot know which were my best hap!'

These doubtful self-speeches made Mopsa yet in a further longing of knowing the matter; so that the pretty pig, laying her sweet burden about his neck: 'My Dorus,' said she, 'tell me these wonders, or else I know not what will befall me. Honey Dorus, tell them me'.

Dorus, having stretched her mind upon a right last, 'Extremely loved Mopsa,' said he, 'the matters be so great as my heart fails me in the telling them; but since you hold the greatest seat in it, it is reason your desire should add life unto it.' Therewith he told her a far-fet tale: how that many millions of years before, Jupiter, fallen out with Apollo, had thrown him out of heaven, taking from him the privilege of a god; so that poor Apollo was fain to lead a very miserable life, unacquainted to work, and never used to beg; that, in this order, having in time learned to be Admetus's herdman, he had (upon occasion of fetching a certain breed of goodly beasts out of Arcadia) come to that very desert, where, wearied with travel and resting himself in the bough of a pleasant ash tree stood a little off from the lodge, he had with pitiful complaints gotten his father Jupiter's pardon, and so from that tree was received again to his golden sphere. But having that right nature of a god, never to be ungrateful, to Admetus he had granted a double life; and because that tree was the chapel of his prosperous prayers, he had given it this quality: that whosoever, of such estate and in such manner as he then was, sat down in that tree, they should obtain whatsoever they wished. This Basilius having understood by the oracle was the only cause which had made him try whether, framing himself to the state of a herdman, he might have the privilege of wishing only granted to that degree. But that having often in vain attempted it, because indeed he was not such, he had now opened the secret to Dametas, making him swear he should wish according to his direction. 'But because', said Dorus, 'Apollo was at that time with extreme grief muffled round about his face with a scarlet cloak Admetus had given him, and because they that must wish must be muffled in like sort, and with like stuff, my master Dametas is gone I know not whither to provide him a scarlet cloak, and tomorrow doth appoint to return with it. My mistress, I cannot tell how, having gotten some inkling of it, is trudged to Mantinea to get herself a cloak before him, because she would have the first wish. My master at his parting of great trust told me this secret, commanding me to see nobody should climb that tree. But now, my Mopsa,' said he, 'I have here the like cloak of mine own, and am not so very a fool as, though I keep his commandment in others, to bar myself. I rest only extremely perplexed because, having nothing in the world I wish for, but the enjoying you and your favour, I think it a much pleasanter conquest to come to it by your own consent than to have it by such a charming force as this is. Now therefore choose, since have you I will, in what sort I shall have you.'

But never child was so desirous of a gay puppet as Mopsa was to be in the tree; and therefore without squeamishness promising all he would, she conjured him by all her precious loves that she might have the first possession of the wishing tree, assuring him that, for the enjoying her, he should never need to climb far.

Dorus, to whom time was precious, made no great ceremonies with her; but helping her up to the top of the tree, from whence likewise she could ill come down without help, he muffled her round about the face so truly that she herself could not undo it. And so he told her the manner was she should hold her mind in continual devotion to Apollo, without making at all any noise, till at the furthest within twelve hours' space she should hear a voice call her by name three times; and that till the third time she must in no wise answer: 'and then you shall not need to doubt your coming down, for at that time', said he, 'be sure but to wish wisely, and in what shape soever he come unto you, speak boldly unto him, and your wish shall have as certain effect as I have a desire to enjoy your sweet loves.' In this plight did he leave Mopsa, resolved in her heart to be the greatest lady of the world, and never after to feed on worse than furmenty.

Thus Dorus, having delivered his hands of his three tormentors, took speedily the benefit of his device, and mounting the gracious Pamela upon a fair horse he had provided for her, he thrust himself forthwith into the wildest part of the desert where he had left marks to guide him from place to place to the next seaport, disguising her very fitly with scarves, although he rested assured he should meet that way with nobody till he came to his bark, into which he meant to enter by night. But Pamela who all this while transported with desire, and troubled with fear, had never free scope of judgement to look with perfect consideration into her own enterprise, but even by the laws of love had bequeathed the care of herself upon him to whom she had given herself, now that the pang of desire with evident hope was quieted, and most part of the fear passed, reason began to renew his shining in her heart, and make her see herself in herself, and weigh with what wings she flew out of her native country, and upon what ground she built so strange a determination. But love, fortified with her lover's presence, kept still his own in her heart, so that as they rid together, with her hand upon her faithful servant's shoulder, suddenly casting her bashful eyes to the ground, and yet bending herself towards him (like the client that commits the cause of all his worth to a well trusted advocate) from a mild spirit said unto him these sweetly delivered words:

'Prince Musidorus (for so my assured hope is I may justly call you, since with no other my heart would ever have yielded to go; and if so I do not rightly term you, all other words are as bootless as my deed miserable, and I as unfortunate as you wicked), my prince Musidorus, I say, now that the vehement shows of your faithful love towards me have brought my mind to answer it in so due a proportion that, contrary to all general rules of reason, I have laid in you my estate, my life, my honour, it is now your part to double your former care, and make me see your virtue no less in preserving than in obtaining, and your faith to be a faith as much in freedom as bondage. Tender now your own workmanship, and so govern your love towards me as I may still remain worthy to be loved. Your promise you remember, which here by the eternal givers of virtue I conjure you to observe. Let me be your own (as I am), but by no unjust conquest. Let not our joys, which ought ever to last, be stained in our own consciences. Let no shadow of repentance steal into the sweet consideration of our mutual happiness. I have yielded to be your wife; stay then till the time that I may rightly be so. Let no other defiled name burden my heart. What should I more say? If I have chosen well, all doubt is past, since your action only must determine whether I have done virtuously or shamefully in following you.'

Musidorus (that had more abundance of joy in his heart than Ulysses had what time with his own industry he stale the fatal Palladium,* imagined to be the only relic of Troy's safety), taking Pamela's hand, and many times kissing it, 'What I am,' said he, 'the gods, I hope, will shortly make your own eyes judges; and of my mind towards you, the mean time shall be my pledge unto you. Your contentment is dearer to me than mine own, and therefore doubt not of his mind whose thoughts are so thralled unto you as you are to bend or slack them as it shall seem best unto you. You do wrong to yourself to make any doubt that a base estate could ever undertake so high an enterprise, or a spotted mind be able to behold your virtues. Thus much only I must confess I can never do: to make the world see you have chosen worthily; since all the world is not worthy of you.'

In such delightful discourses kept they on their journey, maintaining their hearts in that right harmony of affection which doth interchangeably deliver each to other the secret workings of their souls, till with the unused travel the princess being weary, they lighted down in a fair thick wood which did entice them with the pleasantness of it to take their rest there. It was all of pine trees, whose broad heads meeting together yielded a perfect shade to the ground, where their bodies gave a spacious and pleasant room to walk in. They were set in so perfect an order that every way the eye being full, yet no way was stopped; and even in the midst of them were there many sweet springs which did loose themselves upon the

face of the earth. Here Musidorus drew out such provision of fruits
and other cates as he had brought for that day's repast, and laid it
down upon the fair carpet of the green grass. But Pamela had much
more pleasure to walk under those trees, making in their barks
pretty knots* which tied together the names of Musidorus and Pamela,
sometimes intermixedly changing them to Pamedorus and Musimela,
with twenty other flowers of her travailing fancies, which had bound
themselves to a greater restraint than they could without much pain
well endure. And to one tree, more beholding to her than the rest
she entrusted the treasure of her thoughts in these verses:

> Do not disdain, O straight upraised pine,
> That wounding thee, my thoughts in thee I grave;
> Since that my thoughts, as straight as straightness thine,
> No smaller wound—alas! far deeper have.
>
> Deeper engraved, which salve nor time can save,
> Giv'n to my heart by my fore-wounded ey'n:
> Thus cruel to myself, how canst thou crave
> My inward hurt should spare thy outward rine?
>
> Yet still, fair tree, lift up thy stately line,
> Live long, and long witness my chosen smart,
> Which barred desires (barred by myself) impart.
>
> And in this growing bark grow verses mine.
> My heart my word, my word hath giv'n my heart.
> The giver giv'n from gift shall never part.

Upon a root of the tree that the earth had left something barer than
the rest she wrate this couplet:

> Sweet root, say thou, the root of my desire
> Was virtue clad in constant love's attire.

Musidorus, seeing her fancies drawn up to such pleasant contempla-
tions, accompanied her in them, and made the trees as well bear the
badges of his passions, as this song engraved in them did testify:

> You goodly pines, which still with brave ascent
> In nature's pride your heads to heav'nward heave,
> Though you besides such graces earth hath lent,
> Of some late grace a greater grace receive,

By her who was (O blessed you) content,
With her fair hand, your tender barks to cleave,
And so by you (O blessed you) hath sent
Such piercing words as no thoughts else conceive:

Yet yield your grant, a baser hand may leave
His thoughts in you, where so sweet thoughts were spent,
For how would you the mistress' thoughts bereave
Of waiting thoughts all to her service meant?

Nay higher thoughts (though thralled thoughts) I call
My thoughts than hers, who first your rine did rent,
Than hers, to whom my thoughts alonely thrall
Rising from low, are to the highest bent;
    Where hers, whom worth makes highest over all,
    Coming from her, cannot but downward fall.

While Pamela, sitting her down under one of them, and making a
posy of the fair undergrowing flowers, filled Musidorus's ears with
the heavenly sound of her music, which before he had never heard,
so that it seemed unto him a new assault given to the castle of his
heart, already conquered; which to signify, and withal reply to her
sweet notes, he sang in a kind of still but ravishing tune a few
verses. Her song was this, and his reply follows:

Pamela. Like diverse flowers, whose diverse beauties serve
    To deck the earth with his well-coloured weed,
    Though each of them his private form preserve,
        Yet joining forms one sight of beauty breed;
        Right so my thoughts whereon my heart I feed;

Right so my inward parts, and outward glass,
    Though each possess a diverse working kind,
    Yet all well knit to one fair end do pass:
        That he to whom these sundry gifts I bind,
        All what I am, still one, his own, do find.

Musidorus. All what you are still one, his own to find,
    You that are born to be the world's*eye,
    What were it else, but to make each thing blind,
    And to the sun with waxen wings to fly?

No, no, such force with my small force to try
Is not my skill, nor reach of mortal mind.
Call me but yours, my title is most high:
Hold me most yours, then my long suit is signed.

You none can claim but you yourself by right,
For you do pass yourself, in virtue's might.
So both are yours: I, bound with gaged heart;
You only yours, too far beyond desert.

In this virtuous wantonness suffering their minds to descend to each
tender enjoying their united thoughts, Pamela having tasted of the
fruits, and growing extreme sleepy, having been long kept from it
with the perplexity of her dangerous attempt, laying her head in his
lap, was invited by him to sleep with these softly uttered verses:

Lock up, fair lids, the treasures of my heart:
Preserve those beams, this age's only light:
To her sweet sense, sweet sleep, some ease impart—
Her sense too weak to bear her spirit's might.

And while, O sleep, thou closest up her sight
(Her sight where love did forge his fairest dart),
O harbour all her parts in easeful plight:
Let no strange dream make her fair body start.

But yet, O dream, if thou wilt not depart
In this rare subject from thy common right;
But wilt thyself in such a seat delight,

Then take my shape, and play a lover's part:
Kiss her from me, and say unto her sprite,
Till her eyes shine, I live in darkest night.

The sweet Pamela was brought into a sweet sleep with this song,
which gave Musidorus opportunity at leisure to behold her excellent
beauties. He thought her fair forehead was a field where all his
fancies fought, and every hair of her head seemed a strong chain that
tied him. Her fair lids (then hiding her fairer eyes) seemed unto him
sweet boxes of mother of pearl, rich in themselves, but containing
in them far richer jewels. Her cheeks, with their colour most deli-
cately mixed, would have entertained his eyes somewhile, but that

the roses of her lips (whose separating was wont to be accompanied with most wise speeches) now by force drew his sight to mark how prettily they lay one over the other, uniting their divided beauties, and through them the eye of his fancy delivered to his memory the lying (as in ambush) under her lips of those armed ranks, all armed in most pure white, and keeping the most precise order of military discipline. And lest this beauty might seem the picture of some excellent artificer, forth there stale a soft breath, carrying good testimony of her inward sweetness; and so stealingly it came out as it seemed loath to leave his contentful mansion, but that it hoped to be drawn in again to that well closed paradise, that did so tyrannize over Musidorus's affects that he was compelled to put his face as low to hers as he could, sucking the breath with such joy that he did determine in himself there had been no life to a chameleon's, if he might be suffered to enjoy that food. But each of these having a mighty working in his heart, all joined together did so draw his will into the nature of their confederacy that now his promise began to have but a fainting force, and each thought that rase against those desires was received but as a stranger to his counsel, well experiencing in himself that no vow is so strong as the avoiding of occasions; so that rising softly from her, overmastered with the fury of delight, having all his senses partial against himself and inclined to his well beloved adversary, he was bent to take the advantage of the weakness of the watch, and see whether at that season he could win the bulwark before timely help might come. And now he began to make his approaches when (to the just punishment of his broken promise, and most infortunate bar*of his long-pursued and almost-achieved desires) there came by a dozen clownish villains, armed with divers sorts of weapons, and for the rest, both in face and apparel, so forwasted that they seemed to bear a great conformity with the savages; who (miserable in themselves, thought to increase their mischiefs in other bodies' harms) came with such cries as they awaked Pamela (whose sleep had been set upon with two dangers, the one of which had saved her from the other), and made Musidorus turn unto them full of a most violent rage, with the look of a she-tiger when her whelps are stolen away.

But Cleophila (whom I left in the cave hardly bested, having both great wits and stirring passions to deal with) makes me lend her my pen awhile to see with what dexterity she could put by her dangers. Cleophila (who had in one instant both to resist rage and go beyond wisdom, having to deal with a lady that had her wits awake in everything but in helping of her own hurt) saw now no other remedy in her case but to qualify her rage with hope, and to satisfy her wit with plainness. Yet (lest too abrupt a falling into it should yield too great an advantage unto her) she thought good to come to it by degrees, with this kind of insinuation:

'Your wise but very dark speeches, most excellent lady, are woven up in so intricate a manner as I know not how to proportion mine answer unto them; so are your prayers mixed with threats, and so is the show of your love hidden with the name of revenge, the natural effect of mortal hatred. You seem displeased with the opinion you have of my disguising; and yet if I be not disguised, you must needs be much more displeased, hope then (the only succour of perplexed minds) being quite cut off. You desire my affection, and yet you yourself think my affection already bestowed. You pretend cruelty before you have the subjection, and are jealous of the keeping that which as yet you have not gotten. And that which is strangest in your jealousy is both the unnatural unjustice of it (in being loath that should come to your daughter which you deem good), and the vainness, since you two are in so diverse respects that there is no necessity one of you should fall to be a bar to the other. For neither (if I be such as you fancy) can I marry you, which must needs be the only end I can aspire to in her; neither need the marrying of her keep me from a grateful consideration how much you honour me in the love you vouchsafe to bear me.'

Gynecia (to whom the fearful agonies she still lived in made any small reprieval sweet) did quickly find her words falling to a better way of comfort; and therefore with a mind ready to show nothing could make it rebellious against Cleophila but too extreme tyranny, she thus said: 'Alas, too much beloved Cleophila, the thoughts are but outflowings of the mind, and the tongue is but a servant of the thoughts. Therefore, marvel not that my words suffer contrarieties, since my mind doth hourly suffer in itself whole armies of mortal adversaries. But, alas, if I had the use of mine own reason, then should I not need, for want of it, to find myself in this desperate mischief. But because my reason is vanished, so have I likewise no power to correct my unreasonableness. Do you, therefore, accept the protection of my mind (which hath no other resting place), and drive it not, by being unguarded, to put itself into unknown extremities. I desire but to have my affection answered, and to have a right reflection of my love in you. That granted, assure yourself mine own love will easily teach me to seek your contentment, and make me think my daughter a very mean price to keep still in mine eyes the food of my spirits. But take heed that contempt drive me not into despair, the most violent cause of that miserable effect.'

Cleophila (that already saw some fruit of her last determined fancy, so far as came to a mollifying of Gynecia's rage) seeing no other way to satisfy suspicion (which was held open with the continual pricks of love), resolved now with plainness to win trust—which trust she might after deceive with a greater subtlety. Therefore, looking upon her with a more relenting grace than ever she had done before, pretending a great bashfulness before she could come to confess such a fault, she thus said unto her: 'Most worthy lady, I did never think till now that pity of another could make one betray himself, nor that the sound of words could overthrow any wise body's determination; but your words, I think, have charmed me, and your grace bewitched me. Your compassion makes me open my heart to you, and leave unharboured mine own thoughts. For proof of it I will disclose my greatest secret, which well you might suspect, but never know, and so have your wandering hope in a more painful wilderness, being neither way able to be lodged in any perfect resolution. I will, I say, unwrap my most hidden estate, and after make you judge of it—perchance director. The truth is I am a man. Nay, I will say further to you I am born a prince; and to make up your mind in a thorough understanding of me, since I came to this place I may not deny I have had some sprinkling of I know not what good liking to my lady Philoclea. For how could I ever imagine the heavens would have rained down so much of your favour upon me? And of that side there was a show of possible hope, the most comfortable counsellor of love. The cause of this my changed attire was a journey two years ago I made among the Amazons, where having sought to try my unfortunate valour, I met not one in all the country but was too hard for me; till, in the end, in the presence of their queen Senicia, I (hoping to prevail against her) challenged an old woman of fourscore years to fight on horseback to the uttermost with me: who, having overthrown me, for saving of my life made me swear I should go like an unarmed Amazon till the coming of my beard did with the discharge of my oath deliver me of that bondage.'

Here Cleophila ended, not coming to a full conclusion, because she would see what this wrought in Gynecia's mind, having in her speech sought to win a belief of her; and if it might be, by the disgrace of herself to diminish Gynecia's affection. For the first, it had much prevailed, but Gynecia whose end of loving her was not her fighting; neither could her love, too deeply grounded, receive diminishment; and besides she had seen herself sufficient proofs of Cleophila's admirable prowess. Therefore (slightly passing over that point of her feigned dishonour, but taking good hold of the confessing her manly sex), with the shamefast look of that suitor who, having already obtained much, is yet forced by want to demand more, put forth her sorrowful suit in these words:

'The gods', said she, 'reward thee for thy virtuous pity of my overladen soul, who yet hath received some breath of comfort by finding thy confession to maintain some possibility for my languishing hope. But alas, as they who seek to enrich themselves by mineral industry, their first labour is to find the mine, which to their cheerful comfort being found, if after any unlooked-for stop or casual impediment keep them from getting the desired ore, they are so much the more grieved as the late-conceived hope adds torment to their former want; so falls it out with me, happy or hapless woman as it pleaseth you to ordain, who am now either to receive some guerdon of my long woeful labours, or to return into a more wretched darkness, having had some glimmering of my blissful sun. O Cleophila, tread not upon a soul that lies under your feet! Let not the abasing of myself make me more base in your eyes, but judge of me according to that I am and have been, and let my errors be made excusable by the immortal name of love!'

With that (under a feigned rage tearing her clothes) she discovered some parts of her fair body, which, if Cleophila's heart had not been so fully possessed as there was no place left for any new guest, no doubt it would have yielded to that gallant assault. But Cleophila so much the more arming her determination as she saw such force threatened, yet still remembering she must wade betwixt constancy and courtesy, embracing Gynecia and once or twice kissing her: 'Dear lady', said she, 'he were a great enemy to himself that would refuse such offered bliss, in the purchase of which a man's life were blessedly bestowed. Nay, how can I ever yield due recompense for so excessive a favour? But having no more to give you but myself, take that—I must confess a small but a very free present. What other affection soever I have had shall give place to as great perfections, working besides upon the bond of gratefulness.

The gods forbid I should either be so foolish as not to see, or so wicked as not to remember, how much my small deserts are over-balanced by your unspeakable goodness. Nay, happy may I well account my mishap among the Amazons, since that dishonour hath been so true a path to my greatest honour, and the changing of my outward raiment hath clothed my mind in such inward contenta-tion. Take therefore, noble lady, as much comfort to your heart as the full commandment of me can yield you. Wipe your fair eyes, and keep them for nobler services. And now I will presume thus much to say unto you: that you make of yourself for my sake that my joys of my new-obtained riches may be accomplished in you. But let us leave this place, lest you be too long missed; and henceforward quiet your mind from any further care, for I will now to my too much joy take the charge upon me within few days to work your satisfaction and my felicity.'

Thus much she said, and withal led Gynecia out of the cave; for well she saw the boiling mind of Gynecia did easily apprehend the fitness of that lonely place. But indeed this direct promise of a short space, joined with the cumbersome familiar of womankind (I mean modesty), stayed so Gynecia's mind that she took thus much at that present for good payment, remaining with a painful joy and a wearisome kind of comfort, not unlike to the condemned prisoner, whose mind still running upon the violent arrival of his cruel death, hears that his pardon is promised, but not yet signed. In this sort they both issued out of that obscure mansion, Gynecia already half persuaded in herself (O weakness of human conceit!) that Cleophila's affection was turned towards her. For such, alas, are we all! In such a mould are we cast that, with the too much love we bear ourselves being first our own flatterers, we are easily hooked with others' flattery, we are easily persuaded of others' love.

But Cleophila (who had now to play her prize), seeing no way things could long remain in that state, and now finding her promise had tied her trial to a small compass of time, began to throw her thoughts into each corner of her invention, how she might achieve her life's enterprise. For well she knew deceit cannot otherwise be maintained but by deceit. And how to deceive such heedful eyes, and how to satisfy, and yet not satisfy, such hopeful desires, it was no small skill. But both their thoughts were called from themselves with the sight of Basilius, who then lying down by his daughter Philoclea upon the fair (though natural) bed of green grass, seeing the sun what speed he made to leave our west to do his office in the other hemisphere, his inward muses made him in his best music sing this madrigal:

> Why dost thou haste away,*
> O Titan fair, the giver of the day?
> Is it to carry news
> To western wights, what stars in east appear?
> Or dost thou think that here
> Is left a sun whose beams thy place may use?
> Yet stay, and well peruse
> What be her gifts that make her equal thee.
> Bend all thy light to see
> In earthly clothes enclosed a heav'nly spark.
> Thy running course cannot such beauties mark.
> No, no, thy motions be
> Hastened from us with bar of shadow dark,
> Because that thou, the author of our sight,
> Disdainst we see thee stained with other's light.

And having ended: 'Dear Philoclea', said he, 'sing something that may divert my thoughts from the continual taste of their ruinous harbour.'

She (obedient to him, and not unwilling to disburden her secret passion) made her sweet voice to be heard in these words:

> O stealing time, the subject of delay
> (Delay, the rack of unrefrained desire),
> What strange design hast thou my hopes to stay,
> My hopes which do but to mine own aspire?
>
> Mine own? O word on whose sweet sound doth prey
> My greedy soul, with gripe of inward fire.
> Thy title great, I justly challenge may,
> Since in such phrase his faith he did attire.
>
> O time, become the chariot of my joys;
> As thou draw'st on, so let my bliss draw near.
> Each moment lost, part of my hap destroys.
>
> Thou art the father of occasion dear:
> Join with thy son to ease my long annoys.
> In speedy help thankworthy friends appear.

Philoclea brake off her song as soon as her mother with Cleophila came near unto them, rising up with a kindly bashfulness, being not ignorant of the spite her mother bare her, and stricken with the sight of that person whose love made all those troubles seem fair flowers of her dearest garland. Nay, rather, all those troubles made the love increase. For as the arrival of enemies makes a town so fortify itself as ever after it remains stronger, so that a man may say enemies were no small cause to the town's strength; so to a mind once fixed in a well pleasing determination, who hopes by annoyance to overthrow it doth but teach it to knit together all his best grounds, and so perchance of a changeable purpose make an unchangeable resolution. But no more did Philoclea see the wonted signs of Cleophila's affection towards her. She thought she saw another light in her eyes, with a bold and careless look upon her (which was wont to be dazzled with her beauty), and the framing of her courtesies rather ceremonious than affectionate. And that which worse liked her was that it proceeded with such quiet settledness as it rather threatened a full purpose than any sudden passion. She found her behaviour bent altogether to her mother, and presumed in herself she discerned the well acquainted face of his fancies now turned to another subject. She saw her mother's worthiness, and too well knew her affection. These joining their diverse working powers together in her mind (but yet a prentice in the painful mystery of passions) brought Philoclea into a new traverse of her thoughts, and made her keep her careful look the more attentive upon Cleophila's behaviour; who indeed (though with much pain and condemning herself to commit a sacrilege against the sweet saint that lived in her inmost temple, yet strengthening herself in it, being the surest way to make Gynecia bite of her other baits) did so quite overrule all wonted shows of love to Philoclea, and convert them to Gynecia, that the part she played did work in both a full and lively persuasion: to Gynecia, such excessive comfort as the being preferred to a rival doth deliver to swelling desire. But to the delicate Philoclea (whose calm thoughts were unable to nourish any strong debate) it gave so stinging a hurt that, fainting under the force of her inward torment, she withdrew herself to the lodge, and there (weary of supporting her own burden) cast herself upon her bed, suffering her sorrow to melt itself into abundance of tears. At length, closing her eyes, as if each thing she saw were a picture of her mishap, and turning upon her heart side (which with vehement panting did summon her to consider her fortune), she thus bemoaned herself:

'Alas, Philoclea, is this the prize of all thy pains? Is this the reward of thy given-away liberty? Hath too much yielding bred cruelty, or can too great acquaintance make me held for a stranger? Hath the choosing a companion made me left alone, or doth granting desire cause the desire to be neglected? Alas, despised Philoclea, why didst thou not hold thy thoughts in their simple course, and content thyself with the love of thy own virtue which would never have betrayed thee? Ah, silly fool, didst thou look for truth in him that with his own mouth confessed his falsehood; for plain proceeding in him that still goes disguised? They say the falsest men will yet bear outward shows of a pure mind; but he that even outwardly bears the badge of treachery, what hells of wickedness must needs in the depth be contained? But, O wicked mouth of mine, how darest thou thus blaspheme the ornament of the earth, the vessel of all virtue? O, wretch that I am, that will anger the gods in dispraising their most excellent work! O no, O no, there was no fault but in me, that could ever think so high eyes would look so low, or so great perfections would stain themselves with my unworthiness! Alas, why could I not see I was too weak a band to tie so heavenly a heart? I was not fit to limit the infinite course of his wonderful destinies. Was it ever like that upon only Philoclea his thoughts should rest? Ah, silly soul that couldst please thyself with so impossible an imagination; an universal happiness is to flow from him! How was I so inveigled to hope I might be the mark of such a mind? He did thee no wrong, O Philoclea, he did thee no wrong! It was thy weakness to fancy the beams of the sun should give light to no eyes but thine! And yet, O prince Pyrocles (for whom I may well begin to hate myself, but can never leave to love thee), what triumph canst thou make of this conquest? What spoils wilt thou carry away of this my undeserved overthrow? Could thy force find out no fitter field than the feeble mind of a poor maid who at the first sight did wish thee all happiness? Shall it be said the mirror of mankind hath been employed to destroy a hurtless gentlewoman? O Pyrocles, Pyrocles, let me yet call thee before the judgement of thine own virtue! Let me be accepted for a plaintiff in a cause which concerns my life! What need hadst thou to arm thy face with the enchanting mask of thy painted passions? What need hadst thou to fortify thy excellencies with so exquisite a cunning in making our own arts betray us? What needest thou descend so far from thy incomparable worthiness as to take on the habit of weak womankind? Was all this to win the undefended castle of a friend; which being won, thou wouldst after raze? Could so small a cause allure thee, or did not so unjust a cause stop thee? O me, what say I more? This is my case: my love hates me, virtue deals wickedly with me, and he does me wrong whose doing I can never account wrong.'

With that, the sweet lady turning herself upon her weary bed, she haply saw a lute, upon the belly of which Gynecia had written this song what time Basilius imputed her jealous motions to proceed of the doubt she had of his untimely loves. Under which veil she (contented to cover her never ceasing anguish) had made the lute a monument of her mind; which Philoclea had never much marked till now the fear of a competitor more stirred her than before the care of a mother. The verses were these:

> My lute within thyself thy tunes enclose,
> Thy mistress' song is now a sorrow's cry,
> Her hand benumbed with fortune's daily blows,
> Her mind amazed, can neither's help apply.
> Wear these my words as mourning weeds of woes,
> Black ink becomes the state wherein I die.
> And though my moans be not in music bound,
> Of written griefs, yet be the silent ground.
>
> The world doth yield such ill consorted shows
> (With circled course, which no wise stay can try)
> That childish stuff which knows not friends from foes
> (Better despised) bewonder gazing eye.
> Thus noble gold down to the bottom goes,
> When worthless cork aloft doth floating lie.
>   Thus in thyself least strings are loudest found,
>   And lowest stops do yield the highest sound.

Philoclea read them, and throwing down the lute: 'Is this the legacy you have bequeathed me, O kind mother of mine', said she, 'did you bestow the light upon me for this, or did you bear me to be the author of my burial? A trim purchase you have made of your own shame: robbed your daughter to ruin yourself! The birds unreasonable, yet use so much reason as to make nests for their tender young ones; my cruel mother turns me out of mine own harbour. Alas, plaint boots not, for my case can receive no help; for who should give me help? Shall I flee to my parents? They are my murderers. Shall

I go to him who (already being won and lost) must needs have killed all pity? Alas, I can bring no new intercessions; he knows already what I am is his! Shall I come home again to myself? O me, contemned wretch, I have given away myself!'

With that the poor soul beat her breast as if that had been guilty of her faults, neither thinking of revenge nor studying for remedy; but, sweet creature, gave grief a free dominion, keeping her chamber a few days after, not needing to feign herself sick, feeling even in her soul the pangs of extreme pain. But little did Gynecia reck that, neither when she saw her go away from them, neither when she after found that sickness made her hide her fair face—so much had fancy prevailed against nature. But, O you that have ever known how tender to every motion love makes the lover's heart, how he measures all his joys upon her contentment, and doth with respectful eye hang all his behaviour upon her eyes, judge, I pray you, now of Cleophila's troubled thoughts when she saw Philoclea with an amazed kind of sorrow carry away her sweet presence, and easily found (so happy a conjecture unhappy affection hath) that her demeanour was guilty of that trespass. There was never foolish soft-hearted mother that, forced to beat her child, did weep first for his pains, and doing that she was loath to do, did repent before she began, did find half that motion in her weak mind as Cleophila did, now that she was forced by reason to give an outward blow to her passions, and for the lending of a small time to seek the usury of all her desires. The unkindness she conceived Philoclea might conceive did wound her soul; each tear she doubted she spent drowned all her comfort. Her sickness was a death unto her. Often would she speak to the image of Philoclea (which lived and ruled in the highest of her inward part), and use vehement oaths and protestations unto her that nothing should ever falsify the free-chosen vow she had made. Often would she desire her that she would look well to Pyrocles' heart; for, as for her, she had no more interest in it to bestow it any way. 'Alas,' would she say, 'only Philoclea, hast thou not so much feeling of thine own force as to know no new conqueror can prevail against thy conquests? Was ever any dazzled with the moon that had used his eyes to the beams of the sun? Is he carried away with a greedy desire of acorns that hath had his senses ravished with a garden of most delightful fruits? O Philoclea, Philoclea, be thou but as merciful a princess to my mind as thou art a sure possessor, and I shall have as much cause of gladness as thou hast no cause of misdoubting! O no, no! when a man's own heart is the gage of his debt, when a man's own thoughts are willing witnesses to his promise, lastly, when a man is the gaoler over himself, there is little doubt of breaking credit, and less doubt of such an escape.'

In this combat of Cleophila's doubtful imaginations in the end reason (well backed with the vehement desire to bring her matters soon to the desired haven) did overrule the boiling of her inward kindness—though, as I say, with such a manifest strife that both Basilius's and Gynecia's well waiting eyes had marked her muses had laboured in deeper subject than ordinary; which she likewise perceiving they had perceived, awaking herself out of those thoughts, and principally caring how to satisfy Gynecia (whose judgement and passion she stood most in regard of), bowing her head to her attentive ear, 'Madam,' said she, 'with practice of my thoughts I have found out a way by which your contentment shall draw on my happiness.'

Gynecia (delivering in her face as thankful a joyfulness as her heart could hold) said it was then time to retire themselves to their rest; for what with the tumult the day before, and late sitting up for the eclogues, their bodies had dearly purchased that night's quiet. So went they home to their lodge, Cleophila framing of both sides bountiful measures of loving countenances, to either's joy and neither's jealousy, but to the especial comfort of Basilius, whose weaker bowels were straight full with the least liquor of hope; so that (still holding her by the hand and sometimes tickling it) he went by her with the most gay conceits that ever had entered his brains, growing now so hearted in his resolution that he little respected Gynecia's presence, but with a lustier note than wonted, clearing his voice and cheering his spirits, looking still upon Cleophila (whom now the moon did beautify with her shining almost at the full) as if her eyes had been his songbook, he did the message of his mind in singing these verses:

> When two suns do appear
> Some say it doth betoken wonders near,
> As prince's loss or change.
> Two gleaming suns of splendour like I see,
> And seeing feel in me
> Of prince's heart quite lost the ruin strange.

> But now each where doth range
> With ugly cloak the dark envious night;
> Who full of guilty spite,
> Such living beams should her black seat assail—
> Too weak for them our weaker sight doth veil.
>
> 'No', says fair moon, 'my light
> Shall bar that wrong, and though it not prevail
> Like to my brother's rays, yet those I send
> Hurt not the face, which nothing can amend.'

And by that time being come to the lodge, and visited the sweet Philoclea (with much less than natural care of the parents, and much less than wonted kindness of Cleophila), each party, full fraught with diversely working fancies, made their pillows weak props of their overloaden heads. Yet of all other were Cleophila's brains most turmoiled, troubled with love both active and passive, and lastly and especially with care how to use her short limited time to the full performance of her violent affection by some wise and happy diverting her two lovers' unwelcome desires. But Cleophila, having had the night her only counsellor in the busy enterprise she was to undertake, and having all that time mused, and yet not fully resolved how she might join obtaining with preventing, was offended with the day's bold entry into her chamber, as if he had now by custom grown an assured bringer of evil news; which she, taking a cithern to her, did lay to Aurora's charge with these well sung verses:

> Aurora, now thou show'st thy blushing light
> (Which oft to hope lays out a guileful bait,
> That trusts in time to find the way aright
> To ease those pains which on desire do wait)
>
> Blush on for shame that still with thee do light
> On pensive souls (instead of restful bait)
> Care upon care (instead of doing right)
> To overpressed breasts, more grievous weight.
>
> As oh! myself, whose woes are never light,
> Tied to the stake of doubt, strange passions bait;
> While thy known course, observing nature's right,
> Stirs me to think what dangers lie in wait.
>   For mischiefs great, day after day doth show;
>   Make me still fear thy fair appearing show.

'Alas,' said she, 'am I not run into a strange gulf, that am fain for love to hurt her I love; and because I detest the others, to please them I detest? O, only Philoclea, whose beauty is matched with nothing but with the unspeakable beauty of thy fairest mind, if thou didst see upon what a rack my tormented soul is set, little would you think I had free scope now to leap to any new change.'

With that with hasty hands she gat herself up, turning her sight to everything, as if change of object might help her invention. So went she again to the cave, where forthwith it came into her head that should be the fittest place to perform her exploit—of which she had now a kind of confused conceit, although she had not set down in her fancy the meeting with each particularity that might fall out. But as a painter doth at the first but show a rude proportion of the thing he imitates, which after with more curious hand he draws to the representing each lineament, so had her thoughts (beating about it continually) received into them a ground plot of her device, although she had not in each part shaped it according to a full determination. But in this sort, having early visited the morning's beauty in those pleasant deserts, she came to the duke and duchess, and told them that, for the performance of certain her country devotions which only were to be exercised in solitariness, she did desire their leave she might for a few days lodge herself in the cave, the fresh sweetness of which did greatly delight her in that hot country; and that for that small space they would not otherwise trouble themselves in visiting her, but at such times as she would come to wait upon them, which should be every day at certain hours. Neither should it be long she would desire this privileged absence of them. They (whose minds had already taken out that lesson, perfectly to yield a willing obedience to all her desires) with consenting countenance made her soon see her pleasure was a law unto them, both indeed inwardly glad of it: Basilius hoping that her dividing herself from them might yet give him some freer occasion of coming in secret unto her, whose favourable face had lately strengthened his fainting courage; but Gynecia of all other most joyous, holding herself assured that this was but a prologue to the play she had promised her. Thus both flattering themselves with diversely grounded hopes, they rang a bell which served to call certain poor women (which ever lay in cabins not far off to do the household services of both lodges, and never came to either but being called for), and commanded them to carry forthwith Cleophila's bed and furniture of her chamber into the pleasant cave, and to deck it up as finely as it was possible for them, that their souls' rest might rest her body to her best pleasing manner. That was with all diligence performed of them, and Cleophila already in possession of her new chosen lodging where she (like one of Vesta's nuns)*entertained herself for a few days in all show of straitness; yet once a day coming to do her duty to the duke and duchess, in whom the seldomness of the sight increased the more unquiet longing—though somewhat qualified, as her countenance was decked to either of them with more comfort than wonted, especially to Gynecia who (seeing her wholly neglect her daughter Philoclea) had now promised herself a full possession of Cleophila's heart, still expecting the fruit of the happy and hoped-for invention. But both she and Basilius kept such a continual watch about the precincts of the cave that either of them was a bar to the other from having any secret communing with Cleophila.

While in the meantime the sweet Philoclea (forgotten of her father, despised of her mother, and in appearance left of Cleophila) had yielded up her soul to be a prey to sorrow and unkindness, not with raging conceit of revenge (as had passed through the stout and wise heart of her mother), but with a kindly meekness taking upon herself the weight of her own woes, and suffering them to have so full a course in her as it did not a little weaken the state of her body. As well for which cause, as for that she could not see Cleophila without expressing (more than she would) how far now her love was imprisoned in extremity of sorrow, she bound herself to the limits of her own chamber. But Cleophila having now a full liberty to cast about every way how to bring her conceived attempt to a desired success, was oft so perplexed with the manifold difficulty of it that sometimes she would resolve by force to take her away, though it were with the death of her parents; sometimes to go away herself with Musidorus, and bring both their forces, so to win her. But lastly, even the same day that Musidorus, by feeding the humour of his three loathsome guardians, had stolen away the princess Pamela —whether it were that love meant to match them every way, or that indeed Cleophila forbare the practising her device till she found her friend had passed through his—the same day, I say, thus she governed her purpose: having curiously trimmed herself to the beautifying her beauties (that being now at her last trial, she might come to it in her best armour), having put on that kind of mild countenance which doth encourage the looker-on to hope for a gentle answer, according to her late-received manner, she left the pleasant darkness of her melancholy cave to go take her dinner of the duke and duchess, and give unto both them a pleasant food of seeing the owner of their desires. But even as the Persians were anciently wont to leave no rising sun unsaluted, but as his fair beams appeared clearer unto them would they more heartily rejoice, laying upon them a great foretoken of their following fortunes; so was there no time that Cleophila encountered their eyes with her beloved presence but that it bred a kind of burning devotion in them, yet so much the more gladding their greedy souls as her countenance were cleared with more favour unto them—which now being determinately framed to the greatest descent of kindness, it took such hold of her unfortunate lovers that, like children about a tender father from a long voyage returned with lovely childishness hang about him, and yet with simple fear measure by his countenance how far he accepts their boldness, so were these two now thrown into so serviceable an affection that the turning of Cleophila's eye was a strong stern enough to all their motions, wending no way but as the enchanting force of it guided them. But having made a light repast of the pleasant fruits of that country, interlarding their food with such manner of general discourses as lovers are wont to cover their passions in when respect of a third person keeps them from plainer particulars, at the earnest entreaty of Basilius, Cleophila (first saluting the muses with a bass viol hung hard by her) sent this ambassade in versified music to both her ill-requited lovers:

> Beauty hath force to catch the human sight.
> Sight doth bewitch the fancy ill awaked.
> Fancy, we feel, includes all passion's might.
> Passion rebelled, oft reason's strength hath shaked.
>
> No wonder then, though sight my sight did taint,
> And though thereby my fancy was infected,
> Though (yoked so) my mind with sickness faint,
> Had reason's weight for passion's ease rejected.
>
> But now the fit is passed; and time hath given
> Leisure to weigh what due desert requireth.
> All thoughts so sprung are from their dwelling driven,
> And wisdom to his wonted seat aspireth,

Crying in me: 'Eye-hopes deceitful prove;
Things rightly prized, love is the band of love.'

And after her song, with an affected modesty, she threw down her eye, as if the conscience of a secret grant her inward mind made had suddenly cast a bashful veil over her; which Basilius finding, and thinking now was the time to urge his painful petition, beseeching his wife with more careful eye to accompany his sickly daughter Philoclea, being rid for that time of her (who was content to grant him any scope, that she might after have the like freedom), with a gesture governed by the force of his passions, making his knees his best supporters, he thus said unto her:

'If either,' said he, 'O lady of my life, my deadly pangs could bear delay, or that this were the first time the same were manifested unto you, I would now but maintain still the remembrance of my misfortune, without urging any further reward than time and pity might procure for me. But alas, since my martyrdom is no less painful than manifest, and that I no more feel the miserable danger than you know the assured truth thereof, why should my tongue deny his service to my heart? Why should I fear the breath of my words who daily feel the flame of your works? Embrace in your sweet consideration, I beseech you, the misery of my case; acknowledge yourself to be the cause, and think it is reason for you to redress the effects! Alas, let not certain imaginative rules (whose truth stands but upon opinion) keep so wise a mind from gratefulness and mercy, whose never failing laws nature hath planted in us. I plainly lay my death unto you, the death of him that loves you, the death of him whose life you may save. Say your absolute determination, for hope itself is a pain while it is overmastered with fear; and if you do resolve to be cruel, yet is the speediest condemnation, as in evils, most welcome.'

Cleophila who had fully set to herself the train she would keep, yet knowing that who soonest means to yield doth well to make the bravest parley, keeping her countenance aloft: 'Noble prince,' said she, 'your words are too well couched to come out of a restless mind, and thanked be the gods your face threatens no danger of death. These be but those swelling speeches which give the uttermost name to every trifle, which all were worth nothing if they were not enamelled with the goodly outside of love. Truly, love were very unlovely if it were half so deadly as you lovers (still living) term it. I think well it may have a certain childish vehemency which for the time to one desire will engage all the soul, so long as it lasteth. But with what impatience, you yourself show, who confess the hope of it a pain, and think your own desire so unworthy as you would fain be rid of it, and so with overmuch love sue hard for a hasty refusal.'

'A refusal!' cried out Basilius, amazed withal, but pierced with the last, 'Now assure yourself whensoever you use that word definitively it will be the undoubted doom of my approaching death; and then shall your own experience know in me how soon the spirits dried up with anguish leave the performance of their ministry, whereupon our life dependeth. But, alas, what a cruelty is this, not only to torment, but to think the torment slight! The terriblest tyrants would say by no man they killed, he died not; nor by no man they punished, that he escaped free. For of all other there is least hope of mercy where there is no acknowledging of the pain; and with like cruelty are my words, breathed out from a flamy heart, accounted as messengers of a quiet mind. If I speak nothing, I choke myself, and am in no way of relief; if simply, neglected; if confusedly, not understood; if by the bending together all my inward powers they bring forth any lively expressing of that they truly feel, that is a token forsooth the thoughts are at too much leisure. Thus is silence desperate, folly punished, and wit suspected. But, indeed, it is vain to say any more, for words can bind no belief. Lady, I say, determine of me. I must confess I cannot bear this battle in my mind, and therefore let me soon know what I may account of myself; for it is a hell of dolours when the mind, still in doubt for want of resolution, can make no resistance.'

'Indeed,' answered Cleophila, 'if I should grant to your request, I should show an example in myself that I esteem the holy band of chastity to be but an imaginative rule (as you termed it), and not the truest observance of nature, the most noble commandment that mankind can have over themselves (as indeed both learning teacheth and inward feeling assureth). But first shall Cleophila's grave become her marriage bed before my soul shall consent to his own shame, before I will leave a mark in myself of an unredeemable trespass. And yet must I confess that if ever my heart were stirred, it hath been with the manifest and manifold shows of the misery you live in for me. For in truth so it is, nature gives not to us her degenerate children any more general precept than one to help the other, one to feel a true compassion of the other's mishap. But yet if I were never so contented to speak with you (for further never, O Basilius, look for at my hands), I know not how you can avoid your wife's jealous attendance, but that her suspicion shall bring my honour into question.'

Basilius (whose small sails the least wind did fill) was forthwith as far gone into a large promising himself his desire as before he was stricken down with a threatened denial. And therefore, bending his brows as though he were not a man to take the matter as he had done: 'What,' said he, 'shall my wife become my mistress? Think you not that thus much time hath taught me to rule her? I will mew the gentlewoman till she have cast all her feathers, if she rouse herself against me.' And with that he walked up and down, nodding his head as though they mistook him much that thought he was not his wife's master.

But Cleophila, now seeing it was time to conclude: 'Of your wisdom and manhood,' said she, 'I doubt not, but that sufficeth not me; for both they can hardly tame a malicious tongue, and impossibly bar the freedom of thought—which be the things that must be my only witnesses of honour, or judges of dishonour. But that you may see I do not set light your affection, if tonight after your wife be assuredly asleep (whereof by your love I conjure you to have a most precise care) you will steal handsomely to the cave unto me, there do I grant you as great proportion as you will take of free conference with me, ever remembering you seek no more, for so shall you but deceive yourself, and forever lose me.'

Basilius (that was old enough to know that women are not wont to appoint secret night meetings for the purchasing of land), holding himself already an undoubted possessor of his desires, kissing her hand, and lifting up his eyes to heaven, as if the greatness of the benefit did go beyond all measure of thanks, said no more, lest stirring of more words might bring forth some perhaps contrary matter.

In which trance of joy Cleophila went from him, saying she would leave him to the remembrance of their appointment; and for her, she would go visit the lady Philoclea. Into whose chamber being come, keeping still her late-taken-on gravity, and asking her how she did (rather in the way of dutiful honour than any special affection), with extreme inward anguish to them both she turned from her, and taking the duchess Gynecia, led her into a bay window of the same chamber, determining in herself not to utter to so excellent a wit as Gynecia had the uttermost point of her pretended device, but to keep the clause of it for the last instant, when the shortness of the time should not give her spirits leisure to look into all those doubts that easily enter into an open invention. But with smiling eyes, and with a delivered-over grace (feigning as much love to her as she did counterfeit little love to Philoclea), she began with more credible than eloquent speech to tell her that, with much consideration of a matter so nearly importing her own fancy and Gynecia's honour, she had now concluded that the night following should be the fittest time for the joining together their several desires, what time sleep should perfectly do his office upon the duke her husband; and that the one should come to the other into the cave (which place, as it was the first receipt of their promised love, so it might have the first honour of the due performance); that the cause why those few days past she had not sought the like was lest the new change of her lodging might make the duke more apt to mark any sudden event—which now the use of it would take out of his mind. 'And therefore now, most excellent lady,' said she, 'there resteth nothing but that quickly after supper you train up the duke to visit his daughter Philoclea; and then, feigning yourself not well at ease, by your going to bed draw him not long to be after you. In the mean time I will be gone home to my lodging, where I will attend you with no less devotion (but, as I hope, with better fortune) than Thisbe did the too much loving, and too much loved, Pyramus.'*

The blood that quickly came into Gynecia's fair face was the only answer she made, but that one might easily see contentment and consent were both to the full in her—which she did testify with the wringing Cleophila fast by the hand, closing her eyes, and letting her head fall, as if she would give her to know she was not ignorant of her fault, although she were transported with the violence of her evil.

But in this triple agreement did the day seem tedious of all sides, till his never erring course had given place to the night's succession. And the supper, by each hand hasted, was with no less speed ended; when Gynecia, presenting a heavy sleepiness in her countenance, brought up both Basilius and Cleophila to see Philoclea, still keeping her bed, and far more sick in mind than body, and more grieved than comforted with any such visitation. Thence Cleophila (wishing easeful rest to Philoclea) did seem to take that night's leave of this princely crew; when Gynecia, likewise seeming somewhat diseased, desired Basilius to stay awhile with her daughter, while she recommended her sickness to her bed's comfort, indeed desirous to determine again of the manner of her stealing away—to no less comfort of Basilius who, the sooner she was asleep, the sooner hoped to come by his long-pursued prey. Thus both were bent to deceive each other, and to take the advantage of either other's disadvantage.

But Gynecia having taken Cleophila into her bedchamber to speak a little with her of their sweet determination, Cleophila upon a sudden (as though she had never thought of it before): 'Now the gods forbid', said she, 'so great a lady as you are should come to me, or that I should leave it to the hands of fortune if, by either the ill governing of your passion, or your husband's sudden waking, any danger might happen unto you! No! If there be any superiority in the points of true love, it shall be yours; if there be any danger, since myself am the author of this device, it is reason it should be mine. Therefore do you but leave with me the keys of the gate, and upon yourself take my upper garment, that if any of Dametas's house see you they may think you to be myself; and I will presently lie down in your place, so muffled for your supposed sickness as the duke shall nothing know me. And then, as soon as the duke is asleep, will I (as it much better becomes me) wait upon you; and if the uttermost of mischiefs should happen, I can assure you the duke's life shall sooner pay for it than your honour.'

And with the ending of her words she threw off her gown, not giving Gynecia any space to take the full image of this new change into her fancy; but seeing no ready objection against it in her heart, and knowing that there was no time then to stand long disputing, besides remembering the giver was to order the manner of his gift, yielded quickly to this conceit—indeed, not among the smallest causes, tickled thereunto by a certain wanton desire that her husband's deceit might be the more notable. In this sort did Cleophila, nimbly disarming herself, possess Gynecia's place, hiding her head in such a close manner as grievous and overwatched sickness is wont to invite to itself the solace of sleep.

And of the other side the duchess, putting on Cleophila's utmost apparel, went first into her closet, there quickly to beautify herself with the best and sweetest night deckings; but there casting a hasty eye over her precious things (which ever since Cleophila's coming her head, otherwise occupied, had left unseen), she happened to see a bottle of gold, upon which down along were graved these verses:

Let him drink this whom long in arms to fold
Thou dost desire, and with free pow'r to hold.

She remembered the bottle, for it had been kept of long time by the kings of Cyprus as a thing of rare virtue, and given to her by her mother when she being very young married to her husband of much greater age, her mother (persuaded it was of property to force love with love's effects) had made a precious present of it to this her well beloved child—though it had been received rather by tradition to have such a quality than by any approved experiment. This Gynecia (according to the common disposition, not only (though especially) of wives, but of all other kinds of people, not to esteem much one's own, but to think the labour lost employed about it) had never cared to give it to her husband, but suffered his affection to run according to his own scope. But now that love of her particular choice had awaked her spirits, and perchance the very unlawfulness of it had a little blown the coal, among her other ornaments with glad mind she took most part of this liquor, putting it into a fair cup all set with diamonds—for what dare not love undertake, armed with the night and provoked with lust? And thus down she went to the cave-ward, guided only by the moon's fair shining, suffering no other thought to have any familiarity with her brains, but that which did present unto her a picture of her approaching contentment. She that had long disdained this solitary life her husband had entered into now wished it much more solitary, so she might only obtain the private presence of Cleophila. She that before would not have gone alone so far (especially by night, and to so dark a place) now took a pride in the same courage, and framed in her mind a pleasure out of the pain itself. Thus with thick doubled paces she went to the cave, receiving to herself for her first contentment the only lying where Cleophila had done—whose pillow she kissed a thousand times for having borne the print of that beloved head. And so keeping with panting heart her travailing fancies so attentive that the wind could stir nothing, but that she stirred herself as if it had been the pace of the longed-for Cleophila, she kept her side of the bed, defending only and cherishing the other side with her arm; till after a while waiting, counting with herself how many steps were betwixt the lodge and the cave, and oft accusing Cleophila of more curious stay than needed, she was visited as you shall presently hear.

For Basilius, after his wife was departed to her feigned repose, as long as he remained with his daughter to give his wife time of unreadying*herself, it was easily seen it was a very thorny abode he made there, and the discourses with which he entertained his daughter not unlike to those of earnest players when, in the midst of their game, trifling questions be put unto them: his eyes still looking about, and himself still changing places; began to speak of a thing, and brake it off before it were half done; to any speech Philoclea ministered unto him, with a sudden starting and casting up his head, made an answer far out of all grammar; a certain deep musing, and by and by out of it; uncertain motions, unstaid graces. Having borne out the limit of a reasonable time with as much pain as might be, he came darkling into his chamber, forcing himself to tread as softly as he could. But the more curious he was, the more he thought everything creaked under him; and his mind being out of the way with another thought, and his eyes not serving his turn in that dark place, each coffer or cupboard he met, one saluted his shins, another his elbows; sometimes ready in revenge to strike them again with his face. Till at length, fearing his wife were not fully asleep, he came lifting up the clothes as gently as I think poor Pan did when, instead of Iole's bed, he came into the rough embracings of Hercules,* and laying himself down as tenderly as a new bride, rested awhile with a very open ear to mark each breath of his supposed wife. And sometimes he himself would yield a long-fetched sigh, as though that had been a music to draw on another to sleep. Till within a very little while, with the other party's well counterfeited sleep (who was as willing to be rid of him as he was to be gotten thence), assuring himself he left all safe there, in the same order stale out again; and putting on his nightgown, with much groping and scrambling, he gat himself out of the little house. And then did the moonlight serve to guide his feet. Thus with a great deal of pain did Basilius go to her whom he fled, and with much cunning left the person for whom he had employed all his cunning. But when Basilius was once gotten (as he thought) into a clear coast, what joy he then made; how each thing seemed vile in his sight, in comparison of his fortune; how far already he deemed himself in the chief tower of his desires, it were tedious to tell. But once his heart could not choose but yield this song as a fairing of his contentment:

Get hence foul grief,*the canker of the mind;
Farewell complaint, the miser's only pleasure;

Away vain cares, by which few men do find
        Their sought-for treasure.

Ye helpless sighs, blow out your breath to naught;
Tears, drown yourselves, for woe (your cause) is wasted;
Thought, think to end, too long the fruit of thought
        My mind hath tasted.

But thou, sure hope, tickle my leaping heart;
Comfort, step thou in place of wonted sadness;
Forefelt desire, begin to savour part
        Of coming gladness.

Let voice of sighs into clear music run;
Eyes, let your tears with gazing now be mended;
Instead of thought, true pleasure be begun
        And never ended.

Thus imagining as then with himself, his joys so held him up that he never touched ground. Like a right old beaten soldier that knew well enough the greatest captains do never use long orations when it comes to the very point of execution, as soon as he was gotten into the cave, and (to the joyful, though silent, expectation of Gynecia) come close to the bed, never recking his promise to look for nothing but conference, he leapt into that side preserved for a more welcome guest; and laying his lovingest hold upon Gynecia: 'O Cleophila,' said he, 'embrace in your favour this humble servant of yours! Hold within me my heart which pants to leave his master to come unto you!'

In what case poor Gynecia was when she knew the voice and felt the body of her husband, fair ladies, it is better to know by imagination than experience; for straight was her mind assaulted, partly with the being deprived of her unquenched desire, but principally with the doubt that Cleophila had betrayed her to her husband—besides the renewed sting of jealousy what in the mean time might befall her daughter. But of the other side her love, with a fixed persuasion she had had, taught her to seek all reason of hopes; and therein thought best, before discovering of herself, to mark the behaviour of her husband who, both in deeds and words still using her as taking her to be Cleophila, made Gynecia hope that this might be Basilius's own enterprise which Cleophila had not stayed, lest she should discover the matter, which might be performed at another time.

Which hope, accompanied with Basilius's manner of dealing (he being at that time fuller of livelier fancies than many years before he had been), besides the remembrance of her daughter's sickness, and late strange countenance betwixt her and Cleophila, all coming together into her mind (which was loath to condemn itself of an utter overthrow) made her frame herself, not truly with a sugared joy, but with a determinate patience, to let her husband think he had found a very gentle and supple-minded Cleophila; which he, good man, making full reckoning of, did melt in as much gladness as she was oppressed with divers ungrateful burdens.

But Pyrocles (who had at that present no more to play the part of Cleophila) having, as I told you, so naturally measured the manner of his breathing that Basilius made no doubt of his sound sleeping, having lain a pretty while with a quiet unquietness to satisfy his greedy desire, as soon as (by the debate betwixt Basilius's shins and the unregarding forms) he perceived that he had fully left the lodge, after him went he with stealing steps, having his sword under his arm (still doubting lest some mischance might turn Basilius back again), down to the gate of the lodge, which not content to lock fast, he barred and fortified with as many devices as his wit and haste would suffer him, resolving to have full time to accomplish his enterprise, and to have warning enough before they should come at him. For further ends of those ends, and what might ensue of this action, his love and courage well matched never looked after, holding for an assured ground that whosoever in great things will think to prevent all objections must lie still and do nothing. This only generally he remembered: that so long as Gynecia bewrayed not the matter (which he thought she would not do, as well for her own honour and safety as for the hope she might still have of him— which is loath to die in a lover's heart), all the rest would turn but to a pretty merriment, and inflame his lover Basilius again to a new casting about for the missed favour. This determination thus weighed, this first part thus performed, up to Philoclea's chamber door went Pyrocles, rapt from himself with the excessive forefeeling of his near coming contentment. Whatever pains he had taken, what dangers he had run into, and especially those saucy pangs of love, doubts, griefs, languishing hopes, and threatening despairs, came all now to his mind in one rank to beautify this after-following blissful-ness, and to serve for a most fit sauce, whose sourness might give a kind of life to the delightful cheer his imagination fed upon. All the great estate of his father seemed unto him but a trifling pomp, whose good stands in other men's conceit, in comparison of the true comfort he found in the depth of his mind; and the knowledge of any misery that might ensue this joyous adventure was recked of but as a slight purchase of possessing the top of happiness. And yet well he found that extremity of joy is not without a certain joyful pain,* by extending the heart beyond his wonted limits, and by so forcible a holding all the senses to one object, that it confounds their mutual working, not without a charming kind of ravishing them from the free use of their own function. Thus grieved only with too much gladness, being come to the door which should be the entry to his happiness, he was met with the latter end of a song which Philoclea, like a solitary nightingale, bewailing her guiltless punishment and helpless misfortune, had newly delivered over, meaning none should be judge of her passion but her own conscience. The song, having been accorded to a sweetly played-on lute, contained these verses which she had lately with some art curiously written to enwrap her secret and resolute woes:

Virtue, beauty, and speech,* did strike, wound, charm,

My heart, eyes, ears, with wonder, love, delight:

First, second, last, did bind, enforce, and arm,

His works, shows, suits, with wit, grace, and vow's might.

Thus honour, liking, trust, much, far, and deep,

Held, pierced, possessed, my judgement, sense, and will,

Till wrong, contempt, deceit, did grow, steal, creep,

Bands, favour, faith, to break, defile, and kill.

Then grief, unkindness, proof, took, kindled, taught,

Well grounded, noble, due, spite, rage, disdain,

But ah, alas! (in vain) my mind, sight, thought,

      1   2   3   1   2   3

Doth him, his face, his words, leave, shun, refrain,

      1   2   3   1   2   3

For no thing, time, nor place, can loose, quench, ease,

      1   2   3   1   2   3

Mine own, embraced, sought, knot, fire, disease.

The force of love, to those poor folk that feel it, is many ways very strange, but no way stranger than that it doth so enchain the lover's judgement upon her that holds the reins of his mind that whatsoever she doth is ever in his eyes best.* And that best, being by the continual motion of our changing life turned by her to any other thing, that thing again becometh best; so that nature in each kind suffering but one superlative, the lover only admits no positive. If she sit still, that is best; for so is the conspiracy of her several graces held best together to make one perfect figure of beauty. If she walk, no doubt that is best; for besides the making happy the more places by her steps, the very stirring adds a pleasing life to her native perfections. If she be silent, that without comparison is best; since by that means the untroubled eye most freely may devour the sweetness of his object. But if she speak, he will take it upon his death that is best; the quintessence of each word being distilled down into his affected soul. Example of this was well to be seen in the given-over Pyrocles who, with panting breath and sometimes sighs (not such as sorrow, restraining the inward parts, doth make them glad to deliver, but such as the impatience of desire, with the unsurety of never so sure hope, is wont to breathe out), now being at the door, of the one side hearing her voice (which, he thought, if the philosophers said true of the heavenly seven-sphered harmony, was by her not only represented but far surmounted), and of the other having his eyes overfilled with her beauty—for the duke at his parting had left the chamber open, and she at that time lay (as the heat of that country did well suffer) upon the top of her bed, having her beauties eclipsed with nothing but with a fair smock (wrought all in flames of ash-colour silk and gold), lying so upon her right side that the left thigh down to the foot yielded his delightful proportion to the full view, which was seen by the help of a rich lamp which, through the curtains a little drawn, cast such a light upon her as the moon doth when it shines into a thin wood—Pyrocles, I say, was stopped with the violence of so many darts cast by Cupid altogether upon him that, quite forgetting himself, and thinking therein already he was in the best degree of felicity, I think he would have lost much of his time, and with too much love omitted great fruit of his love, had not Philoclea's pitiful accusing of him forced him to bring his spirits again to a new bias. For she, laying her hand under her fair cheek, upon which there did privily trickle the sweet drops of her delightful (though sorrowful) tears, made these words wait upon her moanful song:

'And hath that cruel Pyrocles', said she, 'deserved thus much of me, that I should for his sake lift up my voice in my best tunes, and to him continually, with pouring out my plaint, make a disdained oblation? Shall my soul still do this honour to his unmerciful tyranny, by my lamenting his loss to show his worthiness and my weakness? He hears thee not, simple Philoclea, he hears thee not; and if he did, some hearts grow the harder, the more they find their advantage. Alas, what a miserable constitution of mind have I! I disdain my fortune, and yet reverence him that disdains me. I accuse his ungratefulness, and have his virtue in admiration. O ye deaf heavens, I would either his injury could blot out my affection, or my affection could forget his injury!'

With that, giving a pitiful but sweet screech, she took again the lute and began to sing this sonnet which might serve as an explaining to the other:

> The love which is imprinted in my soul
> With beauty's seal, and virtue fair disguised,
> With inward cries puts up a bitter roll
> Of huge complaints that now it is despised.
>
> Thus, thus, the more I love, the wrong the more
> Monstrous appears, long truth received late,
> Wrong stirs remorsed grief, grief's deadly sore
> Unkindness breeds, unkindness fost'reth hate.
>
> But ah! the more I hate, the more I think
> Whom I do hate, the more I think on him,
> The more his matchless gifts do deeply sink
> Into my breast, and loves renewed swim.
>   What medicine, then, can such disease remove
>   Where love draws hate, and hate engendreth love?

But Pyrocles (that had heard his name accused and condemned by the mouth which of all the world, and more than all the world, he most loved) had then cause enough to call his mind to his own home, and with the most haste he could (for true love fears the accident of an instant) to match the excusing of his fault with accomplishment of his errand thither. And therefore (blown up and down with as many contrary passions as Aeolus sent out winds upon the Trojan relics*guided upon the sea by the valiant Aeneas) he went into her chamber; and with such a pace as reverent fear doth teach he came to her bed side, where kneeling down, and having prepared a long oration for her, his eyes were so filled with her sight that, as if they would have robbed all their fellows of their services, both his heart fainted and his tongue failed, in such sort that he could not bring forth one word, but referred her understanding to his eyes' language. But she in extremity amazed to see him there at so undue a season, and ashamed that her beautiful body made so naked a prospect, drawing in her delicate limbs into the weak guard of the bed, and presenting in her face to him such a kind of pitiful anger as might show this was only a fault, therefore, because she had a former grudge unto him, turning away her face from him, she thus said unto him:

'O Cleophila or Pyrocles (for whether name I use it much skills not, since by the one I was first deceived, and by the other now betrayed), what strange motion is the guide of thy cruel mind hither? Dost thou not think the day torments thou hast given me sufficient, but that thou dost envy me the night's quiet? Wilt thou give my sorrows no truce but, by making me see before mine eyes how much I have lost, offer me due cause of confirming my plaint? Or is thy heart so full of rancour that thou dost desire to feed thine eyes with the wretched spectacle of thine overthrown enemy, and so to satisfy the full measure of thy undeserved rage with the receiving into thy sight the unrelievable ruins of my desolate life? O Pyrocles, Pyrocles, for thine own virtue's sake, let miseries be no music unto thee; and be content to take to thyself some colour of excuse, that thou didst not know to what extremity thy inconstancy, or rather false-hood, hath brought me!'

Pyrocles, to whom every syllable she pronounced was a thunder-bolt to his heart, equally distracted betwixt amazement and sorrow, abashed to see such a stop of his desires, grieved with her pain, but tormented to find himself the author of it, with quaking lips and pale cheer:

'Alas! divine lady,' said he, 'your displeasure is so contrary to my desert, and your words so far from all expectation, that I have least ability now I have most need to speak in the cause upon which my life dependeth. For my troth is so undoubtedly constant unto you, my heart is so assured a witness to itself of his unspotted faith, that having no one thing in me whereout any such sacrilege might arise, I have likewise nothing in so direct a thing to say for myself but sincere and vehement protestations. For, in truth, there may most words be spent where there is some probability to breed of both sides conjectural allegations; but in so perfect a thing as my love is of you, as it suffers no question so it seems to receive injury by any addition of words unto it. If my soul could have been polluted with treachery, it would likewise have provided for itself due furniture of colourable answers; but as it stood upon the naked confidence of his untouched duty, so I must confess it is altogether unarmed against so unjust a violence as you lay upon me. Alas, let not the pains I have taken to serve you be now accounted injurious unto you! Let not the dangerous cunning I have used to please you be deemed a treason against you! Since I have deceived them whom you fear for your sake, do not you destroy me for their sake. What can my words further express? I have rid them both out of the house. There is none here to be either hinderers or knowers of the perfecting the mutual love which once my love wrought in you towards me, but only the almighty powers, whom I invoke to be the triers of my innocency. And if ever my thoughts did receive so much as a fainting in their true affection; if they have not continually, with more and more ardour, from time to time pursued the possession of your sweetest favour; if ever in that profession they received either spot or falsehood, then let their most horrible plagues fall upon me; let mine eyes be deprived of the light, which did abuse the heavenly beams that strake them; let my falsified tongue serve to no use but to bemoan mine own wretchedness; let my heart empoisoned with detestable treason be the seat of infernal sorrow; let my soul with the endless anguish of his conscience become his own tormentor!'

'O false mankind!' cried out the sweet Philoclea, 'how can an impostumed heart but yield forth evil matter by his mouth? Are oaths there to be believed where vows are broken? No, no! Who doth wound the eternal justice of the gods cares little for the abusing their name; and who, in doing wickedly, doth not fear due recompensing plagues, doth little fear that invoking of plagues will make them come ever a whit the sooner. But alas! What aileth this new conversion? Have you yet another sleight to play; or do you think to deceive me in Pyrocles' form, as you have done in Cleophila's? Or rather, now you have betrayed me in both those, is there some third sex left you into which you can transform yourself, to inveigle my simplicity? Enjoy, enjoy the conquests you have already won, and assure yourself you are come to the furthest point of your cunning! For my part, unkind Pyrocles, my only defence shall be belief of nothing; my comfort, my faithful innocency; and the punishment I desire of you shall be your own conscience.'

Philoclea's hard persevering in this unjust condemnation of him did so overthrow all the might of Pyrocles' mind (who saw that time would not serve to make proof by deeds, and that the better words he used, the more they were suspected of deceitful cunning) that, void of all counsel and deprived of all comfort, finding best deserts punished and nearest hopes prevented, he did abandon the succour of himself, and suffered grief so to close his heart that his breath failing him, with a deathful shutting of his eyes, he fell down by her bedside, having had time to say no more but 'Oh, whom dost thou kill, Philoclea?'*

She that little looked for such an extreme event of her doings, starting out of her bed like Venus rising from her mother the sea,* not so much stricken down with amazement and grief of her fault as lifted up with the force of love and desire to help, she laid her fair body over his breast; and throwing no other water in his face but the stream of her tears, nor giving him other blows but the kisses of her well formed mouth, her only cries were these lamentations:

'O unfortunate suspicions,' said she, 'the very mean to lose that we most suspect to lose! O unkind kindness of mine which returns an imagined wrong with an effectual injury! O folly to make quarrels my supplications, or to use hate as the mediator of love! Childish Philoclea, hast thou thrown away the jewel wherein all thy pride consisted? Hast thou with too much haste overrun thyself?'

Then would she renew her kisses, and yet not finding the life return, redouble her plaints in this manner:

'O divine soul,' said she, 'whose virtue can possess no less than the highest place in heaven, if for my eternal plague thou hast utterly left this most sweet mansion, before I follow thee with Thisbe's punishment*of my rash unwariness, hear this true protestation of mine: that, as the wrong I have done thee proceeded of a most sincere but unresistible affection, so led with this pitiful example it shall end in the mortal hate of myself; and if it may be, I will make my soul a tomb of thy memory!'

But as she was rising, perchance to have begun some such enterprise, Pyrocles, severing his eyelids, and having for his first object her beloved beauty (which wrought in him not unlike to those who, lying abroad, are summoned by the morning sun to pay the tribute of their sight to his rising fairness), he was almost in as much danger of having his spirits again overpressed with this too excessive joy; but that she, finding him alive, and forgetting natural bashfulness for the late fear of his loss, with her dear embracements added strength to his life. So that, coming again to the use of his feet, and lifting the sweet burden of Philoclea in his arms, he laid her on her bed again, having so free scope of his serviceable sight that there came into his mind a song the shepherd Philisides had in his hearing sung* of the beauties of his unkind mistress, which in Pyrocles' judgement was fully accomplished in Philoclea. The song was this:

> What tongue can her perfections tell*
> In whose each part all pens may dwell?
> Her hair fine threads of finest gold
> In curled knots man's thought to hold;
> But that her forehead says, 'in me
> A whiter beauty you may see.'
> Whiter indeed; more white than snow
> Which on cold winter's face doth grow.
>
> That doth present those even brows,
> Whose equal lines their angles bows,
> Like to the moon when after change
> Her horned head abroad doth range;
> And arches be to heav'nly lids,
> Whose wink each bold attempt forbids.
>
> For the black stars those spheres contain,
> Their matchless praise* e'en praise doth stain.
> No lamp whose light by art is got,
> No sun which shines, and seeth not,
> Can liken them without all peer,
> Save one as much as other clear;
> Which only thus unhappy be
> Because themselves they cannot see.
>
> Her cheeks with kindly claret spread,

Aurora-like new out of bed,
Or like the fresh queen-apple's side,
Blushing at sight of Phoebus' pride.
Her nose, her chin, pure ivory wears,
No purer than the pretty ears,
Save that therein appears some blood,
Like wine and milk that mingled stood.
In whose incirclets if you gaze
Your eyes may tread a lover's maze,
But with such turns the voice to stray,
No talk untaught can find the way.
The tip no jewel needs to wear;
The tip is jewel of the ear.

But who those ruddy lips can miss,
Which blessed still themselves do kiss?
Rubies, cherries, and roses new,
In worth, in taste, in perfect hue,
Which never part but that they show
Of precious pearl the double row,
The second sweetly-fenced ward
Her heav'nly-dewed tongue to guard,
Whence never word in vain did flow.

Fair under these doth stately grow
The handle of this pleasant work,
The neck, in which strange graces lurk.
Such be, I think, the sumptuous towers
Which skill doth make in princes' bowers.

So good a say invites the eye
A little downward to espy
The lovely clusters of her breasts,
Of Venus' babe the wanton nests,
Like pommels round of marble clear,
Where azured veins well mixed appear,
With dearest tops of porphyry.*

Betwixt these two a way doth lie,
A way more worthy beauty's fame
Than that which bears the milken name.
This leads unto the joyous field
Which only still doth lilies yield;
But lilies such whose native smell

The Indian odours doth excel.
Waist it is called, for it doth waste
Men's lives until it be embraced.

There may one see, and yet not see,
Her ribs in white well armed be,
More white than Neptune's foamy face
When struggling rocks he would embrace.

In these delights the wand'ring thought
Might of each side astray be brought,
But that her navel doth unite
In curious circle busy sight,
A dainty seal of virgin wax
Where nothing but impression lacks.

Her belly there glad sight doth fill,
Justly entitled Cupid's hill;
A hill most fit for such a master,
A spotless mine of alabaster,
Like alabaster fair and sleek,
But soft and supple, satin-like,
In that sweet seat the boy doth sport.
Loath, I must leave his chief resort;
For such an use the world hath gotten,
The best things still must be forgotten.

Yet never shall my song omit
Those thighs (for Ovid's song more fit)
Which, flanked with two sugared flanks,
Lift up their stately swelling banks
That Albion cliffs in whiteness pass,
With haunches smooth as looking glass.

But bow all knees, now of her knees
My tongue doth tell what fancy sees:
The knots of joy, the gems of love,
Whose motion makes all graces move;
Whose bought incaved doth yield such sight,
Like cunning painter shadowing white.*
The gart'ring place*with childlike sign
Shows easy print in metal fine.

But there again the flesh doth rise
In her brave calves like crystal skies,
Whose Atlas is a smallest small,

More white than whitest bone of whale.
　　There oft steals out that round clean foot,
This noble cedar's precious root;
In show and scent pale violets,
Whose step on earth all beauty sets.
　　But back unto her back, my muse,
Where Leda's swan his feathers mews,
Along whose ridge such bones are met,
Like comfits round in marchpane set.
　　Her shoulders be like two white doves,
Perching within square royal rooves,
Which leaded are with silver skin,
Passing the hate-spot ermelin.*
　　And thence those arms derived are;
The phoenix' wings be not so rare
For faultless length and stainless hue.
　　Ah, woe is me, my woes renew!
Now course doth lead me to her hand,
Of my first love the fatal band,
Where whiteness doth for ever sit;
Nature herself enamelled it.
For there with strange compact doth lie
Warm snow, moist pearl, soft ivory.
There fall those sapphire-coloured brooks,
Which conduit-like, with curious crooks,
Sweet islands make in that sweet land.
As for the fingers of the hand,
The bloody shafts of Cupid's war,
With amethysts they headed are.
　　Thus hath each part his beauty's part;
But how the Graces do impart
To all her limbs a special grace,
Becoming every time and place,
Which doth e'en beauty beautify,
And most bewitch the wretched eye!
How all this is but a fair inn
Of fairer guest which dwells within,
Of whose high praise, and praiseful bliss,
Goodness the pen, heav'n paper is;
The ink immortal fame doth lend.

As I began, so must I end:
No tongue can her perfections tell,
In whose each part all pens may dwell.

But do not think, fair ladies, his thoughts had such leisure as to run over so long a ditty; the only general fancy of it came into his mind, fixed upon the sense of that sweet subject. Where, using the benefit of the time, and fortifying himself with the confessing her late fault (to make her now the sooner yield to penance), turning the past griefs and unkindness to the excess of all kind joys (as passion is apt to slide into his contrary), beginning now to envy Argus's thousand eyes, and Briareus's hundred hands,* fighting against a weak resistance, which did strive to be overcome, he gives me occasion to leave him in so happy a plight, lest my pen might seem to grudge at the due bliss of these poor lovers whose loyalty had but small respite of their fiery agonies. And now Lalus's pipe doth come to my hearing, which invites me to his marriage that in this season was celebrated between him and the handsome Kala whom long he had loved; which, I hope your ears, fair ladies, be not so full of great matters that you will disdain to hear.

The end of the third book.

LALUS, not with many painted words, nor false-hearted promises, had won the consent of his beloved Kala, but with a true and simple making her know he loved her; not forcing himself beyond his reach to buy her affection, but giving her such pretty presents as neither could weary him with the giving nor shame her for the taking. Thus the first strawberries he could find were ever in a clean washed dish sent to Kala. Thus posies of the spring flowers were wrapped up in a little green silk and dedicated to Kala's breasts. Thus sometimes his sweetest cream, sometimes the best cake-bread his mother made, were reserved for Kala's taste. Neither would he stick to kill a lamb when she would be content to come over the way unto him. But then lo, how the house was swept, and rather no fire than any smoke left to trouble her. Then love songs were not dainty, when she would hear them, and as much mannerly silence when she would not. In going to church, great worship to Kala, so that all the parish said never a maid they knew so well waited on; and when dancing was about the maypole, nobody taken out but she, and he after a leap or two to show her his own activity, would frame all the rest of his dancing only to grace her. As for her father's sheep, he had no less care of them than his own; so that she might play her as she would, warranted with honest Lalus's carefulness. But if he spied Kala favoured any one of the flock more than his fellows, then that was cherished, shearing him so (when shorn he must be) as might most become him; but while the wool was on, wrapping within it some verses (wherein Lalus had a special gift), and making the innocent beast his unwitting messenger. Thus constantly continuing, though he were none of the fairest, at length he wan Kala's heart, the honestest wench in all those quarters. And so, with consent of both parents (without which neither Lalus would ask nor Kala grant), their marriage day was appointed; which, because it fell out in this time, I think it shall not be impertinent to remember a little our shepherds while the other greater persons are either sleeping or otherwise occupied. Lalus's marriage time once known, there needed no inviting of the neighbours in that valley; for so well was Lalus beloved that they were all ready to do him credit. Neither yet came they like harpies to devour him, but one brought a fat pig, the other a tender kid, a third a great goose; as for cheese, milk and butter were the gossips' presents. Thither came of stranger shepherds only the melancholy Philisides; for the virtuous Coredens*had long since left off all joyful solemnities, and as for Strephon and Klaius, they had lost their mistress, which put them into such extreme sorrows as they could scarcely abide the light of the day, much less the eyes of men. But of the Arcadian-born shepherds, thither came good old Geron, young Histor (though unwilling), and upright Dicus, merry Pas, and jolly Nico; as for Dametas, they durst not presume, his pride was such, to invite him; and Dorus they found might not be spared. And there under a bower was made of boughs (for Lalus's house was not able to receive them), they were entertained with hearty welcome, and every one placed according to his age. The women (for such was the manner of that country) kept together to make good cheer among themselves, from which otherwise a certain painful modesty restrains them. And there might the sadder matrons give good counsel to Kala who, poor soul, wept for fear of that she desired. But among the shepherds was all honest liberty; no fear of dangerous telltales (who hunt greater preys), nor indeed minds in them to give telltales any occasion, but one questioning with another of the manuring his ground, and governing his flock. The highest point they reached to was to talk of the holiness of marriage; to which purpose, as soon as their sober dinner was ended, Dicus instead of thanks sang this song with a clear voice and cheerful countenance:

Let mother earth*now deck herself in flowers,
To see her offspring seek a good increase,
Where justest love doth vanquish Cupid's powers
And war of thoughts is swallowed up in peace
    Which never may decrease,
    But like the turtles fair
    Live one in two, a well united pair,
    Which, that no chance may stain,
O Hymen long their coupled joys maintain.

O heav'n awake, show forth thy stately face;
Let not these slumb'ring clouds thy beauties hide,
But with thy cheerful presence help to grace
The honest bridegroom and the bashful bride,
    Whose loves may ever bide,

Like to the elm and vine,
With mutual embracements them to twine;
In which delightful pain,
O Hymen long their coupled joys maintain.

Ye muses all which chaste affects allow,
And have to Lalus showed your secret skill,
To this chaste love your sacred favours bow,
And so to him and her your gifts distil,
    That they all vice may kill;
    And like to lilies pure
    Do please all eyes, and spotless do endure;
    Where, that all bliss may reign,
    O Hymen long their coupled joys maintain.

Ye nymphs in which the waters empire have,
Since Lalus' music oft doth yield you praise,
Grant to the thing which we for Lalus crave:
Let one time (but long first) close up their days,
    One grave their bodies seize,
    And like two rivers sweet
    When they, though diverse, do together meet,
    One stream both streams contain;
    O Hymen long their coupled joys maintain.

Pan, father Pan, the god of silly sheep,
Whose care is cause that they in number grow,
Have much more care of them that them do keep,
Since from these good the others' good doth flow,
    And make their issue show
    In number like the herd
    Of younglings which thyself with love hast reared,
    Or like the drops of rain;
    O Hymen long their coupled joys maintain.

Virtue, if not a god, yet God's chief part,
Be thou the knot of this their open vow:
That still he be her head, she be his heart,
He lean to her, she unto him do bow;
    Each other still allow,

Like oak and mistletoe,
Her strength from him, his praise from her do grow.
In which most lovely train,
O Hymen long their coupled joys maintain.

But thou foul Cupid, sire to lawless lust,
Be thou far hence with thy empoisoned dart
Which, though of glitt'ring gold, shall here take rust*
Where simple love, which chasteness doth impart,
    Avoids thy hurtful art,
    Not needing charming skill
    Such minds with sweet affections for to fill,
    Which being pure and plain,
    O Hymen long their coupled joys maintain.

All churlish words, shrewd answers, crabbed looks,
All privateness, self-seeking, inward spite,
All waywardness which nothing kindly brooks,
All strife for toys, and claiming master's right,
    Be hence ay put to flight;
    All stirring husband's hate
    Gainst neighbours good for womanish debate
    Be fled as things most vain,
    O Hymen long their coupled joys maintain.

All peacock pride, and fruits of peacock's pride,
Longing to be with loss of substance gay
With recklessness what may thy house betide,
So that you may on higher slippers stay,
    For ever hence away.
    Yet let not sluttery,
    The sink of filth, be counted housewifery;
    But keeping wholesome mean,
    O Hymen long their coupled joys maintain.

But above all, away vile jealousy,
The ill of ills, just cause to be unjust,
(How can he love, suspecting treachery?
How can she love where love cannot win trust?)
    Go snake, hide thee in dust,

Ne dare once show thy face
Where open hearts do hold so constant place;
That they thy sting restrain,
O Hymen long their coupled joys maintain.

The earth is decked with flow'rs, the heav'ns displayed,
Muses grant gifts, nymphs long and joined life,
Pan store of babes, virtue their thoughts well stayed,
Cupid's lust gone, and gone is bitter strife,
    Happy man, happy wife.
    No pride shall them oppress,
    Nor yet shall yield to loathsome sluttishness,
    And jealousy is slain;
    For Hymen will their coupled joys maintain.

'Truly Dicus,' said Nico, 'although thou didst not grant me the prize the last day, when undoubtedly I wan it, yet must I needs say thou for thy part hast sung well and thriftily.'

Pas straight desired all the company they would bear witness that Nico had once in his life spoken wisely: 'For', said he, 'I will tell it to his father, who will be a glad man when he hears such news.'

'Very true,' said Nico, 'but, indeed, so would not thine in like case, for he would look thou shouldst live but one hour longer, that a discreet word wandered out of thy mouth.'

'And I pray thee,' said Pas, 'gentle Nico, tell me what mischance it was that brought thee to taste so fine a meat?'

'Marry, goodman blockhead,' said Nico, 'because he speaks against jealousy, the filthy traitor to true affection, and yet disguising itself in the raiment of love.'

'Sentences, sentences,'* cried Pas, 'alas, how ripe-witted these young folks be nowadays! But well counselled shall that husband be when this man comes to exhort him not to be jealous.'

'And so shall he,' answered Nico, 'for I have seen a fresh example, though it be not very fit to be known.'

'Come, come,' said Pas, 'be not so squeamish. I know thou longest more to tell it than we to hear it.'

But for all his words Nico would not bestow his voice till he was generally entreated of the rest; and then with a merry marriage look he sang this following discourse—for with a better grace he could sing than tell:

A neighbour mine not long ago there was*
(But nameless he, for blameless he shall be)
That married had a trick and bonny lass
As in a summer day a man might see;
   But he himself a foul unhandsome groom,
   And far unfit to hold so good a room.

Now whether moved with self-unworthiness,
Or with her beauty, fit to make a prey,
Fell jealousy did so his brain oppress
That if he absent were but half a day,
   He guessed the worst (you wot what is the worst)
   And in himself new doubting causes nursed.

While thus he feared the silly innocent,
Who yet was good, because she knew none ill,
Unto his house a jolly shepherd went,
To whom our prince did bear a great goodwill,
   Because in wrestling and in pastoral
   He far did pass the rest of shepherds all.

And therefore he a courtier was benamed,
And as a courtier was with cheer received
(For they have tongues to make a poor man blamed
If he to them his duty misconceived);
   And for this courtier should well like his table,
   The goodman bad his wife be serviceable.

And so she was, and all with good intent,
But few days passed while she good manner used,
But that her husband thought her service bent
To such an end as he might be abused.
   Yet, like a coward fearing stranger's pride,
   He made the simple wench his wrath abide.

With chumpish looks, hard words, and secret nips,
Grumbling at her when she his kindness sought,
Asking her how she tasted courtier's lips,
He forced her think that which she never thought.
   In fine, it made her guess there was some sweet
   In that which he so feared that she should meet.

When once this entered was in woman's heart,
And that it had inflamed a new desire,
There rested then to play a woman's part,
Fuel to seek and not to quench the fire;
    But (for his jealous eye she well did find)
    She studied cunning how the same to blind.

And thus she did: one day to him she came
And (though against his will) on him she leaned,
And out gan cry, 'ah wellaway, for shame,
If you help not our wedlock will be stained!'
    The goodman starting, asked what did her move?
    She sighed, and said the bad guest sought her love.

He little looking that she should complain
Of that whereto he feared she was inclined,
Bussing her oft, and in his heart full fain,
He did demand what remedy to find;
    How they might get that guest from them to wend,
    And yet the prince (that loved him) not offend.

'Husband', quoth she, 'go to him by and by,
And tell him that you find I do him love,
And therefore pray him that of courtesy
He will absent himself, lest he should move
    A young girl's heart to that were shame for both,
    Whereto you know his honest heart were loath.

Thus shall you show that him you do not doubt,
And as for me, sweet husband, I must bear.'
Glad was the man when he had heard her out;
And did the same, although with mickle fear.
    For fear he did lest he the young man might
    In choler put, with whom he would not fight.

The courtly shepherd much aghast at this,
Not seeing erst such token in the wife,
Though full of scorn, would not his duty miss,
Knowing that ill becomes a household strife,
    Did go his way, but sojourned near thereby,
    That yet the ground hereof he might espy.

The wife thus having settled husband's brain
(Who would have sworn his spouse Diana was),
Watched when she a further point might gain;
Which little time did fitly bring to pass.
   For to the court her man was called by name,
   Whither he needs must go for fear of blame.

Three days before that he must sure depart,
She written had (but in a hand disguised)
A letter such which might from either part
Seem to proceed, so well it was devised.
   She sealed it first, then she the sealing brake,
   And to her jealous husband did it take.

With weeping eyes (her eyes she taught to weep)
She told him that the courtier had it sent:
'Alas', quoth she, 'thus women's shame doth creep.'
The goodman read on both sides the content;
   It title had: *Unto my only love.*
   Subscription was: *Yours most, if you will prove.*

The pistle self, such kind of words it had:
'My sweetest joy, the comfort of my sprite,
So may thy flocks increase, thy dear heart glad,
So may each thing e'en as thou wishest light,
   As thou wilt deign to read, and gently read,
   This mourning ink in which my heart doth bleed.

Long have I loved (alas, thou worthy art),
Long have I loved (alas, love craveth love),
Long have I loved thyself; alas, my heart
Doth break now tongue unto thy name doth move;
   And think not that thy answer answer is,
   But that it is my doom of bale or bliss.

The jealous wretch must now to court be gone;
Ne can he fail, for prince hath for him sent;
Now is the time we may be here alone,
And give a long desire a sweet content.
   Thus shall you both reward a lover true,
   And eke revenge his wrong suspecting you.'

And this was all, and this the husband read
With chafe enough, till she him pacified,
Desiring that no grief in him he bred
Now that he had her words so truly tried;
  But that he would to him the letter show,
  That with his fault he might her goodness know.

That straight was done, with many a boistrous threat
That to the duke he would his sin declare;
But now the courtier gan to smell the feat,
And with some words which showed little care,
  He stayed until the goodman was departed,
  Then gave he him the blow which never smarted.

Thus may you see the jealous wretch was made
The pander of the thing he most did fear.
Take heed, therefore, how you ensue that trade,
Lest that some marks of jealousy you bear;
  For sure no jealousy can that prevent
  Whereto two parties once be full content.

'Behold,' said Pas, 'a whole dicker of wit! He hath picked out such
a tale, with intention to keep a husband from jealousy, which were
enough to make a sanctified husband jealous, to see subtleties so
much in the feminine gender. But', said he, 'I will strike Nico dead
with the wise words shall flow out of my gorge'; and without further
entreaty thus sang:

Who doth desire that chaste his wife should be,
First be he true, for truth doth truth deserve.
Then such be he, as she his worth may see;
And one man still, credit with her preserve.

Not toying kind, nor causelessly unkind,
Not stirring thoughts, nor yet denying right,
Not spying faults, nor in plain errors blind;
Never hard hand, nor ever reins too light.

As far from want, as far from vain expense
(The one doth force, the latter doth entice);
Allow good company, but keep from thence
All filthy mouths that glory in their vice.

> This done, thou hast no more, but leave the rest
> To virtue, fortune, time, and woman's breast.

'Well concluded', said Nico, 'when he hath done all, he leaves the matter to his wife's discretion. Now whensoever thou marriest, let her discretion deck thy head with Actaeon's ornament!'

Pas was so angry with his wish (being indeed towards marriage) that they might perchance have fallen to buffets, but that Dicus (who knew it more wisdom to let a fray than part a fray) desired Philisides (who as a stranger sat among them, revolving in his mind all the tempests of evil fortunes he had passed) that he would do so much grace to the company as to sing one of his country songs. Philisides knew it no good manners to be squeamish of his cunning, having put himself in their company, and yet loath either in time of marriage to sing his sorrows, more fit for funerals, or by any outward matter to be drawn to such mirth as to betray (as it were) that passion to which he had given over himself, he took a mean way betwixt both and sang this song he had learned before he had ever subjected his thoughts to acknowledge no master but a mistress:

> As I my little flock on Ister bank*
> (A little flock, but well my pipe they couthe)
> Did piping lead, the sun already sank
> Beyond our world, and ere I gat my booth
> Each thing with mantle black the night did soothe,
>   Saving the glow-worm, which would courteous be
>   Of that small light oft watching shepherds see.
>
> The welkin had full niggardly enclosed
> In coffer of dim clouds his silver groats,
> Ycleped stars; each thing to rest disposed:
> The caves were full, the mountains void of goats;
> The birds' eyes closed, closed their chirping notes.
>   As for the nightingale, wood-music's king,
>   It August was, he deigned not then to sing.
>
> Amid my sheep, though I saw naught to fear,
> Yet (for I nothing saw) I feared sore;
> Then found I which thing is a charge to bear,
> For for my sheep I dreaded mickle more
> Than ever for myself since I was bore.

I sat me down, for see to go ne could,
And sang unto my sheep lest stray they should.

The song I sang old Languet had me taught,
Languet, the shepherd best swift Ister knew,
For clerkly rede, and hating what is naught,
For faithful heart, clean hands, and mouth as true.
With his sweet skill my skill-less youth he drew
   To have a feeling taste of him that sits
   Beyond the heav'n, far more beyond our wits.

He said the music best thilke powers pleased
Was jump concord between our wit and will,
Where highest notes to godliness are raised,
And lowest sink not down to jot of ill.
With old true tales*he wont mine ears to fill:
   How shepherds did of yore, how now, they thrive,
   Spoiling their flock, or while twixt them they strive.

   He liked me, but pitied lustful youth.
   His good strong staff my slipp'ry years upbore.
He still hoped well, because I loved truth;
Till forced to part, with heart and eyes e'en sore,
To worthy Coredens*he gave me o'er.
   But thus in oak's true shade recounted he
   Which now in night's deep shade sheep heard of me.

Such manner time there was*(what time I not)
When all this earth, this dam or mould of ours,
Was only woned with such as beasts begot;
Unknown as then were they that builden towers.
The cattle, wild or tame, in nature's bowers
   Might freely roam or rest, as seemed them;
   Man was not man their dwellings in to hem.

The beasts had sure some beastly policy;
For nothing can endure where order nis.
For once the lion by the lamb did lie;
The fearful hind the leopard did kiss;
Hurtless was tiger's paw and serpent's hiss.
   This think I well: the beasts with courage clad
   Like senators a harmless empire had.

At which, whether the others did repine
(For envy harb'reth most in feeblest hearts),*
Or that they all to changing did incline
(As e'en in beasts their dams leave changing parts),
The multitude to Jove a suit imparts,
   With neighing, bleaing, braying, and barking,
   Roaring, and howling, for to have a king.

A king in language theirs they said they would
(For then their language was a perfect speech).
The birds likewise with chirps and pewing could,
Cackling and chatt'ring, that of Jove beseech.
Only the owl still warned them not to seech
   So hastily that which they would repent;
   But saw they would, and he to deserts went.

Jove wisely said (for wisdom wisely says):
'O beasts, take heed what you of me desire.
Rulers will think all things made them to please,
And soon forget the swink due to their hire.
But since you will, part of my heav'nly fire
   I will you lend; the rest yourselves must give,
   That it both seen and felt may with you live.'

Full glad they were, and took the naked sprite,
Which straight the earth yclothed in his clay.
The lion, heart; the ounce gave active might;
The horse, good shape; the sparrow, lust to play;
Nightingale, voice, enticing songs to say.
   Elephant gave a perfect memory;
   And parrot, ready tongue, that to apply.

The fox gave craft; the dog gave flattery;
Ass, patience; the mole, a working thought;
Eagle, high look; wolf, secret cruelty;
Monkey, sweet breath; the cow, her fair eyes brought;
The ermine, whitest skin spotted with naught;
   The sheep, mild-seeming face; climbing, the bear;
   The stag did give the harm-eschewing fear.

The hare her sleights; the cat his melancholy;
Ant, industry; and cony, skill to build;
Cranes, order; storks, to be appearing holy;
Chameleon, ease to change; duck, ease to yield;

Crocodile, tears which might be falsely spilled.
  Ape great thing gave, though he did mowing stand:
  The instrument of instruments, the hand.

Each other beast likewise his present brings;
And (but they drad their prince they oft should want)
They all consented were to give him wings.
And ay more awe towards him for to plant,
To their own work this privilege they grant:
  That from thenceforth to all eternity
  No beast should freely speak, but only he.

Thus man was made; thus man their lord became;
Who at the first, wanting or hiding pride,
He did to beasts' best use his cunning frame,
With water drink, herbs meat, and naked hide,
And fellow-like let his dominion slide,
  Not in his sayings saying 'I', but 'we';
  As if he meant his lordship common be.

But when his seat so rooted he had found
That they now skilled not how from him to wend,
Then gan in guiltless earth full many a wound,
Iron to seek, which gainst itself should bend
To tear the bowels that good corn should send.
  But yet the common dam none did bemoan,
  Because (though hurt) they never heard her groan.

Then gan he factions in the beasts to breed;
Where helping weaker sort, the nobler beasts
(As tigers, leopards, bears, and lions' seed)
Disdained with this, in deserts sought their rests;
Where famine ravin taught their hungry chests,
  That craftily he forced them to do ill;
  Which being done, he afterwards would kill

For murder done, which never erst was seen,
By those great beasts. As for the weakers' good,
He chose themselves his guarders for to been
Gainst those of might of whom in fear they stood,
As horse and dog; not great, but gentle blood.
  Blithe were the commons, cattle of the field,
  Tho when they saw their foen of greatness killed.

But they, or spent or made of slender might,
Then quickly did the meaner cattle find,
The great beams gone, the house on shoulders light;
For by and by the horse fair bits did bind;
The dog was in a collar taught his kind.
   As for the gentle birds, like case might rue
   When falcon they, and goshawk, saw in mew.

Worst fell to smallest birds, and meanest herd,
Who now his own, full like his own he used.
Yet first but wool, or feathers, off he teared;
And when they were well used to be abused,
For hungry throat their flesh with teeth he bruised;
   At length for glutton taste he did them kill;
   At last for sport their silly lives did spill.

But yet, O man, rage not beyond thy need;
Deem it no gloire to swell in tyranny.
Thou art of blood; joy not to make things bleed.
Thou fearest death; think they are loath to die.
A plaint of guiltless hurt doth pierce the sky.
   And you, poor beasts, in patience bide your hell,
   Or know your strengths, and then you shall do well.

Thus did I sing and pipe eight sullen hours
To sheep whom love, not knowledge, made to hear;
Now fancy's fits, now fortune's baleful stours.
But then I homeward called my lambkins dear;
For to my dimmed eyes began t'appear
   The night grown old, her black head waxen grey,
   Sure shepherd's sign that morn would soon fetch day.

According to the nature of diverse ears, diverse judgements straight
followed: some praising his voice; others the words, fit to frame a
pastoral style; others the strangeness of the tale, and scanning what
he should mean by it. But old Geron (who had borne him a grudge
ever since, in one of their eclogues, he had taken him up over-
bitterly) took hold of this occasion to make his revenge and said he
never saw thing worse proportioned than to bring in a tale of he
knew not what beasts at such a banquet when rather some song of
love, or matter for joyful melody, was to be brought forth. 'But', said

he, 'this is the right conceit of young men who think then they speak wiseliest when they cannot understand themselves.' Then invited he Histor to answer him in eclogue-wise; who, indeed, having been long in love with the fair bride Kala, and now prevented, was grown into a detestation of marriage. But thus it was:

Geron   Histor

Geron. In faith, good Histor, long is your delay
    From holy marriage, sweet and surest mean
    Our foolish lusts in honest rules to stay.
I pray thee do to Lalus' sample lean.
    Thou seest how frisk and jolly now he is
    That last day seemed he could not chaw a bean.
Believe me, man, there is no greater bliss
    Than is the quiet joy of loving wife,
    Which whoso wants, half of himself doth miss.
Friend without change, playfellow without strife,
    Food without fullness, counsel without pride,
    Is this sweet doubling of our single life.

Histor. No doubt to whom so good chance did betide
    As for to find a pasture strowed with gold,
    He were a fool if there he did not bide.
Who would not have a phoenix if he could?
    The humming wasp, if it had not a sting,
    Before all flies the wasp accept I would.
But this bad world few golden fields doth bring;
    Phoenix but one, of crows we millions have;
    The wasp seems gay, but is a cumbrous thing.
If many Kalas our Arcadia gave,
    Lalus' example I would soon ensue;
    And think I did myself from sorrow save.
But of such wives we find a slender crew;
    Shrewdness so stirs, pride so puffs up their heart,
    They seldom ponder what to them is due.
With meagre looks, as if they still did smart,
    Puling and whimp'ring, or else scolding flat,
    Make home more pain than following of the cart.
Either dull silence, or eternal chat;
    Still contrary to what her husband says:

If he do praise the dog, she likes the cat.
Austere she is, when he would honest plays;
   And gamesome then, when he thinks on his sheep;
   She bids him go, and yet from journey stays.
She war doth ever with his kinsfolk keep,
   And makes them fremd who friends by nature are,
   Envying shallow toys with malice deep.
And if, forsooth, there come some new-found ware,
   The little coin his sweating brows have got
   Must go for that, if for her lours he care;
Or else: 'Nay, faith, mine is the lucklest lot
   That ever fell to honest woman yet;
   No wife but I hath such a man, God wot.'
Such is their speech who be of sober wit;
   But who do let their tongues show well their rage,
   Lord, what by-words they speak, what spite they spit!
The house is made a very loathsome cage,
   Wherein the bird doth never sing, but cry
   With such a will that nothing can assuage.
Dearly the servants do their wages buy,
   Reviled for each small fault, sometimes for none;
   They better live that in a gaol do lie.
Let other fouler spots away be blown,
   For I seek not their shame; but still, methinks,
   A better life it is to lie alone.

Geron. Who for each fickle fear from virtue shrinks
   Shall in this life embrace no worthy thing;
   No mortal man the cup of surety drinks.
The heav'ns do not good haps in handfuls bring,
   But let us pick our good from out much bad;
   That still our little world may know his king.
But certainly so long we may be glad
   While that we do what nature doth require,
   And for th'event we never ought be sad.
Man oft is plagued with air, is burnt with fire,
   In water drowned, in earth his burial is;
   And shall we not therefore their use desire?
Nature above all things requireth this:
   That we our kind do labour to maintain;

Which drawn-out line doth hold all human bliss.
Thy father justly may of thee complain,
    If thou do not repay his deeds for thee,
    In granting unto him a grandsire's gain.
Thy commonwealth may rightly grieved be,
    Which must by this immortal be preserved,
    If thus thou murder thy posterity.
His very being he hath not deserved
    Who for a self-conceit will that forbear
    Whereby that being ay must be conserved.
And God forbid women such cattle were
    As you paint them; but well in you I find,
    No man doth speak aright who speaks in fear.
Who only sees the ill is worse than blind.
    These fifty winters married I have been;
    And yet find no such faults in womankind.
I have a wife worthy to be a queen,
    So well she can command, and yet obey;
    In ruling of a house so well she's seen.
And yet in all this time betwixt us tway,
    We bear our double yoke with such consent,
    There never passed foul word, I dare well say.
But these be your love-toys which still are spent
    In lawless games, and love not as you should,
    But with much study learn late to repent.
How well last day before our prince you could
    Blind Cupid's works with wonder testify!
    Yet now the root of him abase you would.
Go to, go to, and Cupid now apply
    To that where thou thy Cupid mayst avow,
    And thou shalt find in women virtues lie.
Sweet supple minds which soon to wisdom bow,
    Where they by wisdom's rules directed are,
    And are not forced fond thraldom to allow.
As we to get are framed, so they to spare;
    We made for pains, our pains they made to cherish;
    We care abroad, and they of home have care.
O Histor, seek within thyself to flourish;
    Thy house by thee must live, or else be gone,
    And then who shall the name of Histor nourish?

Riches of children pass a prince's throne;
   Which touch the father's heart with secret joy
   When without shame he saith: 'these be mine own.'
Marry therefore; for marriage will destroy
   Those passions which to youthful head do climb,
   Mothers and nurses of all vain annoy.

Histor. Perchance I will, but now methinks it time
   We go unto the bride, and use this day
   To speak with her, while freely speak we may.

He spake these last words with such affection as a curious eye
might easily have perceived he liked Lalus's fortune better than he
loved his person. But then, indeed, did all arise, and went to the
women; where spending all the day and good part of the night in
dancing, carolling, and wassailing, lastly they left Lalus where he
long desired to be left, and with many unfeigned thanks returned
every man to his home. But some of them, having to cross the way
of the two lodges, might see a lady making doleful lamentations over
a body seemed dead unto them.

But methinks Dametas cries unto me, if I come not the sooner to
comfort him, he will leave off his golden work hath already cost him
so much labour and longing.

Here end the third eclogues.

THE FOURTH BOOK OR ACT

THE everlasting justice (using ourselves to be the punishers of our faults, and making our own actions the beginning of our chastisement, that our shame may be the more manifest, and our repentance follow the sooner) took Dametas at this present (by whose folly the others' wisdom might receive the greater overthrow)* to be the instrument of revealing the secretest cunning—so evil a ground doth evil stand upon, and so manifest it is that nothing remains strongly but that which hath the good foundation of goodness. For so it fell out that Dametas, having spent the whole day in breaking up the cumbersome work of the pastor Dorus, and feeling in all his labour no pain so much as that his hungry hopes received any stay, having with the price of much sweat and weariness gotten up the huge stone which he thought should have such a golden lining, the goodman in the great bed that stone had made found nothing but these two verses written upon a piece of vellum:

> Who hath his hire, hath well his labour placed;
> Earth thou didst seek, and store of earth thou hast.

What an inward discountenance it was to master Dametas to find his hope of wealth turned to poor verses (for which he never cared much) nothing can describe, but either the feeling in oneself the state of such a mind Dametas had, or at least the bethinking what was Midas's fancy when, after the great pride he conceived to be made judge between gods, he was rewarded with the ornament of an ass's ears. Yet the deep apprehension he had received of such riches could not so suddenly lose the colour that had so thoroughly dyed his thick brain but that he turned and tossed the poor bowels of the innocent earth, till the far passing of the night, and the tediousness of his fruitless labour, made him content rather to exercise his discontentation at home than there. Yet forced he was (his horse being otherwise burdened with digging instruments) to return, as he came, most part of the way on foot, with such grudging lamentations as a nobler mind would (but more nobly) make for the loss of his mistress. For so far had he fed his foolish soul with the expectation of that which he reputed felicity that he no less accounted himself miserable than if he had fallen from such an estate his fancy had embraced. So then home again went Dametas, punished in conceit, as in conceit he had erred, till he found himself there from a fancied loss fallen to an essential misery. For entering into his house three hours within night, instead of the lightsome countenance of Pamela (which gave such an inward decking to that lodge as proudest palaces might have cause to envy it), and of the grateful conversation of Dorus (whose witty behaviour made that loneliness to seem full of good company), instead of the loud scolding of Miso, and the busy tumbling up and down of Mopsa (which, though they were so short as quite contrary to the others' praiseworthiness, yet were they far before them in filling of a house), he found nothing but a solitary darkness which, as naturally it breeds a kind of irksome ghastfulness, so it was to him a most present terror, remembering the charge he had left behind, which he well knew imported no less than his life unto him. Therefore, lighting a candle, there was no place a mouse could have dwelled in but that he with quaking diligence sought into. But when he saw he could see nothing of that he most cared for, then became he the right pattern of a wretch dejected with fear. For crying and howling, knocking his head to the wall, he began to make pitiful complaints where nobody could hear him; and with too much dread he should not recover her, leave all consideration how to recover her. But at length, looking like a she goat when she casts her kid, for very sorrow he took in his own behalf, out of the lodge he went running as hard as he could, having now received the very form of hanging into his consideration. Thus running as a man that would gladly have run from himself, it was his foolish fortune to espy by the glimmering light the moon did then yield him one standing aloft among the boughs of a fair ash. He (that would have asked counsel at that time of a dog) cast up his face as if his tooth had been drawing, and with much bending his sight he perceived it was mistress Mopsa, fitly seated there for her wit and dignity. There, I will not say with joy (for how could he taste of joy whose imagination was fallen from a palace to a gallows?), but yet with some refreshing of comfort, in hope he should learn better tidings of her, he began to cry out: 'O Mopsa, my beloved chicken, here am I thine own father Dametas, never in such a towardness to hanging, if thou cannot help me!'

But never a word could his eloquence procure of Mopsa who, indeed, was there attending for greater matters. This was yet a new burden to poor Dametas who thought all the world was conspired against him; and therefore, with a silly choler he began another tune: 'Thou vile Mopsa,' said he, 'now the vengeance of my fatherly curse light overthwart thee if thou do not straight answer me!'

But neither blessing nor cursing could prevail with Mopsa who was now great with child with the expectation of her may-game hopes, and did long to be delivered with the third time being named, which by and by followed; for Dametas, rubbing his elbow, stamping and whining, seeing neither of these take place, began to throw stones at her, and withal to conjure her by the name of hellish Mopsa. But when he had named her the third time, no chime can more suddenly follow the striking of a clock than she, verily thinking it was the god that used her father's voice, throwing her arms abroad, and not considering she was muffled upon so high a tree, came fluttering down like a hooded hawk, like enough to have broken her neck, but that the tree, full of boughs, tossed her from one bough to another, and lastly well bruised brought her to receive an unfriendly salutation of the earth. Dametas, as soon as she was down, came running to her, and finding her so close wrapped, pulled off the scarlet cloak—in good time for her; for, with the soreness of the fall, if she had not had breath given her, she had delivered a foolish soul to Pluto. But then Dametas began afresh to desire his daughter not to forget the pains he had taken for her in her childhood (which he was sure she could not remember), and to tell him where Pamela was.

'O good Apollo,' said Mopsa, 'if ever thou didst bear love to Phaethon's mother, let me have a king to my husband.'

'Alas, what speakest thou of Phaethon?' said Dametas, 'if by thy circumspect means I find not out Pamela, thy father will be hanged tomorrow.'

'It is no matter, though he be hanged,' answered Mopsa, 'do but thou make Dorus a king, and let him be my husband, good Apollo, for my courage doth much prick me towards him.'

'Ah, Mopsa,' cried out Dametas, 'where is thy wit? Dost thou not know thy father? How hast thou forgotten thyself?'

'I do not ask wit of thee, mine own god,' said she, 'but I see thou wouldst have me remember my father, and indeed forget myself. No, no, a good husband!'

'Thou shalt have thy fill of husbands', said Dametas, 'and do but answer me my question.'

'O, I thank thee,' said Mopsa, 'with all my heart, heartily; but let them be all kings.'

Dametas, seeing no other way prevail, fell down on his knees: 'Mopsa, Mopsa,' said he, 'do not thus cruelly torment me; I am already wretched enough. Alas, either help me or tell me thou canst not.'

She (that would not be behind Apollo in courtesy) kneeled down on the other side: 'I will never leave tormenting thee', said Mopsa, 'until thou hast satisfied my longing; but I will proclaim thee a promise-breaker, that even Jupiter shall hear it.'

'Now, by the fostering thou hast received in this place, save my life', said Dametas.

'Now, by this fair ash', answered Mopsa, 'where thou didst receive so great a good turn, grant post-haste to my burning fancy.'

'O where is Pamela?' said Dametas.

'O a lusty husband!' said Mopsa.

Dametas (that now verily assured himself his daughter was mad) began utterly to despair of his life; and therefore amazedly catching her in his arms, to see whether he could bring her to herself, he might feel the weight of a great cudgel light upon his shoulders, and for the first greeting he knew his wife Miso's voice by the calling him 'ribald villain', and asking him whether she could not serve his turn as well as Charita. For Miso having, according to Dorus's counsel, gone to Mantinea, and there harboured herself in an old acquaintance house of hers, as soon as ten of the clock was stricken (where she had remained closely all that while, I think with such an amiable cheer as when jealous Juno sat cross-legged*to hinder the childbirth of her husband's love) with open mouth she went to the magistrate appointed over such matters, and there, with the most scolding invective her rage rather than eloquence could bring forth, she required his aid to take Dametas, who had left his duty to the duke and his daughter to commit adultery in the house of Charita's uncle in the Oudemian street. But neither was the name of Charita remembered, nor any such street known. Yet such was the general mislike all men had of Dametas's unworthy advancement that every man was glad to make himself a minister of that which might redound to his shame. Therefore, with pans, cries and laughters,* there was no suspected place in all the city but was searched for, under the title of, Dametas; Miso ever foremost encouraging them with all the shameful blazings of his demeanour, increasing the sport of hunting her husband with her diligent barking; till at length, having already done both him and herself as much infamous shame as such a tongue in such an action might perform, in the end (not being able to find a thing that was not) to her mare again she went, having neither suspicion nor rage anything mitigated. But (leaving behind her a sufficient comedy of her tragical fancies) away homeward she came, imputing the not finding her husband to any chance rather than to his innocency; for her heart being apt to receive and nourish a bitter thought, it had so swallowed up a determinate condemnation that in the very anatomy of her spirits one should have found nothing but devilish disdain and hateful jealousy. In this sort, grunting out her mischievous spite, she came by the tree even as Dametas was making that ill understood intercession to his foolish Mopsa. As soon as she heard her husband's voice, she verily thought she had her prey; and therefore stealing from her mare as softly as she could, she came creeping and halting behind him, even as he (thinking his daughter's little wits had quite left her great noll) began to take her in his arms, thinking perchance her feeling sense might call her mind parts unto her. But Miso, who saw nothing but through the colour of revengeful anger, established upon the forejudgement of his trespass, undoubtedly resolving that Mopsa was Charita, Dorus had told her of, mumping out her hoarse chafe, she gave him the wooden salutation you heard of. Dametas (that was not so sensible in anything as in blows) turned up his blubbered face like a great lout new whipped: 'Alas, thou woman,' said he, 'what hath thy poor husband deserved to have his own ill luck loaden with thy displeasure? Pamela is lost! Pamela is lost!'

Miso, still holding on the course of her former fancy: 'What tellest thou me, naughty varlet,' said she, 'of Pamela? Dost thou think that doth answer me for abusing the laws of marriage? Have I brought thee children; have I been a true wife unto thee, to be despised in mine old age?'

And ever among she would sauce her speeches with such bastinados that poor Dametas began now to think that either a general madding was fallen, or else that all this was but a vision. But as for visions, the smart of the cudgel put out of his fancy; and therefore again turning to his wife, not knowing in the world what she meant: 'Miso,' said he, 'hereafter thou mayst examine me; do but now tell me what is become of Pamela.'

'I will first examine this drab', said she; and withal let fall her staff as hard as she could upon Mopsa, still taking her for Charita. But Mopsa (that was already angry, thinking she had hindered her from Apollo) leaped up and caught her by the throat, like to have strangled her, but that Dametas from a condemned man was fain to become a judge and part this fray (such a picture of a rude discord where each was out with the other two), and then getting the opportunity of their falling out to hold himself in surety (who was indeed the veriest coward of the three), he renewed his earnest demand of them. But it was a sport to see how the former conceits Dorus had printed in their imaginations kept still such a dominion in them that Miso, though now she found and felt it was her daughter Mopsa yet did Charita continually pass through her thoughts, which she uttered with such crabbed questions to Dametas that he, not possibly conceiving any part of her doubt, remained astonished; and the astonishment increased her doubt. And as for Mopsa, as first she did assuredly take him to be Apollo, and thought her mother's coming did mar the bargain, so now much talking to and fro had delivered so much light into the misty mould of her capacity as to know him to be her father, yet remained there such footsteps of the foretaken opinion that she thought verily her father and mother were hasted thither to get the first wish; and therefore to whatsoever they asked of her, she would never answer, but embracing the tree as if she feared it had been running away: 'Nay,' says she, 'I will have the first wish, for I was here first.'

Which they understood no more than Dametas did what Miso meant by Charita; till at length with much urging them, being indeed better able to persuade both than to meet hand to hand with either, he prevailed so much with them as to bring them into the lodge to see what loss their negligence had suffered. Then, indeed, the near neighbourhood they bare to themselves made them leave other toys, and look into what dangerous plight they were all fallen as soon as the duke should know his daughter's escape. And as for the women, they began afresh to enter into their brawling, whether were in the fault. But Dametas (who did fear that among his other evils the thunderbolt of that storm would fall upon his shoulders) slipped away from them, but with so meagre a cheer as might much sooner engender laughter than pity: 'O true Arcadia,' would he say, tearing his hair and beard, and sometimes for too much woe making unwieldy somersaults, 'how darest thou bear upon thee such a felonious traitor as I am? And you, false-hearted trees, why would you make no noise to make her ungracious departure known? Ah, Pamela, Pamela, how often when I brought thee in fine posies of all coloured flowers, wouldst thou clap me on the cheek, and say thou wouldst be one day even with me? Was this thy meaning: to bring me to an even pair of gallows? Ah, ill-taught Dorus, that came hither to learn good manners of me, did I ever teach thee to make thy master sweat out his heart for nothing, and in the mean time run away with thy mistress? O my dun cow, I did think some evil was towards me ever since the last day thou didst run away from me and hold up thy tail, so pitifully. Did not I see an eagle kill a cuckoo, which was a plain foretoken unto me Pamela should be my destruction? O wife Miso, if I durst say it to thy face, why didst thou suspect thy husband that loves a piece of cheese better than a woman? And thou little Mopsa, that shalt inherit the shame of thy father's death, was it time for thee to climb trees, which should so shortly be my best burial?*O that I could live without death, or die before I were aware! O heart, why hast thou no hands at commandment to dispatch thee? O hands, why want you a heart to kill this villain?'

In this sort did he inveigh against everything, sometimes thinking to run away while it was yet night; but he (that had included all the world within his sheepcote) thought that worse than any death. Sometimes for dread of hanging he meant to hang himself, finding (as indeed it is) that fear is far more painful to cowardice than death to a true courage. But his fingers were nothing nimble in that action, and anything was let enough thereto, he being a true lover of himself without any rival. But lastly, guided by a far greater constellation than his own, he remembered to search the other lodge, where it might be Pamela that night had retired herself. So thither with trembling hams he carried himself; but employing his double key (which the duke for special credit had unworthily bestowed upon him), he found all the gates so barred that his key could not prevail, saving only one trap-door (which went down into a vault by the cellar) which, as it was unknown of Pyrocles, so had he left it unguarded. But Dametas (that ever knew the buttery better than any place) got in that way, and pacing softly to Philoclea's chamber (where he thought most likely to find Pamela), the door being left open, he entered in, and by the light of the lamp he might discern one abed with her, which he, although he took to be Pamela, yet thinking no surety enough in a matter touching his neck, he went hard to the bedside of these unfortunate lovers, who at that time, being not much before the break of day—whether it were they were so divinely surprised to bring their fault to open punishment; or that the too high degree of their joys had overthrown the wakeful use of their senses; or that their souls, lifted up with extremity of love after mutual satisfaction, had left their bodies dearly joined to unite themselves together so much more freely as they were freer of that earthly prison; or whatsoever other cause may be imagined of it—but so it was that they were as then possessed with a mutual sleep, yet not forgetting with viny embracements to give any eye a perfect model of affection. But Dametas, looking with the lamp in his hand, but neither with such a face nor mind, upon these excellent creatures, as Psyche did upon her unknown lover,* and giving every way freedom to his fearful eyes, did not only perceive it was Cleophila (and therefore much different from the lady he sought), but that this same Cleophila did more differ from the Cleophila he and others had ever taken her for. Satisfied with that, and not thinking it good to awake the sleeping lion, he went down again, taking with him Pyrocles' sword (wherewith upon his shirt Pyrocles came only apparelled thither), being sure to leave no weapon in the chamber. And so, making the door as fast as he could on the outside, hoping with the revealing of this fault to make his own the less, or at least that this injury would so fill the duke's head that he should not have leisure to chastise his negligence (like a fool not considering that the more rage breeds the crueller punishment), he went first into the duke's chamber, and not finding him there, he ran down crying with open mouth, the duke was betrayed, and that Cleophila did abuse his daughter. The noise he made, being a man of no few words, joined to the yelping sound of Miso and his unpleasant inheritrix, brought together some number of the shepherds, to whom he, without any regard of first reserving it for the duke's knowledge, spattered out the bottom of his stomach, swearing by him he never knew that Cleophila, whom they had taken all that while to be a woman, was as arrant a man as himself was, whereof he had seen sufficient signs and tokens; and that he was as close as a butterfly with the lady Philoclea. The poor men, jealous of their prince's honour, were ready with weapons to have entered the lodge, standing yet in some pause, whether it were not better first to hear some news of the duke himself, when by the sudden coming of other shepherds, which with astonished looks ran from one cry to the other, their griefs were surcharged with the evil tidings of the duke's death. Turning therefore all their minds and eyes that way, they ran to the cave where they said he lay dead, the sun beginning now to send some promise of his coming light, making haste, I think, to be spectator of the following tragedies.

But of Basilius, thus it had fallen out: the duke, having passed over the night, more happy in contemplation than action, having had his spirits sublimed with the sweet imagination of embracing the much desired Cleophila, doubting lest the cave's darkness might deceive him in the day's approach, thought it now season to return to his wedlock bed, remembering the promise he had made Cleophila to observe due orders towards Gynecia. Therefore departing, but not departing without bequeathing by a will of words, sealed with many kisses, a full gift of all his love and life to his misconceived bedfellow, he went to the mouth of the cave, there to apparel himself; in which doing, the motion of his joy could not be bridled from uttering suchlike words: 'Blessed be thou, O night,' said he, 'that hast with thy sweet wings shrouded me in the vale of bliss! It is thou that art the first gotten child of time. The day hath been but an usurper upon thy delightful inheritance. Thou invitest all living things to comfortable rest. Thou art the stop of strife, and the necessary truce of approaching battles.' And therewith, he sang these verses to confirm his former praises:

> O night, the ease of care, the pledge of pleasure,
> Desire's best mean, harvest of hearts affected,
> The seat of peace, the throne which is erected
> Of human life to be the quiet measure.
>
> Be victor still of Phoebus' golden treasure,
> Who hath our sight with too much sight infected,
> Whose light is cause we have our lives neglected,
> Turning all nature's course to self-displeasure.
>
> These stately stars in their now shining faces,
> With sinless sleep, and silence, wisdom's mother,
> Witness his wrong which by thy help is eased.
>
> Thou art therefore of these our desert places
> The sure refuge, by thee and by no other
> My soul is blest, sense joyed, and fortune raised.

And yet further would his joy needs break forth: 'O Basilius,' said he, 'the rest of thy time hath been but a dream unto thee. It is now only thou beginnest to live; now only thou hast entered into the way of blissfulness. Should fancy of marriage keep me from this paradise? Or opinion of I know not what promise bind me from paying the right duties to nature and affection? O who would have thought there could have been such difference betwixt women? Be not jealous no more, good Gynecia, but yield to the pre-eminence of more excellent gifts; support thyself upon such marble pillars as she doth; deck thy breast with those alabaster bowls that Cleophila doth; then accompanied with such a title, perhaps thou mayst recover the possession of my otherwise-inclined love. But alas, Gynecia, thou canst not show such evidence; therefore thy plea is vain.'

Gynecia heard all this he said, who had cast about her Cleophila's garment wherein she came thither, and had followed Basilius even to the cave's entry, full of inward vexation betwixt the deadly accusation of her own guiltiness and the spiteful doubt she had Cleophila had abused her. But because of the one side, finding the duke did think her to be Cleophila, she had liberty to imagine it might rather be the duke's own unbridled enterprise which had barred Cleophila than Cleophila's cunning deceiving of her; and that of the other part, if she should headily seek a violent revenge, her own honour might be as much interested as Cleophila endangered; she fell to this determination: first, with fine handling of the duke to settle in him a perfect good opinion of her; and then, as she should learn how things had passed, so take into herself new devised counsels. But this being her first action: having given unlooked-for attendance to the duke, she heard with what partiality he did prefer her to herself; she saw in him how much fancy doth not only darken reason but beguile sense; she found opinion mistress of the lover's judgement. Which serving as a good lesson to her wise conceit, she went out to Basilius, setting herself in a grave behaviour and stately silence before him, until he (who at the first thinking her by so much shadow as he could see to be Cleophila, was beginning his loving ceremonies) did now (being helped by the peeping light wherewith the morning did overcome the night's darkness) know her face and his error. Which acknowledging in himself with starting back from her, she thus with a modest bitterness spake unto him:

'Alas, my lord, well did your words decipher your mind; and well be those words confirmed with this gesture. Very loathsome must that woman be from whom a man hath cause to go back; and little better liked is that wife before whom the husband prefers them he never knew. Alas, hath my faithful observing my part of duty made you think yourself ever a whit the more exempted? Hath that which should claim gratefulness been a cause of contempt? Is the being the mother of Pamela become an odious name unto you? If my life hitherto led have not avoided suspicion; if my violated truth to you be deserving of any punishment; I refuse not to be chastised with the most cruel torment of your displeasure; I refuse not misery purchased by mine own merit. Hard I must needs say (although till now I never thought I should have had cause to say) is the destiny of womankind, the trial of whose virtue must stand upon the loving them that employ all their industry not to be beloved. If Cleophila's young years had not had as much gravity hidden under a youthful face as your grey hairs have been but the visor of a far unfitting youthfulness, your vicious mind had brought some fruits of late repentance; and Gynecia might then have been with much more right so basely despised.'

Basilius (that was more ashamed to see himself so overtaken than Vulcan was when with much cunning he proved himself a cuckold) began to make certain extravagant excuses. But the matter in itself hardly brooking any purgation, with the suddenness of the time, which barred any good conjoined invention, made him sometimes allege one thing, to which by and by he would bring in a contrary: one time with flat denial, another time with mitigating the fault; now brave, then humble, use such a stammering defensive that Gynecia (the violence of whose sore, indeed, ran another way) was content thus to fasten up the last stitch of her anger:

'Well, well, my lord,' said she, 'it shall well become you so to govern yourself as you may be fit rather to direct me than to be judged of me, and rather be a wise master of me than an unskilful pleader before me. Remember the wrong you do me is not only to me, but to your children, whom you had of me; to your country, when they shall find they are commanded by him that cannot command his own undecent appetites; lastly to yourself, since with these pains you do but build up a house of shame to dwell in. If from those movable goods of nature*(wherewith in my first youth my royal parents bestowed me upon you) bearing you children and increase of years have withdrawn me, consider, I pray you, that as you are the cause of the one, so in the other, time hath not left to work his never failing effects in you. Truly, truly, sir, very untimely are these fires in you. It is high season for us both to let reason enjoy his due sovereignty. Let us not plant anew those weeds which by nature's course are content to fade.'

Basilius that would rather than his life this matter had been ended, the best rhetoric he had was flat demanding pardon of her, swearing it was the very force of Apollo's destiny which had carried him thus from his own bias; but that now, like far travellers were taught to love their own country, he had such a lesson without book of affection unto her as he would repay the debt of this error with the interest of a great deal more true honour than ever before he had borne her.

'Neither am I to give pardon to you, my lord,' said she, 'nor you to bear honour to me. I have taken this boldness for the unfeigned love I owe you, to deliver my sorrow unto you, much more for the care I have of your well doing than for any other self-fancy. For well I know that by your good estate my life is maintained; neither, if I would, can I separate myself from your fortune. For my part, therefore, I claim nothing but that which may be safest for yourself; my life, will, honour, and whatsoever else, shall be but a shadow of that body.'

How much Basilius's own shame had found him culpable, and had already even in soul read his own condemnation, so much did this unexpected mildness of Gynecia captive his heart unto her, which otherwise perchance would have grown to a desperate carelessness. Therefore, embracing her and confessing that her virtue shined in his vice, he did even with a true resolved mind vow unto her that, so long as he unworthy of her did live, she should be the furthest and only limit of his affection. He thanked the destinies that had wrought her honour out of his shame; and that had made his own striving to go amiss to be the best mean ever after to hold him in the right path.

Thus reconciled to Basilius's great contentation, who began something to mark himself in his own doings, his hard hap guided his eye to the cup of gold wherein Gynecia had put the liquor meant for Cleophila, and having failed of that guest, was now carrying it home again. But he (whom perchance sorrow, perchance some long disaccustomed pains, had made extremely thirsty) took it out of her hands, although she directly told him both of whom she had it, what the effect of it was, and the little proof she had seen thereof, hiding nothing from him, but that she meant to minister it to another patient. But the duke, whose belly had no ears, and much drought kept from the desiring a taster, finding it not unpleasant to his palate, drank it almost off, leaving very little to cover the cup's bottom. But within a while that from his stomach the drink had delivered to his principal veins his noisome vapours, first with a painful stretching and forced yawning, then with a dark yellowness dyeing his skin and a cold deadly sweat principally about his temples, his body by natural course longing to deliver his heavy burden to his earthly dam, wanting force in his knees (which utterly abandoned him), with heavy fall gave soon proof whither the operation of that unknown potion tended. For, with pang-like groans and ghastly turning of his eyes, immediately all his limbs stiffened and his eyes fixed, he having had time to declare his case only in these words: 'O Gynecia, I die! Have care—.' Of what, or how much further he would have spoken, no man can tell. For Gynecia, having well perceived the changing of his colour and those other evil signs, yet had not looked for such a sudden overthrow, but rather had bethought herself what was best for him, when she suddenly saw the matter come to that period, coming to him, and neither with any cries getting a word of him, nor with any other possible means able to bring any living action from him, the height of all ugly sorrows did so horribly appear before her amazed mind that at the first it did not only distract all power of speech from her but almost wit to consider, remaining as it were quick buried in a grave of miseries. Her painful memory had straight filled her with the true shapes of all the forepassed mischiefs. Her reason began to cry out against the filthy rebellion of sinful sense, and to tear itself with anguish for having made so weak a resistance; her conscience (a terrible witness of the inward wickedness) still nourishing this debateful fire; her complaint now not having an end directed to it, something to disburden sorrow; but as a necessary downfall of inward wretchedness, she saw the rigour of the laws was like to lay a shameful death upon her—which being for that action undeserved, made it the more insupportable; and yet in depth of her soul most deserved, made it more miserable. At length, letting her tongue go as her dolorous thoughts guided it, she thus, with lamentable demeanour, spake:

'O bottomless pit of sorrow in which I cannot contain myself, having the firebrands of all furies within me, still falling and yet by the infiniteness of it never fallen! Neither can I rid myself, being fettered with the everlasting consideration of it. For whither should I recommend the protection of my dishonoured fall? To the earth? It hath no life, and waits to be increased by the relics of my shamed carcass. To men, who are always cruel in their neighbours' faults, and make others' overthrow become the badge of their ill-masked virtue? To the heavens? O unspeakable torment of conscience which dare not look unto them; no sin can enter there! O, there is no receipt for polluted minds! Whither, then, wilt thou lead this captive of thine, O snaky despair? Alas, alas, was this the free-holding power that accursed poison hath granted unto me: that, to be held the surer, it should deprive life? Was this the folding in mine arms promised: that I should fold nothing but a dead body? O mother of mine, what a deathful suck have you given me! O Philoclea, Philoclea, well hath my mother revenged upon me my unmotherly hating of thee! O Cleophila, to whom yet, lest any misery should fail me, remain some sparks of my detestable love, if thou hast (as now, alas, my mind assures me thou hast) deceived me, there is a fair scene prepared for thee: to see the tragical end of thy hated lover.'

With that word, there flowed out two rivers of tears out of her fair eyes, which before were dry, the remembrance of her other mischiefs being dried up in a furious fire of self-detestation, love only (according to the temper of it) melting itself into those briny tokens of passion. Then, turning her eyes again upon the body, she remembered a dream she had had some days before, wherein, thinking herself called by Cleophila, passing a troublesome passage, she found a dead body which told her there should be her only rest. This no sooner caught hold of her remembrance than that she (determining with herself it was a direct vision of her fore-appointed end) took a certain resolution to embrace death as soon as it should be offered unto her, and no way to seek the prolonging of her annoyed life. And therefore, kissing the cold face of Basilius:

'And even so will I rest', said she, 'and join this faulty soul of mine to thee, if so much the angry gods will grant me.'

As she was in this plight (the sun now climbing over our horizon), the first shepherds came by; who, seeing the duke in that case, and hearing the noise Dametas made of the lady Philoclea, ran with the doleful tidings of Basilius's death unto him; who presently with all his company came to the cave's entry where the duke's body lay— Dametas, for his part, more glad for the hope he had of his private escape than sorry for the public loss his country received of a prince not to be misliked. But in Gynecia nature prevailed above judgement, and the shame she conceived to be taken in that order overcame for that instant the former resolution; so that, as soon as she saw the foremost of the pastoral troop, the wretched princess ran to have hid her face in the next woods, but with such a mind that she knew not almost herself what she could wish to be the ground of her safety. Dametas (that saw her run away in Cleophila's upper raiment, and judging her to be so) thought certainly all the spirits in hell were come to play a tragedy in those woods, such strange change he saw every way: the duke dead at the cave's mouth; the duchess (as he thought) absent; Pamela fled away with Dorus; his wife and Mopsa in diverse frenzies. But of all other things Cleophila conquered his capacity, suddenly from a woman grown a man, and from a locked chamber gotten before him into the fields, which he gave the rest quickly to understand. For, instead of doing anything as the exigent required, he began to make circles and all those fantastical defences that he had ever heard were fortifications against devils. But the other shepherds (who had both better wits and more faith) forthwith divided themselves; some of them running after Gynecia, taking her to be Cleophila and esteeming her running away a great condemnation of her own guiltiness; others going to their prince to see what service was left for them, either in recovery of his life, or honouring his death. They that went after the duchess had soon overtaken her, in whom now the first fears were stayed, and the resolution to die had repossessed his place in her mind. But when they saw it was the duchess, to whom, besides the obedient duty they owed to her state, they had always carried a singular love for her courteous liberalities and other wise and virtuous parts which had filled all that people with affection and admiration, they were all suddenly stopped, beginning to ask pardon for their following her in that sort, and desiring her to be their good lady as she had ever been. But the duchess (who now thirsted to be rid of herself whom she hated above all things), with such an assured countenance as they have who already have dispensed with shame and digested the sorrows of death, she thus said unto them:

'Continue, continue, my friends! Your doing is better than your excusing; the one argues assured faith, the other want of assurance. If you loved your prince when he was able and willing to do you much good, which you could not then requite to him, do you now publish your gratefulness when it shall be seen to the world there are no hopes left to lead you unto it. Remember, remember, you have lost Basilius: a prince to defend you, a father to care for you, a companion in your joys, a friend in your wants. And if you loved him, show you hate the author of his loss. It is I, faithful Arcadians, that have spoiled this country of their protector. I, none but I, was the minister of his unnatural end. Carry, therefore, my blood in your hands to testify your own innocency. Neither spare for my title's sake, but consider it was he that so entitled me. And if you think of any benefits received by my means, think with it that I was but the instrument, and he the spring. What, stay ye, shepherds, whose great shepherd is gone? You need not fear a woman, reverence your lord's murderer, nor have pity of her who hath not pity of herself.'

With this she presented her fair neck; some by name, others by signs, desiring them to do justice to the world, duty to their good duke, honour to themselves, and favour to her. The poor men looked one upon the other, unused to be arbiters in princes' matters, and being now fallen into a great perplexity betwixt a prince dead and a princess alive. But once for them she might have gone whither she would, thinking it a sacrilege to touch her person, when she, finding she was not a sufficient orator to persuade her own death by their hands:

'Well,' said she, 'it is but so much more time of misery; for my part, I will not give my life so much pleasure from henceforward as to yield to his desire of his own choice of death. Since all the rest is taken from me, yet let me excel in misery. Lead me, therefore, whither you will, only happy because I cannot be more wretched.'

But neither so much would the honest shepherds do, but rather with many tears bemoaned this increase of their former loss, till she was fain to lead them, with a very strange spectacle: either that a princess should be in the hands of shepherds, or a prisoner should direct her guardians, lastly before either witness or accuser a lady condemn herself to death. But in such moanful march they went towards the other shepherds, who in the mean time had left nothing unassayed to revive the duke. But all was bootless, and their sorrows increased the more they had suffered any hopes vainly to arise. Among other trials they made to know at least the cause of his end, having espied the unhappy cup, they gave the little liquor that was left in it to a dog of Dametas, in which within short space it wrought the same effect; although Dametas did so much to recover him that for very love of his life he dashed out his brains. Now all together, and having Gynecia among them (who, to make herself the more odious, did continually record to their minds the excess of their loss), they yielded themselves over to all those forms of lamentation that doleful images do imprint in the honest but over-tender hearts, especially when they think the rebound of the evil falls to their own smart. Therefore, after the ancient Greek manner, some of them remembering the nobility of his birth, continued by being like his ancestors; others his shape which, though not excellent, yet favour and pity drew all things now to the highest point; others his peaceable government, the thing which most pleaseth men resolved to live of their own; others his liberality which, though it cannot light upon all men, yet all men naturally hoping it may be they, makes it a most amiable virtue; some calling in question the great-ness of his power, which increased the compassion to see the present change (having a doleful memory how he had tempered it with such familiar courtesy among them, that they did more feel the fruits than see the pomps of his greatness). All with one consent giving him the sacred titles of good, just, merciful, the father of the people, the life of his country, they ran about his body tearing their beards and garments; some sending their cries to heaven; others inventing particular howling musics; many vowing to kill themselves at the day of his funerals; generally giving a true testimony that men are loving creatures when injuries put them not from their natural course, and how easy a thing it is for a prince by succession deeply to sink into the souls of his subjects—a more lively monument than Mausolus's tomb. Lastly, having one after the other cryingly sung the duke's praise and his own lamentation, they did all desire Agelastus, one notably noted among them as well for his skill in poetry as for an austerely maintained sorrowfulness (the cause of which, as it were too long to tell, so yet the effect of an Athenian senator to become an Arcadian shepherd), to make an universal complaint for them in this universal mischief; who did it in this sestine:*

> Since wailing is a bud of causeful sorrow,
>   Since sorrow is the follower of ill fortune,
>   Since no ill fortune equals public damage,
>   Now prince's loss hath made our damage public,
>   Sorrow pay we unto the rights of nature,
>   And inward grief seal up with outward wailing.
>
> Why should we spare our voice from endless wailing,
>   Who justly make our hearts the seats of sorrow,
>   In such a case where it appears that nature
>   Doth add her force unto the sting of fortune,

Choosing alas, this our theatre public,
Where they would leave trophies of cruel damage?

Then since such pow'rs conspire unto our damage
(Which may be known, but never helped with wailing)
Yet let us leave a monument in public,
Of willing tears, torn hair, and cries of sorrow.
For lost, lost is by blow of cruel fortune
Arcadia's gem, the noblest child of nature.

O nature doting old, O blinded nature,
How hast thou torn thyself, sought thine own damage,
In granting such a scope to filthy fortune,
By thy imp's loss to fill the world with wailing!
Cast thy stepmother eyes upon our sorrow,
Public our loss, so see thy shame is public.

O that we had, to make our woes more public,
Seas in our eyes, and brazen tongues by nature,
A yelling voice, and hearts composed of sorrow,
Breath made of flames, wits knowing naught but
    damage,
Our sports murdering ourselves, our musics wailing,
Our studies fixed upon the falls of fortune.

No, no, our mischief grows in this vile fortune,
That private pangs cannot breathe out in public
The furious inward griefs with hellish wailing;
But forced are to burden feeble nature
With secret sense of our eternal damage,
And sorrow feed, feeding our souls with sorrow.

Since sorrow then concludeth all our fortune,
With all our deaths show we this damage public.
His nature fears to die who lives still wailing.

They did with such hearty lamentation disperse among those
woods their resounding shrieks that, the sun (the perfectest mark of
time) having now gotten up two hours' journey in his daily-changing
circle, their voice, helped with the only answering echo, came to the
ears of the faithful and worthy gentleman Philanax; who at that
time was coming, accompanied with divers of the principal Arcadian
lords, to visit the duke upon this occasion. Fame (the charge of many

ears and governor of many tongues) had delivered to the attentive
ear of Philanax the late drunken commotion of the Phagonians, with
so large an increase that he (who well knew that too much provision
might well lose some charge, but too little might lose all) had speedily
assembled in the frontiers where he lay five hundred horse, and came
with all diligence, giving order more should be in readiness if more
needed. But being come to the very town itself of Phagona (as it was
not out of his way), he there understood how far the virtue of
Cleophila had made Basilius fortunate, and that those dangers feared
were utterly passed; yet to avoid any such other disturbance to his
master's quiet (whom he loved with incomparable loyalty), suffering
those that were pardoned to enjoy the fruits of a prince's word, he
placed garrisons in all the towns and villages anything near the
lodges, over whom he appointed captains of such wisdom and virtue
as might not only with the force of their soldiers keep the inhabitants
from outrage, but might unpartially look to the discipline both of
the men of war and people. That done, thinking it as well his duty
to see the duke as of good purpose, being so near, to receive his
further direction, accompanied as abovesaid, he was this morning
coming unto him, when these unpleasant voices gave his mind an
uncertain presage of his near approaching sorrow. For by and by
he saw the body of his dearly esteemed prince, and heard Gynecia's
waymenting, not such as the turtle-like love is wont to make for the
ever over-soon loss of her only loved make, but with cursings of her
life, detesting her own wickedness, seeming only therefore not to
desire death because she would not show a love of anything. The
shepherds, especially Dametas, knowing him to be the second person
in authority, gave forthwith relation unto him what they knew and
had proved of this dolorous spectacle, besides the other accidents
of his children. But he (principally touched with his master's loss),
lighting from his horse, with a heavy cheer came and kneeled down by
him; where finding he could do no more than the shepherds had for
his recovery, the constancy of his mind surprised before he might
call together his best rules, could not refrain suchlike words:

'Ah, dear master', said he, 'what change it hath pleased the
almighty justice to work in this place! How soon (not to your
loss, who have lived long to nature, and now live longer by your
well deserved glory, but longest of all in the eternal mansion you now
possess), but how soon, I say, to our ruin have you left the frail bark
of your estate! O that the words my most faithful duty delivered unto

you when you first entered this solitary course might have wrought as much persuasion in you as they sprang from truth in me! Perchance your servant Philanax should not now have had cause in your loss to bewail his own overthrow.' And therewith taking himself: 'And, indeed, ill fitteth it me,' said he, 'to let go my heart to womanish complaints, since my prince being undoubtedly well, it rather shows love of myself, which makes me bewail mine own loss. No, the true love must be proved in the honour of your memory; and that must be showed with seeking just revenge upon your unjust and unnatural enemies. And far more honourable it will be for your tomb to have the blood of your murderers sprinkled upon it than the tears of your friends. And if your soul look down upon this miserable earth, I doubt not it had much rather your death were accompanied with well deserved punishment of the causers of it than with the heaping on it more sorrows with the end of them to whom you vouchsafed your affection. Let them lament that have woven this web of lamentation! Let their own deaths make them cry out for your death that were the authors of it!'

Therewith, carrying manful sorrow and vindicative resolution in his face, he rose up, so looking upon the poor guiltless princess, transported with an unjust justice, that his eyes were sufficient heralds for him to denounce a mortal hatred. She (whom furies of love, firebrands of her conscience, shame of the world, with the miserable loss of her husband, towards whom now the disdain of herself bred more love, with the remembrance of her vision wherewith she resolved assuredly the gods had appointed that shameful end to be her resting place, had set her mind in no other way but to death) used suchlike speeches to Philanax as she had done before to the shepherds, willing him not to look upon her as a woman but a monster; not as a princess but a traitor to his prince; not as Basilius's wife but as Basilius's murderer. She told him how the world required at his hands the just demonstration of his friendship. If he now forgot his prince he should show he had never loved but his fortune, like those vermin which suck of the living blood and leave the body as soon as it is dead—poor princess, needlessly seeking to kindle him who did most deadly detest her; which he uttered in this bitter answer:

'Madam,' said he, 'you do well to hate yourself, for you cannot hate a worse creature; and though we feel enough your hellish disposition, yet we need not doubt you are a counsel to yourself of

much worse than we know. But now fear not, you shall not long be
cumbered with being guided by so evil a soul. Therefore prepare
yourself, that if it be possible you may deliver up your spirit so much
purer as you more wash your wickedness with repentance.'

Then, having presently given order for the bringing from Man-
tinea a great number of tents for the receipt of the principal Arca-
dians, the manner of that country being that where the prince died
there should be order taken for the country's government, and in
the place any murder was committed the judgement should be given
there before the body was buried, both concurring in this matter
and already great part of the nobility being arrived, he delivered the
duchess to a gentleman of great trust. And as for Dametas, taking
from him the keys of both the lodges, calling him the moth of his
prince's estate, and only spot of his judgement, he caused him with
his wife and daughter to be fettered up in as many chains and clogs
as they could bear, and every third hour to be cruelly whipped, till
the determinate judgement should be given of all these matters.
That done, having sent already at his first coming to all the quarters
of the country to seek Pamela, although with small hope of over-
taking them, he himself went well accompanied to the lodge where
the two unfortunate lovers were attending a cruel conclusion of their
long-painful, late-pleasant, affection.

Dametas's clownish eyes having been the only discoverers of
Pyrocles' stratagem, he had no sooner taken a full view of them
(which in some sights would rather have bred anything than an
accusing mind) and locked the door upon these two young folks
(now made prisoners for love as before they had been prisoners to
love) but that, immediately upon his going down (whether with noise
Dametas made, or with the creeping in of the light, or rather, as I think,
that as he had but little slept that night so the sweet embracement
he enjoyed gave his senses a very early salve to come to themselves),
but so it was that Pyrocles awaked, grudging in himself that sleep
(though very short) had robbed him of any part of those his highest
contentments, especially considering that he was then to prepare
himself to return to the duke's bed, and at his coming to set such a
comical face of the matter as he should find by the speeches of
Basilius and Gynecia should be most convenient. But being now
fully awaked, he might hear a great noise under the lodge which (as
affection is full of sudden doubts) made him leap out of his bed,
having first with earnest kissing the peerless Philoclea (who then

soundly sleeping was the natural image of exact beauty) received into his sense a full proportion of the greatest delight he could imagine under the moon. But being up, the first ill handsel he had of the ill case wherein he was was the seeing himself deprived of his sword, from which he had never separated himself in any occasion, and even that night, first by the duke's bed, and then there, had laid it as he thought safe, putting great part of the trust of his well doing in his own courage, so armed. For, indeed, the confidence in oneself is the chief nurse of true magnanimity; which confidence notwithstanding doth not leave the care of necessary furnitures for it, and therefore of all the Grecians Homer doth ever make Achilles the best armed. But that, as I say, was his first ill token. But by and by he perceived he was a prisoner before any arrest; for the door, which he had left open, was made so fast of the outside that, for all the force he could employ unto it, he could not undo Dametas's doing. Then went he to the window to see if that way there were any escape for him and his dear lady. But as vain he found all his employment there, not having might to break out, but only one bar, wherein notwithstanding he strained his sinews to the uttermost; and that he rather took out to use for other services than for any possibility he found of escape. For even then it was that Dametas, having gathered together the first-coming shepherds, did blabber out what he had found in the lady Philoclea's chamber. Pyrocles markingly hearkened to all that Dametas said (whose voice and mind acquaintance had taught him sufficiently to know). But when he assuredly perceived all his action with the lady Philoclea was fully discovered, remembering withal the cruelty of the Arcadian laws* which, without exception, did condemn all to death who were found in act of marriage without solemnity of marriage, assuring himself, besides the law, that the duke and duchess would use so much more hate against their daughter as they had found themselves sotted by him in the pursuit of their love; lastly, seeing they were not only in the way of death but fitly encaged for death, looking with a hearty grief upon the honour of love, the fellowless Philoclea (whose innocent soul now enjoying his own goodness did little know the danger of his ever fair, then sleeping, harbour), his excellent wit, strengthened with virtue but guided by love, had soon described to himself a perfect vision of their present condition. Wherein having presently cast a resolute reckoning of his own part of the misery, not only the chief but sole burden of his anguish consisted in the unworthy case which was like to fall upon the best deserving Philoclea. He saw the misfortune, not the mismeaning, of his work was like to bring that creature to end in whom the world, as he thought, did begin to receive honour. He saw the weak judgement of man would condemn that as a death-deserving vice in her which had in truth never broken the bands of a true living virtue. And how often his eye turned to his attractive adamant so often did an unspeakable horror strike his noble heart, to consider so unripe years, so faultless a beauty, the mansion of so pure goodness, should have her youth so untimely cut off, her natural perfections unnaturally consumed, her virtue rewarded with shame. Sometimes he would accuse himself of negligence, that had not more curiously looked to all the house entries; and yet could he not imagine the way Dametas was gotten in. And to call back what might have been to a man of wisdom and courage carries but a vain shadow of discourse. Sometimes he could not choose but, with a dissolution of his inward might, lamentably consider with what face he might look upon his (till then) joy, Philoclea, when the next light waking should deliver unto her should perchance be the last of her hurtless life; and that the first time she should bend her excellent eyes upon him she should see the accursed author of her dreadful end. And even this consideration, more than any other, did so settle itself in his well disposed mind that, dispersing his thoughts to all the ways that might be of her safety, finding a very small discourse in so narrow limits of time and place, at length in many difficulties he saw none bear any likelihood for her life, but his death. For then he thought it would fall out that when they found his body dead, having no accuser but Dametas (as by his speech he found there was not), it might justly appear that either Philoclea in defending her honour, or else he himself in despair of achieving, had left his carcass proof of his fact but witness of her clearness. Having a small while stayed upon the greatness of his resolution, and looked to the furthest of it:

'Be it so,' said the valiant Pyrocles, 'never life for better cause, nor to better end, was bestowed; for if death be to follow this fact (which no death of mine shall ever make me repent), who is to die so justly as myself? And if I must die, who can be so fit executioners as mine own hands which, as they were accessaries to the fact, so in killing me they shall suffer their own punishment?'

But then arose there a new impediment; for Dametas having carried away anything which he thought might hurt as tender a man as himself, he could find no fit instrument which might give him a final dispatch. At length, making the more haste lest his lady should awake, taking the iron bar (which being sharper something at the one end than the other, he hoped, joined to his willing strength, might break off the slender thread of mortality):

'Truly,' said he, 'fortune, thou hast well persevered mine enemy, that wilt grant me no fortune to be unfortunate, nor let me have an easy passage, now I am to trouble thee no more. But,' said he, 'O bar, blessed in that thou hast done service to the chamber of the paragon of life, since thou couldst not help me to make a perfecter escape, yet serve my turn, I pray thee, that I may escape from myself.'

Therewithal, yet once looking to fetch the last repast of his eyes, and new again transported with the pitiful case he left her in, kneeling down he thus prayed unto Jupiter:

'O great maker*and great ruler of this world,' said he, 'to thee do I sacrifice this blood of mine; and suffer, O Jove, the errors of my youth to pass away therein. And let not the soul by thee made, and ever bending unto thee, be now rejected of thee. Neither be offended that I do abandon this body, to the government of which thou hadst placed me, without thy leave, since how can I know but that thy unsearchable mind is I should so do, since thou hast taken from me all means longer to abide in it? And since the difference stands but in a short time of dying, thou that hast framed my heart inclined to do good, how can I in this small space of mine benefit so much all the human kind as in preserving thy perfectest workmanship, their chiefest honour? O justice itself, howsoever thou determinest of me, let this excellent innocency not be oppressed. Let my life pay her loss. O Jove, give me some sign that I may die with this comfort.' And pausing a little, as if he had hoped for some token: 'And whensoever, to the eternal darkness of the earth, she doth follow me, let our spirits possess one place, and let them be more happy in that uniting.'

With that word, striking the bar upon his heart side with all the force he had, and falling withal upon, to give it the througher passage, the bar in truth was too blunt to do the effect; although it pierced his skin and bruised his ribs very sore, so that his breath was almost past him. But the noise of his fall drave away sleep from the quiet senses of the dear Philoclea, whose sweet soul had an early salutation of a deadly spectacle unto her; with so much more astonishment as the falling asleep but a little before she had left herself in the uttermost point of contentment, and saw now before her eyes the most cruel enterprise that human nature can undertake, without discerning any cause thereof. But the lively print of her affection had soon taught her not to stay long upon deliberation in so urgent a necessity. Therefore getting with speed her well accorded limbs out of her sweetened bed (as when jewels are hastily pulled out of some rich coffer), she spared not the nakedness of her tender feet, but I think borne as fast with desire as fear carried Daphne, she came running to Pyrocles; and finding his spirits something troubled with the fall, she put by the bar that lay close to him, and straining him in her most beloved embracement:

'My comfort, my joy, my life,' said she, 'what haste have you to kill your Philoclea with the most cruel torment that ever lady suffered? Do you not yet persuade yourself that any hurt of yours is a death unto me, and that your death should be my hell? Alas, if any sudden mislike of me (for other cause I see none) have caused you to loathe yourself; if any fault or defect of mine hath bred this terriblest rage in you, rather let me suffer the bitterness of it, for so shall the deserver be punished, mankind preserved from such a ruin, and I, for my part, shall have that comfort that I die by the noblest hand that ever drew sword.'

Pyrocles, grieved with his fortune that he had not in one instant cut off all such deliberation, thinking his life only reserved to be bound to be the unhappy news-teller: 'Alas,' said he, 'my only star, why do you this wrong to God, yourself, and me, to speak of faults in you? No, no, most faultless, most perfect lady, it is your excellency that makes me hasten my desired end. It is the right I owe to the general nature that (though against private nature) makes me seek the preservation of all that she hath done in this age. Let me, let me die! There is no way to save your life, most worthy to be conserved, than that my death be your clearing.'

Then did he, with far more pain and backward loathness than the so near killing himself was (but yet driven with necessity to make her yield to that he thought was her safety), make her a short but pithy discourse what he had heard by Dametas's speeches, confirming the rest with a plain demonstration of their imprisonment. And then sought he new means of stopping his breath, but that by Philoclea's labour above her force he was stayed to hear her, in whom a man might perceive what small difference in the working there is betwixt a simple voidness of evil and a judicial habit of virtue. For she, not with an unshaked magnanimity, wherewith Pyrocles weighed and despised death, but with an innocent guiltlessness, not knowing why she should fear to deliver her unstained soul to God, helped with the true loving of Pyrocles, which made her think no life without him, did almost bring her mind to as quiet attending all accidents as the unmastered virtue of Pyrocles. Yet, having with a pretty paleness (which did leave milken lines upon her rosy cheeks) paid a little duty to human fear, taking the prince by the hand, and kissing the wound he had given himself:

'O the only life of my life and, if it fall out so, the comfort of my death,' said she, 'far, far from you be the doing me such wrong as to think I will receive my life as a purchase of your death. But well may you make my death so much more miserable as it shall anything be delayed after my only felicity. Do you think I can account of the moment of death like the unspeakable afflictions my soul should suffer so oft as I call Pyrocles to my mind, which should be as oft as I breathed? Should these eyes guide my steps, that had seen your murder? Should these hands feed me, that had not hindered such a mischief? Should this heart remain within me, at every pant to count the continual clock of my miseries? O no, if die we must, let us thank death he hath not divided so true an union. And truly, my Pyrocles, I have heard my father and other wise men say that the killing oneself is but a false colour of true courage, proceeding rather of fear of a further evil, either of torment or shame. For if it were a not respecting the harm, that would likewise make him not respect what might be done unto him; and hope being of all other the most contrary thing to fear, this being an utter banishment of hope, it seems to receive his ground in fear. Whatsoever (would they say) comes out of despair cannot bear the title of valour, which should be lifted up to such a height that, holding all things under itself, it should be able to maintain his greatness even in the midst of miseries. Lastly, they would say God had appointed us captains of these our bodily forts, which without treason to that majesty were never to be delivered over till they were redemanded.'

Pyrocles (who had that for a law unto him not to leave Philoclea in anything unsatisfied), although he still remained in his former purpose, and knew the time would grow short for it, yet hearing no noise (the shepherds being as then run to Basilius), with settled and humbled countenance, as a man that should have spoken of a thing that did not concern himself, bearing even in his eyes sufficient shows that it was nothing but Philoclea's danger which did anything burden his heart, far stronger than fortune, having with vehement embracings of her got yet some fruit of his delayed end, he thus answered the wise innocency of Philoclea:

'Lady most worthy not only of life but to be the very life of all things, the more notable demonstrations you make of the love so far beyond my desert with which it pleaseth you to overcome fortune in making me happy, the more am I even in course of humanity (to leave that love's force which I neither can nor will leave) bound to seek requital's witness that I am not ungrateful; to do which, the infiniteness of your goodness being such as it cannot reach unto it, yet doing all I can and paying my life, which is all I have, though it be far (without measure) short of your desert, yet shall I not die in debt to mine own duty. And truly, the more excellent arguments you made to keep me from this passage (imagined far more terrible than it is), the more plainly it makes me see what reason I have to prevent the loss, not only Arcadia but all the face of the earth, should receive if such a tree*(which even in his first spring doth not only bear most beautiful blossoms but most rare fruits) should be so untimely cut off. Therefore, O most truly beloved lady, to whom I desire for both our goods that these may be my last words, give me your consent even out of that wisdom which must needs see that (besides your unmatched betterness, which perchance you will not see) it is fitter one die than both. And since you have sufficiently showed you love me, let me claim by that love you will be content rather to let me die contentedly than wretchedly; rather with a clear and joyful conscience than with desperate condemnation in myself that I, accursed villain, should be the mean of banishing from the sight of men the true example of virtue. And because there is nothing left me to be imagined which I so much desire as that the memory of Pyrocles may ever have an allowed place in your wise judgement, I am content to draw so much breath longer as, by answering the sweet objections you alleged, may bequeath (as I think) a right conceit unto you that this my doing is out of judgement, and not sprung of passion. Your father, you say, was wont to say that this like action doth more proceed of fear of further evil or shame than of a true courage. Truly first, they put a very guessing case, speaking of them who can never after come to tell with what mind they did it. And as for my part, I call the immortal truth to witness that no fear of torment can appal me, who know it is but

diverse manners of apparelling death, and have long learned to set
bodily pain in the second form of my being. And as for shame, how
can I be ashamed of that for which my well meaning conscience will
answer for me to God, and your unresistible beauty to the world? But
to take that argument in his own force, and grant it done for avoiding of
further pain or dishonour (for as for the name of fear, it is but an odious
title of a passion given to that which true judgement performeth),
grant I say it is to shun a worse case; and truly I do not see but that
true fortitude, looking into all human things with a persisting resolu-
tion, carried away neither with wonder of pleasing things nor astonish-
ment of unpleasant, doth not yet deprive itself of the discerning the
difference of evils, but rather is the only virtue with which an assured
tranquillity shuns the greater by valiant entering into the less. Thus for
his country's safety he will spend his life; for the saving of a limb he
will not niggardly spare his goods; for the saving of all his body he will
not spare the cutting off a limb*—where indeed the weak-hearted man
will rather die than see the face of a surgeon, who might with as good
reason say that the constant man abides the painful surgery* for fear
of a further evil, but he is content to wait for death itself. But neither is
true, for neither hath the one any fear, but a well choosing judgement;
nor the other hath any contentment, but only fear, not having a heart
actively to perform a matter of pain, is forced passively to abide a
greater damage. For to do requires a whole heart, to suffer falls easiliest
in the broken minds; and if in bodily torments thus, much more in
shame wherein, since valour is a virtue, and virtue is ever limited, we
must not run so infinitely as to think the valiant man is willingly to
suffer any thing, since the very suffering of some things is a certain
proof of want of courage; and if anything unwillingly, among the
chiefest may shame go. For if honour be to be held dear, his contrary
is to be abhorred; and that not for fear, but of a true election. Which is
the less inconvenient, either the loss of some years more or less*(for
once we know our lives be not immortal), or the submitting ourselves
to each unworthy misery which the foolish world may lay upon us? As
for their reason that fear is contrary to hope, neither do I defend fear,
nor much yield unto the authority of hope; to either of which, great
inclining shows but a feeble reason, which must be guided by his
servants; and who builds not upon hope shall fear no earthquake of
despair. Their last alleging of the heavenly powers, as it bears the
greatest name so it is the only thing that at all bred any combat in
my mind. And yet I do not see but that, if God have made us masters

of anything, it is of our own lives, out of which without doing wrong to anybody we are to issue at our own pleasure; and the same argument would as much prevail to say we should for no necessity lay away from us any of our joints, since they being made of him, without his warrant we shall not depart from them; or if that may be for a greater cause, we may pass to a greater degree. And if we be lieutenants of God in this little castle, do you not think we must take warning of him to give over our charge* when he leaves us unprovided of good means to tarry in it?'

'No, certainly do I not,' answered the sorrowful Philoclea, 'since it is not for us to appoint that mighty majesty what time he will help us. The uttermost instant is scope enough* for him to revoke everything to one's own desire. And therefore, to prejudice his determination is but a doubt of goodness in him who is nothing but goodness. But when, indeed, he doth either by sickness or outward force lay death upon us, then are we to take knowledge that such is his pleasure, and to know that all is well that he doth. That we should be masters of ourselves we can show at all no title, nor claim; since neither we made ourselves, nor bought ourselves,* we can stand upon no other right but his gift, which he must limit as it pleaseth him. Neither is there any proportion betwixt the loss of any other limb and that, since the one bends to the preserving all, the other to the destruction of all; the one takes not away the mind from the actions for which it is placed in the world, the other cuts off all possibility of his working. And truly, my most dear Pyrocles, I must needs protest unto you that I cannot think your defence even in rules of virtue sufficient. Sufficient and excellent it were, if the question were of two outward things wherein a man might by nature's freedom determine whether he would prefer shame to pain, present smaller torment to greater following, or no. But to this (besides the comparison of the matters' values) there is added of the one part a direct evil doing, which maketh the balance of that side too much unequal, since a virtuous man, without any respect whether the grief be less or more, is never to do that which he cannot assure himself is allowable before the everliving rightfulness, but rather is to think honours or shames (which stand in other men's true or false judgements), pains or not pains (which yet never approach our souls) to be nothing in regard of an unspotted conscience. And these reasons do I remember I have heard good men bring in: that since it hath not his ground in an assured virtue, it proceeds rather of some other disguised passion.'

Pyrocles was not so much persuaded as delighted by her well conceived and sweetly pronounced speeches. But when she had closed her pitiful discourse and, as it were, sealed up her delightful lips with the moistness of her tears (which followed still one another like a precious rope of pearl), now thinking it high time: 'Be it as you say,' said he, 'most virtuous beauty, in all the rest; but never can God himself persuade me that Pyrocles' life is not well lost for to preserve the most admirable Philoclea. Let that be, if it be possible, written on my tomb, and I will not envy Codrus's honour.'*

With that, he would again have used the bar, meaning if that failed to leave his brains upon the wall, when Philoclea, now brought to that she most feared, kneeled down unto him, and embracing so his legs that without hurting her (which for nothing he would have done) he could not rid himself from her, she did, with all the conjuring words which the authority of love may lay, beseech him he would not now so cruelly abandon her; he would not leave her comfortless in that misery to which he had brought her; that then indeed she would even in her soul accuse him to have most foully betrayed her; that then she should have cause to curse the time that ever the name of Pyrocles came to her ears, which otherwise no death could make her do. 'Will you leave me', said she, 'not only dishonoured as unchaste with you, but as a murderer of you? Will you give mine eyes such a picture of hell before my near approaching death as to see the murdered body of him I love more than all the lives that nature can give?' With that, she sware by the highest cause of all devotions that, if he did persevere in that cruel resolution, she would not only confess to her father that with her consent this act had been committed but, if that would not serve, after she had pulled out her own eyes (made accursed by such a sight), she would give herself so terrible a death as she might think the pain of it would countervail the never dying pain of her mind: 'Now therefore kill yourself, to crown our virtuous action with infamy; kill yourself, to make me (whom you say you love), as long as I after-live you, change my loving admiration of you to a detestable abhorring your name. And so, indeed, you shall have the end you shoot at; for instead of one death you shall give me a thousand, and yet in the mean time deprive me of the help God may send me.'

Pyrocles, even overweighed with her so wisely uttered affection, finding her determination so fixed that his end should but deprive them both of a present contentment, and not avoid a coming evil (as

a man that ran not unto it by a sudden qualm of passion, but by a
true use of reason, preferring her life to his own), now that wisdom
did manifest unto him that way would not prevail, he retired himself
with as much tranquillity from it as before he had gone unto it, like
a man that had set the keeping or leaving of the body as a thing
without himself, and so had thereof a freed and untroubled con-
sideration. Therefore throwing away the bar from him, and taking
her up from the place where he thought the consummating of all
beauties very unworthily lay, suffering all his senses to devour up
their chiefest food, which he assured himself they should shortly
after forever be deprived of: 'Well', said he, 'most dear lady, whose
contentment I prefer before mine own, and judgement esteem more
than mine own, I yield unto your pleasure. The gods send you have
not won your own loss! For my part, they are my witnesses that I
think I do more at your commandment in delaying my death than
another would in bestowing his life. But now', said he, 'as thus far I
have yielded unto you, so grant me in recompense thus much again,
that I may find your love in granting as you have found your
authority in obtaining: my humble suit is you will say I came in by
force into your chamber, for so I am resolved now to affirm, and
that will be the best for us both. But in no case name my name,
that whatsoever come of me my house be not dishonoured.'

Philoclea, fearing lest refusal would turn him back again to his
violent refuge, gave him a certain countenance that might show she
did yield to his request, the latter part whereof indeed she meant for
his sake to perform. Neither could they spend more words together,
for Philanax, with twenty of the noblest personages of Arcadia after
him were come into the lodge. Philanax, making the rest stay below
for the reverence he bare to womanhood, as stilly as he could came
to the door, and opening it, drew the eyes of these two doleful lovers
unto him; Philoclea closing again for modesty's sake within her bed
the richess of her beauties, but Pyrocles took hold of his bar,
minding at least to die before the excellent Philoclea should receive
any outrage. But Philanax rested awhile upon himself, stricken with
admiration at the goodly shape of Pyrocles, whom before he had
never seen, and withal remembering the notable act he had done
(when with his courage and eloquence he had saved Basilius, per-
chance the whole state, from utter ruin), he felt a kind of relenting
mind towards him. But when that same thought came waited on
with the remembrance of his master's death, which he by all

probabilities thought he had been of counsel unto with the duchess, compassion turned to hateful passion, and left in Philanax a strange medley betwixt pity and revenge, betwixt liking and abhorring.

'O lord,' said he to himself, 'what wonders doth nature in our time to set wickedness so beautifully garnished; and that which is strangest, out of one spring to make wonderful effects both of virtue and vice to issue!'

Pyrocles seeing him in such a muse, neither knowing the man nor the cause of his coming, but assuring himself it was not for his good, yet thought best to begin with him in this sort: 'Gentleman,' said he, 'what is the cause of your coming to my lady Philoclea's chamber? Is it to defend her from such violence as I might go about to offer unto her? If it be so, truly your coming is vain, for her own virtue hath been a sufficient resistance. There needs no strength to be added to so inviolate chastity. The excellency of her mind makes her body impregnable, which for mine own part I had soon yielded to confess with going out of this place (where I found but little comfort, being so disdainfully received) had I not been, I know not by whom, presently upon my coming hither so locked into this chamber that I could never escape hence, where I was fettered in the most guilty shame that ever man was, seeing what a paradise of unspotted goodness my filthy thoughts sought to defile. If for that therefore you come, already I assure you your errand is performed. But if it be to bring me to any punishment whatsoever for having undertaken so unexcusable presumption, truly I bear such an accuser about me of mine own conscience that I willingly submit myself unto it. Only thus much let me demand of you, that you will be a witness unto the duke what you hear me say, and oppose yourself, that neither his sudden fury nor any other occasion may offer any hurt to this lady, in whom you see nature hath accomplished so much that I am fain to lay mine own faultiness as a foil of her purest excellency. I can say no more, but look upon her beauty; remember her blood; consider her years; and judge rightly of her virtues, and I doubt not a gentleman's mind will then be a sufficient instructor unto you in this, I may term it, miserable chance, happened unto her by my unbridled audacity.'

Philanax was content to hear him out, not for any favour he owed him, but to see whether he would reveal anything of the original cause and purpose of the duke's death. But finding it so far from that that he named Basilius unto him as supposing him alive, thinking it rather cunning than ignorance: 'Young man,' said he, 'whom I have cause to hate before I have mean to know, you use but a point of skill by confessing the manifest smaller fault, to be believed hereafter in the denial of the greater. But for that matter, all passeth to one end, and hereafter we shall have leisure to seek by torments the truth—if the love of truth itself will not bring you unto it. As for my lady Philoclea, if it so fall out as you say, it shall be the more fit for her years, and comely for the great house she is come of, that an ill-governed beauty have not cancelled the rules of virtue. But howsoever that be, it is not for you to teach an Arcadian what reverent duty we owe to any of that progeny. But', said he, 'come you with me without resistance, for the one cannot avail, and the other may procure pity.'

'Pity,' said Pyrocles with a bitter smiling, disdained with so currish an answer, 'no, no, Arcadian, I can quickly have pity of myself, and I would think my life most miserable which should be a gift of thine. Only I demand this innocent lady's security, which until thou hast confirmed unto me by an oath assure thyself the first that lays hands upon her shall leave his life for a testimony of his sacrilege.'

Philanax with an inward scorn, thinking it most manifest they were both, he at least, of counsel with the duke's death: 'Well', said he, 'you speak much to me of the duke. I do here swear unto you by the love I have ever borne him she shall have no worse (howsoever it fall out) than her own parents.'

'And upon that word of yours I yield', said the poor Pyrocles, deceived by him that meant not to deceive him.

Then did Philanax send for apparel for him, and having arrayed him, delivered him into the hands of a nobleman in the company, everyone desirous to have him in his charge, so much did his goodly presence (in whom true valour shined) breed a delightful admiration in all the beholders. Philanax himself stayed with Philoclea, to see whether of her he might learn some disclosing of this former confusion. But she, sweet lady, whom first a kindly shamefastness had separated from Pyrocles (they being both left in a more open view than her modesty would well bear), then the attending her father's coming and studying how to behave herself towards him for both their safeties had called her spirits all within her, now that upon a sudden Pyrocles was delivered out of the chamber from her, at the first she was so surprised with the extreme stroke of the woeful sight that, like those that in their dream are taken with some ugly vision they would fain cry for help but have no force, so remained she awhile quite deprived, not only of speech, but almost of any other lively action. But when indeed Pyrocles was quite drawn from her eyes, and that her vital strength began to return unto her, now not knowing what they did to Pyrocles, but according to the nature of love fearing the worst, wringing her hands and letting abundance of tears be the first part of her eloquence, bending her amber-crowned head*over her bedside, to the hard-hearted Philanax: 'O Philanax, Philanax,' said she, 'I know how much authority you have with my father; there is no man whose wisdom he so much esteems, nor whose faith he so much reposeth upon. Remember how oft you have promised your service unto me; how oft you have given me occasion to believe that there was no lady in whose favour you more desired to remain. Now my chance is turned, let not your troth turn. I present myself unto you, the most humble and miserable suppliant living; neither shall my desire be great. I seek for no more life than I shall be thought worthy of. If my blood may wash away the dishonour of Arcadia, spare it not; although through me it hath never been willingly dishonoured. My only suit is you will be a mean for me that, while I am suffered to enjoy this life, I may not be separated from him to whom the gods have joined me; and that you determine nothing more cruelly of him than you do of me. But if you rightly judge of our virtuous marriage, whereto our innocencies were the solemnities, and the gods themselves the witnesses, then procure we may live together. But if my father will not so conceive of us, as the fault (if any were) was united, so let the punishment be united also.'

There was no man that ever loved either his prince or anything pertaining unto him with a truer zeal than Philanax did. This made him even to the depth of his heart receive a most vehement grief to see his master made, as it were, more miserable after death. And for himself, there was nothing could have kept him from falling to all tender pity but the perfect persuasion he had that all this was joined to the pack of his master's death, which the speech of marriage made him the more believe. Therefore, first muttering to himself suchlike words: 'the violence the gentleman spake of is now turned to marriage. He alleged Mars, but she speaks of Venus. O unfortunate master, this hath been that fair devil Gynecia, sent away one of her daughters, prostituted the other, empoisoned thee to overthrow the diadem of Arcadia.' But at length thus unto herself he said: 'If your father, madam, were now to speak unto, truly there should nobody be found a more ready advocate for you than myself; for I would suffer this fault, though very great, to be blotted out of my mind by your former led life, and being daughter to such a father. But since among yourselves you have taken him away in whom was the only power to have mercy, you must now be clothed in your own working, and look for no other than that which dead pitiless laws may allot unto you. For my part, I loved you for your virtue; but now where is that? I loved you for your father; unhappy folks, you have robbed the world of him.'

These words of her father were so little understood of the only well understanding Philoclea that she desired him to tell her what he meant to speak in such dark sort unto her of her lord and father, whose displeasure was more dreadful unto her than her punishment; that she was free in her own conscience she had never deserved evil of him but in this last fact, wherein notwithstanding if it pleased him to proceed with patience he should find her choice had not been unfortunate.

He that saw her words written in the plain table of her fair face thought it impossible there should therein be contained deceit; and therefore so much the more abashed: 'Why,' said he, 'madam, would you have me think that you are not of conspiracy with the princess Pamela's flight and your father's death?'

With that word the sweet lady gave a pitiful cry, having straight in her face and breast abundance of witnesses that her heart was far from any such abominable consent. 'Ah, of all sides utterly ruined Philoclea,' said she, 'now indeed I may well suffer all conceit of hope to die in me. Dear father, where was I that might not do you my last service before soon after miserably following you?'

Philanax perceived the demonstration so lively and true in her that he easily acquitted her in his heart of that fact; and the more was moved to join with her in most hearty lamentation. But remembering him that the burden of the state and punishment of his master's murderers lay all upon him: 'Well,' said he, 'madam, I can do nothing without all the states of Arcadia. What they will determine of you, I know not; for my part your speeches would much prevail with me, but that I find not how to excuse your giving over your body to him that for the last proof of his treason lent his garments to disguise your miserable mother in the most vile fact she hath committed. Hard surely it will be to separate your causes, with whom you have so nearly joined yourself.'

'Neither do I desire it,' said the sweetly weeping Philoclea, 'whatsoever you determine of him, do that likewise to me; for I know from the fountain of virtue nothing but virtue could ever proceed.'

Philanax, feeling his heart more and more mollifying to her, renewed the image of his dead master in his fancy, and using that for the spurs of his revengeful choler, went suddenly without any more speech from the desolate lady; to whom now fortune seemed to threaten unripe death and undeserved shame among her least evils. But Philanax, leaving good guard upon the lodge, went himself to see the order of his other prisoners, whom even then as he issued he found increased with unhoped means—the order of which shall be from the beginning thereof declared.

Long methinks it is since anything hath been spoken of the noble prince Musidorus, especially having been left in so impatient a case as he should hardly brook a tedious respite. But so sovereign a possession the charming Philoclea had stolen into that her eldest sister was almost forgotten; who, having delivered over the burden of her fearful cares to the natural ease of a well refreshing sleep, reposing both body and mind upon the trusted support of her princely shepherd, was with the braying cries of a rascal company robbed of her quiet, at what time she was in a shrewd likelihood to have had great part of her trust in Musidorus deceived, and found herself robbed of that she had laid in store as her dearest jewel—so did her own beauties enforce a force against herself. But a greater peril preserved her from the less, and the coming of enemies defended her from the violence of a friend; so that both she at one instant opened her eyes (which in so double a danger had great need to look to themselves) and the every way enraged Musidorus rase from her—enraged betwixt a repentant shame of his promise-breaking attempt and the tyrannical fire of lust (which, having already caught hold of so sweet and fit a fuel, was past the calling back of reason's counsel), and now betwixt the doubt he had what these men would go about and the spite he conceived against their cumbersome presence. But the clowns, having with their hideous noise brought them both to their feet, had soon knowledge what guests they had found. For indeed these were the scummy remnant of those Phagonian rebels whose naughty minds could not trust so much to the goodness of their prince as to lay their hang-worthy necks upon the constancy of his promised pardon. Therefore, when the rest (who as sheep had but followed their fellows) so sheepishly had submitted themselves, these only committed their safety to the thickest part of those desert woods; who, as they were in the constitution of their minds little better than beasts, so were they apt to degenerate to a beastly kind of life, having these few days already framed their gluttonish stomachs to have for food the wild benefits of nature, the uttermost end they had being but to draw out as much as they could the line of a tedious life. In this sort vagabonding in those untrodden places, they were guided by the everlasting justice to be chastisers of Musidorus's broken vow; whom, as soon as they saw turned towards them, they full well remembered it was he that, accompanied with some other honest shepherds, had come to the succour of Cleophila, and had left among some of them bloody tokens of his valour. As for Pamela, they had many times seen her. Thus, first stirred up with a rustical revenge against him, and then desire of spoil to help their miserable wants, but chiefly thinking it was the way to confirm their own pardon to bring the princess back unto her father, whom (they were sure) he would never have sent so far so slightly accompanied, they did, without any other denouncing of war, set all together upon the worthy Musidorus; who, being beforehand as much inflamed against them for the interrupting his vehement pursuit, gave them so brave a welcome that the smart of some made the rest stand further off, crying and prating against him, but like bad curs rather barking than closing; he, in the mean time, placing his trembling lady to one of the fair pine trees, and so setting himself before her as might show the cause of his courage grew in himself, but the effect was only employed in her defence. The villains (that now had a second proof how ill wards they had for such a sword) turned all the course of their violence into throwing darts and stones—indeed, the only way to overmaster the valour of Musidorus who, finding them some already touch, some fall so near his chiefest life Pamela, that in the end some one or other might hap to do an unsuccourable mischief, setting all his hope in despair, ran out from his lady among them; who straight (like so many swine when a hardy mastiff sets upon them) dispersed themselves. But the first he overtook as he ran away, carrying his head as far before him as those manner of runnings are wont to do, with one blow strake it so clean off that, it falling betwixt the hands, and the body falling upon it, it made a show as though the fellow had had great haste to gather up his head again. Another, the speed he made to run for the best game bare him full butt against a tree, so that tumbling back with a bruised face and a dreadful expectation, Musidorus was straight upon him, and parting with his sword one of his legs from him, left him to make a roaring lamentation that his mortar-treading was marred for ever. A third, finding his feet too slow as well as his hands too weak, suddenly turned back, beginning to open his lips for mercy, but before he had well entered a rudely compiled oration, Musidorus's blade was come betwixt his jaws into his throat; and so the poor man rested there for ever with a very ill mouthful of an answer. Musidorus in this furious chafe would have followed some other of these hateful wretches but that he heard his lady cry for help, whom three of that villainous crew had (whilst Musidorus followed their fellows), compassing about some trees, suddenly come upon and surprised, threatening to kill her if she cried, and meaning to convey her out of sight while the prince was making his bloodthirsty chase. But she that was resolved no worse thing could fall unto her than the being deprived of him on whom she had established all her comfort, with a pitiful cry fetched his eyes unto her; who then, thinking so many weapons thrust into his eyes as with his eyes he saw bent against her, made all hearty speed to her succour. But one of them, wiser than his companions, set his dagger to her alabaster throat, swearing if he threw not away his sword he would presently kill her. There was never poor scholar that, having instead of his book some playing toy about him, did more suddenly cast it from him at the child-feared presence of a cruel schoolmaster than the valorous Musidorus discharged himself of his only defence, when he saw it stood upon the instant point of his lady's life; and holding up his noble hands to so unworthy audience:

'O Arcadians, it is I, it is I, that have done you the wrong! She is your princess,' said he, 'she never had will to hurt you; and you see she hath no power. Use your choler upon me that have better deserved it. Do not yourselves the wrong to do her any hurt, which in no time nor place will ever be forgiven you.'

They, that yet trusted not to his courtesy, bad him stand further off from his sword, which he obediently did—so far was love above all other thoughts in him. Then did they call together the rest of their fellows who, though they were few, yet according to their number possessed many places. And then began those savage senators to make a consultation what they should do; some wishing to spoil them of their jewels and let them go on their journey (for that, if they carried them back, they were sure they should have

least part of the prey); others, preferring their old homes to any-
thing, desiring to bring them to Basilius as pledges of their surety;
and there wanted not which cried the safest way was to kill them
both—to such an unworthy thraldom were these great and excellent
personages brought. But the most part resisted to the killing of
the princess, foreseeing their lives would never be safe after such a
fact committed, and began to wish rather the spoil than death of
Musidorus; when the villain that had his leg cut off came scrawling
towards them, and being helped to them by one of the company, began
with a groaning voice and a disfigured face to demand the revenge
of his blood which, since he had spent with them in their defence,
it were no reason he should be suffered by them to die discontented.
The only contentment he required was that by their help with his
own hands he might put his murderer to some cruel death. He would
fain have cried more against Musidorus, but that the much loss of
blood, helped on with this vehemency, choked up the spirits of his
life, leaving him to make betwixt his body and soul an ill-favoured
partition. But they, seeing their fellow in that sort die before their
faces, did swell in new mortal rages, all resolved to kill him, but now
only considering what manner of terrible death they should invent
for him. Thus was a while the agreement of his slaying broken by
the disagreement of the manner of it; and extremity of cruelty grew
for a time to be the stop of cruelty. At length they were resolved
everyone to have a piece of him, and to become all as well hangmen
as judges; when Pamela, tearing her hair and falling down among
them, sometimes with all the sort of humble prayers, mixed with
promises of great good turns (which they knew her estate was able to
perform), sometimes threatening them that, if they killed him and
not her, she would not only revenge it upon them but upon all their
wives and children, bidding them consider that, though they might
think she was come away in her father's displeasure, yet they might
be sure he would ever show himself a father; that the gods would
never if she lived put her in so base estate but that she should have
ability to plague such as they were; returning afresh to prayers and
promises, and mixing the same again with threatenings, brought
them (who were now grown colder in their fellow's cause, who was
past aggravating the matter with his cries) to determine with them-
selves there was no way but either to kill them both or save them
both. As for the killing, already they having answered themselves
that that was a way to make them citizens of the woods for ever,

they did in fine conclude they would return them back again to the
duke, which they did not doubt would be cause of a great reward,
besides their safety from their fore-deserved punishment. Thus
having, either by fortune, or the force of these two lovers' inward
working virtue, settled their cruel hearts to this gentler course, they
took the two horses, and having set upon them their princely pris-
oners, they returned towards the lodge. The villains, having decked
all their heads with laurel branches, as thinking they had done a
notable act, singing and shouting, ran by them in hope to have
brought them the same day again to the duke. But the time was so
far spent that they were forced to take up that night's lodging in the
midst of the woods where, while the clowns continued their watch
about them, now that the night, according to his dark nature, did
add a kind of desolation to the pensive hearts of these two afflicted
lovers, it is said that Musidorus, taking the tender hand of Pamela
and bedewing it with his tears, in this sort gave an issue to the
swelling of his heart's grief:

'Most excellent lady,' said he, 'in what case think you am I
with myself? How unmerciful judgements do I lay upon my soul
now that I know not what god hath so reversed my well meaning
enterprise as, instead of doing you that honour which I hoped (and
not without reason hoped) Thessalia should have yielded unto you,
am now like to become a wretched instrument of your discomfort?
Alas, how contrary an end have all the inclinations of my mind taken!
My faith falls out a treason unto you, and the true honour I bear you
is the field wherein your dishonour is like to be sown. But I invoke
that universal and only wisdom (which examining the depth of
hearts, hath not his judgement fixed upon the event) to bear testi-
mony with me that my desire, though in extremest vehemency, yet
did not so overgo my remembrance but that, as far as man's wit
might be extended, I sought to prevent all things that might fall to
your hurt. But now that all the ill fortunes of ill fortune have crossed
my best framed intent, I am most miserable in that I cannot only
not give you help but, which is worst of all, am barred from giving
you counsel. For how should I open my mouth to counsel you in
that wherein, by my counsel, you are most undeservedly fallen?'

The fair and wise Pamela, although full of cares of the unhappy
turning of this matter, yet seeing the grief of Musidorus only stirred
for her, did so tread down all other motions with the true force of
virtue that she thus answered him, having first kissed him (which

before she had never done),* either love so commanding her (which doubted how long they should enjoy one another) or of a lively spark of nobleness to descend in most favour to one when he is lowest in affliction: 'My dear and ever dear Musidorus,' said she, 'a great wrong you do to yourself that will torment you thus with grief for the fault of fortune. Since a man is bound no further to himself than to do wisely, the chance is only to trouble them that stand upon chance. But greater is the wrong (at least, if anything comes from you may bear the name of wrong) you do unto me to think me either so childish as not to perceive your faithful faultlessness; or perceiving it, so basely disposed as to let my heart be overthrown, standing upon itself in so unspotted a pureness. Hold for certain, most worthy Musidorus, it is yourself I love, which can no more be diminished by these showers of ill hap than flowers are marred with the timely rains of April. For how can I want comfort that have the true and living comfort of my unblemished virtue; and how can I want honour as long as Musidorus (in whom indeed honour is) doth honour me? Nothing bred from myself can discomfort me, and fools' opinions I will not reckon as dishonour.'

Musidorus, looking up to the stars, 'O mind of minds,' said he, 'the living power of all things which dost with all these eyes behold our ever varying actions, accept into thy favourable ears this prayer of mine. If I may any longer hold out this dwelling on the earth which is called a life, grant me ability to deserve at this lady's hands the grace she hath showed unto me; grant me wisdom to know her wisdom, and goodness so to increase my love of her goodness that all mine own chosen desires be to myself but second to her determinations. Whatsoever I be, let it be to her service. Let me herein be satisfied that for such infinite favours of virtue I have some way wrought her satisfaction. But if my last time approacheth, and that I am no longer to be among mortal creatures, make yet my death serve her to some purpose, that hereafter she may not have cause to repent herself that she bestowed so excellent a mind upon Musidorus.'

Pamela could not choose but accord the conceit of their fortune to these passionate prayers, insomuch that her constant eyes yielded some tears, which wiping from her fair face with Musidorus's hand, speaking softly unto him, as if she had feared more that anybody should be witness of her weakness than of anything else she had said:

'You see,' said she, 'my prince and only lord, what you work in me by your too much grieving for me. I pray you think I have no joy but in you, and if you fill that with sorrow, what do you leave for me? What is prepared for us we know not, but that with sorrow we cannot prevent it, we know. Now let us turn from these things, and think how you will have me behave myself towards you in this matter.'

Musidorus, finding the authority of her speech confirmed with direct necessity, the first care came into his mind was of his dear friend and cousin, the prince Pyrocles, with whom at his parting he had concluded what names they should bear if upon any occasion they were forced to give themselves out for great men, and yet not make themselves fully known. Now fearing lest, if the princess name him for Musidorus, the fame of their two being together would discover Pyrocles, holding her hand betwixt his hands a good while together:

'I did not think, most excellent princess,' said he, 'to have made any further request unto you; for having been already to you so unfortunate a suitor, I know not what modesty can bear any further demand. But the estate of one young man whom (next to you, far before myself) I owe more than all the world, one both worthy of all well being for the notable constitution of his mind, and most unworthy to receive hurt by me, whom he doth in all faith and constancy love, the pity of him only goes beyond all resolution to the contrary.'

Then did he, to the princess's great admiration, tell her the whole story so far as he knew of it; and that when they made the grievous disjunction of their long company, they had concluded Musidorus should entitle himself Palladius, prince of Caria, and Pyrocles should be Timopyrus of Lycia.

'Now,' said Musidorus, 'he keeping a woman's habit is to use no other name than Cleophila, but I that find it best of the one side for your honour it be known you went away with a prince, and not with a shepherd; of the other side accounting any death less evil than the betraying that sweet friend of mine, will take this mean betwixt both, and using the name of Palladius (if the respect of a prince will stop your father's fury, that will serve as well as Musidorus) until Pyrocles' fortune being some way established, I may freely give good proofs that the noble country of Thessalia is mine. And if that will not mitigate your father's opinion to me-wards, nature, I hope, working in your excellencies will make him deal well by you. For my part, the image of death is nothing fearful unto me, and this good I shall have reaped by it, that I leave my most esteemed friend in no danger to be disclosed by me. And besides (since I must confess I am not without a remorse of her case) my virtuous mother shall not know her son's violent death hid under the fame will go of Palladius. But as long as her years (now of good number) be counted among the living, she may joy herself with some possibility of my return.'

Pamela, promising him upon no occasion ever to name him, fell into extremity of weeping, as if her eyes had been content to spend all their seeing moistness, now that there was speech of the loss of that which they held as their chiefest light. So that Musidorus was forced to repay her good counsels with sweet consolations, which continued betwixt them until it was about midnight that their thoughts, even weary of their own burdens, fell to a strange kind of uncertainty; and the minds standing only upon the nature of their inward intelligences, left their bodies to give a sleeping respite to their vital spirits, which they (according to the quality of sorrow) received with greater greediness than ever in their lives before— according to the nature of sorrow, I say, that which is past care's remedy. For care, stirring the brain and making thin the spirits, breaketh rest; but those griefs wherein one is determined there is no preventing, do breed a dull heaviness which easily clothes itself in sleep. As it fell out in these personages who, delicately wound up one in another's arms, laid a plot in that picture of death how gladly, if death came, their souls would go together. But as soon as that morning appeared to play her part (which, as you have heard, was laden with so many well occasioned lamentations), their lobbish guard (who all night had kept themselves awake with prating how valiant deeds they had done, when they ran away; and how fair a death their fellow died, who at his last gasp sued to be a hangman) awaked them and set them upon their horses; to whom the very shining force of excellent virtue (though in a very harsh subject) had wrought a kind of reverence in them. Musidorus, as he rid among them (of whom they had no other hold but the hold of Pamela), thinking it want of a well squared judgement to leave any mean unassayed of saving their lives, to this purpose spake to his unseemly guardians, using a plain kind of phrase to make his speech the more credible:

'My masters,' said he, 'there is no man that is wise but hath in whatsoever he doth some purpose whereto he directs his doing, which so long he follows till he see that either that purpose is not worth the pains or that another doing carries with it a better purpose. That you are wise in what you take in hand, I have to my cost learned; that makes me desire you to tell me what is your end in carrying the princess and me back again unto her father.'

'Pardon', said one. 'Reward', cried another.

'Well,' said he, 'take both; although I know you are so wise to remember that hardly they both will go together, being of so contrary a making. For the ground of pardon is an evil. Neither any man pardons, but remembers an evil done. The cause of reward is the opinion of some good act; and whoso rewardeth that, holds the chief place of his fancy. Now one man of one company to have the same consideration both of good and evil, but that the conceit of pardoning, if it be pardoned, will take away the mind of rewarding, is very hard, if not impossible. For either even in justice will he punish the fault, as well as reward the desert, or else in mercy balance the one by the other; so that the not chastising shall be a sufficient satisfying. Thus then you may see that in your own purpose rests great uncertainty; but I will grant that by this your deed you shall obtain your double purpose. Yet consider, I pray you, whether by another mean that may not better be obtained, and then I doubt not your wisdoms will teach you to take hold of the better. I am sure you know anybody were better have no need of a pardon than enjoy a pardon; for as it carries with it the surety of a preserved life so bears it a continual note of a deserved death. This, therefore (besides the danger you may run into, my lady Pamela being the undoubted inheritrix of this state, if she shall hereafter seek to revenge your wrong done her), shall be continually cast in your teeth, as men dead by the law. The honester sort will disdain your company and your children shall be the more basely reputed of, and you yourselves in every slight fault hereafter, as men once condemned, aptest to be overthrown. Now if you will, as I doubt not you will (for you are wise), turn your course and guard my lady Pamela thitherward whither she was going first, you need not doubt to adventure your fortunes where she goes, and there shall you be assured in a country as good and rich as this, of the same manners and language, to be so far from the conceit of a pardon as we both shall be forced to acknowledge we have received by your means whatsoever we hold dear in this life; and so for reward, judge you whether it be not more likely you shall there receive it where you have done no evil, but singular and undeserved goodness, or here where this service of yours shall be diminished by your duty and blemished by your former fault. Yes: I protest and swear unto you by the fair eyes of that lady there shall no gentleman in all that country be preferred. You shall have riches, ease, pleasure, and that which is best to such worthy minds, you shall not be forced to cry mercy for a good fact. You only, of all the Arcadians, shall have the praise in continuing in your late valiant attempt, and not basely be brought under a halter for seeking the liberty of Arcadia.'

These words in their minds (who did nothing for any love of goodness but only as their senses presented greater shows of profit) began to make them waver, and some to clap their hands, and scratch their heads and swear it was the best way; others (that would seem wiser than the rest) to capitulate what tenements they should have, what subsidies they should pay; others to talk of their wives (in doubt whether it were best to send for them or take new where they went); most like fools, not readily thinking what was next to be done, but imagining what cheer they would make when they came there; one or two only of the least discoursers beginning to turn their faces towards the woods which they had left, and come within the plain near to the lodges, when unhappily they espied a troop of horsemen. But then their false hearts had quickly, for the present fear, forsaken their last hopes. And therefore keeping on the way towards the lodge with songs and cries of joy, these horsemen (who were some of them Philanax had sent out to the search of Pamela) came galloping unto them, marvelling who they were that in such a general mourning durst sing joyful tunes, and in so public a ruin wear the laurel tokens of victory. And that which seemed strangest, they might see two among them, unarmed like prisoners, but riding like captains. But when they came nearer, they perceived the one was a lady, and the lady Pamela. Then glad they had by hap found that which they so little hoped to meet withal, taking these clowns (who first resisted them for the desire they had to be the deliverers of the two excellent prisoners), learning that they were of those Phagonians which had made the dangerous uproar, as well under colour to punish that as this their last withstanding them, but indeed their principal cause being because they themselves would have the only praise of their own quest, they suffered not one of them to live. Marry, three of the stubbornest of them they left their bodies hanging upon the trees, because their doing might carry the likelier form of judgement—such an unlooked-for end did the life of justice work for the mighty-minded wretches, by subjects to be executed that would have executed princes, and to suffer that without law which by law they had deserved. And thus these young folks, twice prisoners before any due arrest, delivered of their gaolers but not of their gaol, had rather change than respite of misery. These soldiers (that took them with very few words of entertainment), hasting to carry them to their lord Philanax, to whom they came even as he (going out of the lady Philoclea's chamber) had overtaken Pyrocles whom before he had delivered to the custody of a nobleman of that country.

When Pyrocles (led towards his prison) saw his friend Musidorus with the noble lady Pamela in that inexpected sort returned, his grief (if any grief were in a mind which had placed everything according to his natural worth) was very much augmented; for, besides some small hope he had, if Musidorus had once been clear of Arcadia, by his dealing and authority to have brought his only gladsome desires to a good issue, the hard estate of his friend did no less, nay rather more, vex him than his own; for so, indeed, it is ever found where valour and friendship are perfectly coupled in one heart—the reason being that the resolute man having once digested in his judgement the worst extremity of his own case, and either having quite repelled or at least expelled all passion which ordinarily follows an overthrown fortune, not knowing his friend's mind so well as his own, nor with what patience he brooks his case (which is, as it were, the material cause of making a man happy or unhappy), doubts whether his friend account not himself more miserable, and so, indeed, be more lamentable. But as soon as Musidorus was brought by the soldiers near unto Philanax, Pyrocles not knowing whether ever after he should be suffered to see his friend, and determining there could be no advantage by dissembling a not-knowing of him, leapt suddenly from their hands that held him, and passing with a strength strengthened with a true affection through them that encompassed Musidorus, he embraced him as fast as he could in his arms, and kissing his cheek:

'O my Palladius,' said he, 'let not our virtue now abandon us. Let us prove our minds are no slaves to fortune, but in adversity can triumph over adversity.'

'Dear Timopyrus', answered Musidorus (seeing by his apparel his being a man was revealed), 'I thank you for this best care of my best part. But fear not, I have kept too long company with you to want now a thorough determination of these things. I well know there is nothing evil but within us; the rest is either natural or accidental.'

Philanax (finding them of so near acquaintance) began presently to examine them apart; but such resolution he met within them that by no such means he could learn further than it pleased them to deliver; so that he thought best to put them both in one place with espial of their words and behaviour, that way to sift out the more of these forepassed mischiefs, and for that purpose gave them both unto the nobleman who before had the custody of Pyrocles, by name Sympathus, leaving a trusty servant of his own to give diligent watch to what might pass betwixt them.

No man that hath ever passed through the school of affection needs doubt what a tormenting grief it was to the noble Pamela to have the company of him taken from her to whose virtuous company she had bound her life. But weighing with herself it was fit for her honour, till her doing was clearly manifested, that they should remain separate, kept down the rising tokens of grief, showing passion in nothing but her eyes which accompanied Musidorus even unto the tent whither he and Pyrocles were led. Then with a countenance more princely than she was wont, according to the wont of highest hearts (like the palm tree striving most upward when he is most burdened), she commanded Philanax to bring her to her father and mother, that she might render them account of her doings. Philanax, showing a sullen kind of reverence unto her, as a man that honoured her as his master's heir but much misliked her for her (in his conceit) dishonourable proceedings, told her what was passed, rather to answer her than that he thought she was ignorant of it. But her good spirit did presently suffer a true compassionate affliction of those hard adventures; which, crossing her arms, looking a great while on the ground with those eyes which let fall many tears, she well declared. But in the end remembering how necessary it was for her not to lose herself in such an extremity, she strengthened her well created heart, and stoutly demanded Philanax what authority then they had to lay hands of her person, who being the undoubted heir was then the lawful princess of that dukedom.

Philanax answered: 'Her grace knew the ancient laws of Arcadia bare she was to have no sway of government till she came to one and twenty years of age, or were married.'

'And married I am,' replied the wise princess, 'therefore I demand your due allegiance.'

'The gods forbid', said Philanax, 'Arcadia should be a dowry of such marriages.' Besides, he told her, all the estates of her country were ill satisfied touching her father's death, which likewise according to the statutes of Arcadia was even that day to be judged of, before the body were removed to receive his princely funerals. After that passed, she should have such obedience as by the laws was due unto her, desiring God she would show herself better in public government than she had done in private.

She would have spoken to the gentlemen and people gathered about her, but Philanax, fearing lest thereby some commotion might arise, or at least a hindrance of executing his master's murderers, which he longed after more than anything, hasted her up to the lodge where her sister was, and there with a chosen company of soldiers to guard the place, left her with Philoclea, Pamela protesting they laid violent hands of her, and that they entered into rebellious attempts against her.

But high time it was for Philanax so to do, for already was all the whole multitude fallen into confused and dangerous divisions. There was a notable example how great dissipations monarchal governments are subject unto; for now their prince and guide had left them, they had not experience to rule, and had not whom to obey. Public matters had ever been privately governed, so that they had no lively taste what was good for themselves, but everything was either vehemently desireful or extremely terrible. Neighbours' invasions, civil dissension, cruelty of the coming prince, and whatsoever in common sense carries a dreadful show, was in all men's heads, but in few how to prevent: hearkening on every rumour, suspecting everything, condemning them whom before they had honoured, making strange and impossible tales of the duke's death; while they thought themselves in danger, wishing nothing but safety; as soon as persuasion of safety took them, desiring further benefits as amendment of forepassed faults (which faults notwithstanding none could tell either the grounds or effects of); all agreeing in the universal names of liking or misliking, but of what in especial points infinitely disagreeing; altogether like a falling steeple, the parts whereof (as windows, stones, and pinnacles) were well, but the whole mass ruinous. And this was the general case of all, wherein notwithstanding was an extreme medley of diversified thoughts: the great men looking to make themselves strong by factions; the gentlemen, some bending to them, some standing upon themselves, some desirous to overthrow those few which they thought were over them; the soldiers desirous of trouble as the nurse of spoil; and not much unlike to them (though in another way) were all the needy sort; the

rich, fearful; the wise, careful. This composition of conceits brought
forth a dangerous tumult, which yet would have been more danger-
ous but that it had so many parts that nobody well knew against
whom chiefly to oppose themselves. For some there were that cried
to have the state altered and governed no more by a prince; marry,
in the alteration many would have the Lacedemonian government
of few chosen senators; others the Athenian, where the people's
voice held the chief authority. But these were rather the discoursing
sort of men than the active, being a matter more in imagination than
practice. But they that went nearest to the present case (as in a
country that knew no government without a prince) were they that
strave whom they should make; whereof a great number there were
that would have the princess Pamela presently to enjoy it; some, dis-
daining that she had as it were abandoned her own country, inclining
more to Philoclea; and there wanted not of them which wished
Gynecia were delivered and made regent till Pamela were worthily
married. But great multitudes there were which, having been ac-
quainted with the just government of Philanax, meant to establish
him as lieutenant of the state, and these were the most popular sort
who judged by the commodities they felt. But the principal men in
honour and might, who had long before envied his greatness with
Basilius, did much more spurn against any such preferment of him.
For yet before their envy had some kind of breathing out his rancour
by laying his greatness as a fault to the prince's judgement, who
showed in Dametas he might easily be deceived in men's value. But
now, if the prince's choice by so many mouths should be confirmed,
what could they object to so rightly esteemed an excellency? They
therefore were disposed sooner to yield to anything than to his rais-
ing, and were content (for to cross Philanax) to stop those actions
which otherwise they could not but think good. Philanax himself, as
much hindered by those that did immoderately honour him (which
brought both more envy and suspicion upon him) as by them that
did manifestly resist him, but (standing only upon a constant desire
of justice and a clear conscience) went forward stoutly in the action
of his master's revenge, which he thought himself particularly bound
to. For the rest, as the ordering of the government, he accounted
himself but as one, wherein notwithstanding he would employ all
his loyal endeavour.

But among the noblemen, he that most openly set himself against
him was named Timautus, a man of middle age but of extreme ambi-

tion, as one that had placed his uttermost good in greatness, thinking small difference by what means he came by it; of commendable wit, if he had not made it a servant to unbridled desires; cunning to creep into men's favours, which he prized only as they were serviceable unto him. He had been brought up in some soldiery, which he knew how to set out with more than deserved ostentation; servile (though envious) to his betters, and no less tyrannically minded to them he had advantage of; counted revengeful, but indeed measuring both revenge and reward as the party might either help or hurt him; rather shameless than bold, and yet more bold in practices than in personal adventures; in sum, a man that could be as evil as he listed, and listed as much as any advancement might thereby be gotten. As for virtue, he counted it but a school name. He even at the first assembling together, finding the great stroke Philanax carried among the people, thought it his readiest way of ambition to join with him; which, though his pride did hardly brook, yet the other vice, carrying with it a more apparent object, prevailed over the weaker, so that (with those liberal protestations of friendship which men that care not for their word are wont to bestow) he offered unto him the choice in marriage of either the sisters, so he would likewise help him to the other, and make such a partition of the Arcadian state, wishing him that, since he loved his master because he was his master (which showed the love began in himself), he should rather, now occasion was presented, seek his own good substantially than affect the smoke of a glory by showing an untimely fidelity to him that could not reward it, and have all the fruit he should get in men's opinions; which would be as diverse, as many, few agreeing to yield him due praise of his true heart.

But Philanax, who had limited his thoughts in that he esteemed good (to which he was neither carried by the vain tickling of uncertain fame nor from which he would be transported by enjoying anything whereto the ignorant world gives the excellent name of goods), with great mislike of his offer he made him so peremptory an answer (not without threatening if he found him foster any such fancy) that Timautus went with an inward spite from him whom before he had never loved; and measuring all men's marches by his own pace, rather thought it some further fetch of Philanax (as that he would have all to himself alone) than was any way taken with the lovely beauty of his virtue, whose image he had so quite defaced in his own soul that he had left himself no eyes to behold it. But stayed waiting fit opportunity to execute his desires, both for himself and against Philanax, when by the bringing back of Pamela the people being divided in many motions (which both with murmuring noises and putting themselves into several troops they well showed), he thought apt time was laid before him (the waters being, as the proverb saith, troubled, and so the better for his fishing). Therefore going among the chiefest lords whom he knew principally to repine at Philanax, and making a kind of convocation of them, he inveighed against his proceedings, drawing everything to the most malicious interpretation that malice itself could instruct him to do. He said it was season for them to look to such a weed that else would overgrow them all. It was not now time to consult of the dead but of the living, since such a sly wolf was entered among them that could make justice the cloak of tyranny and love of his late master the destruction of his now being children. 'Do you not see', said he, 'how far his corruption hath stretched that he hath such a number of rascals' voices to declare him lieutenant, ready to make him prince, but that he instructs them matters are not yet ripe for it. As for us, because we are too rich to be bought, he thinks us the fitter to be killed. Hath Arcadia bred no man but Philanax? Is she become a stepmother to all the rest, and hath given all her blessings to Philanax? Or if there be men among us, let us show we disdain to be servants to a servant. Let us make him know we are far worthier not to be slaves than he to be a master. Think you he hath made such haste in these matters to give them over to another man's hand? Think you he durst become the gaoler of his princess but either meaning to be her master or her murderer? And all this for the dear goodwill, forsooth, he bears to the duke's memory, whose authority as he abused in his life so he would now persevere to abuse his name after his death! O notable affection, for the love of the father to kill the wife and disinherit the children! O single-minded modesty, to aspire to no less than to the princely diadem! No, no, he hath veered all this while but to come the sooner to his affected end. But let us remember what we be: in quality, his equals; in number, far before him. Let us deliver the duchess and our natural princesses, and leave them no longer under his authority, whose proceedings would rather show that he himself had been the murderer of the duke than a fit guardian of his posterity.'

These words pierced much into the minds already inclined that way; insomuch that most part of the nobility confirmed Timautus's speech and were ready to execute it, when Philanax came among them and with a constant but reverent behaviour desired them they would not exercise private grudges in so common a necessity. He acknowledged himself a man, and a faulty man; to the clearing or satisfying of which he would at all times submit himself. Since his end was to bring all things to an upright judgement, it should ill fit him to fly the judgement. 'But,' said he, 'my lords, let not Timautus's railing speech (who whatsoever he finds evil in his own soul can with ease lay it upon another) make me lose your good favour. Consider that all well doing stands so in the middle betwixt his two contrary evils that it is a ready matter to cast a slanderous shade upon the most approved virtues. Who hath an evil tongue can call severity cruelty, and faithful diligence diligent ambition. But my end is not to excuse myself, nor to accuse him; for both those, hereafter will be time enough. There is neither of us whose purging or punishing may so much import to Arcadia. Now I request you for your own honours' sake, and require you by the duty you owe to this state that you do presently (according to the laws) take in hand the chastisement of our master's murderers, and laying order for the government; by whomsoever it be done, so it be done, and justly done, I am satisfied. My labour hath been to frame things so as you might determine; now it is in you to determine. For my part, I call the heavens to witness the care of my heart stands to repay that wherein both I and most of you were tied to that prince, with whom all my love of worldly action is dead.'

As Philanax was speaking his last words there came one running to him with open mouth and fearful eyes, telling him that there were a great number of the people which were bent to take the young men out of Sympathus's hands, and as it should seem by their acclamations, were like enough to proclaim them princes.

'Nay,' said Philanax, speaking aloud and looking with a just anger upon the other noblemen, 'it is now season to hear Timautus's idle slanders, while strangers become our lords and Basilius's murderers sit in his throne. But whosoever is a true Arcadian, let him follow me.'

With that, he went towards the place he heard of, followed by those that had ever loved him and some of the noblemen; some other remaining with Timautus, who in the mean time was conspiring by strong hand to deliver Gynecia, of whom the weakest guard was had. But Philanax where he went found them all in an uproar, which thus was fallen out: the greatest multitude of people that were come to the death of Basilius were the Mantineans, as being the nearest city to the lodges. Among these the chief man, both in authority and love, was Kerxenus, he that not long before had been host to the two princes whom, though he knew not so much as by name, yet their noble behaviour had bred such love in his heart towards them as both with tears he parted from them when they left him (under promise to return) and did keep their jewels and apparel as the relics of two demigods. Among others he had entered the prison and seen them, which forthwith so invested his soul both with sorrow and desire to help them (whom he tendered as his children) that, calling his neighbours the Mantineans unto him, he told them all the praises of those two young men, swearing he thought the gods had provided for them better than they themselves could have imagined. He willed them to consider that, when all was done, Basilius's children must enjoy the state, who since they had chosen, and chosen so as all the world could not mend their choice, why should they resist God's doing and their princesses' pleasure? This was the only way to purchase quietness without blood, where otherwise they should at one instant crown Pamela with a crown of gold and a dishonoured title, which whether ever she would forget, he thought it fit for them to weigh. 'Such', said he, 'heroical greatness shines in their eyes, such an extraordinary majesty in all their actions, as surely either fortune by parentage or nature in creation hath made them princes. And yet a state already we have. We need but a man; who, since he is presented unto you by the heavenly providence, embraced by your undoubted princess, worthy for their youth of compassion, for their beauty of admiration, for their excellent virtue to be monarchs of the world, shall we not be content with our own bliss? Shall we put out our eyes because another man cannot see; or rather, like some men when too much good happens unto them, they think themselves in a dream and have not spirits to taste their own good? No, no, my friends, believe me, I am so unpartial that I know not their names, but so overcome with their virtue that I shall then think the destinies have ordained a perpetual flourishing to Arcadia when they shall allot such a governor unto it.'

This, spoken by a man both grave in years and known honest, prevailed so with all the Mantineans that with one voice they ran to deliver the two princes. But Philanax came in time to withstand them, both sides yet standing in arms, and rather wanting a beginning than minds to enter into a bloody conflict; which Philanax foreseeing, thought best to remove the prisoners secretly, and (if need were) rather without form of justice to kill them than against justice (as he thought) to have them usurp the state. But there again arose a new trouble; for Sympathus, the nobleman that kept them, was so stricken in compassion with their excellent presence that, as he would not falsify his promise to Philanax to give them liberty, so yet would he not yield them to himself, fearing he would do them violence. Thus tumult upon tumult arising, the sun, I think, a-weary to see their discords, had already gone down to his western lodging. But yet to know what the poor shepherds did (who were the first descriers of these matters) will not to some ears perchance be a tedious digression.

Here ends the fourth book or act.

THE shepherds, finding no place for them in these garboils, to which their quiet hearts (whose highest ambition was in keeping themselves up in goodness) had at all no aptness, retired themselves from among the clamorous multitude, and (as sorrow refuseth not sorrowful company) went up together to the western side of a hill whose prospect extended it so far as they might well discern many of Arcadia's beauties. And there, looking upon the sun's as then declining race, the poor men sat pensive of their present miseries, as if they found a wearisomeness of their woeful words; till at last good old Geron (who as he had longest tasted the benefits of Basilius's government so seemed to have a special feeling of the present loss), wiping his eyes and long white beard bedewed with great drops of tears, began in this sort to complain:

'Alas, poor sheep',* said he, 'which hitherto have enjoyed your fruitful pasture in such quietness as your wool, among other things, hath made this country famous, your best days are now passed. Now must you become the victual of an army, and perchance an army of foreign enemies. You are now not only to fear home wolves but alien lions; now, I say, now that Basilius, our right Basilius is deceased. Alas, sweet pastures, shall soldiers that know not how to use you possess you? Shall they that cannot speak Arcadian language be lords over your shepherds? For, alas, with good cause may we look for any evil, since Basilius our only strength is taken from us.'

To that all the other shepherds present uttered pitiful voices, especially the very born Arcadians. For, as for the other, though humanity moved them to pity human cases, especially of a prince under whom they had found a refuge of their miseries and justice equally administered, yet they could not so naturally feel the lively touch of sorrow, but rather used this occasion to record their own private sorrows which they thought would not have agreed with a joyful time. Among them the principals were Strephon, Klaius, and Philisides. Strephon and Klaius would require a whole book* to recount their sorrows and the strange causes of their sorrows—another place perchance will serve for the declaring of them. But in short two gentlemen they were both in love with one maid of that country named Urania, thought a shepherd's daughter, but indeed of far greater birth. For her sake they had both taken this trade of life, each knowing other's love, but yet of so high a quality their friend-ship was that they never so much as brake company one from the other, but continued their pursuit, like two true runners both employing their best speed, but one not hindering the other. But after many marvellous adventures, Urania never yielding better than hate for their love, upon a strange occasion had left the country, giving withal strait commandment to these two by writing that they should tarry in Arcadia until they heard from her. And now some months were passed that they had no news of her; but yet rather meaning to break their hearts than break her commandment, they bare it out as well as such evil might be until now that the general complaints of all men called in like question their particular griefs, which eclogue-wise they specified in this double sestine:

Strephon   Klaius

Strephon. Ye goat-herd gods, that love the grassy mountains,
    Ye nymphs, which haunt the springs in pleasant valleys,
    Ye satyrs, joyed with free and quiet forests,
    Vouchsafe your silent ears to plaining music
    Which to my woes gives still an early morning,
    And draws the dolour on till weary evening.

Klaius. O Mercury, foregoer to the evening,
    O heav'nly huntress of the savage mountains,
    O lovely star, entitled of the morning,
    While that my voice doth fill these woeful valleys,
    Vouchsafe your silent ears to plaining music,
    Which oft hath Echo tired in secret forests.

Strephon. I that was once free burgess of the forests,
    Where shade from sun, and sport I sought in evening,
    I that was once esteemed for pleasant music,
    Am banished now among the monstrous mountains
    Of huge despair, and foul affliction's valleys,
    Am grown a screech-owl to myself each morning.

Klaius. I that was once delighted every morning,
    Hunting the wild inhabiters of forests,
    I that was once the music of these valleys,
    So darkened am that all my day is evening,
    Heart-broken so, that molehills seem high mountains,

And fill the vales with cries instead of music.

Strephon. Long since, alas, my deadly swannish music
Hath made itself a crier of the morning,
And hath with wailing strength climbed highest mountains.
Long since my thoughts more desert be than forests.
Long since I see my joys come to their evening,
And state thrown down to over-trodden valleys.

Klaius. Long since the happy dwellers of these valleys
Have prayed me leave my strange exclaiming music,
Which troubles their day's work, and joys of evening.
Long since I hate the night, more hate the morning.
Long since my thoughts chase me like beasts in forests,
And make me wish myself laid under mountains.

Strephon. Meseems I see the high and stately mountains
Transform themselves to low dejected valleys.
Meseems I hear in these ill-changed forests
The nightingales do learn of owls their music.
Meseems I feel the comfort of the morning
Turned to the mortal serene*of an evening.

Klaius. Meseems I see a filthy cloudy evening
As soon as sun begins to climb the mountains.
Meseems I feel a noisome scent the morning
When I do smell the flowers of these valleys.
Meseems I hear (when I do hear sweet music)
The dreadful cries of murdered men in forests.

Strephon. I wish to fire the trees of all these forests;
I give the sun a last farewell each evening;
I curse the fiddling finders-out of music;
With envy I do hate the lofty mountains,
And with despite despise the humble valleys;
I do detest night, evening, day, and morning.

Klaius. Curse to myself my prayer is, the morning;
My fire is more than can be made with forests;
My state more base than are the basest valleys;
I wish no evenings more to see, each evening;
Shamed, I hate myself in sight of mountains,
And stop mine ears lest I grow mad with music.

Strephon. For she, whose parts maintained a perfect music,
  Whose beauties shined more than the blushing morning,
  Who much did pass in state the stately mountains,
  In straightness passed the cedars of the forests,
  Hath cast me, wretch, into eternal evening,
  By taking her two suns from these dark valleys.

Klaius. For she, with whom compared the Alps are valleys,*
  She, whose least word brings from the spheres their music,
  At whose approach the sun rase in the evening,
  Who, where she went, bare in her forehead morning,
  Is gone, is gone from these our spoiled forests,
  Turning to deserts our best pastured mountains.

Strephon. These mountains witness shall, so shall these valleys,

Klaius. These forests eke, made wretched by our music,
  Our morning hymn this is, and song at evening.

  But, as though all this had been but the taking of a taste to their wailings, Strephon again began this dizain, which was answered unto him in that kind of verse which is called the crown:*

Strephon. I joy in grief, and do detest all joys;
  Despise delight, am tired with thought of ease.
  I turn my mind to all forms of annoys,
  And with the change of them my fancy please.
  I study that which most may me displease,
  And in despite of that displeasure's might
  Embrace that most that most my soul destroys;
  Blinded with beams, fell darkness is my sight;
  Dwell in my ruins, feed with sucking smart,
  I think from me, not from my woes, to part.

Klaius. I think from me, not from my woes, to part,
  And loathe this time called life, nay think that life
  Nature to me for torment did impart;
  Think my hard haps have blunted death's sharp knife,
  Not sparing me in whom his works be rife;
  And thinking this, think nature, life, and death
  Place sorrow's triumph on my conquered heart.
  Whereto I yield, and seek no other breath
  But from the scent of some infectious grave;

Nor of my fortune aught but mischief crave.

Strephon. Nor of my fortune aught but mischief crave,
    And seek to nourish that which now contains
    All what I am. If I myself will save,
    Then must I save what in me chiefly reigns,
    Which is the hateful web of sorrow's pains.
    Sorrow then cherish me, for I am sorrow;
    No being now but sorrow I can have;
    Then deck me as thine own; thy help I borrow,
    Since thou my riches art, and that thou hast
    Enough to make a fertile mind lie waste.

Klaius. Enough to make a fertile mind lie waste
    Is that huge storm which pours itself on me.
    Hailstones of tears, of sighs a monstrous blast,
    Thunders of cries; lightnings my wild looks be,
    The darkened heav'n my soul which naught can see;
    The flying sprites which trees by roots up tear
    Be those despairs which have my hopes quite waste.
    The difference is: all folks those storms forbear,
    But I cannot; who then myself should fly,
    So close unto myself my wracks do lie.

Strephon. So close unto myself my wracks do lie;
    Both cause, effect, beginning, and the end
    Are all in me: what help then can I try?
    My ship, myself, whose course to love doth bend,
    Sore beaten doth her mast of comfort spend;
    Her cable, reason, breaks from anchor, hope;
    Fancy, her tackling, torn away doth fly;
    Ruin, the wind, hath blown her from her scope;
    Bruised with waves of care, but broken is
    On rock, despair, the burial of my bliss.

Klaius. On rock, despair, the burial of my bliss,
    I long do plough with plough of deep desire;
    The seed fast-meaning is, no truth to miss;
    I harrow it with thoughts, which all conspire
    Favour to make my chief and only hire.
    But, woe is me, the year is gone about,

And now I fain would reap, I reap but this,
Hate fully grown, absence new sprongen out.
So that I see, although my sight impair,
Vain is their pain who labour in despair.

Strephon. Vain is their pain who labour in despair.
For so did I when with my angle, will,
I sought to catch the fish torpedo fair.*
E'en then despair did hope already kill;
Yet fancy would perforce employ his skill,
And this hath got: the catcher now is caught,
Lamed with the angle which itself did bear,
And unto death, quite drowned in dolours, brought
To death, as then disguised in her fair face.
Thus, thus alas, I had my loss in chase.

Klaius. Thus, thus alas, I had my loss in chase
When first that crowned basilisk*I knew,
Whose footsteps I with kisses oft did trace,
Till by such hap as I must ever rue
Mine eyes did light upon her shining hue,
And hers on me, astonished with that sight.
Since then my heart did lose his wonted place,
Infected so with her sweet poison's might
That, leaving me for dead, to her it went.
But ah, her flight hath my dead relics spent.

Strephon. But ah, her flight hath my dead relics spent,
Her flight from me, from me, though dead to me,
Yet living still in her, while her beams lent
Such vital spark that her mine eyes might see.
But now those living lights absented be,
Full dead before, I now to dust should fall,
But that eternal pains my soul have hent,
And keep it still within this body thrall;
That thus I must, while in this death I dwell,
In earthly fetters feel a lasting hell.

Klaius. In earthly fetters feel a lasting hell
Alas I do; from which to find release,
I would the earth, I would the heavens sell.
But vain it is to think those pains should cease,

Where life is death, and death cannot breed peace.
O fair, O only fair, from thee, alas,
These foul, most foul, disasters to me fell;
Since thou from me (O me) O sun didst pass.
Therefore esteeming all good blessings toys,
I joy in grief, and do detest all joys.

Strephon. I joy in grief, and do detest all joys.
But now an end, O Klaius, now an end,
For e'en the herbs our hateful music stroys,
And from our burning breath the trees do bend.

When they had ended, with earnest entreaty they obtained of Philisides that he would impart some part of the sorrow his countenance so well witnessed unto them. And he (who by no entreaty of the duke would be brought unto it) in this doleful time was content thus to manifest himself:

'The name of Samothea*is so famous that, telling you I am of that, I shall not need to extend myself further in telling you what that country is. But there I was born, of such parentage as neither left me so great that I was a mark for envy nor so base that I was subject to contempt, brought up from my cradle age with such care as parents are wont to bestow upon their children whom they mean to make the maintainers of their name. And as soon as my memory grew strong enough to receive what might be delivered unto it by my senses, they offered learning unto me, especially that kind that teacheth what in truth and not in opinion is to be embraced, and what to be eschewed. Neither was I barred from seeking the natural knowledge of things so far as the narrow sight of man hath pierced into it. And because the mind's commandment is vain without the body be enabled to obey it, my strength was exercised with horsemanship, weapons, and suchlike other qualities as, besides the practice, carried in themselves some serviceable use; wherein I so profited that, as I was not excellent, so I was accompanable. After that by my years, or perchance by a sooner privilege than years commonly grant, I was thought able to be mine own master, I was suffered to spend some time in travel, that by the comparison of many things I might ripen my judgement; since greatness, power, riches, and suchlike standing in relation to another, who doth know none but his own, doth not know his own. Then being home returned, and thought of good hope (for the world rarely bestows a better title upon youth), I continued to use the benefits of a quiet mind; in truth (I call him to witness that knoweth hearts) even in the secret of my soul bent to honesty—thus far you see, as no pompous spectacle, so an untroubled tenor of a well guided life. But alas, what should I make pathetical exclamations to a most true event? So it happened that love (which what it is, your own feeling can best tell you) diverted this course of tranquillity; which, though I did with so much covering hide that I was thought void of it as any man, yet my wound which smarted to myself brought me in fine to this change, much in state but more in mind. But how love first took me I did once, using the liberty of versifying, set down in a song, in a dream indeed it was; and thus did I poetically describe my dream:

Now was our heav'nly vault deprived of the light
With sun's depart; and now the darkness of the night
Did light those beamy stars which greater light did dark.
Now each thing which enjoyed that fiery quickning spark
Which life is called were moved their spirits to repose,
And wanting use of eyes, their eyes began to close.
A silence sweet each where with one concent embraced
(A music sweet to one in careful musing placed);
And mother earth, now clad in mourning weeds, did breathe
A dull desire to kiss the image of our death;
When I, disgraced wretch, not wretched then, did give
My senses such release as they which quiet live,
Whose brains boil not in woes, nor breasts with beatings ache,
With nature's praise are wont in safest home to take.
Far from my thoughts was aught whereto their minds aspire
Who under courtly pomps do hatch a base desire.
Free all my powers were from those captiving snares
Which heav'nly purest gifts defile in muddy cares.
Ne could my soul itself accuse of such a fault
As tender conscience might with furious pangs assault.
But like the feeble flow'r (whose stalk cannot sustain
His weighty top) his top doth downward drooping lean;
Or as the silly bird in well acquainted nest
Doth hide his head with cares but only how to rest,
So I in simple course, and unentangled mind,
Did suffer drowsy lids mine eyes then clear to blind;

And laying down my head, did nature's rule observe,
Which senses up doth shut the senses to preserve.
They first their use forgot, then fancies lost their force,
Till deadly sleep at length possessed my living corse.
A living corse I lay; but ah, my wakeful mind
(Which made of heav'nly stuff no mortal change doth bind)
Flew up with freer wings of fleshly bondage free;
And having placed my thoughts, my thoughts thus placed
    me:
Methought, nay sure I was, I was in fairest wood
Of Samothea land; a land which whilom stood
An honour to the world, while honour was their end,
And while their line of years they did in virtue spend.
But there I was, and there my calmy thoughts I fed
On nature's sweet repast, as healthful senses led.
Her gifts my study was, her beauties were my sport;
My work her works to know, her dwelling my resort.
Those lamps of heav'nly fire to fixed motion bound,
The ever turning spheres, the never moving ground;
What essence dest'ny hath; if fortune be or no;
Whence our immortal souls to mortal earth do flow;
What life it is, and how that all these lives do gather,
With outward maker's force, or like an inward father.
Such thoughts, methought, I thought, and strained my single
    mind
Then void of nearer cares, the depth of things to find.
When lo, with hugest noise (such noise a tower makes
When it blown up with mine a fall of ruin takes;
Or such a noise it was as highest thunders send,
Or cannons thunder-like, all shot together, lend),
The moon asunder rent (O gods, O pardon me,
That forced with grief reveals what grieved eyes did see),
The moon asunder rent; whereat with sudden fall
(More swift than falcon's stoop to feeding falconer's call)
There came a chariot fair by doves and sparrows guided,
Whose storm-like course stayed not till hard by me it bided.
I, wretch, astonished was, and thought the deathful doom
Of heav'n, of earth, of hell, of time and place was come.
But straight there issued forth two ladies (ladies sure
They seemed to me) on whom did wait a virgin pure;

Strange were the ladies' weeds, yet more unfit than strange.
The first with clothes tucked up, as nymphs in woods do range,
Tucked up e'en with the knees, with bow and arrows prest;
Her right arm naked was, discovered was her breast.
But heavy was her pace, and such a meagre cheer*
As little hunting mind (God knows) did there appear.
The other had with art (more than our women know,
As stuff meant for the sale set out to glaring show)
A wanton woman's face, and with curled knots had twined
Her hair which, by the help of painter's cunning, shined.
When I such guests did see come out of such a house,
The mountains great with child I thought brought forth a mouse.
But walking forth, the first thus to the second said:
'Venus, come on.' Said she: 'Diane, you are obeyed.'
Those names abashed me much, when those great names I heard;
Although their fame (meseemed) from truth had greatly jarred.
As I thus musing stood, Diana called to her
Her waiting nymph, a nymph that did excel as far
All things that erst I saw, as orient pearls exceed
That which their mother hight, or else their silly seed;
Indeed a perfect hue, indeed a sweet concent
Of all those graces' gifts the heav'ns have ever lent.
And so she was attired, as one that did not prize
Too much her peerless parts, nor yet could them despise.
But called, she came apace; a pace wherein did move
The band of beauties all, the little world of love.
And bending humbled eyes (O eyes, the sun of sight)
She waited mistress' will, who thus disclosed her sprite:
'Sweet Mira mine', quoth she, 'the pleasure of my mind,
In whom of all my rules the perfect proof I find,
To only thee thou seest we grant this special grace
Us to attend, in this most private time and place.
Be silent therefore now, and so be silent still
Of what thou seest; close up in secret knot thy will.'
She answered was with look, and well performed behest.
And Mira I admired; her shape sank in my breast.
But thus with ireful eyes, and face that shook with spite,
Diana did begin: 'What moved me to invite

Your presence, sister dear, first to my moony sphere,
And hither now, vouchsafe to take with willing ear.
I know full well you know what discord long hath reigned
Betwixt us two; how much that discord foul hath stained
Both our estates, while each the other did deprave,
Proof speaks too much to us that feeling trial have.
Our names are quite forgot, our temples are defaced;
Our off'rings spoiled, our priests from priesthood are displaced.
Is this thy fruit, O strife? those thousand churches high,
Those thousand altars fair now in the dust to lie?
In mortal minds our minds but planets' names preserve;
No knee once bowed, forsooth, for them they say we serve.
Are we their servants grown? no doubt a noble stay;
Celestial pow'rs to worms, Jove's children serve to clay.
But such they say we be; this praise our discord bred,
While we for mutual spite a striving passion fed.
But let us wiser be; and what foul discord brake,
So much more strong again let fastest concord make.
Our years do it require; you see we both do feel
The weak'ning work of time's for ever whirling wheel.
Although we be divine, our grandsire Saturn is
With age's force decayed, yet once the heav'n was his.
And now before we seek by wise Apollo's skill
Our young years to renew (for so he saith he will)
Let us a perfect peace betwixt us two resolve;
Which, lest the ruinous want of government dissolve,
Let one the princess be, to her the other yield;
For vain equality is but contention's field.
And let her have the gifts that should in both remain;
In her let beauty both and chasteness fully reign;
So as, if I prevail, you give your gifts to me;
If you, on you I lay what in my office be.
Now resteth only this: which of us two is she
To whom precedence shall of both accorded be.
For that (so that you like) hereby doth lie a youth
(She beckoned unto me), as yet of spotless truth,
Who may this doubt discern; for better wit than lot
Becometh us; in us fortune determines not.
This crown of amber fair*(an amber crown she held)
To worthiest let him give when both he hath beheld;

And be it as he saith.' Venus was glad to hear
Such proffer made, which she well showed with smiling
    cheer;
As though she were the same as when by Paris' doom
She had chief goddesses in beauty overcome.
And smirkly thus gan say: 'I never sought debate,
Diana dear, my mind to love and not to hate
Was ever apt; but you my pastimes did despise.
I never spited you, but thought you over wise.
Now kindness proffered is, none kinder is than I;
And so most ready am this mean of peace to try.
And let him be our judge; the lad doth please me well.'
Thus both did come to me, and both began to tell
(For both together spake, each loath to be behind)
That they by solemn oath their deities would bind
To stand unto my will; their will they made me know.
I that was first aghast, when first I saw their show,
Now bolder waxed, waxed proud that I such sway might bear;
For near acquaintance doth diminish reverent fear.
And having bound them fast by Styx they should obey
To all what I decreed, did thus my verdict say:
'How ill both you can rule, well hath your discord taught;
Ne yet, for what I see, your beauties merit aught.
To yonder nymph therefore (to Mira I did point)
The crown above you both for ever I appoint.'
I would have spoken out, but out they both did cry:
'Fie, fie, what have we done? ungodly rebel, fie!
But now we must needs yield to what our oaths require.'
'Yet thou shalt not go free,' quoth Venus, 'such a fire
Her beauty kindle shall within thy foolish mind
That thou full oft shalt wish thy judging eyes were blind.'
'Nay then,' Diana, said, 'the chasteness I will give
In ashes of despair, though burnt, shall make thee live.'
'Nay thou', said both, 'shalt see such beams shine in her face
That thou shalt never dare seek help of wretched case.'
And with that cursed curse away to heav'n they fled,
First having all their gifts upon fair Mira spread.
The rest I cannot tell, for therewithal I waked
And found with deadly fear that all my sinews shaked.
Was it a dream? O dream, how hast thou wrought in me

That I things erst unseen should first in dreaming see?
And thou, O traitor sleep, made for to be our rest,
How hast thou framed the pain wherewith I am oppressed?
O coward Cupid, thus dost thou thy honour keep,
Unarmed, alas unwarned, to take a man asleep?

In such, or suchlike, sort in a dream was offered unto me the
sight of her in whose respect all things afterwards seemed but blind
darkness unto me. For so it fell out that her I saw, I say that sweet
and incomparable Mira (so like her which in that rather vision than
dream of mine I had seen), that I began to persuade myself in my
nativity I was allotted unto her; to her, I say, whom even Coredens*
made the upshot of all his despairing desires, and so, alas, from all
other exercises of my mind bent myself only to the pursuit of her
favour. But having spent some part of my youth in following of her,
sometimes with some measure of favour, sometimes with unkind
interpretations of my most kind thoughts, in the end having
attempted all means to establish my blissful estate, and having
been not only refused all comfort but new quarrels picked against
me, I did resolve by perpetual absence to choke mine own ill
fortunes. Yet before I departed these following elegiacs I sent unto
her:

$$- \cup \cup - - - - - - - - \cup \cup - -$$

$$- - - \cup \cup - - \cup \cup - \cup \cup -$$

Unto the caitiff wretch whom long affliction holdeth,
    and now fully believes help to be quite perished,
Grant yet, grant yet a look, to the last monument of his
    anguish,
    O you (alas so I find) cause of his only ruin.
Dread not a whit (O goodly cruel) that pity may enter
    Into thy heart by the sight of this epistle I send;
And so refuse to behold of these strange wounds the recital,
    Lest it might thee allure home to thyself to return
(Unto thyself I do mean, those graces dwell so within thee,
    gratefulness, sweetness, holy love, hearty regard).
Such thing cannot I seek (despair hath giv'n me my answer,
    despair most tragical clause to a deadly request);
Such thing cannot he hope that knows thy determinate
    hardness;
    hard like a rich marble; hard, but a fair diamond.

Can those eyes, that of eyes drowned in most hearty
    flowing tears
  (tears, and tears of a man) had no return to remorse;
Can those eyes now yield to the kind conceit of a
    sorrow,
  which ink only relates, but ne laments, ne replies?
Ah, that, that do I not conceive, though that to me lief were
  more than Nestor's years, more than a king's diadem.
Ah, that, that do I not conceive; to the heaven when a
    mouse climbs
  then may I hope t'achieve grace of a heavenly tiger.
But, but alas, like a man condemned doth crave to be heard
    speak,
  not that he hopes for amends of the disaster he feels,
But finding th'approach of death with an inly relenting,
  gives an adieu to the world, as to his only delight;
Right so my boiling heart, inflamed with fire of a fair eye,
  bubbling out doth breathe signs of his hugy dolours,
Now that he finds to what end his life and love be reserved,
  and that he thence must part where to live only I lived.
O fair, O fairest, are such the triumphs to thy fairness?
  can death beauty become? must I be such a monument?
Must I be only the mark shall prove that virtue is angry?
  shall prove that fierceness can with a white dove abide?
Shall to the world appear that faith and love be rewarded
  with mortal disdain, bent to unendly revenge?
Unto revenge? O sweet, on a wretch wilt thou be revenged?
  shall such high planets tend to the loss of a worm?
And to revenge who do bend would in that kind be re-
    venged,
  as th'offence was done, and go beyond if he can.
All my 'offence was love; with love then must I be chastened,
  and with more by the laws that to revenge do belong.
If that love be a fault, more fault in you to be lovely;
  love never had me oppressed, but that I saw to be
    loved.
You be the cause that I love; what reason blameth a shadow
  that with a body't goes, since by a body it is?
If the love hate you did, you should your beauty have
    hidden;

you should those fair eyes have with a veil covered.
But fool, fool that I am, those eyes would shine from a
    dark cave;
    what veils then do prevail, but to a more miracle?
Or those golden locks (those locks which lock me to bond-
    age)
    torn you should disperse unto the blasts of a wind.
But fool, fool that I am, though I had but a hair of her head
    found,
    ee'n as I am, so I should unto that hair be a thrall.
Or with a fair hand's nails (O hand which nails me to this
    death)
    you should have your face (since love is ill) blemished.
O wretch, what do I say? should that fair face be defaced?
    should my too much sight cause so true a sun to be lost?
First let Cimmerian darkness be my onl'habitation,
    first be mine eyes pulled out, first be my brain perished,
Ere that I should consent to do such excessive a damage
    unto the earth by the hurt of this her heavenly jewel.
O not but such love you say you could have afforded,
    as might learn temp'rance void of a rage's events.
O sweet simplicity, from whence should love be so learned?
    unto Cupid that boy shall a pedant be found?
Well, but faulty I was; reason to my passion yielded,
    passion unto my rage, rage to a hasty revenge.
But what's this for a fault, for which such faith be
    abolished,
    such faith, so stainless, inviolate, violent?
Shall I not? O may I not thus yet refresh the remembrance
    what sweet joys I had once, and what a place I did hold?
Shall I not once object that you, you granted a favour
    unto the man whom now such miseries you award?
Bend your thoughts to the dear sweet words which then
        to me giv'n were;
    think what a world is now, think who hath altered her heart.
What? was I then worthy such good, now worthy so much
    evil?
    now fled, then cherished? then so nigh, now so remote?
Did not a rosed breath, from lips more rosy proceeding,
    say that I well should find in what a care I was had?

With much more: now what do I find but care to abhor me,
    care that I sink in grief, care that I live banished?
And banished do I live, nor now will seek a recov'ry,
    since so she will, whose will is to me more than a law.
If then a man in most ill case may give you a farewell;
    farewell, long farewell, all my woe, all my delight.

Philisides would have gone on in telling the rest of his unhappy
adventures, and by what desperate works of fortune he was become
a shepherd; but the shepherd Dicus desired him he would for that
time leave particular passions, and join in bewailing this general
loss of that country which had been a nurse to strangers as well as a
mother to Arcadians. And so, having purchased silence, Agelastus*
rather cried out than sang this following lamentation:

Since that to death is gone the shepherd high
    Who most the silly shepherd's pipe did prize,
    Your doleful tunes sweet muses now apply.
And you, O trees (if any life there lies
    In trees) now through your porous barks receive
    The strange resound of these my causeful cries;
And let my breath upon your branches cleave,
    My breath distinguished into words of woe,
    That so I may signs of my sorrows leave.
But if among yourselves some one tree grow
    That aptest is to figure misery,
    Let it ambassade bear your griefs to show.
The weeping myrrh I think will not deny
    Her help to this, this justest cause of plaint.
    Your doleful tunes sweet muses now apply.

And thou, poor earth, whom fortune doth attaint
    In nature's name to suffer such a harm
    As for to lose thy gem, our earthly saint,
Upon thy face let coaly ravens swarm;
    Let all the sea thy tears accounted be;
    Thy bowels with all killing metals arm.
Let gold now rust, let diamonds waste in thee;
    Let pearls be wan with woe their dam doth bear;
    Thyself henceforth the light do never see.
And you, O flow'rs, which sometimes princes were,

Till these strange alt'rings you did hap to try,
Of prince's loss yourselves for tokens rear.
Lily in mourning black thy whiteness dye.
    O hyacinth let ai*be on thee still.
    Your doleful tunes sweet muses now apply.

O echo, all these woods with roaring fill,
    And do not only mark the accents last
    But all, for all reach not my wailful will;
One echo to another echo cast
    Sound of my griefs, and let it never end
    Till that it hath all woods and waters passed.

Nay, to the heav'ns your just complainings send,
    And stay the stars' inconstant constant race
    Till that they do unto our dolours bend;
And ask the reason of that special grace
    That they, which have no lives, should live so long,
    And virtuous souls so soon should lose their place?
Ask if in great men good men so do throng
    That he for want of elbow-room must die?
    Or if that they be scant, if this be wrong?
Did wisdom this our wretched time espy
    In one true chest to rob all virtue's treasure?
    Your doleful tunes sweet muses now apply.

And if that any counsel you to measure
    Your doleful tunes, to them still plaining say
    To well felt grief, plaint is the only pleasure.
O light of sun, which is entitled day,
    O well thou dost that thou no longer bidest;
    For mourning night her black weeds may display.
O Phoebus with good cause thy face thou hidest
    Rather than have thy all-beholding eye
    Fouled with this sight while thou thy chariot guidest.
And well (methinks) becomes this vaulty sky
    A stately tomb to cover him deceased.
    Your doleful tunes sweet muses now apply.

O Philomela*with thy breast oppressed
    By shame and grief, help, help me to lament

Such cursed harms as cannot be redressed.
Or if thy mourning notes be fully spent,
   Then give a quiet ear unto my plaining;
   For I to teach the world complaint am bent.
Ye dimmy clouds, which well employ your staining
   This cheerful air with your obscured cheer,
   Witness your woeful tears with daily raining.

And if, O sun, thou ever didst appear
   In shape which by man's eye might be perceived,
   Virtue is dead, now set thy triumph here.
Now set thy triumph in this world, bereaved
   Of what was good, where now no good doth lie;
   And by thy pomp our loss will be conceived.
O notes of mine, yourselves together tie;
   With too much grief methinks you are dissolved.
   Your doleful tunes sweet muses now apply.

Time ever old and young is still revolved
   Within itself, and never taketh end;
   But mankind is for ay to naught resolved.
The filthy snake her aged coat can mend,
   And getting youth again, in youth doth flourish;
   But unto man, age ever death doth send.
The very trees with grafting we can cherish,
   So that we can long time produce their time;
   But man which helpeth them, helpless must perish.
Thus, thus, the minds which over all do climb,
   When they by years' experience get best graces,
   Must finish then by death's detested crime.
We last short while, and build long-lasting places.
   Ah, let us all against foul nature cry;
   We nature's works do help, she us defaces.
For how can nature unto this reply:
   That she her child, I say, her best child killeth?
   Your doleful tunes sweet muses now apply.

Alas, methinks my weakened voice but spilleth
   The vehement course of this just lamentation;
   Methinks my sound no place with sorrow filleth.
I know not I, but once in detestation
   I have myself, and all what life containeth,

Since death on virtue's fort hath made invasion.
One word of woe another after traineth;
  Ne do I care how rude be my invention,
  So it be seen what sorrow in me reigneth.
O elements, by whose (they say) contention*
  Our bodies be in living pow'r maintained,
  Was this man's death the fruit of your dissension?
O physic's power, which (some say) hath refrained
  Approach of death, alas thou helpest meagrely
  When once one is for Atropos*distrained.
Great be physicians' brags, but aid is beggarly;
  When rooted moisture fails, or groweth dry,
  They leave off all, and say death comes too eagerly.
They are but words therefore which men do buy
  Of any since god Aesculapius*ceased.
  Your doleful tunes sweet muses now apply.

Justice, justice is now, alas, oppressed;
  Bountifulness hath made his last conclusion;
  Goodness for best attire in dust is dressed.
Shepherds bewail your uttermost confusion;
  And see by this picture to you presented,
  Death is our home, life is but a delusion.
For see, alas, who is from you absented.
  Absented? nay, I say for ever banished
  From such as were to die for him contented.
Out of our sight in turn of hand*is vanished
  Shepherd of shepherds, whose well settled order
  Private with wealth, public with quiet, garnished.
While he did live, far, far was all disorder;
  Example more prevailing than direction,
  Far was home-strife, and far was foe from border.
His life a law, his look a full correction;
  As in his health we healthful were preserved,
  So in his sickness grew our sure infection;
His death our death. But ah, my muse hath swarved
  From such deep plaint as should such woes descry,
  Which he of us for ever hath deserved.
The style of heavy heart can never fly
  So high as should make such a pain notorious.

Cease muse, therefore; thy dart, O death, apply;
And farewell prince, whom goodness hath made glorious.

Agelastus, when he had ended his song, thus maintained the lamentation in this rhyming sestine, having the doleful tune of the other shepherds' pipes joined unto him:

Farewell O sun, Arcadia's clearest light;
Farewell O pearl, the poor man's plenteous treasure;
Farewell O golden staff, the weak man's might;
Farewell O joy, the woeful's only pleasure.
Wisdom farewell, the skill-less man's direction;
Farewell with thee, farewell all our affection.

For what place now is left for our affection,
Now that of purest lamp is queint the light
Which to our darkened minds was best direction;
Now that the mine is lost of all our treasure,
Now death hath swallowed up our worldly pleasure,
We orphans left, void of all public might?

Orphans indeed, deprived of father's might;
For he our father was in all affection,
In our well doing placing all his pleasure,
Still studying how to us to be a light.
As well he was in peace a safest treasure;
In war his wit and word was our direction.

Whence, whence alas, shall we seek our direction
When that we fear our hateful neighbours' might,
Who long have gaped to get Arcadians' treasure?
Shall we now find a guide of such affection,
Who for our sakes will think all travail light,
And make his pain to keep us safe his pleasure?

No, no, for ever gone is all our pleasure;
For ever wand'ring from all good direction;
For ever blinded of our clearest light;
For ever lamed of our surest might;
For ever banished from well placed affection;
For ever robbed of our royal treasure.

Let tears for him therefore be all our treasure,
And in our wailful naming him our pleasure.
Let hating of ourselves be our affection,
And unto death bend still our thoughts' direction.
Let us against ourselves employ our might,
And putting out our eyes seek we our light.

Farewell our light, farewell our spoiled treasure;
Farewell our might, farewell our daunted pleasure;
Farewell direction, farewell all affection.

The night began to cast her dark canopy over them; and they, even wearied with their woes, bended homewards, hoping by a sleep, forgetting themselves, to ease their present dolours, when they were met with a troop of twenty horsemen. The chief of which asking them for the duke, and understanding the hard news, did thereupon stay among them, and send away with speed to Philanax. But since the night is an ease of all things, it shall at this present ease my memory, tired with these troublesome matters.

Here end the fourth eclogues.

THE LAST BOOK OR ACT

THE dangerous division of men's minds, the ruinous renting of all estates, had now brought Arcadia to feel the pangs of uttermost peril (such convulsions never coming but that the life of that government draws near his necessary period), when to the honest and wise Philanax, equally distracted betwixt desire of his master's revenge and care of the state's establishment, there came (unlooked-for) a Macedonian gentleman who in short but pithy manner delivered unto him that the renowned Euarchus, king of Macedon, having made a long and tedious journey to visit his old friend and confederate the duke Basilius, was now come within half a mile of the lodges, where having understood by certain shepherds the sudden death of their prince, had sent unto him (of whose authority and faith he had good knowledge) desiring him to advertise him in what security he might rest there for that night; where willingly he would (if safely he might) help to celebrate the funerals of his ancient companion and ally; adding he need not doubt, since he had brought but twenty in his company, he would be so unwise as to enter into any forcible attempt with so small force.

Philanax (having entertained the gentleman as well as in the midst of so many tumults he could), pausing a while with himself, considering how it should not only be unjust and against the law of nations not well to receive a prince whom goodwill had brought among them, but in respect of the greatness of his might very dangerous to give him any cause of due offence, remembering withal the excellent trials of his equity which made him more famous than his victories, he thought he might be the fittest instrument to redress the ruins they were in, since his goodness put him without suspicion and his greatness beyond envy. Yet weighing how hard many heads were to be bridled, and that in this monstrous confusion such mischief might be attempted of which late repentance should after be but a simple remedy, he judged best first to know how the people's minds would sway to this determination. Therefore, desiring the gentleman to return to the king his master and to beseech him (though with his pains) to stay for an hour or two where he was till he had set things in better order to receive him, he himself went first to the noblemen, then to Kerxenus and the principal Mantineans who were most opposite unto him, desiring them that, as the night had most blessedly stayed them from entering into civil blood, so they would be content in the night to assemble the people together to hear some news which he was to deliver unto them. There is nothing more desirous of novelties than a man that fears his present fortune. Therefore they, whom mutual diffidence made doubtful of their utter destruction, were quickly persuaded to hear of any new matter which might alter at least, if not help, the nature of their fear; namely the chiefest men who, as they had most to lose so were most jealous of their own case, and were already grown as weary to be followers of Timautus's ambition as before they were enviers of Philanax's worthiness. As for Kerxenus and Sympathus, as in the one a virtuous friendship had made him seek to advance, in the other a natural commiseration had made him willing to protect, the two excellent (though unfortunate) prisoners, so were they not against this convocation; for having nothing but just desires in them, they did not mistrust the justifying of them. Only Timautus laboured to have withdrawn them from this assembly, saying it was time to stop their ears from the ambitious charms of Philanax:

'Let them first deliver Gynecia and her daughters,' said he, 'which were fit persons to hear, and then they might begin to speak; that this was but Philanax's cunning, to link broil upon broil, because he might avoid the answering of his trespasses which, as he had long intended so had he prepared coloured speeches to disguise them.'

But as his words expressed rather a violence of rancour than any just ground of accusation so pierced they no further than to some partial ears; the multitude yielding good attention to what Philanax would propose unto them, who (like a man whose best building was a well framed conscience), neither with plausible words nor fawning countenance, but even with the grave behaviour of a wise father whom nothing but love makes to chide, he thus said unto them:

'I have', said he, 'a great matter to deliver unto you, and thereout am I to make a greater demand of you. But truly, such hath this late proceeding been of yours that I know not what is not to be demanded of you. Methinks I may have reason to require of you, as men are wont among pirates, that the life at least of him that never hurt you may be safe. Methinks I am not without appearance of cause, as if you were cyclops or cannibals, to desire that our prince's body (which hath thirty years maintained us in a flourishing peace) be not torn in pieces or devoured among you, but may be suffered to yield itself (which never was defiled with any of your bloods) to the natural rest of the earth. Methinks not as to Arcadians, renowned for your faith to prince and love of country, but as to sworn enemies of this sweet soil, I am to desire you that at least, if you will have strangers to your princes, yet you will not deliver the seigniory of this goodly dukedom to your noble duke's murderers. Lastly I have reason, as if I had to speak to madmen, to desire you to be good to yourselves; for, before God, what either barbarous violence or unnatural folly hath not this day had his seat in your minds, and left his footsteps in your actions? But in truth I love you too well to stand long displaying your faults; I would you yourselves did forget them, so you did not fall again into them. For my part I had much rather be an orator of your praises. But now, if you will suffer attentive judgement and not fore-judging passion to be the weigher of my words, I will deliver unto you what a blessed mean the heavens have sent unto you, if you list to embrace it. I think there is none among you so young either in years or understanding but hath heard the true fame of that just prince, Euarchus, king of Macedon—a prince with whom our late master did ever hold most perfect alliance. He, even he, is this day come, having but twenty horse with him, within two miles of this place, hoping to have found the virtuous Basilius alive, but now willing to do honour to his death. Surely, surely, the heavenly powers have in so full a time bestowed him on us to unite our disunions. For my part, therefore, I wish that, since among ourselves we cannot agree in so manifold partialities, we do put the ordering of all these things into his hands, as well touching the obsequies of the duke, the punishment of his death, as the marriage and crowning of our princess. He is, both by experience and wisdom, taught how to direct his greatness such as no man can disdain to obey him, his equity such as no man need to fear him; lastly, as he hath all these qualities to help so hath he (though he would) no force to hurt. If, therefore, you so think good, since our laws bear that our prince's murder be chastised before his murdered body be buried, we may invite him to sit tomorrow in the judgement seat; after which done, you may proceed to the burial.'

When Philanax first named Euarchus's landing there was a muttering murmur among the people, as though in that ill-ordered weakness of theirs he had come to conquer their country. But when they understood he had so small a retinue, whispering one with another and looking who should begin to confirm Philanax's proposition, at length Sympathus was the first that allowed it, then the rest of the noblemen; neither did Kerxenus strive, hoping so excellent a prince could not but deal graciously with two such young men; whose authority, joined to Philanax, all the popular sort followed. Timautus, still blinded with his own ambitious haste, not remembering factions are no longer to be trusted than the factious may be persuaded it is for their own good, would needs strive against the stream, exclaiming against Philanax that now he showed who it was that would betray his country to strangers. But well he found that who is too busy in the foundation of a house may pull the building about his ears; for the people, already tired with their own divisions (of which his clampering had been a principal nurse), and beginning now to espy a haven of rest, hated anything that should hinder them from it. And so asked one another whether this were not he whose evil tongue no man could escape; whether it were not Timautus that made the first mutinous oration to strengthen the troubles; whether Timautus, without their consent, had not gone about to deliver Gynecia. And thus inflaming one another against him, they threw him out of the assembly, and after pursued him with stones and staves; so that, with loss of one of his eyes, sore wounded and beaten, he was fain to fly to Philanax's feet for the succour of his life—giving a true lesson that vice itself is forced to seek the sanctuary of virtue. For Philanax, who hated his evil but not his person, and knew that a just punishment might by the manner be unjustly done, remembering withal that, although herein the people's rage might have hit right enough, yet if it were nourished in this, no man knew to what extremities it might extend itself, with earnest dealing and employing the uttermost of his authority, he did protect the trembling Timautus. And then having taken a general oath that they should, in the nonage of the princess, or till these things were settled, yield full obedience to Euarchus, so far as were not prejudicial to the laws, customs, and liberties of Arcadia; and having taken a particular oath of Sympathus that the prisoners should be kept close, without conference to any man, he himself, honourably accompanied with a great number of torches, went to the king Euarchus, whom he found taking his rest under a tree with no more affected pomps than as a man that knew, howsoever he was exalted, the beginning and end of his body was earth.

But first it were fit to be known what cause moved this puissant prince to come in this sort to Arcadia. Euarchus did not further exceed his meanest subject with the greatness of his fortune than he did surmount the greatness of his fortune with the greatness of his mind; in so much that those things which oftentimes the best sort think rewards of virtue, he held them not at so high price, but esteemed them servants to well doing, the reward of virtue being in itself; on which his inward love was so fixed that it never was dissolved into other desires, but keeping his thoughts true to themselves, was neither beguiled with the painted gloss of pleasure nor dazzled with the false light of ambition. This made the line of his actions straight and always like itself, no worldly thing being able to shake the constancy of it; which, among many other times, yielded some proof of itself when Basilius, the mightiest prince of Greece next to Euarchus, did so suddenly without the advice or allowance of his subjects, without either good show of reasonable cause, or good provision for likely accidents, in the sight of the world put himself from the world, as a man that not only unarmed himself but would make his nakedness manifest. This measured by the minds of most princes, even those whom great acts have entitled with the holy name of virtue, would have been thought a sufficient cause (where such opportunity did offer so great a prey into their hands) to have sought the enlarging of their dominions, wherein they falsely put the more or less felicity of an estate. But Euarchus, that had conceived what is evil in itself no respect can make good, and never forgat his office was to maintain the Macedonians in the exercise of goodness and happy enjoying their natural lives, never used war (which is maintained with the cost and blood of the subject) but when it was to defend their right whereon their well being depended. For this reckoning he made: how far soever he extended himself, neighbours he must have; and therefore, as he kept in peace time a continual discipline of war, and at no time would suffer injury, so he did rather stand upon a just moderation of keeping his own in good and happy case than, multiplying desire upon desire, seeking one enemy after another, put both his honour and people's safety in the continual dice of fortune. So that, having this advantage of Basilius's country laid open unto him, instead of laying an unjust gripe upon it (which yet might have been beautified with the noble name of conquest), he straight considered the universal case of Greece deprived by this means of a principal pillar. He weighed and pitied the pitiful case of the Arcadian people, who were in worse case than if death had taken away their prince. For so yet their necessity would have placed someone to the helm; now a prince being, and not doing like a prince, keeping and not exercising the place, they were in so much more evil case as they could not provide for their evil. He saw the Asiatics of the one side, the Latins of the other, gaping for any occasion to devour Greece, which was no way to be prevented but by their united strength, and strength most to be maintained by maintaining their principal instruments. These rightly wise and temperate considerations moved Euarchus to take this laboursome journey, to see whether by his authority he might withdraw Basilius from this burying himself alive, and to return again to employ his old years in doing good, the only happy action of man's life. Neither was he without a consideration in himself to provide the marriage* of Basilius's two daughters for his son and nephew against their return, the tedious expectation of which, joined with the fear of their miscarrying (having been long without hearing any news from them), made him the willinger to ease that part of melancholy with changing the objects of his wearied senses and visiting his old and well approved acquaintance. So, having left his country for the short time of his absence in very perfect state, and having thoroughly settled his late conquests, taking with him a good number of galleys to waft him in safety to the Arcadian shore, he sailed with a prosperous wind to a port not far from Mantinea; where landing no more with him but the small company you have heard of, and going towards the desert, he understood to his great grief the news of the prince's death, and waited in that sort for his safe conduct, till Philanax came; who, as soon as he was in sight of him, lighting from his horse, presented himself unto him in all those humble behaviours which not only the great reverence of the party but the conceit of one's own misery is wont to frame. Euarchus rase up unto him with so gracious a countenance as the goodness of his mind had long exercised him unto, careful so much more to descend in all courtesies as he saw him bear a low representation of his afflicted state. But to Philanax, as soon as by near looking on him he might perfectly behold him, the gravity of his countenance and years not much unlike to his late deceased but ever beloved master, brought his form so lively into his memory, and revived so all the thoughts of his wonted joys with him, that instead of speaking to Euarchus, he stood a while like a man gone a far journey from himself, calling as it were with his mind an account of his losses, imagining that his pain needed not if nature had not been violently stopped of her own course, and casting more loving than wise conceits what a world this would have been if this sudden accident had not interrupted it. And so far strayed he into this raving melancholy that his eyes, nimbler than his tongue, let fall a flood of tears, his voice being stopped with extremity of sobbing—so much had his friendship carried him to Basilius that he thought no age was timely for his death. But at length, taking the occasion of his own weeping, he thus did speak to Euarchus:

'Let not my tears, most worthily renowned prince, make my presence unpleasant or my speech unmarked of you; for the justness of the cause takes away any blame of weakness in me, and the affinity that the same beareth to your greatness seems even lawfully to claim pity in you: a prince, of a prince's fall; a lover of justice, of a most unjust violence. And give me leave, excellent Euarchus, to say it: I am but the representer of all the late flourishing Arcadia, which now with my eyes doth weep, with my tongue doth complain, with my knees doth lay itself at your feet which never have been unready to carry you to the virtuous protecting of innocents. Imagine, vouchsafe to imagine, most wise and good king, that here is before your eyes the pitiful spectacle of a most dolorously ending tragedy, wherein I do but play the part of all this now miserable province which, being spoiled of her guide, doth lie like a ship without a pilot, tumbling up and down in the uncertain waves, till it either run itself upon the rock of self-division or be overthrown by the stormy wind of foreign force. Arcadia, finding herself in these desolate terms, doth speak, and I speak for her, to thee not vainly, puissant prince, that since now she is not only robbed of the natural support of her lord but so suddenly robbed that she hath not breathing time to stand for her safety; so unfortunately that it doth appal their minds, though they had leisure; and so mischievously that it doth exceed both the suddenness and infortunateness of it. Thou wilt lend thine arms unto her, and as a man take compassion of mankind, as a virtuous man chastise most abominable vice, and as a prince protect a people which all have with one voice called for thy goodness, thinking that, as thou art only able, so thou art fully able, to redress their imminent ruins. They do, therefore, with as much confidence as necessity, fly unto you for succour. They lay themselves open to you—to you, I mean yourself, such as you have ever been;

that is to say, one that hath always had his determinations bounded with equity. They only reserve the right to Basilius's blood, the manner to the ancient prescribing of their laws; for the rest, without exception, they yield over unto you as to the elected protector of this dukedom, which name and office they beseech you, till you have laid a sufficient foundation of tranquillity, to take upon you. The particularities, both of their statutes and demands, you shall presently after understand. Now only I am to say unto you that this country falls to be a fair field to prove whether the goodly tree of your virtue will live in all soils. Here, I say, will be seen whether either fear can make you short or the lickerousness of dominion make you beyond justice. And I can for conclusion say no more but this: you must think, upon my words and your answer depend not only the quiet but the lives of so many thousand, which for their ancient confederacy in this their extreme necessity desire neither the expense of your treasure nor hazard of your subjects but only the benefit of your wisdom, whose both glory and increase stands in the exercising of it.'

The sum of this request was utterly unlooked-for of Euarchus, which made him the more diligent in marking his speech, and after his speech take the greater pause for a perfect resolution. For, as of the one side he thought nature required nothing more of him than that he should be a help to them of like creation, and had his heart no whit commanded with fear, thinking his life well passed, having satisfied the tyranny of time with the course of many years, the expectation of the world with more than expected honour, lastly the tribute due to his own mind with the daily offering of most virtuous actions, so of the other he weighed the just reproach that followed those who easily enter into other folk's business with the opinion might be conceived love of seigniory rather than of justice had made him embark himself thus into a matter nothing appertaining unto him. But in the end, wisdom being an essential and not an opinionate thing, made him rather bend to what was in itself good than what by evil minds might be judged not good. And therein did see that, though that people did not belong unto him, yet doing good (which is enclosed within no terms of people or place) did belong unto him. To this, the secret assurance of his own worthiness (which, although it be never so well clothed in modesty, yet always lives in the worthiest minds) did much push him forward, saying unto himself: the treasure of those inward gifts he had were bestowed by the gods upon him to be beneficial and not idle. On which determination resting, and yet willing before he waded any further to examine well the depth of the other's proffer, he thus, with that well appeased gesture unpassionate nature bestoweth upon mankind, made answer to Philanax's most urgent petition:

'Although long experience hath made me know all men (and so princes, which be but men) to be subject to infinite casualties, the very constitution of our lives remaining in continual change, yet the affairs of this country, or at least my meeting so jumply with them, makes me even abashed with the strangeness of it. With much pain I am come hither to see my long-approved friend, and now I find if I will see him, I must see him dead; after for mine own security I seek to be warranted mine own life. And here am I suddenly appointed to be a judge of other men's lives. Though a friend to him, yet am I a stranger to the country; and now of a stranger you would suddenly make a director. I might object to your desire my weakness, which age perhaps hath wrought both in mind and body, and justly I may pretend the necessity of mine own country, to which, as I am by all true rules more nearly tied so can it not long bear the delay of my absence. But though I would and could dispense with these difficulties, what assurance can I have of the people's will, which having so many circles of imaginations can hardly be enclosed in one point? Who knows a people that knows not a sudden opinion makes them hope, which hope, if it be not answered, they fall to hate, choosing and refusing, erecting and overthrowing, according as the presentness of any fancy carries them? Even this their hasty drawing to me makes me think they may be as hastily withdrawn from me; for it is but one ground of inconstancy soon to take or soon to leave. It may be they have heard of Euarchus more than cause; their own eyes will be perhaps more curious judges. Out of hearsay they may have builded many conceits which I cannot, perchance will not, perform. Then will undeserved repentance be a greater shame and injury unto me than their undeserved proffer is honour. And to conclude, I must be fully informed how the patient is minded before I can promise to undertake the cure.'

Philanax was not of the modern minds who make suitors magistrates, but did ever think the unwilling worthy man was fitter than the undeserving desirer. Therefore the more Euarchus drew back, the more he found in him that the cunningest pilot doth most dread the rocks, the more earnestly he pursued his public request unto him. He desired him not to make any weak excuses of his weakness, since so many examples had well proved his mind was strong to overpass the greatest troubles, and his body strong enough to obey his mind; and that, so long as they were joined together, he knew Euarchus would think it no wearisome exercise to make them vessels of virtuous actions. The duty to his country he acknowledged, which as he had so settled as it was not to fear any sudden alteration so, since it did want him, as well it might endure a fruitful as an idle absence. As for the doubt he conceived of the people's constancy in this their election, he said it was such a doubt as all human actions are subject unto; yet as much as in politic matters (which receive not geometrical certainties) a man may assure himself, there was evident likelihood to be conceived of the continuance both in their unanimity and his worthiness, whereof the one was apt to be held and the other to hold, joined to the present necessity, the firmest band of mortal minds. In sum, he alleged so many reasons to Euarchus's mind (already inclined to enter into any virtuous action) that he yielded to take upon himself the judgement of the present cause, so as he might find indeed that such was the people's desire out of judgement and not faction. Therefore, mounting on their horses, they hasted to the lodges, where they found, though late in the night, the people wakefully watching for the issue of Philanax's ambassade, no man thinking the matter would be well done without he had his voice in it, and each deeming his own eyes the best guardians of his throat in that unaccustomed tumult. But when they saw Philanax return, having on his right hand the king Euarchus, on whom now they had placed the greatest burden of their fears, with joyful shouts and applauding acclamations, they made him and the world quickly know that one man's sufficiency is more available than ten thousand's multitude—so ill balanced be the extremities of popular minds, and so much natural imperiousness there rests in a well formed spirit. For, as if Euarchus had been born of the princely blood of Arcadia, or that long and well acquainted proof had engrafted him in their community, so flocked they about this stranger, most of them already from dejected fears rising to ambitious considerations who should catch the first hold of his favour; and then from those crying welcomes to babbling one with another, some praising Philanax for his well succeeding pains, others liking Euarchus's aspect, and as they judged his age by his face, so judging his wisdom by his age. Euarchus passed through them like a man that did neither disdain a people nor yet was anything tickled with their flatteries, but always holding his own, a man might read a constant determination in his eyes. And in that sort dismounting among them, he forthwith demanded the convocation to be made, which accordingly was done with as much order and silence as it might appear Neptune had not more force to appease the rebellious wind than the admiration of an extraordinary virtue hath to temper a disordered multitude. He, being raised up upon a place more high than the rest where he might be best understood, in this sort spake unto them:

'I understand,' said he, 'faithful Arcadians, by my lord Philanax that you have with one consent chosen me to be the judge of the late evils happened, orderer of the present disorders, and finally protector of this country till therein it be seen what the customs of Arcadia require.'

He could say no further, being stopped with a general cry that so it was, giving him all the honourable titles and happy wishes they could imagine. He beckoned unto them for silence, and then thus again proceeded:

'Well,' said he, 'how good choice you have made, the attending must be in you, the proof in me. But because it many times falls out we are much deceived in others, we being the first to deceive ourselves, I am to require you not to have an overshooting expectation of me—the most cruel adversary of all honourable doings—nor promise yourselves wonders out of a sudden liking. But remember I am a man; that is to say, a creature whose reason is often darkened with error. Secondly, that you will lay your hearts void of foretaken opinions, else whatsoever I do or say will be measured by a wrong rule, like them that have the yellow jaundice, everything seeming yellow unto them. Thirdly, whatsoever debates have risen among you may be utterly extinguished, knowing that even among the best men are diversities of opinions, which are no more in true reason to breed hatred than one that loves black should be angry with him that is clothed in white; for thoughts and conceits are the very apparel of the mind. Lastly, that you do not easily judge of your judge; but since you will have me to command, think it is your part to obey. And in reward of this, I will promise and protest unto you that to the uttermost of my skill, both in the general laws of nature, especially of Greece, and particularly of Arcadia (wherein I must confess I am not unacquainted), I will not only see the past evils duly punished, and your weal hereafter established, but for your defence in it, if need shall require, I will employ the forces and treasures of mine own country. In the mean time, this shall be the first order I will take: that no man, under pain of grievous punishment name me by any other name but protector of Arcadia; for I will not leave any possible colour to any of my natural successors to make claim to this, which by free election you have bestowed upon me. And so I vow unto you to depose myself of it as soon as the judgement is passed, the duke buried, and his lawful successor appointed. For the first whereof (I mean the trying which be guilty of the duke's death and these other heinous trespasses), because your customs require such haste, I will no longer delay it than till tomorrow, as soon as the sun shall give us fit opportunity. You may, therefore, retire yourselves to your rest, that you may be the readier to be present at these so great important matters.'

With many allowing tokens was Euarchus's speech heard; who now by Philanax (that took the principal care of doing all due services unto him) was offered a lodging made ready for him (the rest of the people, as well as the small commodity of that place would suffer, yielding their weary heads to sleep), when, lo, the night, thoroughly spent in these mixed matters, was for that time banished the face of the earth. And Euarchus, seeing the day begin to disclose his comfortable beauties, desiring nothing more than to join speed with justice, willed Philanax presently to make the judgement-place be put in order; and as soon as the people (who yet were not fully dispersed) might be brought together, to bring forth the prisoners and the duke's body, which the manner was should in such cases be held in sight, though covered with black velvet, until they that were accused to be the murderers were quitted or condemned—whether the reason of the law were to show the more grateful love to their prince, or by that spectacle the more to remember the judge of his duty. Philanax (who now thought in himself he approached to the just revenge he so much desired) went with all care and diligence to perform his charge.

But first it shall be well to know how the poor and princely prisoners passed this tedious night. There was never tyrant exercised his rage with more grievous torments upon any he most hated than the afflicted Gynecia did crucify her own soul, after the guiltiness of her heart was surcharged with the suddenness of her husband's death; for although that effect came not from her mind, yet her mind being evil, and the effect evil, she thought the justice of God had for the beginning of her pains coupled them together. This incessantly boiled in her breast, but most of all when, Philanax having closely imprisoned her, she was left more freely to suffer the firebrands of her own thoughts; especially when it grew dark and had nothing left by her but a little lamp, whose small light to a perplexed mind might rather yield fearful shadows than any assured sight. Then began the heaps of her miseries to weigh down the platform of her judgement; then began despair to lay his ugly claws upon her. She began to fear the heavenly powers she was wont to reverence, not like a child but like an enemy. Neither kept she herself from blasphemous repining against her creation. 'O gods,' would she cry out, 'why did you make me to destruction? If you love goodness, why did you not give me a good mind? Or if I cannot have it without your gift, why do you plague me? Is it in me to resist the mightiness of your power?' Then would she imagine she saw strange sights, and that she heard the cries of hellish ghosts. Then would she screech out for succour; but no man coming unto her, she would fain have killed herself, but knew not how. At some times again the very heaviness of her imaginations would close up her senses to a little sleep; but then did her dreams become her tormentors. One time it would seem unto her Philanax was haling her by the hair of the head, and having put out her eyes, was ready to throw her into a burning furnace. Another time she would think she saw her husband making the complaint of his death to Pluto, and the magistrates of that infernal region contending in great debate to what eternal punishment they should allot her. But long her dreaming would not hold but that it would fall upon Cleophila, to whom she would think she was crying for mercy, and that he did pass away by her in silence without any show of pitying her mischief. Then waking out of a broken sleep, and yet wishing she might ever have slept, new forms (but of the same miseries) would seize her mind. She feared death, and yet desired death. She had passed the uttermost of shame, and yet shame was one of her cruellest assaulters. She hated Pyrocles as the original of her mortal overthrow, and yet the love she had conceived to him had still a high authority in her passions. 'O Cleophila,' would she say (not knowing how near he himself was to as great a danger), 'now shalt thou glut thy eyes with the dishonoured death of thy enemy—enemy (alas, enemy), since so thou hast well showed thou wilt have me account thee. Couldst thou not as well have given me a determinate denial, as to disguise thy first disguising with a double dissembling? Perchance if I had been utterly hopeless, the virtue was once in me might have called together his forces, and not have been led captive to this monstrous thraldom of punished wickedness.' Then would her own knowing of good inflame anew the rage of despair, which becoming an unresisted lord in her breast, she had no other comfort but in death, which yet she had in horror when she thought of. But the wearisome detesting of herself made her long for the day's approach, at which time she determined to continue her former course in acknowledging anything which might hasten her end; wherein, although she did not hope for the end of her torments (feeling already the beginning of hell-agonies), yet (according to the nature of pain, the present being most intolerable) she desired to change that, and put to adventure the ensuing. And thus rested the restless Gynecia.

No less sorrowful, though less rageful, were the minds of the princess Pamela and the lady Philoclea, whose only advantages were that they had not consented to so much evil, and so were at greater peace with themselves; and that they were not left alone, but might mutually bear part of each other's woes. For when Philanax, not regarding Pamela's princely protestations, had by force left her under guard with her sister, and that the two sisters were matched as well in the disgraces of fortune as they had been in the best beauties of nature, those things that till then bashfulness and mistrust had made them hold reserved one from the other, now fear (the underminer of all determinations) and necessity (the victorious rebel of all laws) forced them interchangeably to lay open; their passions, then so swelling in them as they would have made auditors of stones rather than have swallowed up in silence the choking adventures were fallen unto them. Truly, the hardest hearts which have at any time thought woman's tears to be a matter of slight compassion (imagining that fair weather will quickly after follow), would now have been mollified, and been compelled to confess that, the fairer a diamond is, the more pity it is it should receive a blemish; although no doubt their faces did rather beautify sorrow than sorrow could darken that which even in darkness did shine. But after they had, so long as their other afflictions would suffer them, with doleful ceremonies bemoaned their father's death, they sat down together, apparelled as their misadventures had found them—Pamela in her journeying weeds, now converted to another use; Philoclea only in her nightgown, which she thought should be the raiment both of her marriage and funerals. But when the excellent creatures had, after much panting with their inward travail, gotten so much breathing power as to make a pitiful discourse one to the other what had befallen them, and that, by the plain comparing the case they were in, they thoroughly found that their griefs were not more like in regard of themselves than like in respect of the subject (the two princes, as Pamela had learned of Musidorus, being so minded as they would ever make both their fortunes one), it did more unite, and so strengthen, their lamentation, seeing the one could not any way be helped by the other, but rather the one could not be miserable but that it must necessarily make the other miserable also. That, therefore, was the first matter their sweet mouths delivered, the declaring the passionate beginning, troublesome proceeding, and dangerous ending, their never ending loves had passed; and when at any time they entered into the praises of the young princes, too long it would have exercised their tongues but that their memory forthwith warned them the more praiseworthy they were, the more at that time they were worthy of lamentation. Then again to crying and wringing of hands, and then anew as unquiet grief sought each corner to new discourses; from discourses to wishes; from wishes to prayers— especially the tender Philoclea who, as she was in years younger and had never lifted up her mind to any opinion of sovereignty, so was she apter to yield to her misfortune, having no stronger debates in her mind than a man may say a most witty childhood is wont to nourish, as to imagine with herself why Philanax and the other noblemen should deal so cruelly by her that had never deserved evil of any of them; and how they could find in their hearts to imprison such a personage as she did figure Pyrocles, whom she thought all the world was bound to love as well as she did. But Pamela, although endued with a virtuous mildness, yet the knowledge of herself, and what was due unto her, made her heart full of a stronger disdain against her adversity; so that she joined the vexation for her friend with the spite to see herself, as she thought, rebelliously detained, and mixed desirous thoughts to help with revengeful thoughts if she could not help. And as in pangs of death the stronger heart feels the greater torment, because it doth the more resist to his oppressor, so her mind, the nobler it was set (and had already embraced the higher thoughts), so much more it did repine; and the more it repined, the more helpless wounds it gave unto itself. But when great part of the night was passed over the doleful music of these sweet ladies' complaints, and that leisure (though with some strife) had brought Pamela to know that an eagle when she is in a cage must not think to do like an eagle, remembering with themselves that it was likely the next day the lords would proceed against those they had imprisoned, they employed the rest of the night in writing unto them, with such earnestness as the matter required, but in such styles as the state of their thoughts was apt to fashion.

In the mean time Pyrocles and Musidorus were recommended to so strong a guard as they might well see it was meant they should pay no less price than their lives for the getting out of that place, which they like men indeed (fortifying courage with the true rampire of patience) did so endure as they did rather appear governors of necessity than servants to fortune; the whole sum of their thoughts resting upon the safety of their ladies and their care one for the other, wherein (if at all) their hearts did seem to receive some softness. For sometimes Musidorus would feel such a motion to his friend and his unworthy case that he would fall into such kind speeches: 'My Pyrocles,' would he say, 'how unhappy may I think Thessalia that hath been as it were the middle way to this evil state of yours. For if you had not been there brought up, the sea should not have had this power thus to sever you from your dear father. I have therefore (if complaints do at any time become a man's heart) most cause to complain, since my country, which received the honour of Pyrocles' education, should be a step to his overthrow—if human chances can be counted an overthrow to him that stands upon virtue.'

'O excellent Musidorus,' answered Pyrocles, 'how do you teach me rather to fall out with myself and my fortune, since by you I have received all good, you only by me this affliction. To you and your virtuous mother I in my tenderest years, and father's greatest troubles, was sent for succour. There did I learn the sweet mysteries of philosophy. There had I your lively example to confirm that which I learned. There, lastly, had I your friendship which no unhappiness can ever make me say but that hath made me happy. Now see how my destiny (the gods know, not my will) hath rewarded you. My father sends for you away out of your land, whence, but for me, you had not come. What after followed, you know; it was my love, not yours, which first stayed you here. And therefore, if the heavens ever held a just proportion, it were I, and not you, that should feel the smart.'

'O blame not the heavens, sweet Pyrocles,' said Musidorus, 'as their course never alters, so is there nothing done by the unreachable ruler of them, but hath an everlasting reason for it. And to say the truth of those things, we should deal ungratefully with nature if we should be forgetful receivers of her good gifts, and so diligent auditors of the chances we like not. We have lived,*and have lived to be good to ourselves and others. Our souls (which are put into the stirring earth of our bodies) have achieved the causes of their hither coming. They have known, and honoured with knowledge, the cause of their creation. And to many men (for in this time, place, and fortune, it is lawful for us to speak gloriously) it hath been behoveful that we should live. Since, then, eternity is not to be had in this conjunction, what is to be lost by the separation but time? Which, since it hath his end, when that is once come, all what is past is nothing; and by the protracting, nothing gotten but labour and care. Do not me, therefore, that wrong (who something in years, but much in all other deserts, am fitter to die than you) as to say you have brought me to any evil, since the love of you doth overbalance all bodily mischiefs; and those mischiefs be but mischiefs to the baser minds too much delighted with the kennel of this life. Neither will I any more yield to my passion of lamenting you, which howsoever it might agree to my exceeding friendship, surely it would nothing to your exceeding virtue.'

'Add this to your noble speech, my dear cousin', said Pyrocles, 'that if we complain of this our fortune, or seem to ourselves faulty in having one hurt the other, we show a repentance of the love we bear to those matchless creatures, or at least a doubt it should be over dearly bought, which for my part (and so dare I answer for you) I call all the gods to witness, I am so far from that no shame, no torment, no death, would make me forgo the least part of the inward honour, essential pleasure, and living life I have enjoyed in the presence of the faultless Philoclea.'

'Take the pre-eminence in all things but in true loving', answered Musidorus, 'for the confession of that no death shall get of me.'

'Of that,' answered Pyrocles, soberly smiling, 'I perceive we shall have a debate in the other world—if, at least, there remain anything of remembrance*in that place.'

'I do not think the contrary,' said Musidorus, 'although you know it is greatly held that with the death of body and senses (which are not only the beginning but dwelling and nourishing of passions, thoughts, and imaginations), they failing, memory likewise fails (which riseth only out of them), and then is there left nothing but the intellectual part or intelligence which, void of all moral virtues (which stand in the mean of perturbations) doth only live in the contemplative virtue and power of the omnipotent God (the soul of souls and universal life of this great work); and therefore is utterly void from the possibility of drawing to itself these sensible considerations.'

'Certainly,' answered Pyrocles, 'I easily yield that we shall not know one another, and much less these past things, with a sensible or passionate knowledge; for the cause being taken away, the effect follows. Neither do I think we shall have such a memory as now we have, which is but a relic of the senses, or rather a print the senses have left of things past in our thoughts; but it shall be a vital power of that very intelligence which, as while it was here it held the chief seat of our life, and was as it were the last resort to which of all our knowledges the highest appeal came, and so by that means was never ignorant of our actions (though many times rebelliously resisted, always with this prison darkened), so much more being free of that prison, and returning to the life of all things, where all infinite knowledge is, it cannot but be a right intelligence (which is both his name and being) of things both present and past, though void of imagining to itself anything, but even grown like to his creator, hath all things with a spiritual knowledge before it. The difference of which is as hard for us to conceive as it had been for us when we were in our mothers' wombs to comprehend (if anybody could have told us) what kind of light we now in this life see, what kind of knowledge we now have. Yet now we do not only feel our present being but we conceive what we were before we were born; though remembrance make us not do it, but knowledge. And though we are utterly without any remorse of any misery we might then suffer, even such and much more odds shall there be at that second delivery of ours when, void of sensible memory or memorative passion, we shall not see the colours but lives of all things that have been or can be; and shall, as I hope, know our friendship, though exempt from the earthly cares of friendship, having both united it and ourselves in that high and heavenly love of the unquenchable light.'

As he had ended his speech, Musidorus, looking with a heavenly joy upon him, sang this song unto him he had made before love turned his muse to another subject.

> Since nature's works be good, and death doth serve
> As nature's work, why should we fear to die?
> Since fear is vain but when it may preserve,
> Why should we fear that which we cannot fly?
>
> Fear is more pain than is the pain it fears,
> Disarming human minds of native might;
> While each conceit an ugly figure bears,
> Which were not ill, well viewed in reason's light.
>
> Our owly eyes, which dimmed with passions be,
> And scarce discern the dawn of coming day,
> Let them be cleared, and now begin to see
> Our life is but a step in dusty way.
> > Then let us hold the bliss of peaceful mind,
> > Since this we feel, great loss we cannot find.

Thus did they, like quiet swans, sing their own obsequies, and virtuously enable their minds against all extremities which they did think would fall upon them, especially resolving that the first care they would have should be, by taking the fault upon themselves, to clear the two ladies, of whose case (as of nothing else that had happened) they had not any knowledge; although their friendly host, the honest gentleman Kerxenus, seeking all means how to help them, had endeavoured to speak with them and to make them know who should be their judge. But the curious servant of Philanax forbad him the entry upon pain of death; for so it was agreed upon that no man should have any conference with them for fear of new tumults, in so much that Kerxenus was constrained to retire himself, having yet obtained thus much: that he would deliver unto the two princes their apparel and jewels, which being left with him at Mantinea (wisely considering that their disguised weeds, which were all as then they had, saving a certain mean raiment Philanax had cast upon Pyrocles, would make them more odious in the sight of the judges), he had that night sent for, and now brought unto them. They accepted their own with great thankfulness, knowing from whence it came, and attired themselves in it against the next day; which being indeed rich and princely, they accordingly determined to maintain the names of Palladius and Timopyrus (as before it is mentioned). Then gave they themselves to consider in what sort they might defend their causes (for they thought it no less vain to wish death than cowardly to fear it), till something before morning, a small slumber taking them, they were by and by after called up to come to the answer of no less than their lives imported.

But in this sort was the judgement ordered: as soon as the morning had taken a full possession of the element, Euarchus called unto him Philanax, and willed him to draw out into the midst of the green (before the chief lodge) the throne of judgement seat in which Basilius was wont to sit, and according to their customs was ever carried with the prince. For Euarchus did wisely consider the people to be naturally taken with exterior shows far more than with inward consideration of the material points; and therefore in this new entry into so entangled a matter he would leave nothing which might be either an armour or ornament unto him; and in these pompous ceremonies he well knew a secret of government much to consist. That was performed by the diligent Philanax; and therein Euarchus did sit himself, all clothed in black, with the principal men who could in that suddenness provide themselves of such mourning raiments, the whole people commanded to keep an orderly silence of each side, which was duly observed of them, partly for the desire they had to see a good conclusion of these matters, and partly stricken with admiration as well at the grave and princely presence of Euarchus as at the greatness of the cause which was then to come in question. As for Philanax, Euarchus would have done him the honour to sit by him, but he excused himself, desiring to be the accuser of the prisoners in his master's behalf; and therefore, since he made himself a party, it was not convenient for him to sit in the judicial place.

Then was it a while deliberated whether the two young ladies should be brought forth in open presence. But that was stopped by Philanax, whose love and faith did descend from his master to his children, and only desired the smart should light upon the others whom he thought guilty of his death and dishonour, alleging for this that neither wisdom would they should be brought in presence of the people, which might thereupon grow to new uproars, nor justice required they should be drawn to any shame, till somebody accused them. And as for Pamela, he protested the laws of Arcadia would not allow any judgement of her, although she herself were to determine nothing till age or marriage enabled her.

Then, the duke's body being laid upon a table just before Euarchus, and all covered over with black, the prisoners (namely the duchess and two young princes) were sent for to appear in the protector's name (which name was the cause they came not to knowledge how near a kinsman was to judge of them, but thought him to be some nobleman chosen by the country in this extremity— so extraordinary a course had the order of the heavens produced at this time that both nephew and son were not only prisoners but unknown to their uncle and father, who of many years had not seen them, and Pyrocles was to plead for his life before that throne, in which throne lately before he had saved the duke's life).

But first was Gynecia led forth in the same weeds that the day and night before she had worn, saving that, instead of Cleophila's garment, in which she was found, she had cast on a long cloak which reached to the ground, of russet coarse cloth,* with a poor felt hat which almost covered all her face, most part of her goodly hair (on which her hands had laid many a spiteful hold), so lying upon her shoulders as a man might well see had no artificial carelessness; her eyes down on the ground of purpose not to look on Pyrocles' face, which she did not so much shun for the unkindness she conceived of her own overthrow as for the fear those motions at this short time of her life should be revived which she had with the passage of infinite sorrows mortified. Great was the compassion the people felt to see their princess's estate and beauty so deformed by fortune and her own desert, whom they had ever found a lady most worthy of all honour. But by and by the sight of the other two prisoners drew most of the eyes to that spectacle.

Pyrocles came out, led by Sympathus, clothed after the Greek manner in a long coat of white velvet reaching to the small of his leg, with great buttons of diamonds all along upon it. His neck, without any collar, not so much as hidden with a ruff, did pass the whiteness of his garments, which was not much in fashion unlike to the crimson raiment our knights of the order first put on.* On his feet he had nothing but slippers which, after the ancient manner, were tied up by certain laces which were fastened under his knee, having wrapped about (with many pretty knots) his naked leg. His fair auburn hair (which he ware in great length, and gave at that time a delightful show with being stirred up and down with the breath of a gentle wind) had nothing upon it but a white ribbon, in those days used for a diadem, which rolled once or twice about the uppermost part of his forehead, fell down upon his back, closed up at each end with the richest pearl were to be seen in the world. After him followed another nobleman, guiding the noble Musidorus who had upon him a long cloak after the fashion of that which we call the apostle's mantle, made of purple satin—not that purple which we now have, and is but a counterfeit of the Gaetulian purple (which yet was far the meaner in price and estimation), but of the right Tyrian purple (which was nearest to a colour betwixt our murrey and scarlet).* On his head (which was black and curled) he ware a Persian tiara all set down with rows of so rich rubies as they were enough to speak for him that they had to judge of no mean personage. In this sort, with erected countenances, did these unfortunate princes suffer themselves to be led, showing aright by the comparison of them and Gynecia how to diverse persons compassion is diversely to be stirred. For as to Gynecia, a lady known of great estate and greatly esteemed, the more miserable representation was made of her sudden ruin, the more men's hearts were forced to bewail such an evident witness of weak humanity; so to these men, not regarded because unknown, but rather (besides the detestation of their fact) hated as strangers, the more they should have fallen down in an abject semblance, the more, instead of compassion, they should have gotten contempt; but therefore were to use (as I may term it) the more violence of magnanimity, and so to conquer the expectation of the lookers with an extraordinary virtue. And such effect, indeed, it wrought in the whole assembly, their eyes yet standing as it were in balance to whether of them they should most direct their sight. Musidorus was in stature so much higher than Pyrocles as commonly is gotten by one year's growth; his face, now beginning to have some tokens of a beard, was composed to a kind of manlike beauty; his colour was of a well pleasing brownness; and the features of it such as they carried both delight and majesty; his countenance severe, and promising a mind much given to thinking; Pyrocles of a pure complexion, and of such a cheerful favour as might seem either a woman's face on a boy or an excellent boy's face in a woman; his look gentle and bashful, which bred the more admiration having showed such notable proofs of courage. Lastly, though both had both, if there were any odds, Musidorus was the more goodly and Pyrocles the more lovely. But as soon as Musidorus saw himself so far forth led among the people that he knew to a great number of them his voice should be heard, misdoubting their intention to the princess Pamela (of which he was more careful than of his own life), even as he went (though his leader sought to interrupt him), he thus with a loud voice spake unto them:

'And is it possible, O Arcadians,' said he, 'that you can forget the natural duty you owe to your princess Pamela? Hath this soil been so little beholding to her noble ancestors? Hath so long a time rooted no surer love in your hearts to that line? Where is that faith to your prince's blood, which hath not only preserved you from all dangers heretofore but hath spread your fame to all the nations in the world? Where is that justice the Arcadians were wont to flourish in, whose nature is to render to everyone his own? Will you now keep the right from your prince who is the only giver of judgement, the key of justice, and life of your laws? Do you hope in a few years to set up such another race, which nothing but length of time can establish? Will you reward Basilius's children with ungratefulness, the very poison of manhood? Will you betray your long-settled reputation with the foul name of traitors? Is this your mourning for your duke's death: to increase his loss with his daughters' misery? Imagine your prince do look out of the heavens unto you; what do you think he could wish more at your hands than that you do well by his children? And what more honour, I pray you, can you do to his obsequies than to satisfy his soul with a loving memory, as you do his body with an unfelt solemnity? What have you done with the princess Pamela? Pamela, the just inheritrix of this country; Pamela, whom this earth may be happy that it shall be hereafter said she was born in Arcadia; Pamela, in herself your ornament, in her education your foster child, and every way your only princess; what account can you render to yourselves of her? Truly, I do not think that you all know what is become of her, so soon may a diamond be lost, so soon may the fairest light in the world be put out. But look, look unto it! O Arcadians, be not wilfully robbed of your greatest treasure! Make not yourselves ministers to private ambitions, who do but use yourselves to put on your own yokes! Whatsoever you determine of us (who I must confess are but strangers), yet let not Basilius's daughters be strangers unto you. Lastly, howsoever you bar her from her public sovereignty (which if you do, little may we hope for equity where rebellion reigns), yet deny not that child's right unto her, that she may come and do the last duties to her father's body. Deny not that happiness (if in such a case there be any happiness) to your late duke, that his body may have his last touch of his dearest child.'

With suchlike broken manner of questions and speeches was Musidorus desirous, as much as in passing by them he could, to move the people to tender Pamela's fortune. But at length, by that they came to the judgement place, both Sympathus and his guider had greatly satisfied him, with the assurance they gave him, that this assembly of people had neither meaning nor power to do any hurt to the princess, whom they all acknowledged as their sovereign lady; but that the custom of Arcadia was such, till she had more years, the state of the country to be guided by a protector, under whom he and his fellow were to receive their judgement. That eased Musidorus's heart of his most vehement care, when he found his beloved lady to be out of danger. But Pyrocles, as soon as the duchess of the one side, he and Musidorus of the other, were stayed before the face of their judge (having only for their bar the table on which the duke's body lay), being nothing less vexed with the doubt of Philoclea than Musidorus was for Pamela, in this sort with a lowly behaviour, and only then like a suppliant, he spake to the protector:

'Pardon me, most honoured judge,' said he, 'that uncommanded I begin my speech unto you, since both to you and me these words of mine shall be most necessary. To you, having the sacred exercise of justice in your hand, nothing appertains more properly than truth nakedly and freely set down. To me, being environed round about with many dangerous calamities, what can be more convenient than at least to be at peace with myself in having discharged my conscience in a most behoveful verity. Understand therefore, and truly understand, that the lady Philoclea (to whose unstained virtue it hath been my unspeakable misery that my name should become a blot), if she be accused, is most unjustly accused, of any dishonourable fact which by my means she may be thought to have yielded unto. Whatsoever hath been done hath been my violence, which notwithstanding could not prevail against her chastity. But whatsoever hath been informed, was my force; and I attest the heavens, to blaspheme which I am not now in fit time, that so much as my coming into her chamber was wholly unwitting unto her. This your wisdom may withal consider: if I would lie, I would lie for mine own behoof. I am not so old as to be weary of myself, but the very sting of my inward knowledge, joined with the consideration I must needs have

what an infinite loss it should be to all those who love goodness in
good folks if so pure a child of virtue should wrongfully be des-
troyed, compels me to use my tongue against myself, and receive the
burden of what evil was upon my own doing. Look therefore with
pitiful eyes upon so fair beams, and that misfortune which by me
hath fallen unto her. Help to repair it with your public judgement;
since whosoever deals cruelly with such a creature shows himself a
hater of mankind and an envier of the world's bliss. And this
petition I make even in the name of justice: that before you proceed
further against us, I may know how you conceive of her noble,
though unfortunate, action; and what judgement you will make of it.'

He had not spoken his last word when all the whole people, both
of great and low estate, confirmed with an united murmur Pyrocles'
demand, longing, for the love generally was borne Philoclea, to know
what they might hope of her. Euarchus, though neither regarding
a prisoner's passionate prayer nor bearing over-plausible ears to a
many-headed motion, yet well enough content to win their liking
with things in themselves indifferent, he was content first to seek as
much as might be of Philoclea's behaviour in this matter; which
being cleared by Pyrocles and but weakly gainsaid by Philanax (who
had framed both his own and Dametas's evidence most for her
favour), yet finding by his wisdom that she was not altogether
faultless, he pronounced she should all her life long be kept prisoner
among certain women of religion like the vestal nuns, so to repay the
touched honour of her house with well observing a strict profession
of chastity. Although this were a great prejudicating of Pyrocles'
case, yet was he exceedingly joyous of it, being assured of his lady's
life, and in the depth of his mind not sorry that, what end soever he
had, none should obtain the after-enjoying that jewel whereon he
had set his life's happiness.

After it was by public sentence delivered what should be done
with the sweet Philoclea (the laws of Arcadia bearing that what was
appointed by the magistrates in the nonage of the prince could not
afterwards be repealed), Euarchus (still using to himself no other
name but protector of Arcadia) commanded those that had to say
against the duchess Gynecia to proceed, because both her estate
required she should be first heard and also for that she was taken to
be the principal in the greatest matter they were to judge of.
Philanax incontinently stepped forth, and showing in his greedy
eyes that he did thirst for her blood, began a well thought-on

discourse of her (in his judgement) execrable wickedness. But Gynecia, standing up before the judge, casting abroad her arms, with her eyes hidden under the breadth of her unseemly hat, laying open in all her gestures the despairful affliction to which all the might of her reason was converted, with suchlike words stopped Philanax as he was entering into his invective oration:

'Stay, stay, Philanax,' said she, 'do not defile thy honest mouth with those dishonourable speeches thou art about to utter against a woman, now most wretched, lately thy mistress! Let either the remembrance how great she was move thy heart to some reverence, or the seeing how low she is stir in thee some pity. It may be truth doth make thee deal untruly, and love of justice frames unjustice in thee. Do not therefore (neither shalt thou need) tread upon my desolate ruins. Thou shalt have that thou seekest, and yet shalt not be the oppressor of her who cannot choose but love thee for thy singular faith to thy master. I do not speak this to procure mercy, or to prolong my life. No, no, I say unto you, I will not live; but I am only loath my death should be engrieved with any wrong thou shouldst do unto me. I have been too painful a judge over myself to desire pardon in others' judgement. I have been too cruel an executioner of mine own soul to desire that execution of justice should be stayed for me. Alas, they that know how sorrow can rent the spirits, they that know what fiery hells are contained in a self-condemning mind, need not fear that fear can keep such a one from desiring to be separated from that which nothing but death can separate! I therefore say to thee, O just judge, that I, and only I, was the worker of Basilius's death. They were these hands that gave unto him that poisonous potion that hath brought death to him and loss to Arcadia. It was I, and none but I, that hastened his aged years to an unnatural end, and that have made all this people orphans of their royal father. I am the subject that have killed my prince. I am the wife that have murdered my husband. I am a degenerate woman, an undoer of this country, a shame of my children. What couldst thou have said more, O Philanax? And all this I grant. There resteth, then, nothing else to say, but that I desire you you will appoint quickly some to rid me of my life, rather than these hands which else are destinied unto it; and that indeed it may be done with such speed as I may not long die in this life which I have in so great horror.'

With that, she crossed her arms and sat down upon the ground, attending the judge's answer. But a great while it was before anybody could be heard speak, the whole people concurring in a lamentable cry; so much had Gynecia's words and behaviour stirred their hearts to a doleful compassion. Neither, in truth, could most of them in their judgements tell whether they should be more sorry for her fault or her misery, for the loss of her estate or loss of her virtue. But most were most moved with that which was under their eyes, the sense most subject to pity. But at length the reverent awe they stood in of Euarchus brought them to a silent waiting his determination; who having well considered the abomination of the fact, attending more the manifest proof of so horrible a trespass, confessed by herself, and proved by others, than anything relenting to those tragical phrases of hers (apter to stir a vulgar pity than his mind which hated evil in what colours soever he found it), having conferred a while with the principal men of the country and demanded their allowance, he definitively gave this sentence:

'That whereas, both in private and public respects, this woman had most heinously offended (in private, because marriage being the most holy conjunction that falls to mankind, out of which all families, and so consequently all societies, do proceed, which not only by community of goods but community of children is to knit the minds in a most perfect union which whoso breaks dissolves all humanity, no man living free from the danger of so near a neighbour, she had not only broken it but broken it with death, and the most pretended death that might be; in public respect, the prince's person being in all monarchal governments the very knot of the people's welfare and light of all their doings, to which they are not only in conscience but in necessity bound to be loyal, she had traitorously empoisoned him, neither regarding her country's profit, her own duty, nor the rigour of the laws); that therefore, as well for the due satisfaction to eternal justice and accomplishment of the Arcadian statutes as for the everlasting example to all wives and subjects, she should presently be conveyed to close prison, and there be kept with such food as might serve to sustain her alive until the day of her husband's burial; at which time she should be buried quick in the same tomb with him, that so his murder might be a murder to herself, and she forced to keep company with the body from which she had made so detestable a severance; and lastly death might redress their disjoined conjunction of marriage.'

His judgement was received of the whole assembly as not with disliking so with great astonishment, the greatness of the matter and person as it were overpressing the might of their conceits. But when they did set it to the beam* with the monstrousness of her ugly misdeed, they could not but yield in their hearts there was no overbalancing. As for Gynecia, who had already settled her thoughts not only to look but long for this event, having in this time of her vexation found a sweetness in the rest she hoped by death, with a countenance witnessing she had beforehand so passed through all the degrees of sorrow that she had no new look to figure forth any more, rose up and offered forth her fair hands to be bound or led as they would, being indeed troubled with no part of this judgement but that her death was, as she thought, long delayed. They that were appointed for it conveyed her to the place she was in before, where the guard was relieved and the number increased to keep her more sure for the time of her execution. None of them all that led her, though most of them were such whose hearts had been long hardened with the often-exercising such offices, being able to bar tears from their eyes and other manifest tokens of compassionate sorrow—so goodly a virtue is a resolute constancy that even in ill-deservers it seems that party might have been notably well deserving. Thus the excellent lady Gynecia, having passed five and thirty years of her age even to admiration of her beautiful mind and body, and having not in her own knowledge ever spotted her soul with any wilful vice but her inordinate love of Cleophila, was brought, first by the violence of that ill-answered passion, and then by the despairing conceit she took of the judgement of God in her husband's death and her own fortune, purposely to overthrow herself, and confirm by a wrong confession that abominable shame which, with her wisdom, joined to the truth, perhaps she might have refelled.

Then did Euarchus ask Philanax whether it were he that would charge the two young prisoners, or that some other should do it, and he sit according to his estate as an assistant in the judgement. Philanax told him, as before he had done, that he thought no man could lay manifest the naughtiness of those two young men with so much either truth or zeal as himself, and therefore he desired he might do this last service to his faithfully beloved master as to prosecute the traitorous causers of his death and dishonour; which being done, for his part, he meant to give up all dealing in public affairs, since that man was gone who had made him love them.

Philanax thus being ready to speak, the two princes were commanded to tell their names; who answered, according to their agreement, that they were Timopyrus, despota of Lycia, and Palladius, prince of Caria. Which when they had said, they demanded to know by what authority they could judge of them, since they were not only foreigners, and so not born under their laws, but absolute princes, and therefore not to be touched by laws. But answer was presently made them that Arcadia laws were to have their force upon any were found in Arcadia, since strangers have scope to know the customs of a country before they put themselves in it, and when they once are entered, they must know that what by many was made must not for one be broken, and so much less for a stranger, as he is to look for no privilege in that place to which in time of need his service is not to be expected. As for their being princes, whether they were so or no, the belief stood but in their own words, which they had so diversely falsified as they did not deserve belief. But whatsoever they were, Arcadia was to acknowledge them but as private men, since they were neither by magistracy nor alliance to the princely blood to claim anything in that region. Therefore, if they had offended (which now by the plaintiff and their defence was to be judged) against the laws of nations, by the laws of nations they were to be chastised; if against the peculiar ordinances of the province, those peculiar ordinances were to lay hold of them.

The princes stood a while upon that, demanding leisure to give perfect knowledge of their greatness. But when they were answered that in the case of a prince's death the law of that country had ever been that immediate trial should be had, they were forced to yield, resolved that in those names they would as much as they could cover the shame of their royal parentage, and keep as long as might be (if evil were determined against them) the evil news from their careful kinsfolk. Wherein the chief man they considered was Euarchus, whom the strange and secret working of justice had brought to be the judge over them—in such a shadow or rather pit of darkness the wormish mankind lives that neither they know how to foresee nor what to fear, and are but like tennis balls tossed by the racket of the higher powers. Thus, both sides ready, it was determined, because their causes were separate, first Philanax should be heard against Pyrocles (whom they termed Timopyrus), and that heard, the other's cause should follow, and so receive together such judgement as they should be found to have deserved.

But Philanax, that was even short-breathed at the first with the extreme vehemency he had to speak against them, stroking once or twice his forehead, and wiping his eyes (which either wept, or he would at that time have them seem to weep), looking first upon Pyrocles as if he had proclaimed all hatefulness against him, humbly turning to Euarchus (who with quiet gravity showed great attention), he thus began his oration:

'That which all men who take upon them to accuse another are wont to desire, most worthy protector, to have: many proofs of many faults in them they seek to have condemned; that is to me in this present action my greatest cumber and annoyance. For the number is so great, and the quality so monstrous, of the enormities this wretched young man hath committed that neither I in myself can tell where to begin (my thoughts being confused with the horrible multitude of them), neither do I think your virtuous ears will be able to endure the report of them, but will rather imagine you hear some tragedy invented of the extremity of wickedness than a just recital of a wickedness indeed committed. For such is the disposition of the most sincere judgements that, as they can believe mean faults and such as man's nature may slide into so, when they pass to a certain degree—nay, when they pass all degrees of unspeakable naughtiness—then find they in themselves a hardness to give credit that human creatures can so from all humanity be transformed. But in myself, the strength of my faith to my dead master will help the weakness of my memory; in you, your excellent love of justice will force you to vouchsafe attention. And as for the matter, it is so manifest, so pitiful evidences lie before your eyes of it, that I shall need to be but a brief recounter, and no rhetorical enlarger, of this most harmful mischief. I will, therefore, in as few words as so huge a trespass can be contained, deliver unto you the sum of this miserable fact, leaving out a great number particular tokens of his naughtiness, and only touching the essential points of this doleful case.

This man, whom to begin withal I know not how to name, since being come into this country unaccompanied like a lost pilgrim, from a man grew a woman, from a woman a ravisher of women, thence a prisoner, and now a prince; but this Timopyrus, this Cleophila, this what you will (for any shape or title he can take upon him that hath no restraint of shame), having understood the solitary life my late master lived, and considering how open he had laid himself to any traitorous attempt, for the first mask of his falsehood disguised himself like a woman (which, being the more simple and hurtless sex, might easier hide his subtle harmfulness), and presenting himself to my master (the most courteous prince that lived), was received of him with so great graciousness as might have bound not only any grateful mind, but might have mollified any enemy's rancour. But this venomous serpent, admitted thus into his bosom, as contagion will easily find a fit body for it, so had he quickly fallen into so near acquaintance with this naughty woman, whom even now you have most justly condemned, that this was her right hand; she saw with no eyes but his, nor seemed to have any life but in him, so glad she was to find one more cunning than herself in covering wickedness with a modest veil. What is to be thought passed betwixt two such virtuous creatures, whereof the one hath confessed murder and the other rape, I leave to your wise consideration. For my heart hastens to the miserable point of Basilius's murder, for the executing of which with more facility this young nymph of Diana's bringing up feigned certain rites she had to perform—so furious an impiety had carried him from all remembrance of goodness that he did not only not fear the gods, as the beholders and punishers of so ungodly a villainy, but did blasphemously use their sacred holy name as a minister unto it. And forsooth a cave hereby was chosen for the temple of his devotions, a cave of such darkness as did prognosticate he meant to please the infernal powers; for there this accursed caitiff upon the altar of falsehood sacrificed the life of the virtuous Basilius. By what means he trained him thither, alas, I know not; for if I might have known it, either my life had accompanied my master, or this fellow's death had preserved him. But this may suffice: that in the mouth of the cave where this traitor had his lodging and chapel, when already master shepherd, his companion, had conveyed away the undoubted inheritrix of this country, was Gynecia found by the dead corpse of her husband newly empoisoned, apparelled in the garments of the young lady, and ready, no question, to have fled to some place according to their consort, but that she was by certain honest shepherds arrested. While in the mean time, because there should be left no revenger of this bloody mischief, this noble Amazon was violently gotten into the chamber of the lady Philoclea where, by the mingling of her shame with his misdeed, he might enforce her to be the accessary to her father's death; and under the countenance of her and her sister (against whom they knew we would not rebel), seize as it were with one gripe into their treacherous hands the regiment of this mighty province. But the almighty eye prevented him of the end of his mischief by using a villain, Dametas's hand, to enclose him in there, where with as much fortification as in a house could be made he thought himself in most security. Thus see you, most just judge, a short and simple story of the infamous misery fallen to this country—indeed infamous, since by an effeminate man we should suffer a greater overthrow than our mightiest enemies have been ever able to lay upon us. And that all this which I have said is most manifest, as well of the murdering of Basilius as the ravishing of Philoclea (for those two parts I establish of my accusation), who is of so incredulous a mind, or rather who will so stop his eyes from seeing a thing clearer than the light, as not to hold for assured so palpable a matter? For (to begin with his most cruel misdeed) is it to be imagined that Gynecia (a woman, though wicked, yet witty) would have attempted and achieved an enterprise no less hazardous than horrible without having some counsellor in the beginning and some comforter in the performing? Had she, who showed her thoughts were so overruled with some strange desire as, in despite of God, nature, and womanhood, to execute that in deeds which in words we cannot hear without trembling? Had she, I say, no practice to lead her unto it? Or had she a practice without conspiracy? Or could she conspire without somebody to conspire with? And if one were, who so likely as this, to whom she communicated, I am sure, her mind; the world thinks, her body? Neither let her words, taking the whole fault upon herself, be herein anything available. For to those persons who have vomitted out of their souls all remnants of goodness there rests a certain pride in evil, and having else no shadow of glory left them, they glory to be constant in iniquity; and that, God knows, must be held out to the last gasp without revealing their accomplices, as thinking great courage is declared in being neither afeard of the gods nor ashamed of the world. But let Gynecia's action die with herself. What can all the earth answer for his coming hither? Why alone, if he be a prince? How so richly jewelled, if he be not a prince? Why then a woman, if now a man? Why now Timopyrus, if then Cleophila? Was all this play for nothing? Or if it had an end, what end but the end of my dear master? Shall we doubt so many secret conferences with Gynecia, such feigned favour to the over-soon beguiled Basilius, a cave made a lodging, and the same lodging made a temple of his religion, lastly such changes and traverses as a quiet poet could scarce fill a poem withal, were directed to any less scope than to this monstrous murder? O snaky ambition which can wind thyself in so many figures to slide thither thou desirest to come! O corrupted reason of mankind that can yield to deform thyself with so filthy desires! And O hopeless be those minds whom so unnatural desires do not with their own ugliness sufficiently terrify! But yet even of favour let us grant him thus much more as to fancy that in these foretold things fortune might be a great actor perchance to an evil end, yet to a less evil end all these entangled devices were intended. But I beseech your ladyship, my lady Timopyrus, tell me what excuse can you find for the changing your lodging with the duchess that very instant she was to finish her execrable practice? How can you cloak the lending of your cloak unto her? Was all that by chance too? Had the stars sent such an influence unto you as you should be just weary of your lodging and garments when our prince was destinied to the slaughter? What say you to this, O shameful and shameless creature, fit indeed to be the dishonour of both sexes? But alas, I spend too many words in so manifest and so miserable a matter. They must be four wild horses (which according to our laws are the executioners of men which murder our prince) which must decide this question with you.

Yet see, so far had my zeal to my beloved prince transported me that I had almost forgotten my second part and his second abomination, I mean his violence offered (I hope but offered) to the lady Philoclea, wherewith (as if it had well become his womanhood) he came braving to the judgement seat; indeed, our laws appoint not so cruel a death (although death too) for this fact as for the other. But whosoever well weighs it shall find it sprung out of the same fountain of mischievous naughtiness: the killing of the father, dishonouring the mother, and ravishing the child. Alas, could not so many benefits received of my prince, the justice of nature, the right of hospitality, be a bridle to thy lust, if not to thy cruelty? Or if thou hadst (as surely thou hast) a heart recompensing goodness with hatred, could not his death (which is the last of revenges) satisfy thy malice, but thou must heap upon it the shame of his daughter? Were thy eyes so stony, thy breast so tigerish, as the sweet and beautiful shows of Philoclea's virtue did not astonish thee? O woeful Arcadia, to whom the name of this mankind courtesan shall ever be remembered as a procurer of thy greatest loss! But too far I find my passion, yet honest passion, hath guided me. The case is every way too too much unanswerable. It resteth in you, O excellent protector, to pronounce judgement; which, if there be hope that such a young man may prove profitable to the world, who in the first exercise of his own determinations far passed the arrantest strumpet in luxuriousness, the cunningest forger in falsehood; a player in disguising, a tiger in cruelty, a dragon in ungratefulness, let him be preserved like a jewel to do greater mischief. If his youth be not more defiled with treachery than the eldest man's age, let, I say, his youth be some cause of compassion. If he have not every way sought the overthrow of human society, if he have done anything like a prince, let his naming himself a prince breed a reverence to his base wickedness. If he have not broken all laws of hospitality, and broken them in the most detestable degree that can be, let his being a guest be a sacred protection of his more than savage doings. Or if his whorish beauty have not been as the highway of his wickedness, let the picture drawn upon so poisonous a wood be reserved to show how greatly colours can please us. But if it is as it is, what should I say more—a very spirit of hellish naughtiness? If his act be to be punished, and his defiled person not to be pitied, then restore unto us our prince by duly punishing his murderers; for then we shall think him and his name to live when we shall see his killers to die. Restore to the excellent Philoclea her honour by taking out of the world her dishonour; and think that at this day in this matter are the eyes of the world upon you, whether anything can sway your mind from a true administration of justice. Alas, though I have much more to say, I can say no more; for my tears and sighs interrupt my speech and force me to give myself over to my private sorrow.'

Thus, when Philanax had uttered the uttermost of his malice, he made sorrow the cause of his conclusion. But while Philanax was in the course of his speech, and did with such bitter reproaches defame the princely Pyrocles, it was well to be seen his heart was unused to bear such injuries, and his thoughts such as could arm themselves better against anything than shame. For sometimes blushing, his blood with diverse motions coming and going, sometimes closing his eyes and laying his hand over them, sometimes again giving such a look to Philanax as might show he assured himself he durst not so have spoken if they had been in indifferent place, with some impatience he bare the length of his oration; which being ended, with as much modest humbleness to the judge as despiteful scorn to the accuser, with words to this purpose he defended his honour:

'My accuser's tale may well bear witness with me, most rightful judge, in how hard a case, and environed with how many troubles, I may esteem myself. For if he (who shows his tongue is not unacquainted with railing) was in an agony in the beginning of his speech with the multitude of matters he had to lay unto me (wherein notwithstanding the most evil could fall unto him was that he should not do so much evil as he would), how cumbered do you think may I acknowledge myself who, in things no less importing than my life, must be mine own advocate, without leisure to answer or fore-knowledge what should be objected? In things, I say, promoted with so cunning a confusion as, having mingled truths with false-hoods, surmises with certainties, causes of no moment with matters capital, scolding with complaining, I can absolutely neither grant nor deny. Neither can I tell whether I come hither to be judged, or before judgement to be punished, being compelled to bear such unworthy words, far more grievous than any death unto me. But since the form of this government allows such tongue-liberty unto him, I will pick as well as I can out of his invective those few points which may seem of some purpose in the touching of me, hoping that, as by your easy hearing of me you will show that though you hate evil yet you wish men may prove themselves not evil, so in that he hath said you will not weigh so much what he hath said as what he hath proved, remembering that truth is simple and naked, and that if he had guided himself under that banner, he needed not out of the way have sought so vile and false disgracings of me, enough to make the untruest accusation believed. I will, therefore, using truth as my best eloquence, repeat unto you as much as I know in this matter; and then, by the only clearness of the discourse, your wisdom, I know, will find the difference betwixt cavilling supposition and direct declaration.

This prince Palladius and I being inflamed with love (a passion far more easily reprehended than refrained) to the two peerless daughters of Basilius, and understanding how he had secluded himself from the world, that like princes there was no access unto him, we disguised ourselves in such forms as might soonest bring us to the revealing of our affections. The prince Palladius had such event of his doings that, with Pamela's consent, he was to convey her out of the thraldom she lived in, to receive the subjection of a greater people than her own, until her father's consent might be obtained. My fortune was more hard, for I bare no more love to the chaste Philoclea than Basilius, deceived in my sex, showed to me, insomuch that by his importunacy I could have no time to assail the constant rock of the pure Philoclea's mind, till this policy I found: taking (under colour of some devotions) my lodging to draw Basilius thither with hope to enjoy me, which likewise I revealed to the duchess, that she might keep my place,* and so make her husband see his error, while I in the mean time being delivered of them both, and having locked so the doors as I hoped the immaculate Philoclea should be succourless, my attempt was such as even now I confessed, and I made prisoner there, I know not by what means, when being repelled by her divine virtue, I would fainest have escaped. Here have you the thread to guide you in the labyrinth this man of his tongue had made so monstrous. Here see you the true discourse which he (mountebank fashion) doth make so wide a mouth over. Here may you conceive the reason why the duchess had my garment, because in her going to the cave in the moonshine night she might be taken for me, which he useth as the knot of all his wise assertions; so that, as this double-minded fellow's accusation was double, double likewise my answer must perforce be to the murder of Basilius and violence offered to the inviolate Philoclea. For the first, O heavenly gods, who would have thought any mouth could have been found so immodest as to have opened so slight proofs of so horrible matters? His first argument is a question: who would imagine that Gynecia would accomplish such an act without some accessaries; and if any, who but I? Truly, I am so far from imagining anything that, till I saw these mourning tokens, and heard Gynecia's confession, I never imagined the duke was dead. And for my part, so vehemently and more like the manner of passionate than guilty folks, I see the duchess prosecute herself, that I think condemnation may go too hastily over her, considering the unlikelihood, if not impossibility, her wisdom and virtue so long nourished should in one moment throw down itself to the uttermost end of wickedness. But whatsoever she hath done (which, as I say, I never believed), yet how unjustly should that aggravate my fault? She found abroad, I within doors (for, as for the wearing my garment, I have told you the cause); she seeking, as you say, to escape, I locking myself in a house; without perchance the conspiracy of one poor stranger might greatly enable her attempt, or the fortification of the lodge (as the trim man alleged) might make me hope to resist all Arcadia. And see how injuriously he seeks to draw from me my chiefest clearing by preventing the credit of her words wherewith she hath wholly taken the fault upon herself. An honest and unpartial examiner!—her words may condemn her, but may not absolve me. Thus, void of all probable allegation, the craven crows upon my affliction, not leaving out any evil that ever he hath felt in his own soul to charge my youth withal. But who can look for a sweeter breath out of such a stomach, or for honey from so filthy a spider? What should I say more? If in so inhuman a matter (which he himself confesseth sincerest judgements are loathest to believe), and in the severest law, proofs clearer than the sun are required, his reasons are only the scum of a base malice, my answers most manifest, shining in their own truth. If there remain any doubt of it (because it stands betwixt his affirming and my denial), I offer, nay I desire, and humbly desire, I may be granted the trial by combat*—by combat; wherein, let him be armed, and me in my shirt. I doubt not justice will be my shield, and his heart will show itself as faint as it is false.

Now come I to the second part of my offence, towards the young lady, which I confess, and for her sake heartily lament. But in fine I offered force to her; love offered more force to me. Let her beauty be compared to my years, and such effects will be found no miracles. But since it is thus, as it is, and that justice teacheth us not to love punishment, but to fly to it for necessity, the salve of her honour (I mean as the world will take it, for else in truth it is most untouched) must be my marriage and not my death, since the one stops all mouths, the other becomes a doubtful fable. This matter requires no more words, and your experience, I hope, in these cases shall need no more. For myself, methinks I have showed already too much love of my life to bestow so many. But certainly it hath been love of truth which could not bear so unworthy falsehood, and love of justice that would brook no wrong to myself nor other, and makes me now even in that respect to desire you to be moved rather with pity at a just cause of tears than with the bloody tears this crocodile spends, who weeps to procure death and not to lament death. It will be no honour to Basilius's tomb to have guiltless blood sprinkled upon it, and much more may a judge overweigh himself in cruelty than in clemency. It is hard, but it is excellent where it is found: a right knowledge when correction is necessary, when grace doth more avail. For my own respect, if I thought in wisdom I had deserved death, I would not desire life; for I know nature will condemn me to die, though you do not, and longer I would not wish to draw this breath than I may keep myself unspotted of any horrible crime. Only I cannot, nor ever will, deny the love of Philoclea, whose violence wrought violent effects in me.'

With that he finished his speech, casting up his eyes to the judge, and crossing his hands, which he held on their length before him, declaring a resolute patience in whatsoever should be done with him.

Philanax, like a watchful adversary, curiously marked all that he said, saving that in the beginning he was interrupted by two letters were brought him from the princess Pamela and the lady Philoclea, who having all that night considered and bewailed their estate, careful for their mother likewise, of whom they could never think so much evil. But considering with themselves that she assuredly should have so due trial by the laws as either she should not need their help or should be past their help, they looked to that which nearliest touched them, and each wrate in this sort for him in whom their lives' joy consisted:

The humble-hearted Philoclea wrate much after this manner:

'My lords, what you will determine of me is to me uncertain, but what I have determined of myself I am most certain of; which is no longer to enjoy my life than I may enjoy him for husband whom the gods for my highest glory have bestowed upon me. Those that judge him, let them execute me. Let my throat satisfy their hunger of murder; for, alas, what hath he done that had not his original in me? Look upon him, I beseech you, with indifferency, and see whether in those eyes all virtue shines not; see whether that face could hide a murderer. Take leisure to know him, and then yourselves will say it hath been too great an inhumanity to suspect such excellency. Are the gods, think you, deceived in their workmanship? Artificers will not use marble but to noble uses. Should those powers be so overshot as to frame so precious an image of their own, but to honourable purposes? O speak with him, O hear him, O know him, and become not the putters-out of the world's light! Hope you to joy my father's soul with hurting him he loved above all the world? Shall a wrong suspicion make you forget the certain knowledge of those benefits this house hath received by him? Alas, alas, let not Arcadia for his loss be accursed of the whole earth and of all posterity! He is a great prince. I speak unto you that which I know, for I have seen most evident testimonies. Why should you hinder my advancement? Who, if I have passed my childhood hurtless to any of you, if I have refused nobody to do what good I could, if have often mitigated my father's anger, ever sought to maintain his favour towards you, nay if I have held you all as fathers and brothers unto me, rob me not of more than my life comes unto, tear not that which is inseparably joined to my soul. But if he rest misliked of you (which, O God, how can it be?), yet give him to me. Let me have him; you know I pretend no right to your state. Therefore it is but a private petition I make unto you. Or if you be hard-heartedly bent to appoint otherwise (which, O sooner let me die than know), then, to end as I began, let me by you be ordered to the same end, without for more cruelty you mean to force Philoclea to use her own hands to kill one of your duke's children.'

Pamela's letter (which she meant to send with her sister's to the general assembly of the Arcadian nobility—for so closely they were kept as they were utterly ignorant of the new-taken orders) was thus framed:

'In such a state, my lords, you have placed me as I can neither write nor be silent. For how can I be silent, since you have left me nothing but my solitary words to testify my misery? And how should I write (for as for speech I have none but my gaoler that can hear me), who neither can resolve what to write nor to whom to write? What to write is as hard for me to say as what I may not write, so little hope have I of any success, and so much hath no injury been left undone to me-wards. To whom to write, where may I learn, since yet I wot not how to entitle you? Shall I call you my sovereigns? Set down your laws that I may do you homage. Shall I fall lower, and name you my fellows? Show me, I beseech you, the lord and master over us. But shall Basilius's heir name herself your princess? Alas, I am your prisoner. But whatsoever I be, or whatsoever you be, O all you beholders of these doleful lines, this do I signify unto you, and signify it with a heart that shall ever remain in that opinion: the good or evil you do to the excellent prince was taken with me, and after by force from me, I will ever impute it as either way done to my own person. He is a prince and worthy to be my husband, and so is he my husband by me worthily chosen. Believe it, believe it; either you shall be traitors for murdering of me or, if you let me live, the murderers of him shall smart as traitors. For what do you think I can think? Am I so childish as not to see wherein you touch him you condemn me? Can his shame be without my re-proach? No, nor shall be, since nothing he hath done that I will not avow. Is this the comfort you bring me in my father's death, to make me fuller of shame than sorrow? Would you do this if it were not with full intention to prevent my power with slaughter? And so do, I pray you. It is high time for me to be weary of my life too long led, since you are weary of me before you have me. I say again, I say it infinitely unto you, I will not live without him, if it be not to revenge him. Either do justly in saving both, or wisely in killing both. If I be your princess, I command his preservation. If but a private person, then are we both to suffer. I take all truth to witness he hath done no fault but in going with me. Therefore, to conclude; in judging him, you judge me. Neither conceive with yourselves the matter you treat is the life of a stranger (though even in that name he deserved pity), nor of a shepherd (to which estate love of me made such a prince descend); but determine most assuredly the life that is in question is of Pamela, Basilius's daughter.'

Many blots had the tears of these sweet ladies made in their letters, which many times they had altered, many times torn, and written anew, ever thinking something either wanted or were too much, or would offend, or (which was worst) would breed denial. But at last the day warned them to dispatch; which they accordingly did, and calling one of their guard (for nobody else was suffered to come near them), with great entreaty they requested him that he would present them to the principal noblemen and gentlemen together, for they had more confidence in the numbers' favour than in any one, upon whom they would not lay the lives they held so precious. But the fellow, trusty to Philanax (who had placed him there), delivered them both to him (what time Pyrocles began to speak); which he suddenly opened, and seeing to what they tended by the first words, was so far from publishing them (whereby he feared, in Euarchus's just mind, either the princesses might be endangered or the prisoners preserved, of which choice he knew not which to think the worst) that he would not himself read them over, doubting his own heart might be mollified, so bent upon revenge. Therefore utterly suppressing them, he lent a spiteful ear to Pyrocles, and as soon as he had ended, with a very willing heart desired Euarchus he might accept the combat, although it would have framed but ill with him, Pyrocles having never found any match near him besides Musidorus.

But Euarchus made answer: since bodily strength is but a servant to the mind, it were very barbarous and preposterous that force should be made judge over reason.

Then would he also have replied in words unto him, but Euarchus (who knew what they could say was already said), taking their arguments into his mind, commanded him to proceed against the other prisoner, and that then he would sentence them both together.

Philanax, nothing the milder for Pyrocles' purging himself, but rather (according to the nature of arguing, especially when it is bitter) so much the more vehement, entered thus into his speech against Musidorus, being so overgone with rage that he forgat in this oration his precise method of oratory:

'Behold, most noble protector, to what a state Arcadia is come, since such manner of men may challenge in combat the faithfullest of the nobility, and having merited the shamefullest of all deaths, dare name in marriage the princesses of this country. Certainly, my masters, I must say you were much out of taste if you had not rather enjoy such ladies than be hanged. But the one you have as much deserved as you have dishonoured the other. But now my speech must be directed to you, good master Dorus, who with Pallas' help, pardie, are lately grown Palladius. Too much, too much, this sacred seat of justice grants unto such a fugitive bondslave who, instead of these examinations, should be made confess with a whip that which a halter should punish. Are not you he, sir, whose sheephook was prepared to be our sceptre, in whom lay the knot of all this tragedy? Or else, perchance, they that should gain little by it were dealers in the murder; you only (that had provided the fruits for yourself) knew nothing of it, knew nothing. Hath thy companion here infected thee with such impudency as even in the face of the world to deny that which all the world perceiveth? The other pleads ignorance, and you, I doubt not, will allege absence. But he was ignorant when he was hard by, and you had framed your absence just against the time the act should be committed—so fit a lieutenant he knew he had left of his wickedness that for himself his safest mean was to convey away the lady of us all, who once out of the country, he knew we would come with olive branches of intercession unto her, and fall at his feet to beseech him to leave keeping of sheep and vouchsafe the tyrannizing over us. For to think they are princes, as they say (although in our laws it behoves them nothing), I see at all no reason. These jewels certainly with their disguising sleights they have pilfered in their vagabonding race. And think you such princes should be so long without some followers after them? Truly, if they be princes, it manifestly shows their virtues such as all their subjects are glad to be rid of them. But be they as they are, for we are to consider the matter and not the men. Basilius's murder hath been the cause of their coming. Basilius's murder they have most treacherously brought to pass. Yet that, I doubt not, you will deny as well as your fellow. But how will you deny the stealing away of the princess of this province, which is no less than treason? So notably hath the justice of the gods provided for the punishing of these malefactors as, if it were possible men would not believe the certain evidences of their principal mischief, yet have they discovered themselves sufficiently for their most just overthrow. I say, therefore (to omit my chief matter of the duke's death), this wolvish shepherd, this counterfeit prince, hath traitorously, contrary to his allegiance (having made himself a servant and subject) attempted the depriving this country of our natural princess; and therefore by all right must receive the punishment of traitors. This matter is so assured as he himself will not deny it, being taken and brought back in the fact. This matter is so odious in nature, so shameful to the world, so contrary to all laws, so hurtful to us, so false in him, as if I should stand further in declaring or defacing it, I should either show great doubts in your wisdom or in your justice. Therefore I will transfer my care upon you, and attend, to my learning and comfort, the eternal example you will leave to all mankind of disguisers, falsifiers, adulterers, ravishers, murderers, and traitors.'

Musidorus, while Philanax was speaking against his cousin and him, had looked round about him, to see whether by any means he might come to have caught him in his arms, and have killed him—so much had his disgracing words filled his breast with rage. But perceiving himself so guarded as he should rather show a passionate act than perform his revenge, his hand trembling with desire to strike, and all the veins in his face swelling, casting his eyes over the judgement seat:

'O gods,' said he, 'and have you spared my life to bear these injuries of such a drivel? Is this the justice of this place, to have such men as we are submitted not only to apparent falsehood but most shameful reviling? But mark, I pray you, the ungratefulness of the wretch; how utterly he hath forgotten the benefits both he and all this country hath received of us. For if ever men may remember their own noble deeds, it is then when their just defence and others' unjust unkindness doth require it. Were not we the men that killed the wild beasts which otherwise had killed the princesses if we had not succoured them? Consider, if it please you, where had been Timopyrus's rape, or my treason, if the sweet beauties of the earth had then been devoured? Either think them now dead, or remember they live by us. And yet full often this telltale can acknowledge the loss they should have by their taking away, while maliciously he overpasseth who were their preservers. Neither let this be spoken of me as if I meant to balance this evil with that good, for I must confess that saving of such creatures was rewarded in the act itself, but only to manifest the partial jangling of this vile pickthank. But if we be traitors, where was your fidelity, O only tongue-valiant gentleman, when not only the young princesses but the duke himself was defended from uttermost peril, partly by me, but principally by this excellent young man's both wisdom and valour? Were we that made ourselves against hundreds of armed men openly the shields of his life like secretly to be his empoisoners? Did we then show his life to be dearer to us than our own because we might after rob him of his life, to die shamefully? Truly, truly, master orator, whosoever hath hired you to be so busy in their matters who keep honester servants than yourself, he should have bid you in so many railings bring some excuse for yourself why in the greatest need of your prince, to whom you pretend a miraculous goodwill, you were not then as forward to do like a man yourself, or at least to accuse them that were slack in that service. But commonly they use their feet for their defence, whose tongue is their weapon. Certainly, a very simple subtlety it had been in us to repose our lives in the daughters when we had killed the father. But as this gentleman thinks to win the reputation of a copious talker by leaving nothing unsaid which a filthy mind can imagine,* so think I (or else all words are vain) that to wisemen's judgement our clearness in the duke's death is sufficiently notorious. But at length, when the merchant hath set out his gilded baggage, lastly he comes to some stuff of importance, and saith I conveyed away the princess of this country. And is she indeed your princess? I pray you, then, whom should I wait of else but her that was my mistress by my professed vow, and princess over me while I lived in this soil? Ask her why she went; ask not me why I served her. Since accounting me as a prince you have not to do with me, taking me as her servant, then take withal that I must obey her. But you will say I persuaded her to fly away. Certainly I will for no death deny it, knowing to what honour I should bring her from the thraldom, by such fellows' counsel as you, she was kept in. Shall persuasion to a prince grow treason against a prince? It might be error in me, but falsehood it could not be, since I made myself partaker of whatsoever I wished her unto. Who will ever counsel his king if his counsel be judged by the event, and if he be not found wise shall therefore be thought wicked? But if I be a traitor, I hope you will grant me a correlative to whom I shall be the traitor; for the princess (against whom treasons are considered), I am sure, will avow my faithfulness, without you will say that I am a traitor to her because I left the country, and a traitor to the country because I went with her. Here do I leave out my just excuses of love's force; which, as thy narrow heart hath never had noble room enough in it to receive, so yet those manlike courages that by experience know how subject the virtuous minds are to love a most virtuous creature (witnessed to be such by the most excellent gifts of nature) will deem it a venial trespass to seek the satisfaction of honourable desires—honourable even in the curiousest points of honour, whereout there can no disgrace nor disparagement come unto her. Therefore, O judge, who I hope dost know what it is to be a judge, that your end is to preserve and not to destroy mankind, that laws are not made like lime twigs or nets to catch everything that toucheth them, but rather like sea marks to avoid the shipwrack of ignorant passengers, since that our doing in the extremest interpretation is but a human error, and that of it you may make a profitable event (we being of such estate as their parents would not have misliked the affinity), you will not, I trust, at the persuasion of this brabbler burn your house to make it clean, but like a wise father turn even the fault of your children to any good that may come of it, since that is the fruit of wisdom and end of all judgements.'

While this matter was thus handling, a silent and, as it were, astonished attention possessed all the people; a kindly compassion moved the noble gentleman Sympathus; but as for Kerxenus, everything was spoken either by or of his dear guests moved an effect in him: sometimes tears, sometimes hopeful looks, sometimes whispering persuasions in their ears that stood by him, to seek the saving the two young princes. But the general multitude waited the judgement of Euarchus who, showing in his face no motions either at the one's or other's speech, letting pass the flowers of rhetoric and only marking whither their reasons tended, having made the question to be asked of Gynecia (who continued to take the whole fault upon herself), and having caused Dametas with Miso and Mopsa (who by

Philanax's order had been held in most cruel prison) to make a full declaration how much they knew of these past matters, and then gathering as assured satisfaction to his own mind as in that case he could, not needing to take leisure for that whereof a long practice had bred a well grounded habit in him, with a voice and gesture directed to the universal assembly, in this form pronounced sentence:

'This weighty matter, whereof presently we are to determine, doth at the first consideration yield two important doubts: the first, whether these men be to be judged; the second, how they are to be judged. The first doubt ariseth because they give themselves out for princes absolute, a sacred name and to which any violence seems to be an impiety; for how can any laws (which are the bonds of all human society) be observed if the lawgivers and law rulers be not held in an untouched admiration? But hereto although already they have been sufficiently answered, yet thus much again I may repeat unto you: that whatsoever they be or be not, here they be no princes, since betwixt prince and subject there is as necessary a relation as between father and son, and as there is no man a father but to his child, so is not a prince a prince but to his own subjects. Therefore is not this place to acknowledge in them any principality, without it should at the same time by a secret consent confess subjection. Yet hereto may be objected that the universal civility, the law of nations (all mankind being as it were coinhabiters or world citizens together), hath ever required public persons should be of all parties especially regarded, since not only in peace but in war, not only princes but heralds and trumpets are with great reason exempted from injuries. This point is true, but yet so true as they that will receive the benefit of a custom must not be the first to break it, for then can they not complain if they be not helped by that which they themselves hurt. If a prince do acts of hostility without denouncing war, if he break his oath of amity, or innumerable such other things contrary to the law of arms, he must take heed how he fall into their hands whom he so wrongeth, for then is courtesy the best custom he can claim; much more these men who have not only left to do like princes but to be like princes, not only entered into Arcadia, and so into the Arcadian orders, but into domestical services, and so by making themselves private deprived themselves of respect due to their public calling. For no proportion it were of justice that a man might make himself no prince when he would do evil, and might anew create himself a prince when he would not suffer evil. Thus, therefore, by all laws of nature and nations, and especially by their own putting themselves out of the sanctuary of them, these young men cannot in justice avoid the judgement, but like private men must have their doings either cleared, excused, or condemned.

'There resteth, then, the second point: how to judge well. And that must undoubtedly be done, not by a free discourse of reason and skill of philosophy, but must be tied to the laws of Greece and municipal statutes of this dukedom. For although out of them these came, and to them must indeed refer their offspring, yet because philosophical discourses stand in the general consideration of things, they leave to every man a scope of his own interpretation; where the laws, applying themselves to the necessary use, fold us within assured bounds, which once broken, man's nature infinitely rangeth. Judged therefore they must be, and by your laws judged. Now the action offereth itself to due balance betwixt the accuser's twofold accusation and their answer accordingly applied, the questions being, the one of a fact simply, the other of the quality of a fact. To the first they use direct denial, to the second qualification and excuse. They deny the murder of the duke, and against mighty presumptions bring forth some probable answers, which they do principally fortify with the duchess's acknowledging herself only culpable. Certainly, as in equality of conjectures we are not to take hold of the worst, but rather to be glad we may find any hope that mankind is not grown monstrous (being undoubtedly less evil a guilty man should escape than a guiltless perish), so if in the rest they be spotless, then is this no further to be remembered. But if they have aggravated these suspicions with new evils, then are those suspicions so far to show themselves as to cause the other points to be thoroughly examined and with less favour weighed; since this no man can deny: they have been accidental, if not principal, causes of the duke's death.

'Now, then, we are to determine of the other matters which are laid to them, wherein they do not deny the fact but deny, or at least diminish, the fault. But first I may remember (though it were not first alleged by them) the services they had before done, truly honourable and worthy of great reward, but not worthy to countervail with a following wickedness. Reward is proper to well doing, punishment to evil doing, which must not be confounded no more than good and evil are to be mingled. Therefore it hath been determined in all wisdoms that no man, because he hath done well before, should have his present evils spared, but rather so much the more punished, as having showed he knew how to be good, would against his knowledge be naught. The fact, then, is nakedly without passion or partiality to be viewed. Wherein, he that terms himself Timopyrus denies not he offered violence to the lady Philoclea, an act punished by all the Grecian laws with being thrown down from a high tower to the earth—a death which doth no way exceed the proportion of the trespass; for nothing can be imagined more unnatural than by force to take that which, being holily used, is the root of humanity, the beginning and maintaining of living creatures, whereof the confusion must needs be a general ruin. And since the wickedness of lust is by our decrees punished by death, though both consent, much more is he whose wickedness so overflows as he will compel another to be wicked.

'The other young man confesseth he persuaded the princess Pamela to fly her country, and accompanied her in it—without all question a ravishment no less than the other; for, although he ravished her not from herself, yet he ravished her from him that owed her, which was her father. This kind is chastised by the loss of the head, as a most execrable theft; for if they must die who steal from us our goods, how much more they who steal from us that for which we gather our goods. And if our laws have it so in the private persons, much more forcible are they to be in princes' children, where one steals as it were the whole state and well being of that people, tied by the secret of a long use to be governed by none but the next of that blood. Neither let any man marvel our ancestors have been so severe in these cases, since the example of the Phoenician Europa, but especially of the Grecian Helen,* hath taught them what destroying fires have grown of such sparkles. And although Helen was a wife and this but a child, that booteth not, since the principal cause of marrying wives is that we may have children of our own.

'But now let us see how these young men (truly for their persons worthy of pity, if they had rightly pitied themselves) do go about to mitigate the vehemency of their errors. Some of their excuses are common to both, some peculiar only to him that was the shepherd; both remember the force of love, and as it were the mending up of the matter by their marriage. If that unbridled desire which is entitled love might purge such a sickness as this, surely we should have many loving excuses of hateful mischiefs. Nay rather, no mischief should be committed that should not be veiled under the name of love. For as well he that steals might allege the love of money, he that murders the love of revenge, he that rebels the love of greatness, as the adulterer the love of a woman; since they do in all speech affirm they love that which an ill-governed passion maketh them to follow. But love may have no such privilege. That sweet and heavenly uniting of the minds, which properly is called love, hath no other knot but virtue; and therefore if it be a right love, it can never slide into any action that is not virtuous. The other, and indeed more effectual, reason is that they may be married unto them, and so honourably redress the dishonour of them whom this matter seemeth most to touch. Surely, if the question were what were convenient for the parties, and not what is just in the never-changing justice, there might be much said in it. But herein we must consider that the laws look how to prevent by due examples that such things be not done, and not how to salve such things when they are done. For if the governors of justice shall take such a scope as to measure the foot of the law by a show of conveniency, and measure that conveniency not by the public society but by that which is fittest for them which offend, young men, strong men, and rich men shall ever find private conveniences how to palliate such committed disorders as to the public shall not only be inconvenient but pestilent. The marriage perchance might be fit for them, but very unfit were it to the state to allow a pattern of such procurations of marriage. And thus much do they both allege. Further goes he that went with the princess Pamela, and requireth the benefit of a counsellor, who hath place of free persuasion, and the reasonable excuse of a servant, that did but wait of his mistress. Without all question, as counsellors have great cause to take heed how they advise anything directly opposite to the form of that present government, especially when they do it simply without public allowance, so yet is this case much more apparent; since neither she was an effectual princess, her father being then alive, and though he had been dead, she not come to the years of authority, nor he her servant in such manner to obey her, but by his own preferment first belonging to Dametas, and then to the duke, and therefore, if not by Arcadia laws, yet by household orders, bound to have done nothing without his agreement. Thus, therefore, since the deeds accomplished by these two are both abominable and inexcusable, I do in the behalf of justice, and by the force of

Arcadia laws pronounce that Timopyrus shall be thrown out of a high tower to receive his death by his fall; Palladius shall be beheaded: the time, before sunset; the place, in Mantinea; the executioner, Dametas. Which office he shall execute all the days of his life, for his beastly forgetting the careful duty he owed to his charge.'

This said, he turned himself to Philanax and two of the other noblemen, commanding them to see the judgement presently performed. Philanax, more greedy than any hunter of his prey, went straight to lay hold of the excellent prisoners who, casting a farewell look one upon the other, represented in their faces as much unappalled constancy as the most excellent courage can deliver in outward graces. Yet if at all there were any show of change in them, it was that Pyrocles was something nearer to bashfulness, and Musidorus to anger, both overruled by reason and resolution. But as with great number of armed men Philanax was descending unto them, and that Musidorus was beginning to say something in Pyrocles' behalf, behold Kerxenus that with arms cast abroad and open mouth came crying to Euarchus, holding a stranger in his hand that cried much more than he, desiring they might be heard speak before the prisoners were removed. Even the noble gentleman Sympathus aided them in it, and taking such as he could command, stopped Philanax betwixt entreaty and force from carrying away the princes until it were heard what new matters these men did bring. So again mounting to the tribunal, they hearkened to the stranger's vehement speech, or rather appassionate exclaiming.

But first you will be content to know what he was, and what cause and mean brought him thither. It is not, I hope, forgotten how in the first beginning of Musidorus's love, when in despite of his best-grounded determinations he became a slave to affection, how leaving the place of his eye-infection, he met with the shepherd Menalcas, by the help of whose raiment he advanced himself to that estate which he accounted most high because it might be serviceable to that fancy which he had placed most high in his mind; and how, lest by his presence his purpose might be revealed, he hired him to go into Thessalia, writing by him to a trusty servant of his that he should arrest him until he knew his further pleasure. Menalcas faithfully performed his errand, and was as faithfully imprisoned by Kalodoulus, for such was the gentleman's name to whom Musidorus directed him. But as Kalodoulus performed the first part of his duty in doing the commandment of his prince, so was he with abundance of sincere loyalty extremely perplexed when he understood of Menalcas the strange disguising of his beloved master. For as the acts he and his cousin Pyrocles had done in Asia and Egypt had filled all the ears of the Thessalians and Macedonians with no less joy than admiration, so was the fear of their loss no less grievous unto them when by the noise of report they understood of their lonely committing themselves to the sea, the issue of which they had yet no way learned. But now that by Menalcas he perceived where he was, guessing the like of Pyrocles, comparing the unusedness of this act with the unripeness of their age, seeing in general conjecture they could do it for nothing that might not fall out dangerous, he was somewhile troubled with himself what to do, betwixt doubt of their hurt and doubt of their displeasure. Lastly he resolved his safest and honestest way was to reveal it to the king Euarchus, that both his authority might prevent any damage, and under his wings he himself might remain safe. Thitherward, therefore, he went. But being come to the city of Pella, where he had heard the king lay, he found him not long before departed towards Arcadia. This made him, with all the speed he could, follow Euarchus, as well to advertise him, if need were, as to do his prince service in his uncle's thither coming. And so it happened that, being even this day come to Mantinea, and as warily as he could inquiring after Euarchus, he straight received a strange rumour of these things, but so uncertainly as popular reports carry so rare accidents. But this by all men he was willed: to seek out Kerxenus, a great gentleman of that country, who would soonest satisfy him of all those occurrents. Thus instructed, he came even about the midst of Euarchus's judgement to the desert, where seeing great multitudes, and hearing unknown names of Palladius and Timopyrus, and not able to press to the place where Euarchus sat, he inquired for Kerxenus, and was soon brought unto him, partly because he was generally known unto all men, and partly because he had withdrawn himself from the press when he perceived by Euarchus's words whither they tended, not being able to endure his guests' condemnation. He inquired forthwith of Kerxenus the cause of the assembly, and whether he had heard of Euarchus. Who with many tears made a doleful recital unto him, both of the amazon and shepherd, setting forth their natural graces, and lamenting their pitiful undoing. But his description made Kalodoulus immediately know the shepherd was his duke, and so judging the other to be Pyrocles, and speedily communicating it to Kerxenus, who he saw did favour their case, they brake the press with astonishing every man with their cries. And being come to Euarchus, Kalodoulus fell at his feet, telling him those he had judged were his own son and nephew, the one the comfort of Macedon, the other the only stay of Thessalia, with many suchlike words, but as from a man that assured himself in that matter he should need small speech; while Kerxenus made it known to all men what the prisoners were. To whom he cried they should salute their father, and joy in the good hap the gods had sent them; who were no less glad than all the people amazed at the strange event of these matters. Even Philanax's own revengeful heart was mollified when he saw how from diverse parts in the world so near kinsmen should meet in such a necessity; and withal the fame of Pyrocles and Musidorus greatly drew him to a compassionate conceit, and had already unclothed his face of all show of malice.

But Euarchus stayed a good while upon himself, like a valiant man that should receive a notable encounter, being vehemently stricken with the fatherly love of so excellent children, and studying with his best reason what his office required. At length, with such a kind of gravity as was near to sorrow, he thus uttered his mind:*

'I take witness of the immortal gods', said he, 'O Arcadians, that what this day I have said hath been out of my assured persuasion what justice itself and your just laws require. Though strangers then to me, I had no desire to hurt them; but leaving aside all considerations of the persons, I weighed the matter which you committed into my hands with my most unpartial and furthest reach of reason, and thereout have condemned them to lose their lives, contaminated with so many foul breaches of hospitality, civility, and virtue. Now, contrary to all expectation, I find them to be mine only son and nephew; such upon whom you see what gifts nature hath bestowed; such who have so to the wonder of the world heretofore behaved themselves as might give just cause to the greatest hopes that in an excellent youth may be conceived; lastly, in few words, such in whom I placed all my mortal joys, and thought myself now near my grave to recover a new life. But, alas, shall justice halt, or shall she wink in one's cause which had lynx's eyes in another's? Or rather, shall all private respects give place to that holy name? Be it so, be it so. Let my grey hairs be laid in the dust with sorrow. Let the small remnant of my life be to me an inward and outward desolation, and to the world a gazing stock of wretched misery. But never, never, let sacred rightfulness fall. It is immortal, and immortally ought to be preserved. If rightly I have judged, then rightly have I judged mine own children, unless the name of a child should have force to change the never-changing justice. No, no, Pyrocles and Musidorus, I prefer you much before my life, but I prefer justice as far before you. While you did like yourselves, my body should willingly have been your shield; but I cannot keep you from the effects of your own doing. Nay, I cannot in this case acknowledge you for mine; for never had I shepherd to my nephew, nor never had woman to my son. Your vices have degraded you from being princes, and have disannulled your birthright. Therefore, if there be anything left in you of princely virtue, show it in constant suffering that your unprincely dealing hath purchased unto you. For my part, I must tell you, you have forced a father to rob himself of his children. Do you, therefore, O Philanax, and you my other lords of this country, see the judgement be rightly performed in time, place, and manner as before appointed.'

With that, though he would have refrained them, a man might perceive the tears drop down his long white beard, which moved not only Kalodoulus and Kerxenus to roaring lamentations, but all the assembly dolefully to record that pitiful spectacle. Philanax himself could not abstain from great shows of pitying sorrow, and manifest withdrawing from performing the king's commandment. But Musidorus, having the hope of his safety and recovering of the princess Pamela (which made him most desire to live) so suddenly dashed, but especially moved for his dear Pyrocles, for whom he was ever resolved his last speech should be, and stirred up with rage of unkindness, he thus spake:

'Enjoy thy bloody conquest, tyrannical Euarchus,' said he, 'for neither is convenient the title of a king to a murderer, nor the remembrance of kindred to a destroyer of his kindred. Go home and glory that it hath been in thy power shamefully to kill Musidorus. Let thy flattering orators dedicate crowns of laurel unto thee, that the first of thy race thou hast overthrown a prince of Thessalia. But for me, I hope the Thessalians are not so degenerate from their ancestors but that they will revenge my injury and their loss upon thee. I hope my death is no more unjust to me than it shall be bitter to thee. Howsoever it be, my death shall triumph over thy cruelty. Neither as now would I live to make my life beholding unto thee.

But if thy cruelty hath not so blinded thy eyes that thou canst not see thine own hurt, if thy heart be not so devilish as thou hast no power but to torment thyself, then look upon this young Pyrocles with a manlike eye, if not with a pitiful. Give not occasion to the whole earth to say "see how the gods have made the tyrant tear his own bowels". Examine the eyes and voices of all this people, and what all men see, be not blind in thine own case. Look, I say, look upon him in whom the most curious searcher is able to find no fault but that he is thy son. Believe it, thy own subjects will detest thee for robbing them of such a prince, in whom they have right as well as thyself.'

Some more words to that purpose he would have spoken, but Pyrocles (who oft had called to him) did now fully interrupt him, desiring him not to do him the wrong to give his father ill words before him, willing him to consider it was their own fault and not his unjustice; and withal to remember their resolution of well suffering all accidents, which this impatience did seem to vary from. And then kneeling down with all humbleness, he took the speech in this order to Euarchus:

'If my daily prayers to the almighty gods had so far prevailed as to have granted me the end whereto I have directed my actions, I should rather have been now a comfort to your mind than an example of your justice, rather a preserver of your memory by my life than a monument of your judgement by my death. But since it hath pleased their unsearchable wisdoms to overthrow all the desires I had to serve you, and make me become a shame unto you, since the last obedience I can show you is to die, vouchsafe yet, O father (if my fault have not made me altogether unworthy so to term you), vouchsafe, I say, to let the few and last words your son shall ever speak not to be tedious unto you. And if the remembrance of my virtuous mother (who once was dear unto you) may bear any sway with you, if the name of Pyrocles have at any time been pleasant, let one request of mine (which shall not be for my own life) be graciously accepted of you. What you owe to justice is performed in my death. A father to have executed his only son will leave a sufficient example for a greater crime than this. My blood will satisfy the highest point of equity. My blood will satisfy the hardest hearted of this country. O save the life of this prince; that is the only all I will with my last breath demand of you. With what face will you look upon your sister when, in reward of nourishing me in your greatest need, you take away, and in such sort take away, that which is more dear to her than all the world, and is the only comfort wherewith she nourisheth her old age? O give not such an occasion to the noble Thessalians for ever to curse the match that their prince did make with the Macedonian blood. By my loss there follows no public loss, for you are to hold the seat, and to provide yourself perchance of a worthier successor. But how can you, or all the earth, recompense the damage that poor Thessalia shall sustain, who sending out (whom otherwise they would no more have spared than their own eyes) their prince to you, and you requesting to have him, by you he should thus dishonourably be extinguished? Set before you, I beseech you, the face of that miserable people when no sooner shall the news come that you have met your nephew but withal they shall hear that you have beheaded him. How many tears they shall spend, how many complaints they shall make, so many just execrations will light upon you. And take heed, O father (for since my death answers my fault while I live I may call upon that dear name), lest seeking too precise a course of justice, you be not thought most unjust in weakening your neighbour's mighty estate by taking away their only pillar. In me, in me, this matter began; in me, let it receive his ending. Assure yourself, no man will doubt your severe observing the laws when it shall be known Euarchus hath killed Pyrocles. But the time of my ever farewell approacheth. If you do think my death sufficient for my fault, and do not desire to make my death more miserable than death, let these dying words of him that was once your son pierce your ears. Let Musidorus live, and Pyrocles shall live in him, and you shall not want a child.'

'A child', cried out Musidorus, 'to him that kills Pyrocles!'

With that again he fell to entreat for Pyrocles, and Pyrocles as fast for Musidorus, each employing his wit how to show himself most worthy to die, to such an admiration of all the beholders that most of them, examining the matter by their own passions, thought Euarchus (as often extraordinary excellencies, not being rightly conceived, do rather offend than please) an obstinate-hearted man, and such a one, who being pitiless, his dominion must needs be insupportable. But Euarchus, that felt his own misery more than they, and yet loved goodness more than himself, with such a sad assured behaviour as Cato killed himself withal,* when he had heard the uttermost of that their speech tended unto, he commanded again they should be carried away, rising up from the seat (which he would much rather have wished should have been his grave), and looking who would take the charge, whereto everyone was exceeding backward.

But as this pitiful matter was entering into, those that were next the duke's body might hear from under the velvet wherewith he was covered a great voice of groaning; whereat every man astonished, and their spirits, appalled with these former miseries, apt to take any strange conceit. When they might perfectly perceive the body stir, then some began to fear spirits, some to look for a miracle, most to imagine they knew not what. But Philanax and Kerxenus, whose eyes honest love (though to diverse parties) held most attentive, leapt to the table, and putting off the velvet cover, might plainly discern, with as much wonder as gladness, that the duke lived. Which how it fell out in few words shall be declared.

So it was that the drink he had received was neither (as Gynecia first imagined) a love potion nor (as it was after thought) a deadly poison, but a drink made by notable art, and as it was thought not without natural magic, to procure for thirty hours such a deadly sleep as should oppress all show of life. The cause of the making of this drink had first been that a princess of Cyprus, grandmother to Gynecia, being notably learned (and yet not able with all her learning to answer the objections of Cupid), did furiously love a young nobleman of her father's court, who fearing the king's rage, and not once daring either to attempt or accept so high a place, she made that sleeping drink, and found means by a trusty servant of hers (who of purpose invited him to his chamber) to procure him, that suspected no such thing, to receive it. Which done, he no way able to resist, was secretly carried by him into a pleasant chamber in the midst of a garden she had of purpose provided for this enterprise, where that space of time pleasing herself with seeing and cherishing of him, when the time came of the drink's end of working (and he more astonished than if he had fallen from the clouds), she bade him choose either then to marry her, and to promise to fly away with her in a bark she had made ready, or else she would presently cry out, and show in what place he was, with oath he was come thither to ravish her. The nobleman in these straits, her beauty prevailed; he married her and escaped the realm with her, and after many strange adventures were reconciled to the king, her father, after whose death they reigned. But she, gratefully remembering the service that drink had done her, preserved in a bottle (made by singular art long to keep it without perishing) great quantity of it, with the foretold inscription. Which wrong interpreted by her daughter-in-law, the queen of Cyprus, was given by her to Gynecia at the time of her marriage; and the drink, finding an old body of Basilius, had kept him some hours longer in the trance than it would have done a younger.

But a good while it was before good Basilius could come again to himself. In which time Euarchus (more glad than of the whole world's monarchy to be rid of his miserable magistracy, which even in justice he was now to surrender to the lawful prince of that country) came from the throne unto him, and there with much ado made him understand how these intricate matters had fallen out. Many garboils passed through his fancy before he could be persuaded Cleophila was other than a woman. At length, remembering the oracle, which now indeed was accomplished (not as before he had imagined), considering all had fallen out by the highest providence, and withal weighing in all these matters his own fault had been the greatest, the first thing he did was with all honourable pomp to send for Gynecia (who, poor lady, thought she was leading forth to her living burial), and (when she came) to recount before all the people the excellent virtue was in her, which she had not only maintained all her life most unspotted but now was content so miserably to die to follow her husband. He told them how she had warned him to take heed of that drink. And so, with all the exaltings of her that might be, he publicly desired her pardon for those errors he had committed. And so kissing her, left her to receive the most honourable fame of any princess throughout the world, all men thinking (saving only Pyrocles and Philoclea who never bewrayed her) that she was the perfect mirror of all wifely love. Which though in that point undeserved, she did in the remnant of her life duly purchase with observing all duty and faith, to the example and glory of Greece—so uncertain are mortal judgements, the same person most infamous and most famous, and neither justly.

Then with princely entertainment to Euarchus, and many kind words to Pyrocles (whom still he dearly loved, though in a more virtuous kind), the marriage was concluded, to the inestimable joy of Euarchus (towards whom now Musidorus acknowledged his fault), betwixt these peerless princes and princesses; Philanax for his singular faith ever held dear of Basilius while he lived, and no less of Musidorus who was to inherit that dukedom, and therein confirmed to him and his the second place of that province, with great increase of his living to maintain it; which like proportion he used to Kalodoulus in Thessalia. Sympathus, Euarchus took with him into Macedon, and there highly advanced him. But as for Kerxenus, Pyrocles (to whom his father in his own time gave the whole kingdom of Thrace) held him always about him, giving him in pure gift the great city of Abdera.

But the solemnities of these marriages, with the Arcadian pastorals* full of many comical adventures happening to those rural lovers, the strange story of the fair queens Artaxia of Persia and Erona of Lydia, with the prince Plangus's wonderful chances, whom the latter had sent to Pyrocles, and the extreme affection Amasis, king of Egypt, bare unto the former, the shepherdish loves of Menalcas with Kalodoulus's daughter, and the poor hopes of the poor Philisides in the pursuit of his affections, the strange continuance of Klaius's and Strephon's desire, lastly the son of Pyrocles named Pyrophilus, and Melidora the fair daughter of Pamela by Musidorus, who even at their birth entered into admirable fortunes, may awake some other spirit to exercise his pen in that wherewith mine is already dulled.

The last book or act.

APPENDIX A: A DEBATE ON VERSIFICATION

DICUS said that since verses had their chief ornament, if not end, in music, those which were just appropriated to music did best obtain their end, or at least were the most adorned; but those must needs most agree with music, since music standing principally upon the sound and the quantity, to answer the sound they brought words, and to answer the quantity they brought measure. So that for every semibreve or minim, it had his syllable matched unto it with a long foot or a short foot, whereon they drew on certain names (as dactylus, spondeus, trocheus, etc.), and without wresting the word did as it were kindly accompany the time, so that either by the time a poet should straight know how every word should be measured unto it, or by the verse as soon find out the full quantity of the music. Besides that it hath in itself a kind (as a man may well call it) of secret music, since by the measure one may perceive some verses running with a high note fit for great matters, some with a light foot fit for no greater than amorous conceits. 'Where', said he, 'those rhymes we commonly use, observing nothing but the number of syllables, as to make it of eight, ten, or twelve feet (saving perchance that some have some care of the accent), the music, finding it confused, is forced sometimes to make a quaver of that which is rough and heavy in the mouth, and at another time to hold up in a long that which, being perchance but a light vowel, would be gone with a breath; and for all this comes at length a hink, tink, blirum and lirum, for a rhyming recompense, much like them that, having not skill to dance (proportioning either slowly or swiftly his foot according to his ear), will yet for fellowship clap his feet together to make a noise. And this is the cause we have such hives full of rhyming poets, more than ever there were owls at Athens, where of the other there were but few in all ages come to our hands, but they dearly esteemed.'

Lalus on the other side would have denied his first proposition, and said that since music brought a measured quantity with it, therefore the words less needed it, but as music brought time and measure, so these verses brought words and rhyme, which were four beauties for the other three. And yet to deny further the strength of his speech, he said Dicus did much abuse the dignity of poetry to apply it to music, since rather music is a servant to poetry, for by the one the ear only, by the other the mind, was pleased. And therefore what doth most adorn words, levelled within a proportion of number, to that music must be implied; which if it cannot do it well it is the musician's fault and not the poet's, since the poet is to look but to beautify his words to the most delight, which no doubt is more had by the rhyme, especially to common ears to which the poet doth most direct his studies, and therefore is called the popular philosopher. And yet in this the finest judgement shall have more pleasure, since he that rhymes observes something the measure but much the rhyme, whereas the other attends only measure without all respect of rhyme; besides the accent which the rhymer regardeth, of which the former hath little or none. 'And therefore', said Lalus, 'meseems rather those kind of poets are such manner dancers which, not binding them to return to one cadence, are ever kicking of their heels, and leave the pleasant observation of the chief cause. And where by the number of our kind you object too much facility, although easily no fault, yet they that will bind themselves to rhyme as the Tuscan and Arcadian shepherds do, you shall not find them so thick. And for the few of the other kind, the cause is that many did write, but few wrote well, and therefore few lasted to the posterity; and the same no doubt will fall to a great number of rhymes, which die as soon as they are born, and few remain to come out of wardship.'

Dicus would have replied to have showed his evasions, but Basilius, after he had moderated betwixt them, and said that in both kinds he wrote well that wrote wisely, and so both commendable, rose, remembering Cleophila's hurt, and therefore (though unwilling) persuaded her to take that far spent night's rest. And so of all sides they went to recommend themselves to the elder brother of Death.

Here endeth the first Eclogues.

APPENDIX B: 'THE LAD PHILISIDES': A *CANZONE*

The lad Philisides
Lay by a river's side,
In flowery field a gladder eye to please;
His pipe was at his foot,
His lambs were him beside;
A widow turtle near on bared root
Sate wailing without boot;
Each thing, both sweet and sad,
Did draw his boiling brain
To think, and think with pain,
Of Mira's beams, eclipsed by absence bad.
And thus, with eyes made dim
With tears, he said, or sorrow said for him:

'O earth, once answer give:
So may thy stately grace
By north or south still rich adorned live;
So Mira long may be
On thy then blessed face,
Whose foot doth set a heaven on cursed thee;
I ask—now answer me—
If th'author of thy bliss,
Phoebus, that shepherd high,
Do turn from thee his eye,
Doth not thyself, when he long absent is,
Like rogue all ragged go,
And pine away with daily wasting woe?

'Tell me, you wanton brook:
So may your sliding race
Shun loathed-loving banks with cunning crook;
So in you ever new
Mira may look her face,
And make you fair with shadow of her hue,
So when to pay your due

To mother sea you come,
She chide you not for stay,
Nor beat you for your play:
Tell me, if your diverted streams become
Absented quite from you,
Are you not dried? Can you yourself renew?

'Tell me, you flowers fair,
Cowslip and columbine:
So may your make, this wholesome spring-time air,
With you embraced lie,
And lately thence untwine,
But with dew-drops engender children high;
So may you never die,
But pulled by Mira's hand
Dress bosom hers, or head,
Or scatter on her bed:
Tell me, if husband spring-time leave your land,
When he from you is sent,
Wither not you, languished with discontent?

'Tell me, my seely pipe:
So may thee still betide
A cleanly cloth thy moistness for to wipe;
So may the cherries red
Of Mira's lips divide
Their sugared selves to kiss thy happy head;
So may her ears be led,
Her ears, where music lives,
To hear, and not despise,
Thy liribliring cries:
Tell, if that breath which thee thy sounding gives
Be absent far from thee,
Absent alone canst thou then piping be?

'Tell me, my lamb of gold:
So may'st thou long abide
The day well fed, the night in faithful fold;
So grow thy wool of note
In time, that, richly dyed,
It may be part of Mira's petticoat;
Tell me, if wolves the throat

Have caught of thy dear dam,
Or she from thee be stayed,
Or thou from her be strayed,
Canst thou, poor lamb, become another's lamb?
Or rather, till thou die,
Still for thy dam with bea-waymenting cry?

'Tell me, O turtle true:
So may no fortune breed
To make thee, nor thy better-loved, rue;
So may thy blessings swarm
That Mira may thee feed
With hand and mouth; with lap and breast keep warm:
Tell me, if greedy arm
Do fondly take away
With traitor lime the one,
The other left alone;
Tell me, poor wretch, parted from wretched prey,
Disdain not you the green,
Wailing till death; shun you not to be seen?

'Earth, brook, flowers, pipe, lamb, dove,
Say all, and I with them:
'Absence is death, or worse, to them that love.'
So I, unlucky lad,
Whom hills from her do hem,
What fits me now but tears, and sighings sad?
O fortune too too bad:
I rather would my sheep
Th'had'st killed with a stroke,
Burnt cabin, lost my cloak,
Than want one hour those eyes which my joys keep.
O, what doth wailing win?
Speech without end were better not begin.

'My song, climb thou the wind
Which Holland sweet now gently sendeth in,
That on his wings the level thou may'st find
To hit, but kissing hit,
Her ears, the weights of wit.
If thou know not for whom thy master dies,
These marks shall make thee wise:
She is the herdess fair that shines in dark,
And gives her kids no food but willow's bark.'

This said, at length he ended
His oft sigh-broken ditty,
Then rase; but rase on legs with faintness bended,
With skin in sorrow dyed,
With face the plot of pity,
With thoughts, which thoughts their own
   tormentors tried,
He rase, and straight espied
His ram, who to recover
The ewe another loved
With him proud battle proved:
He envied such a death in sight of lover,
And always westward eyeing,
More envied Phoebus for his western flying.

EXPLANATORY NOTES

3 *THE COUNTESS OF PEMBROKE*: Sidney's sister Mary, born 1561, married Henry Herbert, second Earl of Pembroke, in 1577. She was his third wife, and about thirty years younger than him. Much of the *Old Arcadia* may have been written while Sidney was staying with his sister at Wilton.

4 *Arcadia*: this account of Arcadia, deriving from such classical sources as Polybius and Virgil's *Eclogues*, is probably covertly a eulogy of England, uniquely peaceful among Northern European countries in the late sixteenth century, and celebrated by Sidney in his *Defence of Poetry* as particularly rich in poetic potential. According to Polybius, it was the Arcadians' practice of music and poetry up to the age of thirty that kept the country at peace: when one city in Arcadia abandoned it they immediately fell into civil strife (Polybius, *The Histories*, Loeb ed., IV. 20–1).

5 *Delphos, there by the oracle*: the Delphic Oracle, which Sidney would have read about in Plato's *Laws* and many other sources, 'was primarily concerned with questions of religion, how in particular circumstances men were to be reconciled with the gods, and evil averted' (Sir Paul Harvey, *Oxford Companion to Classical Literature*, 1941).

7 *Let your subjects . . . uncertain changes*: this passage closely parallels the final paragraph of Sidney's own letter of advice to his sovereign, dissuading her from marriage with the Duke of Alençon (*Misc. Prose*, ed. Duncan-Jones and van Dorsten, 1973, 56–7).

9 *the beauty of the world, Philoclea*: this phrase links Philoclea with Sidney's Stella, for Sir John Harington suffixed his transcription of *Astrophel and Stella* x: 'Sr. Phillip Syd: to the beuty of the worlde' (Ruth Hughey ed., *The Arundel Harington Manuscript of Tudor Poetry*, 1960, 1. 117).

the younger, but chiefer: Pyrocles is heir to a kingdom, Musidorus is only a duke; but 'chiefer' may also identify Pyrocles as the stronger centre of narrative interest.

10 *traverses*: crosses, barriers.

11 *desert*: uninhabited countryside; cf. Shakespeare, *As You Like It*, II. i. 23, II. vii. 110, and *passim*.

13 *the mind itself must, like other things, sometimes be unbent*: in a letter to Hubert Languet in 1574 Sidney had commented on 'the age in which we live: an age that resembles a bow too long bent, it must be unstrung or it will break'.

15 *poets whose liberal pens can as easily travel over mountains as molehills*: cf. Shakespeare, *A Midsummer Night's Dream*, v. i. 2–22.

16 *even as Apollo is painted*: this was a popular motif in Italian Renaissance painting; see for instance the treatment of the subject by Pollaiuolo in the National Gallery, London.

17 *the reasonable part of our soul is to have absolute commandment*: an argument derived from Plato. Henricus Stephanus's edition of Plato's works, with introductions by Serranus, was sent to Sidney in 1579.

18 *a launder, a distaff-spinner*: a reference to the legend of Hercules being taken captive by Omphale, queen of Lydia: he was dressed as a woman and set to spin, while she took his club and lion skin. In the *Defence of Poetry* Sidney refers to this myth as breeding both 'delight and laughter', and in the *New Arcadia* Pyrocles wears a jewel depicting the transvestite Hercules.

21 *quiet schools*: debating schools in universities or Inns of Court; the Divinity School at Oxford is a surviving example which Sidney would have known.

22 *crossing his arms*: a standard gesture of melancholy.

24 *an eagle ... grieved him*: this is a wordless *impresa*, or personal emblem, representing Pyrocles's willing subjection to the feminine power of Philoclea.

25 *Pygmalion*: Pygmalion fell in love with a statue of his own making (Ovid, *Metamorphoses*, x).

28 *Like great god Saturn ... Momus' grace*: a series of paradoxes: Saturn is ugly, Venus wanton, Pan rough-haired, Juno bad-tempered, Iris changeable (fast = steadfast), Cupid blind and Vulcan lame. 'Momus' is a standard classical name for a carping fault-finder.

rudeness, which the duke interpreted plainness: cf. *King Lear*, i. i. 131, 'Let pride, which she calls plainness, marry her'.

29 *Maid Marian*: after the classical oaths invented for Dametas earlier, Sidney here slips into the vernacular: 'Maid Marian' in May games and morris dances was a man dressed as a woman, and it may be that Dametas is suspicious of Cleophila's femininity. Cf. E. K. Chambers, *The Mediaeval Stage* (1903), i. 196.

Latona's: Diana's mother, who turned some Lycian peasants who muddied the pool where she was drinking into frogs (Ovid, *Metamorphoses*, vi).

33 *Penthesilea*: name taken from the Amazon fighting for Troy in Virgil's *Aeneid*, i. 491, though there she is slain by Achilles, rather than by Pyrrhus. 'Senicia' seems to be Sidney's invention.

34 *a perfect white lamb*: this *impresa*, as MSS of earliest versions of the *Old*

Arcadia call it, is a self-explanatory image of the gentle Pamela needlessly confined by her father's caprice. It may be compared with real emblematic jewels, e.g., 'a lambe of mother-of-pearle' given by Fulke Greville to the Queen as a New Year's gift in 1578/9.

black eye ... whiteness: Philoclea resembles Sidney's Stella (cf. note on p. 9) in having a fair complexion and dark eyes.

40 *contentment of the mind*: Sidney here draws on various commonplaces about contentment, e.g. 'Content is a kingdom' (M. P. Tilley, *Proverbs in English C16 and C17*, C623); cf. also *Henry VI*, III. i. 64.

41 *eclogue*: the word seems to be used here to mean 'dialogue', 'poetic debate'. *OED* gives as Sense 2 'Erroneously for: conversation, discourse', citing a first example from 1613.

43 *Arethusa when she ran from Alpheus*: the nymph Arethusa was pursued while bathing by the river-god Alpheus, and was metamorphosed into a fountain (Ovid, *Metamorphoses*, v).

her heart gave her she was a man: Sidney makes a more complex use of disguise than do most of his immediate successors, such as Shakespeare, in allowing one character, Gynecia, to penetrate the disguise, while another, Dametas, is distinctly suspicious.

48 *Pallas with the spoils of Gorgon*: Perseus gave the head of the Gorgon, which he had killed, to Minerva (Pallas Athene).

Hercules killing the Nemean lion: the first of the seven labours of Hercules.

50 *whose pen ... an unthought-on song*: this comment allows us to accept as a record of extempore versification the highly intricate poems that compose the Arcadian eclogues. Such a difference between a text as performed and as written out exists with many masques and entertainments, Sidney's own *Lady of May* probably being an example (cf. *Misc. Prose*, 17–20).

52 *Come, Dorus, come*: this singing competition is one of the earliest in English. The more modest one in *The Lady of May* may have been written a year or so earlier, as may the August eclogue in Spenser's *Shepheardes Calender* (1579). Theocritus and Virgil offered models, but Sidney was more immediately influenced by the Second Eclogue in Sannazaro's *Arcadia* and the Third Song in Gil Polo's continuation of Montemayor's *Diana*. The exacting three- and two-syllable rhymes set up by Lalus for Dorus to follow conform with Sidney's praise, in the *Defence of Poetry*, of English as a language rich in such rhymes (*Misc. Prose*, 120).

54 *Once, O sweet once*: presumably a dramatic projection into the past of Pamela falling down 'flat upon her face' at the sight of the she-bear a matter of minutes before the interrupted 'pastorals' were begun.

57 *Argus*: the herdsman transformed to a many-eyed dog by Juno and set to watch over Jove's mistress Io, transformed to a cow (Ovid, *Metamorphoses*, i).

58 *Pan . . . Syrinx*: Pan pursued the nymph Syrinx who was transformed into a reed, from which he made the seven-reeded pan-pipe (Ovid, *Metamorphoses*, i).

60 *this pitiful story*: the story of Erona, the only major digression in the *Old Arcadia*, is placed in the First Eclogues probably for two reasons: it illustrates the political chaos and personal misery which can be brought about by 'cupidinous' love in a person of royal status; and it shows Pyrocles and Musidorus as active agents of heroic goodness, who are at that moment urgently needed to rescue Erona from prison and death. Though they persuade themselves (p. 63) that they have plenty of time to devote themselves to the 'present action' before they need to reveal themselves to Plangus, the Erona story implicitly reproaches them for the frivolity of their sojourn in Arcadia.

64 *Philisides*: Sidney's poetic persona, formed from his own names, Phili[ppus] Sid[n]e[iu]s, but also meaning 'star-lover', from the Greek φιλειν (to love) and Latin *sidus* (star or constellation). His role is very much reduced in the revised *Arcadia*.

65 *Ruin's relic*: the old spelling 'relique' gives an indication of the likely pronunciation.

He water ploughs, and soweth in the sand: a classical commonplace; cf. Ovid, *Heroides*, v. 115–16. Sidney's immediate source, however, was lines 10–12 of Sannazaro's Eighth Eclogue:

> Nel' onde solca e nel'arene semena;
> E'l vago vento spera in rete accogliere
> Chi sue speranze fonda in cor de femina.

66 *And to conclude, thy mistress is a woman*: cf. Sir Edward Dyer, 'A Fancy', lines 47–8:

> O fraile unconstant kynd, and safe in trust to noe man!
> Noe woomen angels be, and loe, my mystris is a woeman.

(R. M. Sargent, *Life and Lyrics of Sir Edward Dyer*, 1968, 186.)

the loveliest shepherd: apparently a tribute to Sidney's friend Dyer; see previous note.

67 *other sports*: for this catalogue of activities which restrain love, cf. Ovid, *Remedia Amoris*, 715–16 and 178–210.

69 *blow point, hot cockles, or else at keels*: three rustic games: in the first small pieces of wood were blown through a tube, the second was a form of blind man's buff, and the third ninepins.

Life is naught but time: cf. Sidney's letter to Edward Denny in 1580: 'when you say that you lose your time, you do indeed lose so much of your life'.

70 *swan's example*: this fable, explaining the swan's muteness by its former biting tongue, appears to be Sidney's invention.

71 *choler adusted*: medical term for 'dry choler', the cause of melancholy.

Nota: this list of rules for writing quantitative verse in English is found in only one of the *Old Arcadia* MSS, that at St John's College, Cambridge, which was Jean Robertson's copy-text. A slightly different version, entitled 'Rules in mesured verses in English which I observe', is contained in the Ottley MS of Sidney's poetry in the National Library of Wales. For an account of Sidney's theories, see Derek Attridge, *Well-weighed syllables* (1974), 173–6.

72 *sapphics*: it is appropriate that the first poem sung by Pyrocles while he is disguised as a woman should be in the verse form associated with the best known Greek poetess.

75 *None can speak of a wound with skill, if he have not a wound felt*: proverbial; cf. *Romeo and Juliet*, II. ii. 1, 'He jests at scars, that never felt a wound.'

76 *these trees*: the tree catalogue was a commonplace going back to classical poetry; e.g. Ovid, *Metamorphoses*, x. Familiar English examples are Chaucer's *Knight's Tale*, 2920–4, and Spenser's *Faerie Queene*, I.i. Sidney's immediate model may have been the opening prose of Sannazaro's *Arcadia*. In his revised *Arcadia* a hiatus marks a place where Sidney seems to have intended to write a prose tree catalogue (*Works*, ed. Feuillerat, i. 216).

89 *throwing a great number of sheep's eyes*: looking amorously.

95 *Sic vos non vobis*: 'Thus you are honoured, not for yourself'. Sidney was fond of this motto, using another version of it, *Sic nos non nobis*, when he took part in the royal entertainment *The Four Foster Children of Desire* on 15 May 1581. His immediate source may have been G. Ruscelli's *Imprese Illustri* (Venice, 1566), 65, where the motto is applied to a hive of bees, image of useful labour. He offered a copy of this book to Languet in 1573. A four-line epigram which expands the motto is possibly also by Sidney, for it comes in between two of his poems in a commonplace book associated with his circle:

> The silly Bird, the Bee, the Horse,
> The Oxe, that tilles and delves,
> They build, bring hony, beare & draw
> For others: not themselves.
>
> (BL MS Harley 7392, f. 38.)

Sidney appears to confuse Castor and Pollux, for according to Ovid

(*Metamorphoses*, vi) Pollux was born a god and Castor deified at his brother's request.

To thy memory principally: one of several hints that Philoclea is the narrator's central focus of sympathy. If the word 'memory' here implies that Philoclea is now dead, it is the only such hint; 'memory' may rather mean 'thought, recollection'.

98 *Caeneus*: from a story in Ovid's *Metamorphoses* (xii) of a woman, Caenis, who was changed by Neptune into a man, Caeneus.

99 *disastered*: used in its etymological sense, 'ill-starred'.

100 *as the old governess of Danae is painted*: Jupiter made love to Danae in the form of a shower of gold (Ovid, *Metamorphoses*, vi). In Titian's later renderings of the subject an old governess is included, who holds up her hands to catch some of the gold not meant for her. Sidney probably refers to copies or engravings after Titian; cf. K. Duncan-Jones, 'Sidney and Titian', in *English Renaissance Studies: Presented to Helen Gardner* (1980), 1–11.

104 *in a sandy bank*: sand was a stock image of changeability, and especially of women's fickleness; cf. note on p. 65, and also Spenser's *Amoretti*, lxxv. Sidney seems here to be alluding to the opening song of Montemayor's *Diana*, which he translated in *Certain Sonnets*, 28; in it the forsaken Sireno recalls Diana writing the words 'sooner die then change my state' in a 'sandie bank'. Robert Sidney was later to translate the same song (cf. Robert Sidney, *Poems*, ed. P. J. Croft, 1984, 268–9).

106 *Pygmalion's mind*: Pygmalion made a statue which was metamorphosed into a real woman (Ovid, *Metamorphoses*, x); it is striking that Sidney applies the metaphor to Philoclea, not to the male Pyrocles.

107 *with as much rageful haste as the Trojan women went to burn Aeneas's ships*: Virgil, *Aeneid*, v. 60 ff.

108 *scorn which Pallas showed to the poor Arachne*: Arachne, who outdid Athene in a weaving contest, provoked the goddess's wrath and was transformed into a spider (Ovid, *Metamorphoses*, vi). Spenser's *Muiopotmos* (1590) is an elaboration of the myth.

111 *a face of wood of the outside*: i.e., closely barred wooden gates.

Phagona: the name, from φαγών, glutton, suggests the town's character.

114 *Persians, whom you have in present fear*: not a well-developed theme, Arcadia's peacefulness being stressed by and large, rather than her vulnerability to assault: but in the Erona episode, pp. 60–3, an additional motive for the princes' rescuing Erona from Otanes, King of Persia, was 'the natural hate the Greeks bare the Persians'.

115 *a sheep's draught*: a bitter medicine.

121 *Dorus, tell me*: this poem makes remarkably successful use of trisyllabic rhyme, or 'that, which the Italians term *sdrucciola*' (*Misc. Prose*, 120), which is literally 'sliding' rhyme. Though not a formal singing contest, the exacting rhymes initiated by Dicus and followed by Dorus give this debate about love a strongly competitive flavour.

123 *construction*: Dicus introduces a fresh complication into the verse by initiating internal rhymes, though abandoning the triple terminal rhymes in favour of single ones: Dorus, however, introduces double rhyming twelve lines later, which Dicus builds up to triple rhyme again ten lines later.

124 *Nico Pas Dicus*: a comic singing contest, parodying Virgil's Third Eclogue; cf. note on p. 52.

125 *by my hat*: cf. Chaucer, *Parlement of Fowles*, line 589.

126 *barleybreak*: a rustic game for three couples, the middle pair being in 'hell'. The longest poem Sidney wrote, 'Lamon's Tale' (OP 4 in Ringler's edition), includes an extended description of a game of barley break played by Strephon, Geron, Pas, Urania, Cosma and Nous.

128 *Tell me . . . foregoes*: Virgil's Third Eclogue also contained two riddles. Sidney's have not been satisfactorily explained.

129 *With cries first born*: combined with the preceding image of players on a 'filthy stage', this line must have contributed to *King Lear*, IV. vi. 184–5:

> When we are born, we cry that we are come
> To this great stage of fools.

Links with the *Arcadia* in *King Lear* are discussed in K. Muir's Arden edition (1952), xxxvii–xlii.

132 *but a baiting place*: cf. Basilius's visit to the oracle at the beginning of the *Old Arcadia*, misguidedly 'making a perpetual mansion of this poor baiting place of man's life'.

let my life long time: cf. the final line of Petrarch's *Trionfo della Morte*, as translated by Sidney's sister, the Countess of Pembroke, in which Laura tells her lover:

> Thow without me long time on earth shalt staie.

(Text edited by F. B. Young, *PMLA* xxvii, 1912, 52–75.) Like Sidney's poem, Petrarch's *Trionfo* is a philosophical dialogue in *terza rima*.

133 *The ass did hurt*: a reference to Aesop's *Fables*, in which an ass, trying to compete with a playful young dog, fawns on his master and kicks him (Caxton translation, 1550, fol. 62ᵛ).

134 *monthly they should send him*: this story may be based on that of Theseus and the Minotaur, the Cretan monster which devoured seven youths and

　　　seven maidens every year until Theseus killed him. Plutarch opens his
　　　Lives with the life of Theseus, no doubt well known to Sidney.

135　*a horse-load of a mast*: a very heavy pole.

140　*eclogue with*: again, as on pp. 41 and 120, 'eclogue' seems to carry the sense
　　　'dialogue'.

142　*creatures*: metre demands that this is pronounced as three syllables.

143　*Anacreon's kind of verses*: this poem is not only in an 'Anacreontic' metre,
　　　but is thematically based on the first poem in the *Anacreontea*, θελω λεγειν
　　　Ατρειδας, in which the poet wants to sing of heroic subjects but finds
　　　that his lyre will sound of nothing but love. For an account of the poem's
　　　structure, cf. K. Duncan-Jones, 'Sidney's Anacreontics', note forthcom-
　　　ing in *RES*, May 1985.

144　*phaleuciacs*: a term apparently invented by Sidney for 'Phaleucian
　　　hendecasyllabics', a metre used by Catullus. The somewhat grotesque
　　　military imagery of this poem links it with *Astrophel and Stella* 29.

145　*asclepiadics*: a difficult metre, which Sidney is unable to adhere to
　　　consistently, originated by the Greek poets Sappho and Alcaeus and
　　　extensively used by Horace. The first two lines were used as the
　　　beginning of no. 10 in John Dowland's *Second Book of Songs or Airs* (1600).
　　　Together with Philisides's echo poem, this is thought by Ringler to be an
　　　early poem imperfectly revised and blended into the Second Eclogues.

148　*stanzas*: *OED* gives this as the earliest use of the word in English; earlier
　　　writers had used the term 'staff' or 'stave'.

151　*traffic*: trading, referring back to the 'merchant man' image in the
　　　preceding song.

153　*hearty*: heartfelt, sincere.

154　*departure*: separation—see Glossary.

157　*the river Tagus*: river in Spain reputed from antiquity to run over golden
　　　gravel; cf. Wyatt's epigram:

　　　　　　Tagus, fare well, that westward with thy stremes
　　　　　　Torns up the grayns of gold alredy tryd . . .

　　　　　　　　(Wyatt, *Poems*, ed. Muir and Thomson, XCIX.)

164　*the valiant Aristomenes*: probably a reference to Pindar's Pythian Ode
　　　VIII, praising Aristomenes as winner of a wrestling match. In his *Defence
　　　of Poetry* Sidney vigorously defended the value of Pindar's poetry against
　　　the charge that he 'many times praiseth highly victories of small moment'
　　　(*Misc. Prose*, 97). He would no doubt have known the edition of Pindar by
　　　Henricus Stephanus Estienne (Paris, 1560). This seems a more likely
　　　source than Alciati's *Emblemata* (cf. Robertson, 452). But another possible
　　　source is Apuleius's friend 'Aristomenus' in *The Golden Ass*.

what time for the discord fell out in Arcadia he lived banished: Sidney not only takes pains to establish the ancientness of Arcadia, but at several points implies a previous history—though in this instance Musidorus may be beguiling Dametas with fake history.

166 *no one good*: not one benefit, source of consolation.

168 *as hard as brawn made hard by art*: up to this point the rustic images, even the 'fair great ox's eyes', have had an attractive if deliberately naïve effect: this image, however, presenting the country girl as a piece of pressed meat, might betray to an audience more discerning than Miso Musidorus's distaste for peasant love-making.

Oudemian street: meaning 'street without inhabitants'.

169 *Alecto*: one of the Furies, shown with torches and her head covered with serpents; cf. Virgil, *Aeneid*, vii, 417.

Medea: mistress of Jason, who took revenge on Jason for abandoning her by murdering their two children. There is a picture of the subject by Veronese (now in the Accademia, Venice). No doubt Sidney also knew Seneca's tragedy *Medea*.

173 *the fatal Palladium*: the image of Pallas Athene on which Troy's safety was believed to depend; cf. *Iliad*, x; Ovid, *Metamorphoses*, xiii.

174 *making in their barks pretty knots*: similar loving inscriptions on trees by Angelica and Medoro trigger off Orlando's madness in *Orlando Furioso*, xxiii. Harington has a marginal gloss to the passage, in his translation, 'Of the use of writing in trees all good Poets have testified', referring to Propertius and Ovid.

175 *world's*: the metre requires this to be pronounced as two syllables.

177 *just punishment . . . infortunate bar*: the narrator allows us to see Musidorus either as a foul promise breaker, or as a much suffering lover whose opportunism is only natural.

182 *Why dost thou haste away*: together with the parallel poem on p. 187, this appears to be the earliest English madrigal.

190 *one of Vesta's nuns*: the Vestal Virgins, who guarded the sacred flames in the Temple of Vesta in Ancient Rome.

194 *shall my wife become my mistress?*: Basilius uses 'mistress' here purely in the sense of 'authority', but in view of later events there is no doubt some dramatic irony.

195 *Thisbe . . . Pyramus*: the unhappy lovers whose story is told in Ovid's *Metamorphoses*, iv. 55–166. The story was exceptionally popular with Elizabethan writers; cf. *A Midsummer Night's Dream*, v. i., and G. Bullough, *Narrative and Dramatic Sources of Shakespeare's Plays* (1966), i. 374–5.

198 *unreadying*: see Glossary.

   Pan ... Hercules: A story told in Ovid's *Fasti*, ii. 303–58. Sidney had
   previously used the story in *The Lady of May*:

> When wanton Pan, deceived with lion's skin.
> Came to the bed, where wound for kiss he got.
>
>   (*Misc. Prose*, 30.)

   Iole is not named in Ovid's account, and he probably intended to refer,
   rather, to Omphale. However, many other writers besides Sidney
   confused these two mistresses of Hercules; cf. V. Skretkowicz, 'Hercules
   in Sidney and Spenser', *N & Q* ccxxv (1980).

   Get hence foul grief: an imitation of the classical verse form sapphics
   (see note on p. 72), but in accentual rather than quantitative metre.

201 *extremity of joy is not without a certain joyful pain*: Cleophila's painful
   joy should perhaps be contrasted with the untempered crude excitement
   of Basilius in the same position—'he never touched ground'. Cf. also
   Astrophel and Stella, 85. 3–4.

   Virtue, beauty, and speech: Sidney's most elaborate use of 'correlative
   verse'.

202 *ever in his eyes best*: the passage following is echoed by Shakespeare in
   The Winter's Tale, IV. iv. 136–46.

204 *relics*: survivors of the Trojan war; cf. Virgil, *Aeneid* 1.

206 *Oh, whom dost thou kill, Philoclea?*: the strategy of Pyrocles here may
   derive from that of Chaucer's Troilus; cf. *Troilus and Criseyde* iii. 1092
   and *passim*.

   like Venus rising from her mother the sea: Venus Anadyomene, familiar to
   us in Botticelli's 'Birth of Venus'.

   Thisbe's punishment: suicide; Thisbe killed herself on finding her lover,
   Pyramus, dead. Cf. note on p. 95.

207 *a song the shepherd Philisides had in his hearing sung*: some of the images in
   this poem occur in the Fifth Song of *Astrophil and Stella*, which Ringler
   believes to have been originally a poem addressed by Philisides to his
   unkind mistress 'Mira'. Cf. Appendix B.

   What tongue can her perfections tell: this Ovidian 'blason', or catalogue of
   a lady's beauties, was extensively revised by Sidney. It became one of his
   most popular poems, occurring in many manuscript commonplace books
   and in *England's Parnassus* (1600). Puttenham described it as 'excellently
   well handled'. In its context in the *Old Arcadia* the poem stands in place of
   an act of love: while the audience enjoy the poetic celebration of
   Philoclea's body, Pyrocles enjoys the real thing.

   Their matchless praise: this is the reading of the *Old Arcadia* manuscripts;
   Robertson follows the 1590 printed edition in giving 'The matchless pair'.

However, this seems likely to be an early example of Sidney's text being emended; 'matchless praise' fits in with the next four lines: no similes of 'praise' are adequate to 'praise' her eyes. Cf. also *Astrophel and Stella*, 35. 13–14.

208 *porphyry*: a reddish crystal.

209 *Like cunning painter shadowing white*: perhaps a reference to miniature painting, in which density was given to colour by the use of white.

the gart'ring place: the place just above the knee where garters were tied.

210 *the hate-spot ermelin*: the white ermine was thought to hate dirt so much that it would die rather than allow its coat to be stained. Sidney used an ermine with the motto '*Rather dead than spotted*' in the *New Arcadia* (*Works*, ed. Feuillerat, i. 108).

211 *Argus's thousand eyes, and Briareus's hundred hands*: Argus was the dog full of eyes set by Juno to watch over Io (cf. note on p. 57); Briareus was a mythical Greek hundred-handed giant, one of the sons of Uranus and Ge.

212 *otherwise occupied*: a subdued reminder that while Lalus is enjoying the reward for his honest and constant courtship, Pyrocles is in bed with Philoclea, Musidorus is eloping with Pamela, and Gynecia has, as she thinks, poisoned her husband Basilius.

213 *Coredens*: a mysterious figure who has been identified with Sidney's friend Dyer, or, by Ringler, with Edward Wotton, who returned to England from Vienna with Sidney in 1575—'*cored[i]ens*'. While the identification with Wotton is plausible, the etymology seems very strained, since Wotton was not permanently a fellow traveller. Like Philisides, Strephon and Klaius, he is a melancholy lover, and I suspect that his name is '*cor edens*', or 'heart-eater'.

Let mother earth: one of the earliest epithalamia in English. The verse form is based on that of a wedding poem in Montemayor's *Diana*; cf. Ringler, 411–12. We should notice that Cupid, who dominates the extra-marital loves of the princes and the Arcadian royal family, is here firmly banished.

215 *shall here take rust*: in his palinodic sonnet 'Leave me ô love' (*Certain Sonnets*, 32) Sidney bids his soul reject earthly love, to 'grow rich in that which never taketh rust'.

216 *Sentences, sentences*: sententiae, or, in this case, 'empty aphorisms'.

217 *A neighbour mine not long ago there was*: it is appropriate to Nico's coarse-grained rusticity that his discourse is in the form of a *fabliau*, but it cannot be said that Sidney distinguishes himself in this genre.

221 *As I my little flock on Ister bank*: this poem reflects Sidney's friendship with the Huguenot statesman Hubert Languet, who instructed him in political

wisdom. Sidney and Languet were together 'on Ister bank', i.e. in Vienna, on the Danube, in August 1573 and August 1574. It is the poem of Sidney's which brings him closest to Spenser, being written in 'old rustic language', such as he was to criticize in the *Defence of Poetry*. More specifically, it is analogous to the February Eclogue of *The Shepheardes Calender*, a beast fable taught to the poet Thenot, in his youth, by an older poet, Tityrus.

222 *naught*: evil.

With old true tales: writing to Sidney in 1579 Daniel Rogers referred to Languet as he who 'guided you through the histories and origins of states' (Robertson, 463).

worthy Coredens: see note on p. 213. It seems likeliest that Coredens corresponds with Edward Wotton, who was with Sidney in Vienna in 1574/5, and returned to England with him; cf. the opening passage of the *Defence of Poetry*.

Such manner time there was: this passage derives partly from Ovid's accounts of the Golden Age (*Metamorphoses*, i and xv) and partly from Isaiah 11: 6–8. Greville recalls Sidney's myth in 'A Treatise of Monarchy', stanza 122 (*Remains*, ed. G. Wilkes, 1965, 65).

223 *envy harb'reth most in feeble hearts*: a parody of the Chaucerian commonplace, 'Pittee renneth sone in gentil herte'.

230 *by whose folly the others' wisdom might receive the greater overthrow*: cf. *Much Ado About Nothing*, v. i. 227–8: 'what your wisdoms could not discover, these shallow fools have brought to light'.

233 *when jealous Juno sat cross-legged*: story from Ovid, *Metamorphoses*, ix. 273 ff.

pans, cries and laughters: this probably means with 'metal vessels beaten in order to flush out the game' (Robertson, 467), rather than 'Pan's cries', or, as in the 1593 edition, '*Panike* cries'.

236 *trees, which should shortly be my best burial?*: Dametas anticipates his wooden coffin.

237 *as Psyche did upon her unknown lover*: Psyche broke her unknown lover's command and looked at him with a lamp, discovering him to be Cupid (Apuleius, *Golden Ass*, xxii).

240 *movable goods of nature*, i.e. beauties.

243 *folding in mine arms promised*: i.e. by the verses on the bottle of potion, p. 197.

246 *this sestine*: MSS representing early drafts of the *Old Arcadia* read 'fashion' or 'sort' for 'sestine'. Both the word and form were unfamiliar to Sidney's first readers, this being the earliest use of the word cited in the *OED*, and

the earliest example in English of the verse form. For a learned account of
the structural and symbolic patterns of the sestina see Alastair Fowler,
Conceitful Thought (1975), 39–43.

251 *the cruelty of the Arcadian laws*: this law (which Robertson links with
Orlando Furioso, iv. 59, xxv. 22–70), has not been mentioned to the reader
until this point: if it had, it would have cast a dark shadow over the
seduction scene at the end of Book 3.

253 *O great maker*: this prayer anticipates the heroism of Pamela's prayer in the
New Arcadia, said to have been used by Charles I (*Works*, ed. Feuillerat, i.
382–3), but with the major difference that Pyrocles is only partly praying,
and partly justifying his intended suicide.

256 *such a tree*: perhaps a reference to the orange tree, bearing fruit and
blossom at once, which Sidney was to use as part of a symbolic suit of
armour in the *New Arcadia* (*Works*, i. 462).

257 *for the saving of all his body he will not spare the cutting off a limb*: a painfully
prophetic example of a choice of the lesser evil. Amputation of Sidney's
shattered leg in October 1586 might possibly have saved his life.

the constant man abides the painful surgery: Fulke Greville's description of
the wounded Sidney's 'constant and obedient posturing of his body' to the
surgeons' art may owe something to this image (*Life of Sidney*, ed. Nowell
Smith, 133).

the loss of some years more or less: cf. Du Plessis Mornay's *Discourse of
Death*, as translated by the Countess of Pembroke (1592), sig. D4ᵛ and
passim.

258 *we must take warning of him to give over our charge*: Spenser puts this
argument into the mouth of Despair, *Faerie Queene*, I. ix. 41.

The uttermost instant is scope enough: on a material level, this turns out to
be prophetic of the unexpected happy ending. On a spiritual level, it
recalls St Augustine's *Misericordia Domini inter pontem et fontem*, adapted
in the epitaph recorded by Camden on a man killed falling from his
horse:

> Betwixt the stirrup and the ground
> Mercy I asked, mercy I found.
>   (*Remains*, 1605, 55.)

neither we made ourselves, nor bought ourselves: though a virtuous pagan,
Philoclea seems here to apprehend the Christian concept of redemption.

259 *Codrus's honour*: a legendary king of Athens who was killed for his country;
he was so much honoured that the Athenians would have no king in
succession to him.

263 *amber-crowned head*: Astrophel in *Astrophel and Stella* 91 confesses himself

382 EXPLANATORY NOTES

attracted by 'Some beauty's piece, as amber-coloured head| Milk hands, rose cheeks...'.

269 *it is said that*: this phrase, omitted in the 1593 edition, is a rare hint that the story is mediated through tradition.

269–70 *which before she had never done*: Pamela does not know that Musidorus has already kissed her when asleep (p. 177), still less that only the timely arrival of brigands prevented him from raping her.

284 *poor sheep*: coming in the next set of Eclogues after Philisides's beast fable, Geron's address to the sheep of Arcadia has definite political connotations—cf. 'Worst fell to smallest birds, and meanest herd' (p. 225).

Strephon and Klaius would require a whole book: various attempts have been made to explain the significance of the gentlemen Strephon and Klaius and their lost mistress Urania; see for instance K. Duncan-Jones, 'Sidney's Urania', *RES* xvii (1966), 124–32; Alastair Fowler, *Conceitful Thought* (1975), 56–8. Whatever their precise significance in neo-Platonic terms, it is clear that these companionable lovers of an unattainable and absent mistress exemplify a higher kind of love than that of Pyrocles and Musidorus.

285 *double sestine*: cf. note on p. 246. This is the only poem in the *Arcadia* which has stimulated a sizeable body of criticism; see for instance W. Empson, *Seven Types of Ambiguity* (1930), 45–50; J. C. Ransom, *The New Criticism* (1941), 108–14; David Kalstone, *Sidney's Poetry: Contexts and Interpretations* (1965), 71–83; Alastair Fowler, *Conceitful Thought* (1975), 38–58.

286 *mortal serene*: see Glossary. The dews of evening and morning were thought to bring fatal diseases with them; cf. *Julius Caesar*, II. i. 261–3.

287 *she, with whom compared the Alps are valleys*: a hyperbole perhaps not here intended to be ridiculous, as it is in Lewis Carroll's *Through the Looking Glass*: 'I've seen hills, compared with which this is a valley'.

dizain ... crown: 'dizains', or ten-line stanzas ending in couplets, seem to have been first referred to by Gascoigne in *Certayne notes of Instruction* (1575). This appears to be the first English reference to the 'crown' (cf. Donne's 'La Corona' sonnets), a sequence of stanzas or sonnets in which the first line of each repeats the final line of its predecessor, the last line of all repeating the first. Sidney's brother Robert was to attempt a 'Crown of sonnets' (*Poems*, ed. P. J. Croft, 1984, 174–81).

289 *I sought to catch the fish torpedo fair*: in the *New Arcadia* the torpedo fish, an electric ray, is used as an *impresa* on his shield by the accident-prone Amphialus (*Works*, ed. Feuillerat, i. 455).

crowned basilisk: a mythical crowned serpent whose gaze was fatal; cf. Pliny, *Natural History*, viii. 33.

290 *Samothea*: Britain. Sidney probably took the name from Harrison's *Description of Britaine* prefixed to Holinshed's *Chronicles* (1577). He recommended the reading of Holinshed to Edward Denny in 1580. Cf. K. Duncan-Jones, 'Sidney in Samothea', *RES* xxv (1974), 174-7.

293 *meagre cheer*: sour expression.

294 *crown of amber fair*: presumably signifying 'amber' coloured hair, which Sidney admired; cf. note on p. 263.

296 *even Coredens*: cf. note on p. 213. Like Urania, Mira has two lovers, an older and a younger. Sir Edward Dyer's 'Amaryllis', in which Amaryllis is unsuccessfully wooed by 'Coridon' and 'Charamell', who are metamorphosed respectively into the flower heartsease and an owl, may relate in some way to Sidney's stories about friendly rivals (Dyer, *Poems*, ed. Sargent, 1968, 192-5).

299 *Agelastus*: MSS of earlier versions of the *Old Arcadia* show that Sidney originally intended Dicus to utter this lament. Along with the November eclogue in Spenser's *Shepheardes Calender*, this is one of the earliest pastoral elegies in English. It is partly modelled on the Eleventh Ecloga in Sannazaro's *Arcadia*, which is also in *terza rima*; cf. Ringler, 419-21.

300 *ai*: the letters of lament imagined by Greek poets as inscribed on the hyacinth after the metamorphosis of the young Hyacinthus. Cf. Moschus, *Elegy on Bion*, v.5 ff.; Ovid, *Metamorphoses*, x. 215; and Milton's 'Lycidas', 106, 'that sanguine flower inscrib'd with woe'.

O Philomela: the nightingale, imagined as pricking her breast against a thorn as she sings; cf. *Certain Sonnets* 4. Whereas the courtly Agelastus invokes the help of the nightingale, Philisides in his juvenile beast fable (pp. 221-5) recites without the aid of 'wood-musique's king'.

302 *O elements, by whose (they say) contention*: a Renaissance commonplace; cf. Marlowe, *Tamburlaine I*, II. vii. 18-20.

Atropos: the Fury who cuts off the thread of man's life.

Aesculapius: the god of medicine.

in turn of hand: 'in the twinkling of an eye'.

303 *Farewell O Sun*: the first stanza of this poem was quoted by C. S. Lewis as an example of 'Golden' poetry, but his use of the 1593 text, in which 'woeful's' in line 4 was given as 'joyfulls', made him dismiss this line as 'vapid', and criticize the whole poem as 'empty': a striking example of the need for sound texts as a foundation for criticism (*English Literature in the Sixteenth Century*, 1954, 326-7).

310 *provide the marriage*: a surprising revelation to the reader that it had been planned all along that Pyrocles and Musidorus should marry the Arcadian

princesses—a scheme which they have jeopardized by their direct approaches.

321 *We have lived*: C. S. Lewis praised this 'magnificent *viximus*' as a good example of the 'less Arcadian' side of Sidney's style (*English Literature in the Sixteenth Century*, 1954, 337). It may be, however, that we should see the princes' claims to heroism at this point as rather specious.

if, at least, there remain anything of remembrance: this discussion of memory has various possible sources: J. Serranus's commentary on Plato's *Phaedo*; Xenophon's *Cyropaedia*, viii. 7; and Du Plessis Mornay's *De la Verité*, which Sidney partly translated, ch. xiv.

325 *russet coarse cloth*: this rough dress reflects Gynecia's self-hatred, and may be contrasted with the ample 'russet velvet' worn by Pamela as a token of unwilling obedience to the pastoral regime (p. 33).

the crimson raiment our knights of the order first put on: apparently a reference to the surcoats of the Knights of the Garter.

326 *Gaetulian . . . scarlet*: various ancient kinds of purple are discussed by Pliny, *Natural History*, ix. 60–3, where it is made clear that Tyrian purple was by far the most highly prized.

332 *set it to the beam*: weigh it in the balance (see Glossary).

340 *that she might keep my place*: Pyrocles avoids revealing Gynecia's passion for him, suggesting that he and she were virtuously conspiring to deflect Basilius's love into an honest course.

341 *trial by combat*: Pyrocles's vigorous challenge to Philanax may be compared with Sidney's own challenge to the man who libelled his uncle, whom he is willing to meet for the purpose 'in any place of Europe' ('Defence of the Earl of Leicester', *Misc. Prose*, 140).

347 *leaving nothing unsaid which a filthy mind can imagine*: cf. Sidney's 'Defence of Leicester', ed. cit., opening paragraph and *passim*.

351 *Phoenician Europa . . . Grecian Helen*: Jove in the form of a bull carried off Europa; their sons Minos and Rhadamanthus were inexorable judges in the underworld. Helen of Troy's abduction by Paris was the cause of the Trojan war.

355 *But Euarchus . . . mind*: several models existed for Euarchus's steadfastness in continuing his sentence on his own son and nephew. The closest analogue is Livy's story of Lucius Junius Brutus, who condemned his sons to death for their plot to restore Tarquinius (ii. 5, 5–9). Bodin, whose *Six Livres de la Republique* (Paris, 1576) Sidney recommended to his brother Robert in October 1580, devoted his fourth chapter to the ancient Roman law by which fathers had the right of life and death over their children.

358 *such a sad assured behaviour as Cato killed himself withal*: the suicide of Cato of Utica after the death of Pompey was a favourite Renaissance example of stoical determination.

361 *with the Arcadian pastorals*: this seems to point to a culminating fifth set of Eclogues, which either for haste or for some other reason Sidney did not write.

GLOSSARY

This glossary, adapted from Jean Robertson's Oxford edition, will be found useful as a guide to unfamiliar words and usages in the 'Old' *Arcadia*. It is presented here without Miss Robertson's notes on *OED* first citations and pre-datings, and without page and line references. Readers must therefore work out for themselves which sense is the relevant one in a particular context. Many words dealt with in the Glossary occur in the text only once or twice in the senses given here. Miss Robertson's aim was 'to gloss only words which are not immediately familiar, and words used in senses which are no longer the familiar ones. In the case of the latter, the occurrences of the words in their older senses only are given. Thus *salve*, "salutation", will be found, but not *salve*, "ointment, cure".'

A

abroad *adv.* widely apart; stretched out

absented *pp. adj.* removed (from customary residence)

abuse *v.* deceive

accident *n.* event; happening (not necessarily bad)

accompanable *adj.* fit to go with as a companion

accord *n.* harmony; *v.* make to harmonize with or proportionate to; **accorded** *pp.* harmonized; made proportionate

activity *n.* skill, esp. in athletics

adamant *n.* loadstone; magnet

adherent *n.* that which is attached to as a circumstance; *adj.* attached to as a circumstance

adusted *pp. adj.* **choler adust** *n.* medical state characterized by dryness of the body, heat, thirst, etc.

advantage *n.* chance; favourable opportunity

affect *n.* affection; emotion;

affected *pp. adj.* full of affection, aimed at; assumed; put-on; **affection** *n.* emotion; **affectionated** *pp. adj.* passionate

after-live *v.* survive; **after-liver** *n.*

agreeable *adj.* consistent with

ai *interj.* the Greek cry of lament

aland *adv.* ashore

alarum *n.* alarm

all to- *used as an intensive*

allowance *n.* agreement; permission; acceptance; **allowing** *adj.* agreeing; assenting

alonely *adv.* solely

ambassade *n.* message sent by an ambassador; ambassador and his train

annoyed *pp. adj.* full of grief and vexations

apostle's mantle *n.* long cloak

apparent *adj.* manifest; plainly seen

appassionate *adj.* full of passion

appeased *pp. adj.* calm and collected

apply *v.* accommodate to

appropriated *pp.* suited; made to fit with

approved *pp. adj.* proved by experience

arbitrage *n.* arbitration

ardency *n.* ardour; warmth of feeling

arrant *adj.* thorough-going; out-and-out; **arrantest** *superl.*

artificial *adj.* artistic

asclepiadics *n. pl.* asclepiads (quantitative verse form)

askances *conj.* as though

assistants *n. pl.* audience; those present at an event

attaint *v.* condemn, infect

attend *v.* wait for

attent *pp. adj.* intent; attentive to; **attentive** *adj.* listening carefully

attractive *adj.* drawing

auditor *n.* listener; disciple

available *adj.* availing; advantageous

B

bait *n.* resting place; **baiting place** *n.* stopping place for refreshment and changing horses on a journey

bale *n.* ill fortune; unhappiness

basilisk *n.* fabulous monster that kills by its glance

bastinados *n. pl.* blows (seemingly not on the soles of the feet)

beam *n.* scales; **set it to the beam**, weigh it in the balance

beaten *pp. adj.* inured to; experienced

become *v.* befit; suit

beholding *pres. p.* under obligation; holding the eyes; looking attractive

behoveful *adj.* useful; necessary

beldam *n.* old woman; witch

benamed *pp.* described as

best *n.* best course

bested *pp.* beset; pressed

bettering *n.* improvement; **betterness** *n.* superiority

bewonder *v.* fill with amazement

bewray *v.* divulge

blabber *v.* blurt

blaze *v.* emblazon; picture; **blazings** *n. pl.* advertisements

blea *v.* baa

bless *v.* wound

blockish *adj.* obtuse

blow point *n.* children's game

bob *n.* and *v.* blow; hit

book *n.* **without book**, by rote; from memory

booth *n.* temporary dwelling place

bootless *adj.* useless

bore *pp.* born

botch *n.* ulcer; boil

bought *n.* curve; bend

brabbler *n.* caviller about trifles

brave *adj.* boastful; magnificent; **bravery** *n.* bravado

brawl *n.* a kind of dance

brickle *adj.* brittle

brim *adj.* breme; fierce

briny *adj.* salt

burden *n.* bass or undersong

bussing *pres. p.* kissing

busy *adj.* meddlesome; officious

by-word *n.* epithet of scorn

C

caitiff *n.* despicable creature; *adj.* wretched; miserable

calmy *adj.* tranquil

camisado *n.* night attack (orig. one in which the attackers wore nightshirts over their armour for mutual recognition)

canker *n.* cancer

capitulate *v.* specify; make conditions

captive *v.* captivate; take prisoner; **captiving** *pres. p. adj.* capturing

careful *adj.* full of cares; anxious; **careless** *adj.* without anxiety or cares

carking *pres. p. adj.* causing anxiety

casting *pres. p.* deliberating

cates *n. pl.* choice victuals; delicacies

causeful *adj.* having good cause; well grounded

chafe *n.* rage; **chafing** *pres. p.* raging

charming *adj.* magical

chase *n.* prey; that which is hunted; **in chase**, whilst pursuing

chat *n.* talk

chaw *v.* chew

chiefer *comp. adj.* more important

chumpish *adj.* sullen; grumpy

Cimmerian *adj.* dark as the dwellings of the Cimmerii

circumspect *adj.* attentive to all the circumstances

cithern, cittern *n.* a sort of guitar, strung with wire, and played with a plectrum

clampering *vbl. n.* clumsy disturbance of the peace

clause *n.* close, final point

clearing *vbl. n.* removal of suspicion of guilt; **clearness** *n.* innocence

clerkly *adj.* learned

coaly, colly *adj.* coal black

cockered *pp. adj.* pampered

cockles *n. pl.* hot cockles, a children's game

cockling *n.* young one; child

coinhabiters *n. pl.* dwellers in together.

colour *n.* rhetorical flourish; pretext; *v.* justify; supply a pretext for; **colourable** *adj.* plausible; **coloured** *pp. adj.* deceitful; plausible

comfit *n.* sweetmeat

commodity *n.* opportunity; advantage

common *adj.* shared by all alike

compact *n.* combination; joining together

con *v.* **con thank**, acknowledge gratitude

conceit *n.* idea; conception

concent *n.* harmony

conclusion *n.* legal impediment or stoppage

confection *n.* combination of objects

conjoined *pp. adj.* connected; coherent

consort *n.* agreement; **consorted** *pp. adj.* tuned in harmony; agreeing

contemned *pp. adj.* despised

contentation *n.* contentment

convoy *n.* channel; way

corner *adj.* secret; sly

corrosive *n.* exacerbation of grief

corse *n.* corpse

couthe *v. 3rd pers. pl. past* knew

coyed *pp.* appeased; coaxed

cradle *adj.* youngest

crapal *n.* toad stone

craven *n.* coward

crouch *n.* crutch

crown *n.* poem composed of linked stanzas, where the last line of each stanza forms the first line of the next, and the last line of the whole sequence repeats the line that began it

crud *n.* curd

cry *n.* pack of people; **cryingly** *adv.* with lamenting shouts

cumber *n.* trouble; burden; *v.* trouble; be a burden; **cumbersome** *adj.* troublesome; burdensome; **cumbrous** *adj.* troublesome

cunning *n.* skill; knowledge; *adj.* skilful; **cunningest** *superl. adj.* most skilful

curbed *pp. adj.* bent; curved

curious *adj.* careful; carefully made; **curiousest** *superl. adj.* most careful; **curiously** *adv.* carefully; exquisitely

currish *adj.* quarrelsome; mean-spirited

D

daintiness *n.* fastidiousness

damage *n.* loss; detriment; injury

dark *v.* darken; **darkling** *adv.* in the dark

deadly *adj.* dying

debateful *adj.* contentious

deceit *n.* deception

deface *v.* destroy; defame

defensive *n.* defence

delicacy *n.* luxury

demean *n.* demeanour; **demeanour** *n.* behaviour

denizened *pp. adj.* naturalized

depart *n.* departure; *v.* separate; **departure** *n.* parting; separation

deprave *v.* vilify; defame

descrier *n.* discoverer

desireful *adj.* desirable

despaired *pp. adj.* cast into despair; without hope

despota *n.* despot; ruler

destined *pp.* destined

determinate *adj.* resolute; determined

dicker *n.* half a score

disaccustomed *pp. adj.* no longer used to

disannul *v.* cancel; annul

disastered *pp. adj.* stricken with disaster; ill starred

discomfort *v.* defeat the plans of

discontentation *n.* discontent; displeasure

discountenance *n.* abashment; **discountenanced** *pp.* abashed

disdained *pp. adj.* affronted by; offended at

disgrace *n.* affront; **disgracing** *pres. p. adj.* affronting

disguisement *n.* disguise

disjoined *pp. adj.* separated

disjunction *n.* separation

disparagement *n.* marriage to one of inferior rank

distrain *v.* compel by confiscation or seizure to perform a legal obligation

disuse *v.* cease to be accustomed to

diversified *pp. adj.* diverse; different

dividing *vbl. n.* separating

dizain *n.* poem in ten stanzas of ten lines each

downfall *n.* downpour

drivel *n.* drudge; foul slut

E

efficacy *n.* power to produce effects

eft *adv.* moreover; again

emmet *n.* ant

enclosed *pp. adj.* kept in control and hidden

engrieved *pp.* aggravated; exacerbated

ensue *v.* pursue

entireness *n.* absolute devotion; friendship

ermelin, ermion *n.* ermine

erst *adv.* before

essential *adj.* actual; real (as opposed to 'imaginative', 'fancied', and 'opinionate')

estimation *n.* esteem; appreciation

event *n.* outcome; consequence

exigent *n.* occasion requiring immediate action

F

fact . deed

faintly *adv.* timidly

fairing *n.* complimentary gift

fantastical *adj.* imaginary

far-fet *adj.* far-fetched

fearful *adj.* full of fear

feeling *adj.* sympathetic; deeply felt;

touching; **feelingly** *adv.* with feeling; on one's own pulses

fellowless *adj.* without fellow; peerless

fixed *pp.* rigid and immobile

flix *n.* flux; dysentery

foen *n. pl.* foes

fond *adj.* foolish

forcible *adj.* able to be taken by force

fore-appointed *pp. adj.* predestined

forefeeling *n.* anticipation; **forefelt** *pp. adj.* felt in anticipation

foregoer *n.* forerunner; harbinger

fore-judging *pres. p. adj.* prejudging

forepassed *pp. adj.* that had occurred previously

foresightful *adj.* foreseeing

foretaken *pp. adj.* taken previously

forlorn hope *n.* lit. 'lost troop', a picked body of men, detached to the front to begin the attack

forwasted *pp. adj.* wasted away

forworn *pp. adj.* ancient; grown old

framed *pp.* disposed

franzy *n.* frenzy

free-holding *pres. p. adj.* possessing the tenure of

fremd *adj.* unfriendly

freshly *adv.* vigorously

frisk *adj.* full of life and spirit

fugitive *adj.* fleeing

furmenty *n.* frumenty, dish made of hulled wheat boiled in milk, and seasoned with cinnamon, etc.

furniture *n.* equipment

G

gan *v. used as an intensive*, did *rather than* began

garboil *n.* confusion; tumult

gat *v.* arrived at

geometrical *adj.* that can be determined by scientific measurement

german *n.* **cousin german**, first cousin

ghastful *adj.* ghastly; **ghastfulness** *n.* ghastliness; **ghastly** *adv.* in a horrified way

gittern *n.* cithern (q.v.); a musical stringed instrument

glad *v.* make or become happy; rejoice

glass *v.* see or look at the reflection of; **glasses** *n. pl.* hand mirrors

gloire *n.* glory

glorious *adj.* boastful; **gloriously** *adv.* boastfully

glut *n.* act of feeding to excess; gluttony; **gluttonish** *adj.* voracious

grateful *adj.* pleasing

Grew *n.* Greek

H

halidom *n.* holy relic; **by my halidom**, a frequent oath

handsel *n.* omen or token; earnest

harbour *n.* place of rest, refreshment, and entertainment

hard *adv.* hard by; close to

hardy *adj.* courageous

harness *n.* armour; **harnished** *pp.* [an eye-rhyme for **varnished**] clad in armour

harquebus *n.* the common form of movable gun

hatch *v.* conceal

headily *adv.* impetuously

heartless *adj.* lacking courage

hent *pp.* seized

hight *pp.* called

historify *v.* relate the history of

hoise *v.* raise (sail) by means of tackle, etc.

hostry *n.* hostelry; inn

humourist *n.* person governed by his humours; fantasist

hurtless *adj.* harmless; **hurtlessly** *adv.* unhurtably

I

imaginative *adj*. imaginary, fantastic

immodest *adj*. arrogant; impudent

imp *n*. offspring

impair *v*. grow worse; **impairing** *vbl. n*. worsening

implied *pp*. accommodated to

imported *pp*. concerned

impostumed *pp. adj*. diseased; corrupted

impresa *n*. emblem; device

incaved *pp*. hollowed; bent inwards

incirclet *n*. light circular curl or spiral

indifferency *n*. lack of prejudice

infortunate *adj*. inopportune; unlucky; **infortunateness** *n.;* **infortune** *n*. misfortune; misadventure

inhabiter *n*. dweller-in; inhabitant

inheritrix *n*. heiress

inly *adj*. inward

insolence *n*. pride and ambition

interested *pp*. interested; concerned

interlude *n*. stage play

intricate *adj*. perplexingly entangled

inward *adj*. secret

iwis *adv*. indeed

J

jarl *v*. quarrel

jaundice *n*. black jaundice; yellow jaundice

joyed *pp. adj*. gladdened; filled with joy

jump *adj*. exact; **jumply** *adv*. exactly

jurat *n*. sworn witness

just *adv*. precisely

K

keels *n. pl*. kayles, ninepins or skittles

ken *v*. recognize

kind *n*. nature; **kindly** *adj*. natural; *adv*. naturally; according to nature

L

lamentable *adj*. lamenting; plaintive; sorrowful

launder *n*. woman who washes clothes; laundress

lay *n*. lair

learn *v*. show; teach

let *n*. hindrance

license *v*. give leave of departure to

lickerousness *n*. greedy desire

lighten *v*. give light to; **lightsome** *adj*. bright

loathsomely *adv*. with loathing

lobbish *adj*. clownish

lour *n*. gloomy, sullen look

lucklest *superl. adj*. most unlucky

luxuriousness *n*. lecherousness

lyra *n*. lyre, harp

M

madding *vbl. n*. madness

madrigal *n*. song of one stanza with long and short lines and varying rhyme scheme

magistracy *n*. condition of being a ruler

main *adj*. mighty; **mainly** *adv*. vehemently

make *n*. mate

malapert *adj*. impudent; presumptuous

manage *v*. perform the movements proper to a trained horse

mankind *adj*. masculine; virago-like

manwood *adj*. fierce like a man

marchpane *n*. marzipan

marting *pres. p. adj*. trading

masteries *n. pl*. **trying of masteries**, testing strength and skill in competitive feats

match *n*. wick or cord prepared for firing cannon, etc.

mate *n*. checkmate; defeat; **mated** *pp. adj*. downcast; sorrowful

matter *v.* form matter; fester

maugre *prepr.* in spite of

may-game *adj.* trivial

meagre *adj.* spiteful; sour

meanness *n.* low estate

medley *n.* confusion

memorative *adj.* pertaining to the memory

mettle *n.* disposition; temperament

mew *n.* cage for a hawk; *v.* put a hawk in a cage while moulting

mickle *adv.* much

mischief *n.* misfortune; evil deed

miser *adj.* wretched

mismeaning *vbl. n.* evil intention

moanful *adj.* expressing grief

mollified *pp.* softened

monarchal *adj.* ruled by a monarch

moony *adj.* belonging to the moon

mortal *adj.* deadly

mote *v.* may

mould *n.* shape

mountainets *n. pl.* hillocks

mountebank *adj.* characteristic of an itinerant quack

mowing *pres. p.* pulling faces; grimacing

muddy *adj.* confused

muett *adj.* mute

mumping *pres. p.* muttering

municipal *adj.* pertaining to the internal laws of a state

murrey *n. and adj.* purple-red colour of the mulberry

N

namely *adv.* particularly

nar *comp. adv.* nearer

ne *adv.* not; nor

necessary *adj.* fated; unavoidable

next *adj.* nearest

nis *v.* is not

noised *pp. adj.* sounded; **noisome** *adj.* harmful; noxious

noll *n.* head

not *v.* know not

O

occasion *n.* opportunity

occurrents *n. pl.* events

opinionate *adj.* fancied: supposed

original *n.* origin

oughts *n. pl.* things of no consequence; noughts

ounce *n.* lynx

out *adj.* confused; lacking in judgement

overshot *pp. adj.* wide of the mark; mistaken or deceived

owe *v.* own

owly *adj.* having poor vision in daylight

P

pack *n.* gang; set of criminals

pain *n.* difficulty; **painful** *adj.* taking trouble or pains

painted *pp. adj.* having the false colours of rhetoric

pantable *n.* pantofle; slipper

paragon *n.* touchstone; trial for comparison

pardie *interj.* by God

partage *n.* share

partakers *n. pl.* sharers

pass *v.* surpass; alleviate

passenger *n.* traveller

passionated *pp. adj.* activated by passion; made sorrowful

pastor *n.* shepherd; **pastorals** *n. pl.* pastoral games and pastimes

pattern *n.* model for comparison

peculiar *adj.* especial; particular to

pedant *n.* schoolmaster

peise *v.* weigh

pelf *n.* wealth

period *n.* end

pewing *pres. p.* (of a bird) crying plaintively

phaleuciacs *n. pl.* phaleucian hendecasyllables

pie *n.* magpie

pilled *adj.* (1) bereft of feathers; (2) plundered

pinching *pres. p. adj.* painful

pistle *n.* epistle

pitfall, pitfold *n.* small trap for catching birds

plain *v.* utter complaints; **plainfulness** *n.* mournfulness; state of being full of complaints; **plaining** *vbl. n.* complaining; **plaintful** *adj.* full of complaints

platform *n.* basis

plausible *adj.* willing; accepting

plum *adj.* plump

points *n. pl.* tagged laces for attaching hose to doublet

policied *pp. adj.* civilly organized; **policy** *n.* system of government; **politic** *adj.* political

pommel *n.* round, globe-shaped object

pomps *n. pl.* ceremonies

poor *adj.* incompetent

portraiture *n.* portrait; portrayal

prentice *n.* apprentice

presently *adv.* immediately; **presentness** *n.* immediacy

prest *adj.* ready

pretend *v.* claim; **pretended** *pp. adj.* purposed, designed

prevent *v.* forestall

prime *n.* first hour of morning

prize *n.* reward; **play a prize,** engage in a contest

proof *n.* experience; **prove** *v.* experience; find

provoking *pres. p. adj.* stirring up, calling forth (feeling and interest)

puddled *pp. adj.* confused; unclear

puling *pres. p.* crying

puppet *n.* doll; automaton

purgation *n.* purge (med.)

purled *pp. adj.* trimmed, either with gold thread or frills

purling *pres. p. adj.* murmuring

Q

quab *v.* tremble; palpitate

quaint *adj.* full of conceits; fanciful; cunning

queen-apple *n.* variety of red apple

queint *pp.* quenched

quick *adv.* alive

quitted *pp.* acquitted

R

race *n.* strong current

rampire *n.* rampart

rathe *adj.* early

ravening *n.* laying waste; **ravenous** *adj.* seeking for prey; **ravin** *n.* rapine; robbery

rayed *pp.* diseased

reasonable *adj.* having the power of reason

rebeck *n.* musical instrument with three strings

receipt *n.* reception; receiver

recklessness *n.* neglect

reclaimed *pp. adj.* (of a hawk) reduced to obedience

recomfort *n.* solace, comfort

recommend *v.* consign; commit

record *v.* repeat quietly or sadly

recovery *n.* remedy

red *v. past* advised; **rede** *n.* advice

refection *n.* recreation; refreshment

refelled *pp.* refuted; disproved

refrain *v.* restrain; hold back

regiment *n.* rule; government

rehearsal *n.* recital

reins *n. pl.* loins

relent v. soften; cause to relent; **relenting** vbl. n. slackening

remorsed pp. adj. affected with remorse

renting n. rending; tearing

resound n. a returned or echoed sound

reverence n. gesture of respect

richness n. richness; precious quality

rine n. rind; bark

rosed pp. adj. redolent of roses

rouse v. (of a hawk) shake the feathers

rudeness n. uncouthness

runagate n. vagabond

S

sadder comp. adj. more serious; graver; **saddest** superl. adj. most serious; gravest

salve n. salutation

sample n. example

satrapas n. satrap, governor of a province under the ancient Persian monarchy

say n. assay; foretaste

scape n. escape

scimitars n. a kind of sword

scope n. purpose; aim

scrawling pres. p. crawling

scrip n. wallet; small bag

secret n. method or process hidden from all but the initiated

seech v. [an eye-rhyme for **speech**] seek

seigniory n. lordship; sovereignty

self-conceit n. good opinion of oneself

self-fancy n. idea of pleasing oneself

self-liking adj. self-indulgent

selfness n. self-centredness; egoism

self-respect n. private, personal, or selfish end

semblance n. appearance

sensible adj. sensitive; of the senses; **sensibly** adv. feelingly, with sensitivity; **sensive** adj. having senses; sensitive

sentence n. wise saying; maxim

serene n. harmful dew of summer evenings

sestine n. sestina

several adj. separate

shepherdish adj. belonging to, or typical of, a shepherd; **shepherdry** n. business of a shepherd

shift v. change one's clothing

short adj. below standard

shrewdly adv. severely; **shrewdness** n. shrewishness; severity

sicker adv. certainly

sieve n. small net for snaring birds

sightfulness n. power of seeing; ability to see

silly adj. ignorant; simple

singled pp. separated

singularity n. distinction due to superiority

skill n. knowledge; v. know; **it skills not**, it does not matter; **skill-less** adj. without knowledge or understanding

skipjack n. pert, shallow-brained fellow

sleek adj. smooth; **sleekstone-like** adv. in the manner of a slick or sleek stone used for smoothing or polishing

sleightly adv. cunningly; craftily

smackering vbl. n. inclination towards

smirkly adv. simperingly

snakish adj. venomous; **snaky** adj. venomous; deceitful

sneb v. snub

sort n. way; manner

sotted pp. besotted; made foolish

sparefulness *n.* frugality

spent *pp.* destroyed

spill *v.* destroy; spoil

spite *v.* act spitefully towards

splay *adj.* (of foot) broad; turned outward

spoil *n.* despoliation

sprent *pp.* sprinkled

squeamish *adj.* averse, unwilling to do something

stain *v.* deprive of lustre, usually in a musical connection

stark *adv.* absolutely

starting *pres. p. adj.* causing one to start or be startled

stay *n.* stop; hindrance; condition

stead *v.* succour; help

stepmother *adj.* cruel (unlike a true parent)

stomacher *n.* waistcoat

stone *n.* touchstone (for testing purity of metals)

store *n.* plenty

stour *n.* time of turmoil

straight *adv.* immediately

straitly *adv.* closely

stroke *v.* with adv. or similar extension, bring into a specified position

stroy *v.* destroy

sublimed *pp.* elevated

suddenly *adv.* immediately

surfeit *adj.* excessive; intemperate

suspectful *adj.* suspicious

swannish *adj.* pertaining to a swan

swink *n.* toil; labour

sylvan *adj.* pertaining to woods

T

table *n.* picture; **pair of tables**, writing tablets; **table-talk**, familiar conversation at meals

tarantula *n.* tarantism; hysterical dancing disease, supposed to be caused by the bite of the tarantula spider

taster *n.* domestic official whose job it was to taste food and drink about to be served to his master, in order to detect poison, etc.

tell *v.* count

temper *n.* quality; nature; **tempered** *pp. adj.* adjusted

thee *v.* thrive; prosper

thilke *dem. pron.* these

tho *adv.* then

thralled *pp. adj.* captivated

througher *comp. adj.* of **through**

tickled *pp. adj.* pleasurably excited

tie *v.* enforce

tine *n.* a very little time

tire *v.* (of a hawk) prey upon

torpedo *n.* electric ray or cramp fish

touch *v.* censure; **touched** *pp. adj.* tainted

towardness *n.* advancement; furtherance

trace *n.* track; path

train *v.* decoy; deceive; persuade

travailed *pp. adj.* oppressed with cares

traversed *pp.* passed through; experienced

treen-dish *n.* wooden platter

trick *adj.* trim; handsome; **tricked** *pp.* dressed

trim *adj.* (with irony) fine; pretty

trunk *n.* pipe used as speaking-tube or ear-trumpet

trussed *pp.* with the points attaching hose to doublet tied up

try *v.* experience

tway, *n.* two

U

unaptness *adj.* lack of aptitude

unassayed *pp.* untested, unattempted

unbashed *pp. adj.* unabashed

uncomfortable *adj.* lacking in comfort or consolation

uncouth *adj.* unnatural

undecent *adj.* unbecoming; indecent

undeserved *pp. adj.* unwarranted

uneath *adv.* scarcely

unendly *adj.* unending

unentangled *pp. adj.* at liberty

unhap *n.* misfortune; misery

unharboured *pp.* dislodged; without refuge

unlikely *adj.* unseemly; unsuitable

unmeet *adj.* improper

unreachable *adj.* beyond the reach of man

unreadying *n.* undressing

unrefrained *adj.* unchecked

unsearchable *adj.* not to be searched

unsensible *adj.* without good sense

unstaid *adj.* instable, **unstaidness** *n.* instability

unsurety *n.* incertainty; insecurity

untouched *pp. adj.* unviolated

untried *pp. adj.* unsmelted

untrussed *pp.* with the points attaching hose to doublet undone

unused *pp. adj.* unusual; unaccustomed

upbore *v. past* bore up

use *n.* accustomed practice; **used** *pp.* accustomed

utmost *adj.* outermost

V

vagabonding *pres. p.* wandering about like vagabonds

vail *v.* **vail bonnet** *fig.*, yield; acknowledge submission

vainness *n.* futility; vanity

varnished *pp.* embellished

veered *pp.* changed course or direction

vindicative *adj.* vindictive

viny *adj.* closely entwined

W

wanhope *n.* despair

warbled *pp. adj.* injured by warbles (swellings, generally on animals, caused by the larvae of gadflies)

warefulness *n.* watchfulness

waste *n.* destruction; *pp.* destroyed

watered *adj.* filled with water

waymenting *n.* lamenting

weed *n.* dress; clothing

welkin *n.* firmament

whereupon *adv.* upon which

whether *rel. pron.* which of two

whilom *adv.* once

winy *adj.* drunken

without *prep.* outside; beyond

witold *n.* cuckold

woned *pp.* inhabited

wormish *adj.* wretched

wrack *n.* ruin; wreck

wrought *pp. adj.* embroidered

wrying *pres. p.* twisting, contorting

Y

ycleped *pp.* called

yclothed *v. past* clothed

younker *n.* youngster; gay young man

ywroughten *pp. adj.* embroidered

INDEX OF FIRST LINES OF POEMS